SMELLS LIKE WEEIA SPIRIT

I0555604

ELLE BOCA

POYEEN PUBLISHING

Published by Poyeen Publishing
2901 Clint Moore Road #265
Boca Raton, FL 33496

ISBN: 978-1-932534-16-0

Sign up to receive news and updates about Elle Boca titles and special offers at

elleboca.poyeen.com/weeia-marshals/smells-like-weeia-spirit

Other titles by Elle Boca:

Unelmoija: The Dreamshifter
Unelmoija: The Mindshifter
Unelmoija: The Spiritshifter
Unelmoija: The Timeshifter
Unelmoija: Paradox
In the Garden of Weeia
Gypsies, Tramps and Weeia
Weeia on My Mind

Author's Note

This is an original work of fiction. Any relationship to real people is unintentional and a coincidence. At times I took literary liberties, creating fictional places, modifying existing locations, names, addresses, and so forth as necessary to adapt to the story. The setting is Earth. The geographic boundaries of the book encompass the city of Paris, France and its environs, real and imagined. I relied on personal experiences, online and print sources (some of which are listed below). Any errors are my own.

How Paris Became Paris The Invention of the Modern City by Joan DeJean
The Other Paris by Luc Sante
The Seven Ages of Paris

Acknowledgements

I am deeply grateful to my beta readers who made time from their busy lives and commitments to read my unfinished manuscript and share honest and kind feedback: Melissa Manes, and fellow author Nicholas Rossis. I extend a warm welcome and special thank you to new beta readers Sandy Berg, Anne Marvin, Katija van der Heijde, Mary van Ede, and Wendy Wright.

Table of Contents

To Elisabeth and Marie Therese

"Paris is a counterpart in the social order to what Vesuvius is in the natural order: a menacing, hazardous massif, an ever-active hotbed of revolution. But just as the slopes of Vesuvius, thanks to the layers of lava that cover them, have been transformed into paradisal orchards, so the lava of revolutions provides uniquely fertile ground for the blossoming of art, festivity, fashion."

Walter Benjamin

Chapter 1

Beside me, Sébastien looked almost giddy, like a kid heading to his favorite candy store with permission to buy anything he wanted. The more he radiated anticipation of our impending appointment, the more my mood soured and my gut wrenched. While he looked forward to our career day participation at his old school, I dreaded it.

A tall gate painted black with gold tips surrounded the estate of the Académie Superieur de Goin, our destination. It was prestigious among French Weeia, many of whom had attended the school in their youth. From the main entrance I could see the historic buildings inside. Because it was a Weeia high school, and some of the students were from France's most prominent families, security was tight. Armed staff manned posts at all access points, cameras recorded movement around the perimeter, and a private security company was on call for emergencies.

My colleague had explained these precautions in detail on the express train from Paris to Melun in the Seine-et-Marne Department east and south of the city. From Melun, we had picked up a rental car and driven just past the small town Mennecy-la-Forêt.

I had thought his excitement couldn't grow further until we neared the guarded entrance and he broke into a broad smile, proving me wrong. Pulling into a parking space, he shut off the car and jumped out to greet the guard.

"How nice to see you," the uniformed man said in a warm tone to my direct report.

"You too, Benjamin," Sébastien replied, exchanging the customary French greeting kisses with the man. "How's Véronique?"

"Same old ball—" glancing at me, he interrupted himself,

looking sideways in discomfort.

Sébastien saved him from the awkwardness by introducing me, "Danni, meet Benjamin Maud, one of the finest guards to ever work at Goin." The man stood a tad straighter on hearing Sébastien's words. "Benjamin, meet my boss, the fearless Danielle Metreaux."

Benjamin's eyes lit up for an instant as he said, "A pleasure, marshal. I've heard a lot about you. That collar from the Most Wanted list won you many fans. You can count me among them."

Embarrassed, I mumbled something unintelligible in reply, retrieving my hand as soon as I could. The man reeked of stale tobacco, making me hope I never smelled like that despite my fondness for snus. While snus is a tobacco product, it isn't smoked. Instead, users place the round pouches between their teeth and gums, which delivers a mild, satisfying nicotine dose without the tar and toxins of cigarettes or cigars. Even so, I wasn't proud of my habit.

After we shook hands and Sébastien promised to stay in touch, Benjamin waved us through without so much as a glance at my identification. I could feel his eyes on us as we walked into the prestigious estate.

Seeing the cobbled stones, which covered the entrance and stretched all the way across a courtyard to an imposing three-story building, made me glad I had worn my practical boots. Following a friend's advice, I had bought dressy new shoes for the event, but they were in my closet where they could do no harm. Walking in heels on such an uneven surface wouldn't have been fun. I had no idea how so many Parisian women managed to make their way around the city in stylish attire and insanely high heels.

I had been rehearsing in my mind what I would say when my turn to speak arrived, and concentrating on not twisting an ankle on the charming pathways. As a result, I wasn't as alert and observant as I would normally be on my first visit to a place. Something, I wasn't aware of what, made me turn left. Sensing danger, in an instant I pulled Sébastien back, jerking his arm at an odd angle and wresting a guttural sound from his throat, "Aargh."

He lost his footing and I fared only a bit better. The scent of burning stone and greenery caught our attention. A scorch mark marred the ground near where we had stood moments before. Two teenage boys, so intent on each other that they didn't appear aware of us, were fighting on the grass just off the pathway.

"You okay?" I asked Sébastien.

He nodded, asking me in return, "You?"

"Startled, is all," I said, alert for danger.

He moved toward the boys faster than I would have expected from his composed manner. He pulled them apart by the scruff of their uniform collars. The shorter one of the two swung a punch at Sébastien while the other one kicked his shin.

"Stop it," Sébastien roared. "I'm a marshal."

When that failed and the boys began to fight again Sébastien zapped them with a minor electric charge, using his marshal's badge. It wasn't the same as an electric baton, but had a feature for emergencies such as that one. Surprise lit their faces. Their taut muscles reflecting anger slackened. Their arms fell to their sides and they remained unmoving on the ground, dazed.

I couldn't think why I had let Sébastien talk me into participating in career day at the Weeia high school on the outskirts of Paris. Yes, that Paris, the one in France, not Paris, Maine or Paris, Texas. Some days I still pinched myself to make sure I was awake and it was me who had landed one of the dream assignments of my graduating class at the Marshals Academy.

Sébastien and I worked as marshals, policing superhumans called Weeia living in secret among humans.

Although most Weeia had low-level mundane abilities, there were Weeia with no abilities and some whose abilities could be dangerous if used the wrong way or abused. Our job was to protect Weeia and humans from each other and to make sure no one revealed our existence to humans. Because there were few Weeia living in Paris, most of our workdays were ordinary and without excitement, so almost any excuse to break the routine was welcome.

On a good day, I wasn't the most gregarious person. On a bad day, some might describe me as a grump. I would not admit that to Sébastien or that I was jittery about our speaking engagement. I opened my mouth to ask why they were fighting with such ferocity. Before I could say a word, grunting and a thwack sound I didn't recognize distracted me.

I followed the unexpected noises to discover two slightly older boys wrestling, if you could call it that. One of them sought to break the hold the other had on his torso. Succeeding, he turned toward his mate, his brows furrowed in concentration, and his lips pulled back in a vicious snarl. They were so engaged in their dispute they took no notice of me. For a microsecond, I thought the fight was over, except that my feet no longer connected to anything. I fell backward, hitting the ground with a jarring thud. The grappler hit the ground nearby.

My stomach twisted in discomfort. The effects of too much alcohol the previous night at dinner combined with my nervousness due to our upcoming public speaking engagement were making me queasy. I had never been a party goer or much of a drinker. My boyfriend Iaen, on the other hand, liked to socialize and roped me into joining him. He understood the demands of my job, my having to work late nights and weekends, the need to know policy I had to follow, and the occasional wackiness that came with being a marshal.

When I arrived at his riverboat home bedraggled and tired

he would scoop me into his sexy arms and make it all better. The least I could do was tag along when he asked for my company. Although some days all I wanted when I got home was to kick my shoes off and put my feet up, he often had to attend an event, have dinner with acquaintances, or socialize. That was how he did business. A glass of wine or three with dinner wasn't a problem, but we had attended an aged-rum tasting. I was getting the strong impression that rum and I didn't get along.

A scene from the previous night's tasting popped into my head unbidden. "If this is your first time, you might want to take it easy," the rum expert told a middle-aged man with a balding head and a paunch. In response to his blank stare, she continued. "These are some of the best aged fine rums in the world, on par with cognac. They're emboldened by the nuances of the soil, yet delicate and dynamic at the same time."

I didn't know what she meant. Descriptions with words like nuances of the soil were beyond me. I only cared if the rum tasted good.

"See the deep amber hue of this one?" She lifted the bottle, allowing the light to filter through the expensive liquid. The prices of the bottles on the table were as high as premium champagnes. "It was aged eight years in oak barrels." The bald man appeared unimpressed, gulping the samples as she doled them out in tiny crystal glasses.

Iaen also drank the brown beverage with gusto and abandon. If he could do it, I figured I would be okay. I drank the servings in the tasting, trying to keep up with the elaborate descriptions and pairing recommendations. I woke up with a hangover. I thought of calling in sick, something I never did, but the event had been planned weeks earlier and I had promised to be there.

There where? I was still stunned from falling back onto the grass when I fell up into the air. Disoriented, up felt like down and down was up. I twisted around and almost gagged. Using my tongue, I dislodged the unfamiliar object that had gotten into my open mouth and was threatening to slide down my gullet.

I spit it out in disgust. Watching the clump of grass with soil still attached to it did nothing to dispel my rising anger. I spit a second time to get rid of the remaining grit and grassy taste. Weightlessness and almost eating a piece of turf added to my hangover made for an unpleasant combination.

"Oh yeah?" the boy who had fallen near me said to the other. "If you use your gravity twisting I'll use my—"

He never had a chance to finish because he dropped from his half upright position. Again my sense of direction wobbled and I fell. Of course, I knew about gravity twisters and we had learned defenses against them at the Academy, but we had practiced with simulations. This was the real deal. An irresistible sensation took hold of me. Doubling, I retched dinner and the half a pastry and coffee I had wolfed before heading out early that morning. Once the discomfort passed, annoyance replaced it.

"That's it," I bellowed. "I'm Marshal Danielle Metreaux and I'm ordering you to halt what you're doing."

I emphasized marshal. My voice awakened the two as if from a dream. They turned toward me and back to each other, ire taking hold of them once again. It was as if they had no control over their own impulses. The hands of the boy who had been clinging to the other when I had first seen them yellowed. From a kneeling stance he raised them in the air. I couldn't make out what he was saying, but it was clear he was threatening the other boy. Before he did anything further, I slapped him hard. That had the desired effect. Seeing Sébastien arrive with the corner of my eye I barked for him to take the other boy away while I pulled the first one's hands behind his back.

"What's going on?" I asked the teenager in front of me.

The tension was gone from his body. He dropped his eyes, looking confused and ashamed.

"I'm not sure, uh," he stuttered. He hung his head down, slouching. At the end of a long silence he asked, "Can I go?"

"After you give me your name, we'll see about that," I replied, not knowing what steps to take since it was the school's problem. "Let's go to the guard's office. You walk ahead of me. What ability—"

Before I could finish my question he interrupted, "Caustic blast," he said.

Sébastien and the gravity twister were already with Benjamin in his covered enclosure. The boy's expression was sullen. His eye was swollen and a cut on his lower lip was bleeding.

"Someone from security is coming to collect all of them," my colleague told me, making eye contact with the boy in front of me to let him know he was included.

Benjamin called from behind Sébastien to the boy, who did as he was asked without objecting. I sighed with relief. Criminals I could handle. With them, I could use whatever force I considered necessary. Subduing school children with out of control abilities was another matter. They had to be handled with extra care. That was more up Sébastien's alley than mine. I would rather tackle a most-wanted fugitive any day.

Chapter 2

"You don't look so good." My colleague's words, spoken so only I could hear them, shook me out of my reverie.

"Unlike you, who always manage to land on your feet and shine like a movie star," I said in a sharp tone I regretted the instant I spoke.

Ignoring my snarky tone, his eyebrows came together in a concerned expression as he zoomed his attention in on me, asking, "Are you hurt?"

Leave it to Sébastien to be concerned about me even when I'm sharp with him for no reason. If he wasn't such a nice guy who always had my back, he would get under my skin in a big way. Instead, he had a calming effect on me.

"I don't think so. Why do you ask?"

"There's a weird stain on your blouse that wasn't there before," he said, pausing to inspect it. "I thought it could be blood."

Glancing down at my top, I saw what he was talking about. As soon as my eyes paused on the uneven spot, I became aware of the pungent odor of vomit. My gorge and anger threatened to rise at the same time. It was a new ensemble I had bought for career day at the Académie. I was wearing it for the first time that day. I pressed the frustration down with an effort.

"Your clothes aren't even wrinkled," I replied in a kinder tone than before, dismissing his concern with a gesture of my hand, hoping he wouldn't notice I had thrown up all over myself.

Although I masked my mood since it wasn't Sébastien's fault that we had encountered the misbehaving teens, I remained miffed at him for pressuring me to attend career day in the first place. "It's part of our job to be out in the community. We should get to know the people we serve," he had said.

And by we, he meant me, because I was the non-Parisian new arrival with a thick French Canadian accent the locals mocked. I was the one who didn't much like communicating with people, human or Weeia. Growing up, making friends had been difficult, and as a young adult it had become worse.

My family name was tarnished; rumors pursued me wherever I went. To make matters worse, I knew only a bare minimum about what happened. When I was a little girl, my parents perished during a marshals' operation under a cloud of suspicion. The marshals service denied any death benefits, leaving me with no money.

I was lucky that my aunt and uncle had raised me as their own. I couldn't have asked for better, more loving relatives, but Weeia high society didn't accept me because I grew up on a rural farm and never learned the rules of their games. It didn't help that I was a pudgy and plain country mouse, as I had heard Madame Marmotte describe me behind my back.

In addition to fashion model looks, he was blessed with many positive attributes. He was gregarious, Parisian born and bred with impeccable social instincts, from a prominent family, and well-loved. He was right, of course. It would be easier to do my job with the support of the community. It didn't mean I had to like it.

The unfairness of life stung. Weeia lived longer than humans, and their abilities often gave them advantages over humans. Unlike many Weeia, I lived on limited income and had to plan my budget to buy new clothes. He was wealthy and could afford to replace his bespoke clothes with little effort, yet his ensemble was pristine. I had saved my pennies to buy my modest outfit, which had become wrinkled from the fall and had vomit, soil, and grass stains. It might be ruined, not to mention that I would look a sight at the presentation.

"I'll wait for security if you two prefer to head on in," Benjamin said.

"Given their actions of a few minutes ago, I would feel more comfortable staying here to make sure that's the end of it," Sébastien said.

His eyes met mine seeking confirmation. I nodded. Four boys had been a handful for the two of us and we were marshals. There was no need to point out to Benjamin that he was no marshal. We would wait to make sure they were picked up without further issues.

"Yes, it would be better knowing they're away from prying eyes near the gate," Benjamin said, looking relieved.

Moments later a van pulled up to take the boys. The driver offered us a ride, but we declined as we were going to another building in the estate.

"How far to where we're going?" I asked

"It's five minutes at a brisk pace," Sébastien said as he headed toward what looked like the main building.

Behind us, the new-looking front gate became a two-meter fence that surrounded the property. Sébastien saw the direction of my eyes.

"A tall, thick, and prickly hedge runs the entire length of the fence," he said. "It's not exactly impenetrable, but you have to be determined to get in, and well-maintained trip wires will alert security immediately. While the rest of the green areas fronting the castle are decorative, the plants near the hedge are poisonous. Students aren't supposed to play by the fence. It's off-limits. I wonder why those boys were there."

In front of us, the early morning sun warmed the façade of the stately stone structure. Its muted color was a stark contrast against the cobalt blue of the cloudless sky. A double staircase spiraled up toward twin carved wood doors, forming a commanding entrance worthy of a dignitary.

As if reading my thoughts, Sébastien explained, "It was

once the king's residence. The carriages would drive up to the staircase, where he would make his royal arrival an event to behold, or so the lore says. In the twelfth century, when the royal family built Fontainebleau nearby, Goin fell into neglect. It was too expensive to maintain both castles."

"So it was a castle," I said.

"For a few years," he replied. "Many—"

Before he could finish, a lingering piercing sound, between a wail and a howl, assaulted us. It was more than unpleasant. It hurt. We became alert in an instant. We walked in the direction it had originated. A short distance from where we stood, two girls argued. As with the boys before them, they were too agitated and consumed with their interaction to pay any attention to us. I had brought some of our gear, which included ear plugs, for our career day presentation. I took out a set for each of us, handing one to Sébastien and placing the other set in my ears to protect myself.

Auditory attacks could cause permanent hearing loss, brain damage, and in extreme cases, death. We had no idea what control the teen had over her ability or how willing she might be to exercise it. It didn't matter. It wasn't safe to take chances. We could tell which girl it was because the other one fell to her knees, bending forward with her hands covering her ears, grimacing, and whimpering.

The girl with the auditory ability stood ramrod straight with her head tilted sideways. An odd smile marred her face. I noticed the tattoo on the side of her neck stretched almost imperceptibly when she used her ability. I signaled for Sébastien to approach them from the front, making himself visible and nonthreatening, while I approached from the opposite side. I took a defensive position. He could use his mind reading ability to anticipate any attack from the girl.

Sébastien had the good looks of a celebrity, and he could charm the stripes off a zebra. I doubted teenage girls would be immune to the potent combination. My hope was to distract them with the eye candy that was Sébastien so we could tone down the situation with a minimum of fuss.

It worked. Sébastien caught tattoo girl's attention. As I expected, she wanted to talk to him. Soothing words calmed her down long enough for me to pull the other girl to her feet and away from her schoolmate. She remained silent when I asked her what had happened. I escorted her back to Benjamin's guardhouse, where he called for the van to return for her.

I found Sébastien and tattoo girl where I had left them. She was unmoving and wore a stunned expression, like a hare in a spotlight in the pitch dark of midnight.

"I don't know what happened," she half mumbled, holding her head in her hands. I thought it odd she appeared baffled instead of ashamed. "It's not like Claire and I are besties, but we've never had a fight." She watched Sébastien as if to make sure he was listening or perhaps she wanted his approval. He was studying her, wondering, I imagined, if she was telling the truth. She must have been reassured by his interest because she continued in a shaky voice, "Uh, I've never, ever you know, used my ability like that before. I didn't even know I could. I know it is dangerous."

I stepped into the conversation, rebuking her, "Yes, you have to be very, very careful when you use your ability. That's the kind of lesson you should've learned here."

"I did," she blurted. "I mean, you know, it was like I couldn't control what I was doing, you know? I've never felt that way before. I was mad, no it was more than that, you know? And, I couldn't, you know, like, do anything to stop myself."

She sounded like she was describing something that had happened to someone else or something that had no importance. There was no regret, only surprise, in her words.

"Let's get you back," Sébastien replied in a gentler voice

than I thought she deserved given her lack of remorse. "There's a van at the guardhouse waiting to take you to school."

She nodded her agreement, glancing up at him and flashing him a shy smile as if he had just invited her to the prom. As usual Sébastien seemed oblivious to the effect he had on the opposite sex.

"What's going on here?" I blurted in frustration and annoyance at no one in particular as soon as the van drove away with tattoo girl on board.

Benjamin shrugged, returning to his enclosure without a word as if to distance himself from the students' odd behavior. Sébastien took a deep breath, shaking his head from side to side, indicating he was as clueless as I was.

We walked in silence toward the main building. I was thinking and not ready to speak. I assumed he was too.

Chapter 3

We made our way with alacrity to report on the incidents at the Académie. A staff person directed us to a second office where we completed paperwork outlining what we had witnessed and the steps we had taken. Sébastien insisted we pop by the headmistress's office after that, as she was a friend of his family's. Of course she was.

When my direct report first arrived at the Paris office, his puppy-like earnest eagerness, handsome looks, high-society pedigree, ubiquitous connections, and wealth had bugged me no end. He could have taken a fast track within his family's empire. He could have traveled the world.

Assuming he had joined the Marshals Service out of a misguided aspiration I couldn't fathom, to spite his parents or for grins, I had been a grumpy boss at best. He had been gracious when I had been less than welcoming and downright unpleasant. His patience had proved important. In the short months we had worked together, he had demonstrated he was more than a pretty face. He was a competent, if inexperienced, young marshal. We had become good colleagues and friends.

Back then, Sébastien's smooth handling of what for me would have been awkward social situations might have annoyed me. That day at the Académie, I was grateful he was there to deal with the stuffy headmistress's assistant with the tight bun atop her head to match the expression on her face. Judging by the wrinkled brow, you would think we had caused the unexplained disturbances among the students rather than defusing them. I was glad I had used illusion, my Weeia ability, to keep the vomit stain from showing. It required a little effort on my part, but made me look presentable. It would work like a charm, provided we didn't get close enough for her to notice the smell.

The headmistress was not available. Sensing that my presence was not helping, I stepped away from the desk and let Sébastien chat with her assistant in private. They spoke for several minutes until her phone rang. She picked it up and dismissed us both with a wave of her hand.

"That went well," Sébastien said as we left the expansive wood paneled office into the hallway.

Surprised, I snorted, "Coulda fooled me. I hate to see what she's like when things don't go well."

"Like her boss she has a bit of a strict demeanor, but beneath the severe façade is—" he said.

I couldn't help myself and interrupted him before he could finish the sentence, "Let me guess, a spiky solid steel core?"

His lips spread into a smile that revealed his perfect white teeth, melting a fraction of my frustration. He waited for me to let him continue. Sébastien's easygoing personality soothed my volatile temper. It was as if he could see the nice me beneath my tough public façade.

"Maybe," he said, still showing his amusement. "Protecting the school and the headmistress is what she lives for. It may not be obvious, but she's thankful we were here today. It could've been much worse and she knows it. She trusts that we will keep the situation under wraps."

"You mean she trusts you'll do her bidding," I said as the annoyance returned. "If she expects us not to report this because of your family ties to the Académie and your status as an alumnus, I've got news for her. She acted like it was settled without even addressing the issue with me. What am I, chopped liver?"

Sébastien's shoulders dropped in an unconscious movement. His smile vanished.

"We can't sweep three back-to-back incidents of aggressive behavior that nobody can explain under the rug," I said, feeling bad for taking him down a notch even if he deserved it. "If we dig, I wonder whether there have been other incidents before today. She's more likely to tell you if I'm not around. After our presentation, ask her about it."

"Uh, I was getting to that," he said. "You'll be happy to know our presentation has been cancelled. Well, postponed really, to a date and time of our convenience."

I let out a breath I hadn't known I was holding or maybe I had been holding it for so many days I had gotten used to it. I was relieved to be rid of my public speaking commitment for that day even if it meant it wasn't gone altogether. In general, I preferred to do tough things right away so I could relax. In that case, I was grateful for the delay. My mood lifted in an instant.

I was so lost in my inner thoughts of relief, it took a moment for me to realize Sébastien was watching me, unmoving. Feeling self-conscious I returned his gaze.

"There's more," I said. "I can tell by your hesitant stance I'm not going to like it, am I?"

He wavered. I pressed him by remaining silent.

"She already spoke with Francois," he said in a kind voice.

I could have sworn I caught a flash of pity on his face. As the head of the Paris office, Francois was my immediate boss. To say he had treated me with disdain since my arrival wasn't doing justice to his behavior. That would have been bad enough, but it had gotten worse with my handsome colleague's arrival. Francois had treated Sébastien to a welcome lunch when he had reported for duty without ever inviting me. I had found out only by accident.

"Huh?" I snorted, uncomprehending for a moment.

"He's an alumnus too," Sébastien said, the pity flashing lightning fast behind his eyes. "She called him as soon as she heard what had happened. He agreed to keep the incidents unreported for now."

If he had punched me in the gut, I would have regained my composure better. As it was, anger threatened to overwhelm me. I hit the wall with my fist hard enough that it hurt, muttering the mouthful of foul words in case any students walked by, they wouldn't understand what I said.

On the best of days, Francois couldn't muster the interest to do his job, visit the office or even read regular reports. Only under extreme pressure had he intervened in a dangerous case, and afterward he had taken credit for work I had done. I had been de facto acting head of the office from day one. Now he had no problem getting in the middle of the situation at the Académie without so much as a courtesy call to me.

I opened my mouth to vent my ample anger at Sébastien and closed it after uttering an unintelligible sound. Not trusting myself to keep my cool, I turned away from him and we walked in silence out of the prestigious educational institution to make our way back to the office. By the time we got there, I was calmer and more composed, thanks in part to Sébastien's understanding. A couple of his jokes hadn't hurt either.

"After we check in, I'm heading home to change and getting a bite to eat," I announced as we reached the alarm pad at the outer gate of the marshals building where we worked.

The smell of the drying vomit was starting to bother me. Plus, I didn't want to risk any further damage to the expensive outfit. The truth was that my regular clothes would be more comfortable by far than the froufrou ensemble. And, if I was lucky, I might catch Iaen for lunch or at a minimum a heartwarming hug along the way.

We seldom had visitors, so I was surprised to see an exotic-looking stranger sitting in my office. She had olive skin, bleached blond hair with black roots, piled in an uneven bun, and thick, almost black eyebrows. A black and gold-toned headband sat atop her head more as an adornment than serving any purpose. She got up as soon as she saw us. She was of medium height, wearing a black velour workout zippered jacket. The matching pants had the brand name of an easy to forget designer written in large block white letters across the outer side of each sleeve. A wide gold ring hung from a necklace, resting atop the v-line of the jacket. Long earrings in gold and purple dangled from her ears. She wore two gold bangles on her left forearm and one shiny black one on her right forearm.

Permanent narrow worry lines ran across her forehead and two deep lines marred the space between her eyebrows. I suspected the narrow lines that extended outward from her black eyes were from smiling. Anxiety, fear and wariness formed an uncertain expression as I approached.

"Do you speak English?" she asked, looking from me to Sébastien and back to me.

"Yes," we answered in unison.

"Your assistant, she, uh, only speaks French," she said. It was close to lunchtime and Madame Marmotte, who manned our office, was nowhere to be seen. I imagined she had taken an early lunch. "She indicated I should wait here. I hope that was alright." She wrung her hands, telegraphing worry that I might send her away. "I'm sorry to show up unannounced. I couldn't find a phone number and—"

Her voice trailed off and she fell silent as if afraid to continue. The quiet allowed me a moment to think. Although she sounded American or Canadian, I heard a hint of an accent I couldn't place. It told me her first language was not English. I was wondering why Madame Marmotte had invited her into the building and left without letting us know she was there when I heard Sébastien speak.

"I'm Sébastien Poyager," he said, extending his hand.

After they shook hands I spoke, "I'm Dannielle Metreaux."

"Susanna Hassan," she said, shaking my hand.

"How may we help you?" I asked.

"Are these the Weeia headquarters for Europe?" she asked, speaking at such a gunfire pace I had trouble understanding at first. In response to our silence she continued, "I'm Weeia, from, from Syria." She paused before saying the name of her country. "I'm here seeking asylum for my family."

"I don't understand," I said, buying myself time to think. I had no idea there were Weeia in the Middle East. That explained the accent. "Did you just arrive from Syria?"

I had heard about the millions of displaced people around the world. Principal among them were hundreds of thousands of Syrians who had fled their country, escaping frequent violence and bombings. The United Nations had launched a fundraising campaign highlighting the plight of tens of thousands of children and families, split apart and uprooted from the only life they had ever known.

"Yes," she said. "I came straight here as soon as I arrived in Paris. I waited outside the building for several hours until I saw your assistant arrive. I may have startled her. Please tell her I'm sorry if I did."

"I will. You mentioned your family. Are you here alone?" Sébastien asked, referring to the same issue that had caught my attention.

The news reports had given me the impression the Middle Eastern and African migrants were poor, uneducated Arab speakers, mostly men. This lone woman, speaking fluent English and wearing western clothes wasn't what I thought of when someone referred to migrants. That she claimed she was Weeia and had a family threw me for a loop.

While she was distracted answering his question I pulled out my badge with a minimum of fuss and tuned on the Weeia signatures feature. Although to human eyes, marshals badges appeared like unremarkable phones, they were far from that. For a marshal, her badge was an important tool. My badge had the added benefit of having been fine-tuned with the latest software by Ernie Satuan, the Marshals

Academy tech guru and my friend. Within seconds, it registered three Weeia in the room. She was one of us.

"I wasn't sure how long it would take me to make contact with the Weeia authorities to request asylum," she replied. "I left my children with someone. They were fast asleep and I couldn't carry them both."

She looked tired, no, exhausted. There were dark circles under her eyes, and anxiety seemed to blend into her every word as if she feared we might harm her.

"What about your husband?" I asked.

"He's in Berlin, Germany," she said in a soft voice as if it saddened her to say it out loud. "He made the sea crossing by himself and reached an *erstaufnahmerichtung,* where he tried to apply for admission."

I had heard the word on the news. Sébastien was attentive to her response, giving me the impression he had too.

"What does erstaufnahmerichtung mean?" I asked.

"It's German. From what my husband said it's a processing center for refugees, I think," she said.

"Why Berlin?" Sébastien asked. "Isn't it harder to reach than the southern cities?"

"Yes, but once you get to Germany, it doesn't make a huge difference in distance after traveling from Syria across the Mediterranean," she said. "There's already an established Syrian community in Berlin, so he thought it would be better to go to a place where there are others like us. Also, he hoped it would be faster and easier for him to apply there. Unfortunately, many others have gone to Berlin too. He was told that because so many people arrived in Germany at the same time, they have to wait three to six months before they can apply for asylum."

"That's not too bad," Sébastien said.

"No, but while he waits, he can't find a job and without money, he can't help us," she said. "Informally they told him he's likely to be accepted for asylum, but he has to wait to be processed. Until then, he's in a kind of limbo without official aid or a chance to work."

"Where were you while he traveled to Germany? Did you wait in Syria?" Sébastien asked.

"At first I did," she said. "After he left, things improved for a while. Then the barrel bombs started to drop more frequently. Nobody was safe. I saw the bodies of babies and children, pregnant women, old men, my neighbors." She stopped, looking to one side. She drew in her breath and her expression darkened as if she was remembering. "The White Helmets, you've heard of them perhaps, gave us hope, but they weren't enough."

"White Helmets, that rings a bell," I said, straining to figure out where I had heard the term.

"Yes, there was a documentary about them," Sébastien said. "My parents watched it. They said they hadn't understood exactly what was going on there until they saw the film."

"The situation in Syria, I can't describe it," she said in a half moan. "Before we left, every day I woke up wondering how I would feed my family, if that would be the day our luck ran out, if our home would be bombed, if we would—" Her voice broke. "Worse yet, I worried about what might happen to my children if I died and they survived." As if answering my silent question about relatives she went on. "My parents were far away and struggling themselves. Many of our relatives and friends suffered worse than we did. The few neighbors who remained had their hands full. I stayed up at night worrying about who would look after my babies if the worst happened." She glanced away while an anguished expression grew on her face. "One horrible day when I thought we would die, I decided to accept a friend's offer of help. He turned out to be not such a good friend and the offer was more of a sale of transportation services. In the end, we managed to arrive in Turkey."

"If you were safe in Turkey, why come here? Wasn't it dangerous?" I asked without thinking, placing my hands on my hips.

Her eyes darted from side to side like a trapped animal and her breathing sped up. Sébastien winced. Seeing her distress, it occurred to me that I might have made her feel threatened somehow without meaning to do it. I dropped my hands and adopted a more relaxed stance. After a moment she nodded as if to acknowledge my gesture and answered my question.

"Safe is a relative idea," she said, breathing deeply. "No one was bombing our home, but we weren't safe." She emphasized the next to last word. "We were prisoners in a camp with thousands and thousands of other people, little money, no regular food, and no help from the government."

"Prisoners?" Sébastien asked in a gentle tone.

"Exactly, we weren't allowed to leave," she replied.

She shrugged. Crossing one arm over the other she hugged herself like a person seeking comfort or warmth. I preferred not to imagine the bad moments she had experienced in the last few years of her life.

"I thought they had camps with tents, supplies, and even schools," Sébastien said. "The European Union has given Turkey millions of euros for that."

"Yeah, a boatload of money," I said.

"There were tents, some medicine and food, but it was never enough," she said. "People are desperate, sick, and hungry. We stayed at two different camps. They were awful. When we got there, we kept our hopes up, thinking it would be days before my husband sent money and called for us to join him in Germany." Sorrow spread over her face like a fast moving shadow when the winter sun dips over the horizon for the last time at the end of the day. "For weeks, we've been waiting to hear from him, scrambling to find shelter and something to feed my children. I don't care if I go without dinner or anything at all, but they're growing. They need to eat. There are sick people. Disease is spreading like wildfire. You have to watch even the smallest rations and anything you own. Nothing is too small for a thief, a food ration, a scarf, a sweater, or old shoes. They'll take anything. Robbery is a way of life, and it's a violent place. You have to be strong to survive."

"How is it that you speak English with an American accent?" Sébastien asked.

I had noticed that too. Also, she sounded educated, like she was a university graduate.

"I worked for an NGO," she said as if that answered all our questions. My puzzlement must have shown because she explained, "For several years I managed operations for an American non-governmental organization. I'm an organic chemist and my husband is a dentist. We had a good life and now it's shattered. We have nothing left." Her brows furrowed and her lips tightened in a worried expression. "What do I do to request assistance from the Weeia authorities?"

Sébastien turned to me. I had no idea.

"I, I don't know," I said in a halting voice. "It's never come up before." It hadn't crossed my mind either. "I didn't know there were Weeia in the Middle East. Frankly, I'm not sure asylum requests are something we have the authority to handle. We'll look into it and get back to you."

Her shoulders slumped. She looked down at her feet as if she didn't want us to see her face at that moment. I felt bad for her.

"Do you have a place to stay?" Sébastien, ever the thoughtful man, asked.

"I found a group of refugees when we arrived last night," she said.

"We'll find out about the procedure and let you know," I said. "What's your phone number?"

"I don't have a phone number anymore," she said, looking at me as if I had asked her for an alien transporter device instead of the most common electronic mode of communication in Europe.

"How do we reach you?" I asked.

She turned away toward the door. There was a long silence as she walked two steps away from us and back.

"I'll come back," she said in such a soft tone I had difficulty making out the words.

"It may take an hour or a few days to find out," I said, feeling frustrated.

She had to have an address or a phone number where she was staying. Was she trying to be difficult?

"Where exactly are the refugees you found?" Sébastien asked.

"Uh, I don't know the city," she said. "We were at a school, Jean-Jauré, but the police arrived and moved most of the group."

"That's the Lycée Jean-Jauré in the nineteenth," Sébastien, who knew the city better than I did, said. "I heard something about it on the news. Is that where they are?"

"No, we had to leave. There were men in uniforms with machine guns and bulletproof vests," she said. "They weren't kidding around. Fifty of us managed to escape the roundup. Some locals helped us go somewhere else." She pulled a dirty crumpled piece of paper. I caught a glimpse as she lifted it to read it. It looked like it had a name and instructions scribbled on it. "I wrote the name of the streets nearby, boulevard de la Bastille and boulevard Bourdon."

"I know where that is," he said.

"Do you have a toilet I can use?" the woman asked.

"Of course," I said, pointing her toward the office bathroom.

Chapter 4

"I think they're under a bridge," Sébastien said as soon as she was out of earshot. "There's a small canal that links the Seine and the Canal Saint Martin, the Bassin de l'Arsenal. It's a quiet neighborhood near the Gare de Lyon. I bet they're camped out there. She's probably ashamed to tell us she has nowhere to stay. They're on the street."

My heart sank at the thought of that woman and her children, fellow Weeia, homeless. I had met some of the people who called the city streets home and knew it could be rough going and dangerous.

"I saw you pull out your badge," he said. "Were you checking to see if she's Weeia?"

"Yes, she is," I said, half paying attention. Protocol required that I ask the head of the Paris office, Francois, permission before assigning them housing within the marshals complex. He didn't answer my calls and never came by the office. Even if I counted Madame Marmotte, who did as little as possible around the office, we were on our own, Sébastien and I. "We have plenty of space here. Until we find some answers they can stay in the complex."

He opened his mouth and closed it without uttering a word. I watched and waited, giving him an opportunity to weigh in before saying anything else.

"You know this is a can of worms, right?" he asked.

"I guess," I said, hoping he was wrong.

"It's the right thing to do, but that won't make it any easier," he said. "No matter what we do, we're going to make someone unhappy. If we do nothing—"

Before he could finish speaking I interrupted him, "We can't stand by and do nothing."

"I know," he said. His placating tone reminded me he was

on my side. "Many noses are going to be bent out of shape when they discover we're housing Middle Eastern refugees here."

"It's a mother and her two kids," I replied, aware he was right.

"That won't matter much," he said.

"We could keep it on the down low," I said, certain as I spoke the words, that wouldn't be possible for more than a day or two, if at all.

His unbelieving look and matching smile confirmed it. Madame Marmotte was the equivalent of the town crier. Once the family arrived, Madame Marmotte would tell everyone she knew, and she knew a surprising number of Weeia. When it came to putting in a day's work, she moved with the alacrity of the proverbial tortoise, but when it came to gossip, she transformed into the notorious hare.

"Yeah, no," he said. "You and I can keep a secret, but with Odile here there's no chance." He called Madame Marmotte Odile. I didn't share that privilege. She was fond of Sébastien. Since the day I had first set foot in the office, she had made no secret of her dislike for me, describing me in unflattering terms when she thought I wasn't around. "She'll find out. You know she will, and once that happens there's no stopping her. She will start with Francois. I support you one hundred percent. We just have to be aware we'll get splattered with a massive dose of repercussions."

"Fair 'nough," I said. "For now, let's get them off the streets. We'll deal with the naysayers after that."

"Works for me," he said just as the woman reentered the office.

She had settled the loose strands of hair down that had been in disorder, straightened her clothes, and looked more relaxed. I wondered if she had needed to use the facilities during our entire conversation.

"We have a temporary solution," I announced with far

more confidence than I felt. "If you don't mind dust and dirt in the hallways of a mostly empty compound, we have an apartment available where you and your children can stay for a few days."

I left out any mention of the rodents and insects I had fought when I stayed there, figuring there was no point in making it sound as bad as the outdoors. The apartment itself should be free of pests, although it would take much more work for the rest of the complex to reach a similar state. The muscles on her face tightened and her eyes narrowed as if she was trying to spot the catch in the offer.

"You do?" she asked in an almost squeaky voice.

Her stance was tentative and she crossed her arms as if defending herself from something that was too good to be true. It occurred to me that she might be worried about having to pay.

"Yes, it's free of charge," I said. She watched me and waited. I paused to make sure my words had sunk in. "Within the marshals complex you should be fairly safe. There are some rules you must follow. You mustn't tell anyone you're Weeia, which I'm sure you know, and you can't tell anyone where you're going or bring anyone to the complex. As long as you do that, we can figure out the rest together. How does that sound?"

Her mouth opened and closed. After turning from me to Sébastien and back she mumbled something in an unfamiliar language I assumed was Arabic.

"I don't know what to say," she replied after a long while in a trembling voice that threatened tears.

"You don't need to say anything," I replied.

The emotion in her voice tugged at my heartstrings. While I knew nothing of what she had lived through to reach us, I understood what it was like to be alone in Paris for the first time. Despite a bumpy start and a chilly welcome at the office, my arrival had been a picnic by comparison. I was fluent in French and arrived in the city with housing included and the promise of a new and exciting job.

"Remember, it's only temporary," I added. I didn't have the authority to offer her permanent housing or asylum for that matter. As it was, I was stretching my authority. The approval might fall on Francois as the head of the Paris marshals office. Given that it was a delicate subject, it might even be above his rank. "For now, let's go get your kids."

"How old are they?" Sébastien asked.

That brought a shy smile to her lips. Susanna had a confidence and strength that belied the meekness I picked up when we first met. I was glad we had found a way to help her even if it was temporary as I feared it would be.

"Akka is five and Chandi is two," she said. "They'll be so happy when they hear the good news."

Sébastien drove. He was an excellent driver, but like everyone in the city when we sat behind the wheel it was like someone was chasing him, and not in a good way.

"It's best if you don't tell anyone about us," I said as we neared our destination.

"Good thinking," my colleague said as he parked the van in a space that seemed too small for the vehicle. "It's a block and a half away from here, but not within sight of where we are. Walk to the corner then turn right and keep straight and you'll be at the top of the canal. There are stairs on either side."

"How did you know where to go?" she asked.

"I grew up in Paris," he said.

"Go by yourself and get the kids," I said. "We'll be waiting for you here. Say you were in touch with your husband and you plan to join him in Germany. Can you do that?"

"Yes," she said, stepping off the van with caution as if we might disappear at any moment.

When she reached the corner, she looked back at us for a

long while before moving on. I thought I saw her lip tremble, but it might have been my imagination.

"It's been ten minutes," Sébastien said.

"It may take a while for her to gather her kids and say good-bye," I said.

"I'm going to the corner," he said.

"Okay," I agreed, wanting to admonish him to remain unseen and choking down the urge.

An hour after we arrived, Sébastien, Susanna and her two children returned. The kids were scruffy and smelled far worse than they looked. They carried their meager possessions tight against their bodies. I had been able to ignore Susanna's pungent body odor when she was alone. In combination with her offspring, the smell was so unpleasant we opened our windows without saying a word.

The children sat in the back with their mother, chatting in the same language she had used earlier. They stared at us when they thought we weren't looking and turned away when we glanced in their direction.

"Do they speak any English?" Sébastien asked.

"Akka knows a few words, don't you, sweetie?" Susanna said. Her daughter nodded several times. "Chandi was only learning Arabic when we had to flee. Since there was no school and we planned to live in Germany I hadn't worried about it."

We bought sheets, towels, soap, laundry detergent, shampoo, some t-shirts, and food on our way back. Shopping with the children proved a challenge as they hadn't been to a market since they had left Syria, and it was difficult for their mother to keep them under control. Between their unwashed stench and boisterous behavior, the other shoppers gave us a wide birth. I felt such pity for the scrawny things and their mother with her own haggard appearance, I couldn't find it in me to complain. Sébastien seemed to know, as usual, how to win everybody over.

Despite the language barrier and culture within minutes of meeting him, Akka and Chandi became his friends.

On our return we ran into Madame Marmotte as she was heading out. She didn't say anything. She didn't have to because the distaste on her face when she saw us was unmistakable. Where Susanna and her children's faces were bright with excitement, Madame Marmotte was in a sourer mood than usual, which was saying something. It was like watching a thunderstorm approaching a clear sky.

I suspected she had waited for us, because it was past her usual departure time and she was never one to work late. Gossip that she was, she spent the better part of the day in the office on the phone exchanging stories with her friends, I imagined she was curious about the unexpected foreign woman she had left waiting for us.

"The cat is out of the bag," Sébastien said, emphasizing cat and grinning, after she had gone.

"I had hoped we would have until tomorrow," I said. "How long before she expresses her displeasure, do you think?"

"Hmm, not long," he said, his grin broadening. "She has many qualities, but tolerance may not be among them."

"This is so nice," Susanna said in an admiring voice when we entered my former apartment.

"I used to live here," I said, remembering the state it had been in when I had first arrived. It had taken considerable work to clean and modernize it enough for it to be habitable. Then, I had spent many more hours making it comfortable and cozy. It had been empty since I had moved to an apartment in the swanky Left Bank. I was glad to see it put to good use. "You should have everything you need. The appliances are new. There's hot water and a washer and dryer if you want to do laundry."

It took the rest of the day to settle the small family into the apartment and explain the do's and don'ts of the marshals complex. I had thought of calling Tadas and Giedrius, our resident handymen in the complex, to lend us a hand. But by the time we returned from picking up the children, it was early evening, a time they set aside for their families. Since France's laws tended to protect workers over employers, their workdays were never overfull. Still, theirs was hard manual labor and I imagined they were tired. I didn't want to interrupt them. While Sébastien and I didn't benefit from the same protections, and our hours were erratic and at times long, we had flexibility in our schedules and greater say in our employment terms than Tadas and Giedrius.

I was grateful when Sébastien volunteered to stay with me and help out. It was more a matter of solidarity than because the task was unpleasant or hard. He was backing me up in case my actions weren't well received by our boss and the office admin. After we took care of the most important issues we bid Susanna good night. The look of gratitude on her face as her kids played safe and carefree in the living room reassured me that we had made the right decision.

Chapter 5

"Hey gorgeous, how was your day?" Iaen asked when I arrived at his boat tired and wired from the day's events.

I always felt welcome and special when we were together. It wasn't that we didn't ever disagree, we often did. Our lives were opposites in many respects, but Iaen's way of always looking at life as if the glass was half full lightened even my darkest moods. He made me feel pretty, despite my own sense of inadequacy, and my body's tendency to be chunkier than the local ladies. French women spent more hours on their appearance than I could spare even on my days off work.

After removing my shoes, I boarded his spotless wooden vessel, which he babied like a beloved pet. Docked in the heart of the city, it was a short walk from my apartment. He lived a stone's throw from the busy Ile de la Cité, one of two islands on the Seine River and the location of the famous Notre Dame Cathedral. His boat was below the street and might as well have been a world away. Few tourists or Parisians bothered to walk down as far as his craft. The quay was well lit and quiet, except for the gentle lapping of water against the yacht's hull. At that hour of the night, there was seldom traffic on the river to make a wake. I half noticed the familiar musty odor of the murky water, remembering how the mayor had vowed to clean the polluted river so people could swim in it.

The view of the sparkling lights along the Right Bank and the Ile de la Cité was mesmerizing. It made me feel lucky yet again to be living there. It also made me wonder if that was why Paris was called the City of Lights. I would ask Iaen. He loved the city above all others and knew a lot about its history.

I had texted him that I would be late and wasn't sure if he would be home when I arrived, so I was pleased to see him. As soon as I was within reach, he encircled me in an amorous embrace and we kissed until my toes tingled with desire. On the deck behind him, I noticed the table set with wine glasses, pretty cloth napkins, placemats, and candles. He loved candles. The smell of food made me realize I was hungry. Sébastien and I had been so busy getting Susanna and her children to the supermarket and settled in my old apartment that we had forgotten to eat. As if echoing my thoughts loud gurgling sounds rose from my belly, making Iaen chuckle.

"I'm famished," he said as he tore the foil from the top of a bottle of wine. "I don't need to ask if you're hungry. Do you want to hang out for a few minutes before we eat?"

Dinner together would be perfect. I smiled, feeling loved and grateful to have such a wonderful man in my life. His eyes reflected my joy.

"Naw," I replied. "I'm ready whenever you are. Can I help with anything?"

"Everything is taken care of," he said, pouring a glass of rosé and handing it to me. "You had a long day, so sit your cute tail down and keep me company while I serve the salad."

I set the glass on the folding wood table and reached for a slice of baguette from the breadbasket, spreading a thin layer of butter on it. I had been running before going to work in the mornings and added twice a week strenuous workouts to my routine. But Iaen's excellent cooking and the wonderful meals served at many of the places we went had been expanding my hips so I was watching what I ate.

"You'll never believe what happened today," I said.

"Oh?" he asked.

Often, I couldn't discuss much about my day with Iaen. A self-made entrepreneur with a penchant for dodgy deals,

Iaen moved in edgy grey circles, whereas my job required me to move in black and white ones with little to no room for blurry lines. While it was the hint of sexy bad boy that had first attracted me to Iaen, it was his gentle romantic center that had roped me in hook, line, and sinker.

"Uh, I think I can tell you, if you promise to keep it to yourself," I said, convinced Susanna's presence wouldn't remain secret for long with Madame Marmotte in the know.

He paired his index and his thumb running them in the air in front of his lips and making a twisting motion as if locking them and throwing away the key. Then, he dropped to his knees and mimed searching for the key and placing it in his pants pocket.

"Fine, you got me," I said, laughing despite myself. "I wouldn't tell you if it was really secret. Still, keep it under wraps please."

"Will do," he said, carrying two blond wood salad bowls brimming with greens and yummy bits to the table.

We sat down. My stomach grumbled in anticipation, distracting me for an instant. I took a sip of wine.

"We received an asylum request," I blurted.

"For—" he asked as his brows knitted together in confusion, a gesture I found endearing.

"A Syrian woman fleeing the war showed up at the office with her two kids in tow, asking for asylum," I said.

"At your office?" he still seemed baffled. "Not getting it. Please spell it out."

"She's Weeia," I explained. "Did you know there were Weeia in the Middle East?"

"Never gave it much thought," he said, pensive. I took a forkful of salad. "I suppose there's no reason why there wouldn't be superhumans in other parts of the world. I just haven't met any. I take it you're sure she's Weeia?" I nodded. "What's she like?"

"She seemed nice enough, brave, a bit desperate, shy,

confident, quiet," I said, thinking how the woman had made such as strong impression on me that I had decided to offer her shelter.

"Why desperate?" he asked, lifting a mouthful of salad.

"I like the dressing," I said. "Did you make it?"

"Yes, the secret is good balsamic vinegar. It takes two minutes," he said.

"To answer your question, they arrived illegally last night without money, friends, or speaking the language," I said.

Frowning he asked, "If she doesn't speak French how did you communicate?"

"Luckily, she speaks excellent English," I replied. "I'm not sure what would've happened otherwise. Apparently, she waited for hours until morning. We were out when she arrived. She had a hard time convincing Madame Marmotte to let her inside the office to wait."

"Oh?"

"She's not the friendliest of people on a good day," I said. "She thinks her only equals are French Weeia. With an exotic looking stranger who shows up out of the blue, speaks no French, and smells like a homeless person, you have the formula for Madame Marmotte to turn her nose up in the air." I had experienced a heavy dose of her stuffy attitude. It wasn't fun and I was her boss. "Poor woman, she left her small children with other refugees, virtual strangers, under a bridge while she went to our office. They were all dirty, hungry, and afraid. It's hard to describe. I can't imagine what the trek to Paris from Turkey must've been like."

"I guess the mood in France isn't welcoming for asylum seekers," he said. "The fear of bombings and attacks has turned into paranoia and anti-Muslim attitudes."

"That's a horrible situation for all those people," I said. "Their lives will never be the same. I can't imagine what it must be like to be caught in the middle of a war."

"What happened to her husband and the rest of her

family?" he asked between bites.

"Last she heard, he was in Berlin, waiting to apply for refugee status," I said.

"Why didn't they travel together?"

"It was too risky for the whole family to make the crossing by sea and they thought the camps in Turkey would be a better place for her and the little ones," I said.

"Why didn't she join him in Germany instead of coming to Paris?" he asked.

"Sébastien and I wondered the same thing," I replied. "She said she tried, but it's become very difficult to reach Germany. Her mother had told her years ago that if she ever had an emergency she should contact the Weeia. She knew there was an office in Paris. When she realized she wouldn't be able to get to Germany, she came here."

"So were you able to help her?" he asked, picking up our empty salad plates and taking them to the galley.

"Yes and no," I replied. "I don't have the authority to grant her request for asylum. That's a policy issue above my pay grade."

"But?"

"Uh, yeah, I offered her my old apartment to stay in for a few days while I find out what's what," I said, eyeing the pasta filled plates he was carrying with increasing hunger.

"Parmesan?" he asked.

"Yes," I said with enthusiasm. "Bring it on."

Iaen grated cheese over my pasta until I raised my hand in a gesture of surrender. He did the same with his dish before taking the hard cheese chunk back to the galley and sitting down across the table from me.

"We picked up her kids and brought them back," I said after a couple of bites. "It's delicious. This white clams in wine sauce dish is the bomb." He smiled and nodded to let me know he had heard my praise. "Have I ever told you you're a good cook?"

"Once or twice," he said, looking pleased.

"More like a dozen," I replied.

"Perhaps, but I never get tired of praise," he said as he rubbed his toes against mine under the table. "I think you actually told me I'm a handsome, wonderful, and outstanding cook."

I smiled. His caresses drove me to distraction. After a few moments, I drew in a resigned breath and said, "If you keep that up your wonderful dinner is going to get cold and I may not be held responsible."

That earned me a chuckle. He tucked his feet back to his side of the table.

When I still didn't react he prodded me, "You were saying?"

"Huh?" I managed.

"You were telling me about the migrant woman and her family," he said with a naughty twinkle in his eyes.

"Oh, yes. I remember," I said. "Between the two of us we bought her food and some basics and got her settled in. You should've seen the gratitude on her face when we left."

"Listen to you," he said, his eyes crinkling and his lips spreading apart with amusement. "You want people to think you're so tough, made of stone, but beneath the surface you're really full of doughnut jelly."

I threw my cloth napkin at him, thankful it dropped halfway across on the tabletop because I didn't want the pretty, handwoven napkin to be stained with oil from the pasta sauce. He grinned as he picked up the napkin and handed it back to me. Getting up, he topped our glasses with fresh chilled rosé, and planted a kiss on my forehead when he was done.

"That's one of the things I love about you," he said.

He had told me he loved me again. Iaen was better at expressing his feelings and more affectionate than I was. He didn't just tell me how he felt in the heat of passion or after having one glass of wine too many. He told me in the morning on a Sunday, and in the afternoon when he greeted me with a welcome hug. The previous week, he had said he loved me with a lingering look in his eyes like there was something else he wanted to say. Instead of telling him I loved him in reply, I stood like a deer in the headlights, frozen in place and mute.

"What's that?" I asked distracted by the subject of love.

"I said you're a warrior princess on the outside and mushy on the inside," he replied.

"Mushy? Did you just call me mushy?" I asked in mock fury.

"Yep, what are you gonna do about it?" he asked, emphasizing the second word.

"I'll think of something," I said, my voice hoarse with desire.

Chapter 6

It was a gray and cloudy Paris morning, not unusual. A light drizzle fell on the city, making the streets slick and washing the fresh dog poo off the narrow sidewalks.

I had a spring in my step after a night with Iaen and was looking forward to an uneventful day at work. I figured it would be at least a few days before Francois graced us with a call or visit. I had taken two steps out the door when my phone rang. I recognized the name on the caller ID. It belonged to Yolanda, the Weeia healer.

"Hello," I said, surprised to hear from her.

Her soothing voice with a thick accent filled my ear, "Hello, Danni. Sorry to call so early. I was hoping you could spare a few minutes."

Yolanda was the person we went to when we became ill. She was the Weeia equivalent of a doctor, shrink, and nutritionist all rolled into one hard-to-describe being. Beneath the exotic appearance, I sensed a strong woman with a colorful background. She had saved my life not long after I arrived in Paris, and for that, she had earned my gratitude and respect.

"Shoot," I said.

"Can you come by now?" she asked in what for anyone else would've been a serene voice, yet for her was an urgent one.

"On my way," I said, picking up my pace along with the car keys, and wondering what was up.

She worked at home. Her private space was on one side and her office for healing consultations on the other. I had visited the work space on more than one occasion. Her house was near the Sacre Coeur Basilica, a popular tourist attraction and church in the eighteenth arrondissement north of where I lived. Paris had been a walled city in the past and while the walls had been taken down decades earlier, remnants of the wall and gates and the division they represented remained intact in many ways. The city was divided into twenty arrondissements, starting in the center with the first one and moving in a clockwise shape to reach the final one in the northeast of town.

I crossed the Seine River via the Pont Neuf Bridge on the Ile de la Cité to reach the rue du Pont Neuf on the Right Bank. I stayed on the one-way street until it dead-ended at Les Halles, forcing me to turn left to find the rue du Louvre. I continued to rue Montmartre to rue du Faubourg Montmartre, rue de Rochechouart, rue de Clignancourt to rue Lamarck and from there to her house.

In a number of ways, it was a contrast to go from my flat neighborhood in the center of the city to her hilly one close to the edge of the city. During the forty-five minutes it took me to reach the artsy quirky area, I wondered what had made the healer summon me. I had the impression she wouldn't ask me to her home-cum-business without a good reason.

As I approached the building, I recognized the peeling cream paint on the exterior walls. The pale color stood out against the many green plants of different sizes and shapes growing almost wild around the front of the house, and in planters crowded near the entrance and below the windows.

Sale, pronounced sah-leh, her Yorkie mix pooch, barked a greeting before I had a chance to ring the doorbell. From inside, a woman's voice told me to enter. Sale danced a happy jig as soon as I did. I crouched down to pet her while I waited for her owner to appear.

"I'll be there in a moment," she said from further inside.

An instant passed before the healer glided into the room. She had a way of walking that gave the impression she glided just above the ground as if she wasn't subject to the rules of gravity. She had a healthy look accentuated by rich cinnamon-toned skin, the kind sun worshipers spent years cultivating, and a thin and ethereal appearance like someone made of air. I knew first hand that she wasn't that frail. She was strong and energetic. When I faltered, on a previous visit, and almost fell, she caught me with ease.

Her brown hair was like a living being, held in part by waist length Rasta braids. Short curly strands of sun bleached hair escaped the braids and stood at attention in no particular order, away from her head, forming a halo around it. She wore a purple tie-dyed dress that reached her ankles and purple suede shoes. Her sole item of jewelry was a ring with a large sparkling see-through medium blue stone on her index finger.

"Thank you for coming so quickly," she said after the usual exchange of kisses. "I'm sure you're busy so I'll get straight to the point."

I wasn't that busy and I was always curious to learn more about her. While many Weeia in her position of importance would boast and gossip, she was discreet and mysterious, keeping to herself, which made me wonder what her story was. I didn't mind the visit, although there was something about her place that gave me the willies. The odd and unfamiliar odors reminded me of a sick ward or a hospital. Dozens of jars filled with unidentifiable contents, some floating in clear liquid, others so dark as to make a guess impossible, lined the shelves.

"Sure," I said, distracted by my thoughts and at the same time giving her a chance to tell me why she had summoned me.

If someone else had called me the way she had, I might've been grumpy, but she had a way about her that calmed my nerves. Also, from the little I knew of her, I was sure she would only ring me for something important. The serious look on her face and the tension in her body confirmed my suspicions.

"A man died in my arms last night," she said, speaking as if she was weighing every word before allowing it to breach her lips. "You may have heard about it already."

I shook my head from side to side, asking, "Weeia?"

"Of course," she replied in an impatient tone. "It was late when his family called me. He was from out of town and I had never met him before." Her eyes focused to one side as if pulling the memories from some point I couldn't see. "I went to their apartment as soon as I got the call. When I arrived, he was breathing with much difficulty, wheezing and conscious, but unable to speak. Red splotches on the skin around his neck made me think he had an allergic reaction. I thought it would be a matter of minutes to treat him. As soon as I opened my second sight I realized that wouldn't be the case."

"Your second sight?" I blurted.

"As a healer I see the energy of other Weeia," she said in the same impatient tone. "I usually shut down my ability until I need it. So much information all at once becomes exhausting. It's like hitting the pause button on a video player until you're ready to watch a recording. When I open my sight, I use it to diagnose patients. It allows me to see familiar patterns of energy flow and identify problems."

I had no idea that was what she did. I had never given it much thought, assuming it was intuitive and hard to understand. She focused her gaze on my eyes, gauging my comprehension. I moved my head down and back up a tiny bit to confirm I was following her explanation.

"That was something I had never seen before," she said in a soft voice, a mixture of awe and something else I couldn't identify. Her brows furrowed, confirming my impression. "And not in a good way."

"What do you mean?" I asked.

"An allergy, I get," she said. "I've treated many over the

years successfully. They're straightforward. Since there are only five or six groups of foods that make people sick, I start with that and I can usually tell what caused a reaction fairly quickly."

"But?"

"It looked like an allergic reaction, but that's where his case became weird," she said. "His family said nothing similar to that had ever happened before and he suffered from no allergies. That's not unheard of. Some people develop allergies all of a sudden, but they don't often up and die out of the blue. If it was a reaction to something that killed him, I don't think it was anything he ate. I can't prove it. It's what my gut tells me, and I trust my gut."

"Can you only treat food allergies?" I asked, remembering how well she had ministered to my illness.

"Yes, well, I can treat many plant-related allergies, and other allergic reactions, if I know what caused them," she said. "Given enough time to find the cause, I can fix many ailments, including allergies. In his case, the redness was minor. Normally, I would've advised my patient to avoid whatever had caused the rash, provided him an herbal beverage to tone down the body's response, and a salve to sooth the irritated skin. Last night, there was nothing I could do, no time."

"Bear with me, Yolanda, I'm trying to understand what happened," I said. "Stop me if I make any mistakes. The guy last night had a small red spot on his neck, which you diagnosed as an unknown allergy. He was already in bad shape when you got there and before you could figure out what was wrong with him, he died. And, you think whatever made his neck red was minor. It wasn't what killed him. You think that although it's the only visible symptom, it's not the reason he died, correct?"

She let out her breath as if a weight had been lifted off her shoulders and said, "Yes. I've been thinking about it since I got back. I checked my reference books and talked with colleagues." I had no idea healers had reference books. I had it in my head that they worked off the seat of their pants, feeling their way through their craft. "There's no other explanation. His reaction was way worse than I've ever seen from a skin condition. I tried to treat it." Her lips puckered in an anxious expression as if she had sucked on a bitter orange. "Nothing I did worked. I watched helplessly as the energy drained from his body until he had nothing left. It doesn't make sense."

"I wonder why the family hasn't called it in," I said.

"I had a feeling they might not report it," she said. "I'm not sure it had anything to do with him."

"Oh?"

"This may come as a surprise to you, Danni, but not everyone welcomes a visit from a marshal," she said.

The tightness in her face relaxed as a half-smile appeared. It was so unexpected I wasn't sure what to respond.

"The guidelines indicate I should alert the marshals since I can't explain the cause of death and because of how quickly it all happened," she said. "It's up to you what to do next."

"You think I should investigate it," I said, reading the answer on her face before she shrugged in reply. I struggled to grasp what was making her uneasy so I took a stab in the dark. "And you'd rather I didn't mention you."

"I would be grateful if you could leave me out of official reports," she said, returning to her familiar soothing style of speaking.

"I'll do what I can," I said.

"Thank you," she replied. "Now if you don't mind, I have a patient waiting."

Chapter 7

Yolanda had returned to her patient and left me in the privacy of her foyer. After glancing at me once, Sale followed in her footsteps. I liked the spunky dog and envied her cozy relationship with and loyalty to the healer. For a second it made me wish for a pet, but there was no time in my life for one.

"I'm leaving the healer's and heading to 3 rue du Dragon Rouge in the twentieth," I said when Sébastien answered my audio call on his badge. Unless video was necessary, I usually opted for audio. "It's off rue de Ménilmontant. Meet me there as soon as you can."

"Are you okay?" he asked with concern in his voice.

"I'm fine," I replied. "I'm here about a possible new case. I'll fill you in when we meet."

"Sweet," he said, his tone changing in an instant.

"Don't mention Yolanda to Madame Marmotte," I said in a firmer tone than necessary.

"Got it," he said. "What's the nearest metro station?"

In Paris, all the streets had names and there was no obvious way to know where in the city a street was located just from its name. Even lifelong residents used subway stations as reference points when searching for an address.

"I think it's between Jourdain and Ménilmontant," I replied.

"I'll find it. See you in a few," he said.

It was a little more than seven kilometers from Yolanda's house in the eighteenth arrondissement to rue du Dragon Rouge in the twentieth arrondissement. I could take the boulevard Périphérique, a multilane highway that circled Paris, or drive southeast through the city. In theory, the boulevard Périphérique, should have been the faster alternative. In practice, the times I had been on the boulevard, it had been congested and slow-moving. The first time I had taken the boulevard, I had expected pretty scenery and views of the city's iconic attractions. But it wasn't a pretty road. Overpasses felt like short tunnels, the car exhaust and darkness seemed worse than in the heart of town. Colorful yet ugly graffiti lined many sections of the highway. In its overpasses and short tunnels, the car exhaust and darkness seemed worse than in the heart of town. Colorful yet ugly graffiti lined many sections of the highway.

In addition, navigating my way around the boulevard was challenging because I didn't know the exits well. Drivers shifted lanes often and new arrivals eager to speed up merged onto already crowded roads only to brake to a sudden halt when they reached the inevitable gridlock. Despite the usual turtle-like pace, some people, in particular those riding motorcycles, squeezed through the gaps, missing neighboring cars and trucks by a hair's breadth. Impressed by their prowess, I was also fearful of an accident. The office car required a significant effort to acquire, and I preferred it not be damaged, leaving me at the mercy of public transportation again. Hopping on the expressway might double my driving time and would certainly jack up my blood pressure.

Although driving the city route meant I would be caught in at least one traffic jam, I preferred that option. I was more familiar driving within the urban core than on suburban streets and highways. Within the twenty arrondissements the flow of vehicles was at times manic and some drivers could be rude. At the same time, by glancing ahead I had an idea of what to expect. If I could see bumper-to-bumper cars ten blocks in front of me I knew we would all be crawling along for the foreseeable future. Where I knew the streets, I might be able to anticipate the degree of congestion.

Plus, on each drive I learned a little bit about the routes, the avenues, and the neighborhoods I passed. From the Sacre Coeur, making my way south to north in that part of town at that hour of the day hadn't been bad. After a few minutes I made a final left turn to reach the street, where I started looking for a parking spot. Fifteen minutes later, I found one not too far from rue du Dragon Rouge. I walked the rest of the way.

When I arrived, Sébastien was already there. He wore casual clothes, bright red pants, a navy blue sports jacket, and matching shirt. While I paid no attention to brand names or specific styles in vogue, I knew he wore custom-tailored clothing made from the finest natural fibers, as his sister had once explained. He chose colors and patterns that would have made me seem chunkier and less fashionable than I was, and on him they worked well. As was often the case, he looked like he had stepped out of a fashion magazine. As usual, he was full of energy and had the same eager attitude I remembered well from the day we met several months earlier.

"Did you fly?" I asked. "Never mind. I bet you know a shortcut."

"Yep," he said, grinning like a Cheshire cat.

Sébastien knew the city like the back of his hand. He knew the shortcuts, the traffic patterns, the dodgy neighborhoods, the streets favored by strike groups, and the one-way streets. As we worked together, I had come to appreciate the advantages.

"What's so urgent?" he asked.

"There's been a suspicious death," I said in a soft voice to keep from being overheard by people passing us on the sidewalk. "Did anyone report a death last night?"

"Not that I know of," he said, matching my soft tone. "Odile didn't mention anything. I got to the office before she did. There were no messages and nobody called while I was there. It was quiet. Was it a homicide?"

"No, nothing like that," I said. "A middle-aged man visiting from Normandy died suddenly from what may have been an allergy."

"That doesn't sound suspicious," he said, waiting for me to continue.

"Not at first, but Yolanda's never come across a case like his before," I replied. "She can't explain the allergen, the source of the allergy. What's even worse is she didn't know the cause of death. She said he didn't respond to any of her efforts to revive him. She watched feeling helpless as the man's energy drained from his body until he passed away without saying anything." He watched me with interest. "You kept her involvement to yourself, right?"

Sébastien was trustworthy and I was confident he had done as I had asked, but I had to make sure. My question didn't appear to bother him.

"Of course," he said. "Keep in mind that Odile is pretty plugged in to the latest gossip. Even if it wasn't reported officially, I bet she knows already or will know when we return to the office. It's uncanny how she finds out about everything that goes on in Paris. She probably heard about it after it happened last night."

I grunted in reply. He smiled, amused.

After a minute I said, "At the end of the day, I don't care if she finds out from someone else as long as nobody thinks Yolanda was the one who told us. She didn't want her patients thinking she was betraying their trust."

"Yeah, I understand," Sébastien said. "She has to walk a fine line. The marshals guidelines require that she report anything suspicious, even though she doesn't work for us. At the same time, her patients need to trust that what they tell her and whatever happens at her clinic will remain in confidence. If she doesn't protect their privacy, they'll be afraid to see her. From what I've heard, it's an issue for healers in general. With Yolanda it's a sensitive topic. That she called you means she has a high opinion of you." He rolled his eyes in an exaggerated comedic motion. "Consider it a good sign."

"I didn't know it was such a big deal," I said, grateful for his insights and light-hearted humor.

"I think it is, oh trustworthy Marshal Metreaux," he whispered and mock bowed.

"By the way, do you know Robert Previn or the Previn Family?" I asked.

"Not off the top of my head," he said, focusing his eyes in the distance as if seeking data from his brain's hard drive. He was well-connected, and the Weeia population in the city not that large, so it had been worth a shot. "Now what?"

"We'll speak with the family and take a look at the body, but we need an explanation of how we found out," I said, wondering what to say to the man's relatives when we knocked on their door unannounced.

"Well, there's always social media," Sébastien volunteered.

"We're not supposed to—" I never finished the sentence. His muffled guffaw interrupted me. He pulled out his smart phone and started tapping at a rapid clip as he spoke. "I guess people don't always follow the rules."

"Did you when you were a teenager?" he asked. Before I could reply he added, "Oh, don't answer that. It was silly of me to ask. Of course you did." It was my turn to roll my eyes. "Fortunately for us, most people, adults and teenagers, don't always do what they're supposed to do. Although it's not officially allowed, it's not expressly forbidden, as in no penalties have been enforced. Tons of Weeia use social media apps. Here, take a gander."

He passed me his fancy smartphone. The expensive titanium and leather confection was exceptional, making me wonder where he bought it. I strained to see the backlit electronic screen. The sun's reflection on the page made it hard to read.

"What am I looking at?" I asked.

In response, he took off his jacket and raised it above my head, shading the smartphone so I could see well. On the screen were posts by someone from the Brosse and Previn household dated that day about a death in the family.

"Wow," was all I managed. "I'll remind them. No, I guess I won't, at least not today. That will just make them clam up." He nodded in an approving fashion. "But now we have an explanation for how we heard about it in case they ask, and if necessary, we can leverage it to insist they answer our questions. We won't mention it unless we have no choice. Good work."

I was sure he stretched a tiny bit taller on hearing the compliment. I wasn't generous with my praise and had been striving to do better in my new supervisory role. I had opposed a trainee posting for the Paris office under me when it was offered. Despite my objections, Sébastien arrived and although it had been an adjustment, I was glad to work with him.

"Once we speak with them and see the body what will we do?" he asked.

"It depends," I said, pausing to think through my reply as I spoke, "on their attitude and the condition of the body. If what we find confirms, or at least doesn't contradict, Yolanda's report we'll have to look into his death."

"What does that mean exactly?" he asked. "If the healer doesn't know why he died how are we supposed to figure it out? We're not healers."

"True, but an expert told us something is wrong," I said. "We can trace his movement since he arrived in Paris, find out what kind of person he was, if he was a drug user, how well he got along with his family, if he had any enemies. There's also the possibility that if he was allergic to whatever killed him, one of his family members might be too. They could be in danger. Also, we'll need to file a report and request a Body Retrieval."

"What about Francois?" he asked.

"I sent him a message already. As usual, he hasn't replied," I said. "I doubt he has even opened it. If he follows his usual pattern, he isn't going to be happy when we go above his head, and report to Portland directly."

"I could go to his apartment or to the club to try to catch him," he said. "Can we delay the request?"

"Not really," I replied. "It's best if we take action, per the guidelines, quickly and decisively."

"OMG, you're quoting verbatim, aren't you?" he laughed.

I blushed. Doing my best to ignore the good-natured jibe and not get upset I continued.

"If the case meets the requirements and we don't order it immediately, the funeral home will take the body. Then it could get complicated," I said.

Ever the diplomat, he pressed on, lobbying for Francois's participation. I understood he meant well, but it was starting to annoy me.

"He might know the family," he said. "That would be helpful, wouldn't it?"

"Possibly," I conceded. "There's also the chance the family might not want us to investigate, if they have something to hide for example. Our job is to avoid or reduce the involvement of third parties such as a funeral home. Yes, I'm quoting from the manual. While I would prefer to have Francois in the loop, if there's one lesson he's taught me since I got here is that I can't count on him to be around when I need him."

That wasn't one hundred percent true, but Francois shirked his duties at every opportunity. Before Sébastien arrived, more than once my safety or my life or both had been on the line because he hadn't had my back. On the flip side, when it came to taking credit for something I had done well with little or no help from him he didn't hesitate.

"How bad would it be if we waited until tomorrow to interview the family?" he asked.

"I don't know," I said, hesitating. "Until we meet them and get a feel for the situation it's impossible to tell if this is a fluke or if someone committed a crime. What if someone else dies because we didn't look into this right away? Will you be glad we waited?" The more I thought about it, the surer I was of what we had to do. "You're welcome to call him. Maybe he'll take your call. I'm willing to wait for you to do that."

"Thanks," he said, calling our boss as he spoke. A couple of minutes later he hung up adding, "There's no answer."

I felt bad for Sébastien. He was friends with Francois but he was feeling the sting of disappointment I knew so well.

Chapter 8

An elderly woman exiting from 3 rue du Dragon Rouge held the door for us. Sébastien took two long strides to keep the heavy wood door open, thanking her as she walked away.

Once inside we reached a second set of heavy wood doors. They were locked. To one side there was a small board with names next to corresponding buttons.

"We'll have to ring them," Sébastien said. In response to my single nod, he pressed the plastic button by the name Brosse.

"Yes?" a disembodied woman's voice asked.

"Good morning, ma'am, I'm here to see Mr. or Mrs. Previn. Are you Mrs. Previn?"

"Yes, are you from the funeral home?" the woman asked.

"I'm here about a related matter," he said. "My name is Sébastien Poyager from the Office. My colleague Danielle Metreaux and I need to speak with you. May we come up?"

For response, we heard a loud buzz followed by a metallic click. I pushed the door and entered. Sébastien followed me. We glanced at each other as the elevator doors opened before we had a chance to press the call button.

"There's a camera," he said, pointing to the upper corner inside the elevator as the doors shut.

"Once we get to their floor, we can look for the door with their name," I said.

"I think it's going to stop at their front door," he said. "If I'm not mistaken there's only one apartment per floor. A friend lives in a building with a similar design."

"I see," I said. "Take the lead."

He beamed with pleasure. As my colleague had predicted, when the elevator stopped, the doors opened. Seconds later, a woman I estimated to be in her forties, opened another set of doors from the inside. She gestured with her hand for us to enter. Mascara streaks ran down her face. Her eyes were red and puffy. The stale odor of cigarette smoke mixed with an unfamiliar perfume reached me as we stepped inside. Despite her fragile and bedraggled appearance, she didn't hesitate.

"Sabine Brosse," she said by way of greeting, extending her hand to shake ours. "Brosse is my husband's name. Previn was my name before I married."

"Are you alone?" Sébastien asked after we had identified ourselves a second time.

It was standard procedure for us to make sure we had privacy before discussing marshals business. If she had company, humans in particular, we would have to wait for their departure or speak with her in private.

"Yes," she said with obvious annoyance. "You're from the marshals office."

"Yes," I confirmed, wondering if she recognized our names or had anticipated our visit.

"Please accept our deepest condolences," Sébastien said with the ease of a diplomat. Pain flashed across her face at his words, her lips pursed together and lines appeared on her forehead. "We're so sorry to call on you at this difficult time. We have a few routine questions."

"Of course," she said, straightening her blouse and running her hand over the loose strands of tousled bleached blond hair that had escaped from her ponytail. A dark stain marred one side of the paisley-patterned red top and wrinkles covered part of the bottom. "If you would follow me."

We walked down a six-foot-wide corridor to a single large living and dining room, the click-clack of her heels on the wood floor the only sound. Nearest to us was the dining room with seating for ten. The spacious living room was messy, with cushions askew, overflowing ashtrays, and empty glasses and bottles littering the area. Our host stood by an armchair at the tablecloth-covered dining table, inviting us to sit by motioning with her hand and nodding her head.

Once we were seated, she asked in a tight tone, "How may I help you, marshals?"

"We are here to confirm the death of a member of your household," Sébastien said in a soft voice. When she failed to respond after a pause he continued. "What is the exact name of the deceased and your relationship to him?"

"Robert Previn," she said in a flat voice. "My older brother. He isn't exactly a member of our household. He lives, lived in Honfleur."

"Normandy?" Sébastien asked. She nodded. "Why was he in Paris?"

"He was here on business and visiting us for a few days," she said.

She stopped speaking as if she didn't want to say anything else. We waited, allowing an uncomfortable silence to fill the room. To my surprise, the interior of the apartment was quiet. It made me think they had soundproofed the windows. She focused her attention on her hands resting on her lap. Her nails were painted red in a similar shade to her top. It had taken a few weeks of spotting vermillion-clad people of all shapes and sizes for me to realize red was in fashion.

"When the kids were little, he used to come every month," she said still staring at her hands. "He's their favorite uncle." Her voice trembled. She wiped her eyes with one hand. "Now that they're teenagers, they spend less time with their uncle during his visits, so he came less frequently. Still, they're heartbroken. I've been away myself and only just returned. I wish I had spent—"

We waited until she regained her composure. She raised her head, looking straight at nothing in particular as far as I could tell.

"Mrs. Brosse, we need you to tell us what happened,"

Sébastien said in the same soft voice.

"I don't know," she blurted. "One minute he and my son were joking and horsing around as usual, the next he was gasping for air and shaking uncontrollably. We called the healer immediately." Her eyes expanded as if she was seeing a ghost floating in front of her. "She came right away, but she couldn't revive him. She said it was too late. If only we had a better healer."

Her voice dropped at the end, making it difficult to tell what followed. She turned her attention to us, directing an angry glance at me.

"What do you want anyway? He's dead," she said.

Her clipped words burst out of her with such force she startled me and I stood halfway up. As soon as I realized there was no danger, I sat back down. Once again, we allowed her a few moments to compose herself.

"Because it's an unexplained death, we'll need to look into it," Sébastien said.

"And we need to see him," I added in the softest voice I could muster.

I felt sympathy for her. Her anguish was clear to see, but her aggressive behavior was unwarranted and put me on the defensive. Her hand lifted in a slow motion as if it was stuck with molasses to her lap, requiring every ounce of energy she had to pry it free. With a sudden flutter of her wrist, she indicated the living room. I had seen many reactions to trauma and death on the job, yet people still managed to surprise me. For the first time since we had entered the room, I noticed an off-white throw atop the sofa. Because it was almost the same color as the sofa, I had missed it. Once I noticed it, I realized it must have been covering the body, no wonder she was on edge. We were in the same room as her dead brother.

I motioned to Sébastien to keep her talking while I walked over to examine the man's remains. Lifting the blanket, I confirmed Robert Previn's unmoving body was beneath the fabric. He could almost have been sleeping. It wasn't the first time I saw a cadaver, but it always unnerved me. Pushing back the uncomfortable feelings, I examined his neck, noticing the red rash Yolanda had mentioned, and took several photos. Nodding to Sébastien was my confirmation that I was about to request a Body Retrieval from our headquarters in Portland, Maine.

After I tried Francois one last time with the same results, I opened my badge to make the call to the marshals' main office stateside. As I stepped back into the hallway for privacy, I heard Sébastien tell the dead man's sister in a hushed tone what was to follow. A sad moan escaped her lips. A moment later, she began sobbing. I guessed the tough attitude had been her way of dealing with the grief, which was finding an outlet as we waited.

The six-hour time difference meant it was before dawn in Maine. It didn't appear to make much difference. Within fifteen minutes, two uniformed marshals arrived. To avoid startling Mrs. Brosse, I had given them the coordinates of the entrance foyer.

"I'm Marshal Metreaux," I said to the two women when they arrived. "The body is in the living room beneath a blanket. The man's sister is in the same room with my colleague."

"Betty Sue Rond," a petite brunette with a southern twang said without extending her hand.

"Marshal Stevens. Lead the way," the second woman, a beefy older woman with short black hair, commanded in a curt voice.

"We're in a bit of a rush," Betty Sue said. She walked next to me and her colleague followed a few steps behind us. Before I had a chance to apologize for calling so early she continued. "Don't have much time for social niceties. What's the situation? The body intact?"

"As far as I know," I replied. Lowering my voice to a whisper so Mrs. Brosse wouldn't hear our conversation I added, "I only looked at his head and face. There's no blood, if that's what you mean."

"Do you suspect there is any contagious disease?" Marshal Stevens asked.

"Uh, I don't think so," I said, hesitating. "There's evidence of what may have been an allergic reaction, but I don't know for a fact that it was the cause of death. It's because we have no idea what he died of that I'm asking for your help."

The two women moved with efficiency and speed. As soon as we reached Robert Previn's remains they took off their slim backpacks. They both had large cameras with complicated looking flashes mounted on top. Each one took photos of the living area and the body. When they were done, Betty Sue pulled a thick khaki canvas bag out of her backpack, and they inserted the body in it. Marshal Stevens pulled out a black bag of a material that looked like triple thick plastic. They inserted the canvas bag inside the black bag, sealing it with plastic zip ties, and lifting it with a practiced motion exited the room back the way we had come in.

Once in the foyer, they each said a brief good-bye and pressed their index finger on their badge. In a nanosecond, they and the body faded from my sight. The entire process from arrival to departure took eight minutes. If only we could solve cases that fast.

Chapter 9

After the Body Retrieval staff left, I walked back to the dining table. I was glad Mrs. Brosse had stopped sobbing. Sébastien had done a good job of distracting her while they had removed her brother's body.

"I need to see the deceased's belongings," I began.

Sébastien took over, "Mrs. Brosse, it would be a big help if we could take a look at your brother's room and anything he had with him while he was in Paris."

She rose as if waking from a deep sleep and started walking. We followed her until we reached a bedroom near the living room.

"There's not much," she said in a shaky voice. "He usually traveled light, except for the gifts he brought for us, especially the kids. I'll be around if you need me."

Sébastien focused on the wall-to-wall built-in closet while I examined his suitcase and the dresser. The suitcase was empty. The only items on the polished wood dresser were a hairbrush and a bottle of cologne with a brand I had never heard of before. Out of curiosity more than anything, I examined the glass bottle. It had an old style label with modern block letters that spelled Parfumerie Tartan. It looked expensive.

"That belongs to my son," Mrs. Brosse said, startling me because I thought she had stepped away. "Robert must've borrowed it."

"I've heard of them," Sébastien chimed in. "The perfume shop on the Island?"

By the Island, he meant the Ile Saint Louis, a residential island on the Seine River connected to the Ile de la Cité and the Left and Right banks by bridges. Among wealthy Parisians willing to live in distinguished old buildings oozing history, most with stairs only, it was a prestigious address within the city's central fourth arrondissement.

"I think so," she said, brushing a stray hair out of her eye. "It's popular with my kids. I think their mates shop at that place. I didn't know he had Christian's bottle, but it wouldn't have bothered my son. They were close."

Fifteen minutes later, we were leaving the Brosse and Previn home. I felt sorry for the family. It was bad enough to lose a loved one. When loss included uncertainty, such as an unknown cause of death, it made everything worse.

"What was your impression?" I asked Sébastien as we reached the car.

"Of?" he asked.

"The sister," I said.

"Hard to tell," he said, surprising me. Sébastien had a big heart. I was expecting he would speak well of her rather than wobbling. "Her loss was genuine, but I got the feeling she was hiding something."

"Oh?"

"She was too quick to assign fault to others, first Yolanda, then us," he said. "She was kinder when I spoke with her one-on-one, but she was looking for a scapegoat."

"Sometimes people play the blame game because they feel responsible or guilty," I said. "They didn't spend enough time with their relative or they weren't nice the last time they spoke, stuff like that."

"It could be something like that," he said. "Maybe she blames herself for her brother's death or she suspects someone in her family was involved."

"You personally know or know of half the Weeia population in the city," I said, exaggerating not at all. "Do you think there was wrongdoing?"

"Dunno," he said, exhaling. "My contacts are mostly from school or through my family. The name doesn't sound familiar."

"They don't move in your exclusive circles," I said, summarizing so he wouldn't have to say it in so many words. "That what you're trying to tell me?"

He nodded before changing the subject away from his high society life. I let it go.

"How long before we hear back from Portland with the results of the autopsy?"

"A few days, a week at most," I said. "In the meantime, let's check on the family from a distance for now; and, visit that perfume shop."

"Do you think the perfume is what gave him the rash?" he asked.

"It's possible," I said. "It's not like we have any other clues."

"It's a reputable shop, from what I've heard," he said.

"What have you heard?" I asked.

"Not a whole lot, except it's exceptionally expensive. Caroline has complained, or more accurately boasted about their prices," he said. I guessed his sister, Caroline, who I had met on a couple of occasions, spent more on clothes in a fashion season than I had spent on my wardrobe in my entire adult life. "She probably shops there because the prices are stratospheric. Anyway, I think it's Weeia owned and there's only that one location on The Island. Did you notice the label?"

"Mhmm," I said in a noncommittal tone, wondering if I had missed a clue somehow. "There wasn't much to it."

"Exactly," he said as if pointing to the obvious. "If I were a betting man, I would wager a princely sum, the label designer created it for a particular audience. Specifically, it had that understated, sophisticated, only those in the know recognize it style that allows sellers to charge double or triple what they would with an off-the-shelf label. A big part of what you pay for when you buy a brand is the name."

I thought for a second. Since famous name brand products

cost much more than no name ones, I never bought them unless they were deeply discounted. I opted for the cheapest available item that would serve my purpose. I didn't need to impress anyone so I didn't care an iota about the tag.

"What do you mean?" I asked.

"Think of champagne, whisky, laundry detergent, nuts, any product that's fungible, that you can replace with another and might not be able to tell the difference," he said. "For example, blind taste tests prove consumers prefer some brands of coffee and colas over others, and sometimes California over French wine. Even when they're told about it, they're willing to pay a premium for products with a more desirable brand name. In my marketing class, we read that making something exclusive or hard to get increases its desirability."

"And you think Parfumerie Tartan is doing that," I said.

"I don't know what specifically they're doing, but the packaging tells me they're going for an elite clientele," he said. "Like wine, tequila, champagne, and vodka with so many varieties flooding the market; to sell a product at a premium they have to do something to stand out. Every Tom, Dick, and Harriett celebrity has lent his or her name to a scent, and those are just the well-known international brands. If your product is more or less the same as the next guy's, you have to dress it up to make it special. That's where the packaging, the bottle, the box, the label, even the font and the colors become important."

"Aren't you full of knowledge?" I said, half amused.

"At least some of that college money my parents spent is paying off," he said, shrugging as if it was no big deal. "You may have noticed my family believes my talents are wasted as a marshal. They would much rather see me taking over the reins of the business."

"I had no idea," I said, winning a grin.

"As if you hadn't heard me rant a million times about their

frustration at my becoming a marshal," he said.

Their attitude over his pursuit of a career as a marshal was like a thorn in Sébastien's side that poked at him every day. Sébastien wanted to prove himself to himself.

"Maybe nine-hundred and ninety-nine," I said, feeling empathy.

"They think I can't make it as a marshal," he said. "That I'm not smart enough or tough enough, and I should stick to the safety of my station in life and the easy business that's my inheritance." He paused to make air quotes when he said station in life. "Never mind what I want to do."

"Is that why you became a marshal when you could've stuck to the cushy life you were born into?" I asked. "To show off?"

"Naw," he said in a good-humored tone. "You're goading me. You know perfectly well I want to be a marshal for myself, to make a difference, to catch the bad guys like that mindshifter Ursell, because it's right. I want to make a difference, not sit at a desk like one of my father's fat executives, who spend more time thinking about the latest suit styles than the state of the world. If in the process, I show my family and friends that I'm more than just my parents' heir then so much the better. And, why not use the tools at my disposal, like my education, to accomplish my goal?"

"Good for you," I said, meaning it. Lifting the keys in the air I asked. "Wanna drive?"

"Of course," he said, signaling with his hand in the air. He kept it open for me to throw the key ring his way.

After pressing the button to unlock the doors, I did as he asked. He caught the keys with ease. He knew his way around the city far better than I did. Plus, finding parking on The Island in the middle of the day would be a bear, and he was more patient for that sort of thing than I was.

Chapter 10

From rue de Ménilmontant we went to rue des Pyrenees, making a right onto rue Orfila to avenue Gambetta and rue du Chemin Vert. As we drove from one arrondissement to the next the streets changed. At first, the change was subtle and slow. The further into the city we drove the more upscale the neighborhood, and the cleaner and prettier in general. In the fourth arrondissement there were fewer faded and torn promotional posters and graffiti-covered walls than in the twentieth.

Our destination was on rue Budé, a short one-way street that traversed the island from south to north three blocks west from the beginning of rue Saint Louis en l'Ile on the east end of the island.

The Brosse's corner of town had the hustle and bustle of day-to-day activities of students, workers, and parents. Although the Ile Saint Louis was hopping with tourists on the weekends, at midday on a weekday it was much calmer than the city surrounding it. The few narrow streets of the gentrified neighborhood were lined with parked cars and peppered with motorized and pedestrian traffic. It was a picturesque village within one of Europe's largest metropolitan areas. The Island was home to a church, preschool, pharmacy, post office, produce vendor, bank, deli, bookstore, famous ice cream maker, two butchers, two grocery stores, three bakeries, and lots of shops, art galleries and restaurants. Its elderly residents were often unseen behind the decaying facades of the imperfect historic buildings, which lent the neighborhood a distinguished graffiti-free character.

"I don't know how you do it," I said to Sébastien. "You're a magician at parking. Will the car behind us be able to get out?"

Door to door it was less than three miles to drive southwest to the island in the heart of the city. It only took us twenty-five minutes, not counting the ten minutes of circling like birds of prey searching for a street parking spot to open. I took advantage of every visit to the Island to explore a new corner. Almost every one of its streets was narrow and one-way only. They were wide enough for parking on one side and a single car to drive through with little space to spare. Pedestrians made their way along the streets themselves and on narrow cobblestoned sidewalks. The busiest streets were lined with souvenir shops, cafes, restaurants, small clothing stores, and specialty food shops. A few boutique hotels hid in quaint rectangular courtyards.

Judging by what I had seen the times I had jogged around the island all manner of people found their way to its popular paths. Cobblestone stairs led one level below to the riverside, which was favored by smokers, dog walkers, and smelly homeless drunks. The air beneath the bridges reeked of urine. On pretty days, there were almost always tourists snapping pictures of the iconic Notre Dame Cathedral on the Ile de la Cité, the neighboring island. Blessed with a reputation as a city of romance, Paris attracted brides and grooms from near and far, with professional photography teams in tow. They loved to take photos by the Seine.

The Ile Saint Louis provided a seemingly endless supply of unique places to discover. A crowded bookstore chock full of print travel books from floor to ceiling defied the twenty-first century's obsession with digital reading. The tea shop opened only a few hours each week. There was a fine jewelry store, housed in a former butchery on one of the short streets on the west end of the island, offering custom-made designs. The near barren display case had a handwritten sign indicating customers should call for an appointment. An odd shop on the southern bank sold used designer items. Glancing through its windows, I had seen vintage clothing, antiques, a monocycle, home furnishings, and luggage so scratched I wondered if it was functional despite a price as high as a new car.

"Easy peasy," he said.

I let out a peal of laughter at his colloquialism. He winked, which made me laugh more. I had to admit that being around Sébastien lifted my mood.

"Where did you learn that expression?" I asked.

"From my fellow students at the Marshals Academy, of course," he replied. "Apparently, it's short for easy peasy lemon squeezy."

"I never knew that," I said.

"I was curious, so I looked it up," he said. "It's from a British TV commercial from the 70s."

"For what?" I asked as we exited the car and walked toward the address, on the southeast corner of rue Saint Louis en l'Ile and rue Budé.

"Guess," he replied.

"No idea, instant spaghetti sauce?"

"Dishwashing detergent," he said, glancing around in search of the shop. "This is it. The good news is we found it. The bad news is it's closed until after lunch."

"Of course it is, but how do you know?" I asked, miffed and baffled at once. "I haven't even seen the shop."

"There," he said, pointing to it. The shop facade didn't stand out in the slightest. There was no signage, nothing to indicate it was commercial space. If it hadn't been because we knew the address it could have been another one of the many private entrances to hidden residential courtyards that were common on the Island. "See? And there's a sign on the door."

"Who can read that? It looks like it was handwritten by an elf with disappearing ink," I said in mock annoyance.

"I can tell you've been hanging around Iaen too long," he

said, grinning. "He's the elf fan."

I shrugged. If that had happened when I first arrived in Paris, I would have been upset. Over the months, I had made the French capital my home I had come to terms with the erratic opening days and hours small businesses kept due in part to the country's strict labor laws.

"It's too far to go to the office. We'll have to grab a bite around here," I said.

"Club okay with you?" he asked.

"Only if I pay," I said, feeling uncomfortable that as a club member Sébastien signed for his meals and as his guest my cash wasn't welcome.

"No way," he replied. "You treated the last time at that trendy gastropub in the tenth."

"You say trendy and gastropub like they're bad words," I replied.

"When it comes to food trendy definitely is," he said, his smile fading as his expression became neutral. "Trendy places are about people watching, interior designer décor, and what's in fashion rather than good food. At mealtimes, I'm interested in having a gourmet meal."

"And what's wrong with gastropubs?" I asked. "Aren't gastropubs owned by talented up-and-coming chefs who, because they offer mostly inexpensive wines and are in affordable neighborhoods, can charge a fraction of what similar gourmet restaurants cost?"

"That was the theory when the trend began, but in practice gastropub is kind of a bad word too," he said. His expression softened. "The best of the best chefs are recruited to work at established restaurants, where they learn the ropes and perfect their craft. Those who don't make the cut sometimes open gastropubs because they're stubborn or control freaks, or have little talent. My father's friend, who owns a famous restaurant on the Cote d'Azur, says that gastropubs are where wanna be chefs work until they fail or become proper chefs."

"I thought the food was okay at Spo," I said, pushing down my defensive reaction.

For once, I had picked our lunch place after reading about it in an entertainment publication's roundup of new eateries. Sébastien's selections were always spot on, but the prices had a tendency to break my puny budget. I set out to impress him with an affordable foodie lunch.

"It was fine," he said, his puckered mouth and wrinkled nose belying his words.

He didn't have to say the food at the member's only Weeia club on the Island was better by far. While my palate, like my table manners, wasn't as sophisticated as his, I liked to eat and could distinguish between amazing and acceptable meals. Although the menus at the club never had prices, I suspected it was much better value for money too.

At the club, I felt like a fish out of water. Sébastien's family was among the most prominent and wealthiest Weeia in the country, so nobody ever challenged my being a guest of his or gave me any grief. Their snubs were in the form of subtle glances, condescending tones, and facial expressions that made it clear I was not one of them.

They made sure I knew I wasn't from their social circle and didn't have the manners that went with it. I didn't dress the part, and couldn't afford to if I wanted to, which I didn't. Although my wardrobe had received a significant boost since my arrival in the city, and I had gone to great lengths to stand out less than I had at the beginning, I was nowhere close to passing as one of the club's socialite members.

"All right," I conceded. "You win. The club it is. I'll pay for the next non-club meal."

He was a gracious winner, hiding his smile a millisecond after I spoke. I saw it, but couldn't rustle up the energy to be annoyed. I was looking forward to the gourmet lunch that awaited us too much. I didn't feel bad because, while I couldn't compete with his checkbook's reach, I had invited him to join us for dinner at home a bunch of times and Iaen was a good cook, if I said so myself.

Two hours later, we walked back to the shop with full bellies and contented. The handwritten sign was gone. Hard-to-see display cases behind a huge glass wall were the only confirmation we had arrived at a commercial space. There was no hint of the type of business. It could have been an art gallery, a photography studio, or a high-end bathroom fixtures boutique like many I had seen on the popular boulevard Saint-Germain in the Latin Quarter. It was only after pushing the glass and wood door back that I realized a handful of steps led down from the street level into a small room with unpolished rock walls and a low ceiling.

Except for the bright electric lights, modern décor, and shelves stocked with row after row of near identical simple boxes, I might have traveled back in time to when river pirates stashed their loot in secret island basements. On more than one stay at home night Iaen, a history buff, had read stories to me about the Paris of centuries past. He swore despite the island's well-heeled inhabitants there had also been river pirates in not-so-reputable corners on the Ile Saint Louis of the time. I suspected he was pulling my leg.

I didn't see or hear anyone else in the room. That wasn't unusual in tiny businesses where often the owner or a member of the family would greet customers in person. If a shopkeeper was busy with a customer when you arrived, you waited. I glanced at the stark bare walls, shiny wood floors, and distinctive lamps, trying to imagine who would be drawn to shop at a store without a counter or even a chair. Finding only more questions, I returned to thinking about my boyfriend and his love of books and times of old while we waited.

When a nondescript and overweight man in his thirties I had not realized was near me asked, "How may I assist you?" I was so startled, I took a step back.

"Are you the owner?" Sébastien asked in an authoritative voice.

"I am," the man replied.

For a man who sold overpriced colognes he sure wasn't welcoming. His body language was standoffish. I took advantage of Sébastien's intervention to observe him. A glance at my badge confirmed he was Weeia. I nodded to Sébastien to let him know. The shop owner's skin was so pale; I could see the blue lines of veins beneath it like underground rivers. A cleft lip gave his face an oddness I had trouble ignoring. Perhaps that explained his attitude. The pungent smell of body odor was unexpected in a man who made his living selling fragrances. Without realizing what I was doing I placed the palm of my hand over my lips to keep the worst of the stink from entering my mouth.

"Are you alone?" Sébastien asked.

"What's this about?" he asked, standing his ground. "I have no cash on the premises. Besides, there's nothing to steal and my security is state-of-the-art."

If I had been a thief, I might've wondered why if he had nothing to steal, he had such strong security. But I had bigger fish to fry and I wanted to flee the horrible smell of the man as soon as we got some answers, if not sooner.

He had malformed and missing teeth. His limp, curly medium brown hair hung about shoulder length. It was bad enough that his scalp was greasy and unwashed. To make matters worse, his efforts to cover several bald spots by combing his hair to one side were so awkward the result was to draw more attention to his head.

"We're not thieves, Mr.," Sébastien said, enunciating each word, and letting the end of the sentence hang to allow the man to fill in his name.

"Mathis Tartan," the man said after a long minute.

He was young to own a store in such a coveted neighborhood. I wondered if it belonged to his family and he was an employee, or if he had inherited the business the way Sébastien would inherit his father's humongous company.

"We're here to have an important conversation with you, Mr. Tartan. I'm Sébastien Poyager and my colleague is Danielle Metreaux."

It wasn't uncommon for Weeia area residents to know our names even if we hadn't met in person since we represented the highest Weeia authority in town. Depending on the situation and the rank, marshals could have the authority of a Weeia cop, judge, jury, and executioner. I thought a saw a flash of recognition, but I couldn't be sure. Mr. Tartan was hard to read. When not expressing open displeasure, he wore a sort of neutral scowl.

"Marshals?" he asked without extending his hand.

"Correct," I said.

"The sooner you confirm we can have a private conversation the sooner we can leave," Sébastien said.

I prayed there would be no handshaking. The thought of touching the man's hand made me shrink back in disgust.

"How may I assist you?" he asked. I released my breath, grateful that for a change we could dispense with politeness and bypass the usual greeting formality. In a reflex movement, I rubbed my hand against my pant leg. "My records are in order." When we didn't reply he continued. "I offer courtesy discounts to officers of the law like yourselves."

"Thank you, Mr. Tartan, but we're here on official business," I said. "One of your bottles was found next to the body of a man who died yesterday under possibly suspicious circumstances. There were signs he suffered an allergic reaction of some kind."

"Oh?" he asked.

"That's right, Mr. Tartan," Sébastien said. "There was a fiery red eruption along the man's neck. It could be where he applied your cologne." I watched the shopkeeper for a reaction, but there was none. "His name was Robert Previn. Did you know him?"

"I have many customers," Mr. Tartan said, glancing away from Sébastien as if there was something he didn't want him to see in his eyes. "I don't remember all their names."

"He was Weeia," Sébastien said in a tone that indicated Mr. Tartan should pay attention to how he replied. "I'm sure you're better able to recall Weeia names, aren't you?"

"I suppose so," he said, deadpan. "I don't recall a customer by the name of Robert Previn. If there is nothing else, I have an appointment with an important client."

For the first time since we had arrived, Mr. Tartan appeared less than disinterested. If I had to guess at his emotion, I would have said he was nervous. It made me want to pressure him by offering to wait until after his appointment. I was about to say something when I caught myself. He wasn't an endearing man and he smelled awful, yet other than finding one of his products near the dead man, we had nothing to link him to Mr. Previn, or accuse him of wrongdoing.

"Thank you for your time," I said.

"If you think of anything, please call our office," Sébastien said. "I assume you know the number?"

Mr. Tartan nodded. He also released some of the tension in his body as we moved toward the door.

"One last question, Mr. Tartan," I said. "Help me understand, what is it that you sell?"

"Isn't it obvious? Perfume," he snorted.

"Just garden variety perfume with nothing added?" I asked.

"I don't do anything illegal, if that's what you mean," he said.

His whole icy attitude turned sour, giving me the impression I had struck a nerve. It was the only lead we had, so I pushed for more.

"That wasn't what I asked," I said. "Is there anything special in your products?"

"Everything I use is derived from natural products, organic when available," he said. "I comply with all human and Weeia laws and have the documents to prove it."

I was about to ask another question when a man in his twenties entered the store. He wore brand name clothes. I didn't remember the brand names that matched the labels, but I had seen them before. He had striking features; the kind that make you look twice. More than handsome, he came across as strong-willed. He greeted the shop owner by name, sparing a glance at Sébastien and even less effort on me.

"Excuse me, my client is here," Mr. Tartan said, and without wasting another second on us, he turned his attention to welcoming the new arrival.

I noticed they didn't shake hands. They walked toward the back and disappeared behind an old wood door. Perhaps the man was as squeamish as I was regarding the shopkeeper's stench. There wasn't much else to see in the front of the boutique so we too left.

Chapter 11

"What do you think?" Sébastien asked once we were back on rue Saint Louis en l'Ile walking back toward the car.

"He clearly was avoiding or lying about something," I said, weighing my words. "And he's not the most likable or fresh-smelling man I've come across, but—"

My comment about the man's odor elicited a guffaw from Sébastien. He stopped walking and looked at me. Although I was his boss, we were close in age and had developed a comfortable friendship beyond our work duties. As a result, we had an informal work relationship that lent itself to candid conversations, the kind I never had with my previous bosses. I also had not shared the close bond with them that Sébastien and I had. I knew he had my back. He had proven that a number of times. I had his.

"Fresh smelling? That's what I call the understatement of the year," he said, still laughing. "The man is foul." He emphasized the last word. "All I could think about the whole time we were there was how soon we could leave."

I had felt the same way. My first reaction had been anger. I pressed down on it and considered the situation. It was under my control. I could leave at any time. That calmed me enough to continue. As usual, Sébastien had been polite and showed none of his discomfort.

"It was hard to notice," I said, and with an effort kept a straight face.

His eyes grew wide in disbelief as he said, "Yeah, right. It's hard to imagine he's the owner of a perfume shop. That must be one of the top ironies we've come across lately."

"I know, right?" I fessed up. "I was dreading having to shake his hand."

"Argh, me too," Sébastien said. "And his hair was so…

awful."

"Maybe he has a medical condition," I said, striving to be understanding. "That prevents him from showering or using deodorants."

"Does it also prevent him from brushing his teeth, changing his clothes, and using shampoo?" Sébastien asked.

"I don't know about all that, but there are conditions that make sufferers' skin sensitive," I said.

"Yes, lately my mom has been going on about all the chemicals they use to extend the shelf life of food products and cosmetics, and how they cause cancer," he said. "Still, there are natural products he could use. How can he let himself get so rank?"

"Dunno," I said. I wasn't one for expensive name brand perfumes, but cleanliness was a priority in my life. "I'll take two showers a day if it's very hot or if I've been sweating a lot. I keep deodorant at the office just in case. I can't relate. Maybe it's a culture thing."

That won me a burst of laughter, melodic and full of amusement. The cheer reached his eyes, which crinkled.

"No, don't even think about saying that it's because he's French," he said.

Just to goad him I said, "If the shoe fits."

"The shoe doesn't fit," he said. "Well, I'll admit there are French people with poor hygiene, but I think there are people of all nationalities with bad habits. We don't by any means have the monopoly on stinky people." I grinned. "You're busting my chops, aren't you?"

"Maybe a little," I said, enjoying the brief comic moment. "Anyway, back to Mr. Tartan, while I can't say he was warm and fuzzy there's no proof he knew the deceased, no motive, nothing that places him at the Brosse home. The only link is the cologne that didn't even belong to the deceased. For now, unless you have any other ideas, all we can do is wait for the autopsy results, and in the meantime look into Robert

Previn's final hours for clues as to who or what might've killed him."

"You're the boss," he said in an agreeable tone. "Where to now?"

"Back to the office to do some good old-fashioned research," I said. "We need to know who Robert Previn was. Let's start with the usual vitals. The family is circling its wagons. I get the feeling they won't be forthcoming so we'll need to find out what caused their loved one's death on our own."

"What about the kids?" Sébastien asked. "Mrs. Brosse said they were close to their uncle, and that the boy wouldn't mind that his uncle had borrowed his cologne. Maybe, they'll talk to us."

"It's worth a shot," I said, not wanting to rain on his parade. "Before we talk to them, let's get the facts straight."

"I'll get right on it as soon as we're back," he said. "You up for some sparring?"

"Yeah, it's been a day or two since I kicked your ass," I said.

We both laughed. I was the better fighter, but my beating him on the mat was a running joke with us. The drive back to the office took us through familiar congested streets. We were almost there when we were forced to stop by a garbage truck blocking the one-way street in front of our building. There wasn't enough space to pass the truck and a line of several cars snaked behind us so we sat, cooling our heels for ten minutes.

That was the way of life in Paris. It bugged me, but I had learned weeks earlier there wasn't much I could do to change it. I decided to concentrate my efforts on issues where my influence had at least a chance of having an effect. Once the truck began creeping forward, the cars behind us honked. By then it made little difference. We were glad when we reached the entrance to our marshals complex.

"Home sweet home," Sébastien said.

"I'm going to check on our guests," I said. "I'll be in the office in a few minutes."

When I arrived at my old apartment it was empty. Making a mental plan to return later, I went to the office. Sébastien was catching Madame Marmotte up. As was her habit, she ignored me and focused her attention on Sébastien, who in her eyes could do no wrong. If it hadn't been because Sébastien and I were friends her attitude would have gotten me hot and bothered.

I had experienced anger management issues as long as I could remember, at least as far back as the death of my parents. Since I arrived in Paris, I had made an effort to improve my outbursts. At first, it had been difficult with Francois and Madame Marmotte's disdainful attitude. Because they were unkind to me, I felt justified when I got upset.

On a phone conversation during which I complained and moaned about them, in hindsight in an immature fashion, Marla, one of few friends I had while attending the Marshals Academy, had advised me to get a grip. She said it wasn't appropriate for an L3 marshal to lose her temper the way I did. At the time, it had hurt. I was less than gracious and downright ungrateful in my reply.

She made a good point, although it took me a week or two to admit it. I began with baby steps, thinking before responding with words I regretted as soon as I spoke them. Discovering it was less difficult than I had anticipated I continued, taking a deep breath when I felt the ire rise, and letting it out before taking action or even speaking. Iaen hadn't said a word, but I knew he was supportive. A couple of weeks earlier, I had begun meditating after Marla mentioned she was meditating and it had done wonders for her concentration. While I wasn't sure how much it reduced my anger, I felt refreshed at the end of each meditation.

One of the side effects was that Madame Marmotte's bad attitude bothered me less than it ever had. On most occasions, when she said something I didn't like I ignored her, returning to whatever I was doing without any interruption.

After grazing the door to my office with his knuckles in a near moot knock, Sébastien entered, sporting his usual upbeat expression. I was fishing my new coffee mug from my desk drawer when he spoke.

"That was quick," he said. "Everything okay?"

"Far as I know," I replied. "They were out. I imagine they were taken under the Tadas and Giedrius families' wings."

"Of course," he said. "They're probably fattening them up and cooing over the kids."

"That's what I figured," I said.

I had thought of asking if Madame Marmotte had anything to report and decided if there was news I needed to know about he would have mentioned it. I yawned, remembering why I wanted the cup in my hand. A second later, he yawned too.

"That's what we get for gorging on yummy club food in the middle of the day," I said.

"There were lots of salad choices," Sébastien said. "It's our own fault for picking the naughty items. Traditional cassoulet isn't exactly light fare. And the wine is mandatory to digest the cassoulet."

"I need coffee," I said, heading to the kitchen with my mug in hand.

We each fueled ourselves with a strong cup of coffee and began digging for information on Robert Previn. There were old entries in his file for minor drug offenses and one traffic ticket five years in the past, all from human police. There were no citations from marshals. An hour later, the office phone rang and to my shock Madame Marmotte answered it.

Be still, my beating heart, I told myself, quoting from a

poem I had memorized. Having Sébastien in the office had benefits beyond those of a regular new staff member. Madame Marmotte did actual work when he was around. Since I had begun ignoring her jibes she avoided me for the most part. Eager to please the man in the office she had taken to her duties like a duck to water, or as much as I imagined she ever would, ever since Sébastien's arrival.

"Yes, of course," she said to the person on the phone in a deferential tone. "Would you like to speak with one of the marshals?" I assumed whoever it was had said no because she didn't call us. "I'm sure they'll be there as soon as possible. Yes, I will. Goodbye."

I went back to the document I was reading, assuming she would inform Sébastien about the call and he would follow-up. Since they hadn't wanted to speak with us to explain the situation, I imagined it was a minor issue he could take care of on his own. It would be good for him to gain more experience. We received so few calls, I went out of my way to allow him opportunities to take the lead or go solo, provided the danger was minimal, whenever possible.

"Sébastien," Madame Marmotte called.

"Yes?" he asked.

"That was the headmistress of the Académie," she said. "There's a situation. She insists you report to her immediately."

"In Goin?" he asked.

"Yes," Madame Marmotte said.

"We're not students she calls to her office," I said, irritated the headmistress thought she could send for us whenever she wanted. Madame Marmotte told Sébastien when she should have told me or both of us. So much for not letting her annoy me. "She has her own security staff and a security company on retainer. We don't work for her. Right now, we're working on a case about a Weeia who died. It's important that we investigate quickly before the trail cools.

Besides, it's a long way to the school. Going there would take up the rest of our day. She'll have to wait until we can spare some time."

"What exactly did she say was the situation?" Sébastien asked in a much kinder tone than mine.

I tried not to be upset at him. It wasn't his fault that Madame Marmotte treated him better than me. I couldn't blame him for having more patience and better people skills than I did. It was just that sometimes I wished he wasn't so perfect.

"I didn't understand everything," Madame Marmotte replied. "She spoke quickly. I think someone was waiting for her. She said it was similar to when you were there before, that you would know. She sounded like it was urgent." Looking at me, she added, "If you decide to wait and someone gets hurt, that's on you. I did my job and passed on her message."

I snorted, I couldn't help myself. It was unladylike, but I had never pretended to be a lady. I was a marshal. It wasn't my job to be sensitive about people's feelings or polite. When it came to her criticism about my French Canadian accent, my wardrobe, and my country mouse manners I had grown a tough skin. She had a right to her opinion. When we met, I had made an effort to get along with her. She had shown me little respect, and I no longer cared much what she thought.

So what if I was unrefined? For all that, she believed herself superior, she didn't realize or didn't care that it was rude to criticize me behind my back. Besides, I was proud to be from Quebec Province. It was a beautiful area of Canada. Thinking about it, I became a touch homesick. It was true that I spent as little as possible on clothes, which made my wardrobe unimpressive for a Parisian and a social wannabe like her. I was on a budget after all.

If a sophisticated wardrobe was a job requirement, the

marshals could provide me a clothing allowance. Since they didn't, it was nobody's business how I dressed. As long as I respected basic social norms, she had no right to snub her nose at my functional clothes and try to humiliate me. As to my manners, my aunt and uncle had brought me up on their farm. Although they did their best to teach me all they could, I cared little for what I considered useless city rules for the idle rich. Since I didn't belong in those circles there was no reason I should be bound by their rules.

When it came to badmouthing me about doing my job she knew better. I had proven myself since my arrival in Paris more than once. Anything she said about me in that regard was unmerited and spiteful. She, of all people, had no right to talk to me about doing my job. She spent most of her office hours wasting time, filing her nails, touching up her makeup, gossiping with friends and acquaintances, and being a general busybody. I wanted to tell her what I thought about her snippy tone and her attitude. As usual, a glance her way made me pity her. For all her bravado, she was frail, had trouble walking, and an unhealthy appearance. Unlike most Weeia who were well-off, she lived on a modest income, which was why she was forced to work for the marshals when it was obvious she would much rather be at home.

Chapter 12

I took a deep breath, releasing it in several slow ones and shook my head a smidgen to rid myself of the negative feelings she inspired. It was a technique I had been using with some success, an add-on to my meditation. Feeling better, I turned my attention to Sébastien. I could tell he was eager to say something. I imagined he wanted to drop everything to respond to her request.

"I take it you think we should go to Goin," I said in a sharper tone than he deserved.

"From what I know of her the headmistress is calm," he said. "She deals with student issues all the time. She's no stranger to unexpected situations, has lots of experience handling crises and disciplining any wrongdoing. I think she's never called for the marshals before. Asking for outside help is a loss of face for her. She's a proud woman. I don't think she would do it if she had a choice."

"I'll take that as a yes," I said. He angled his head to one side, pursed his lips and nodded in response. "Fine, the Robert Previn investigation can take a backseat. He's already dead. Let's deal with the living. Car or train?"

"The train is faster, but we don't know how late we might have to stay and the trains stop running around 10 p.m.," he said.

"Car it is," I said, grabbing the keys from my desk drawer and handing them to him. "I can get us out of the city, but you know the way to Goin better than I do."

Because of the rain, the one and a quarter hour drive to Goin took two hours. With practiced ease Sébastien traversed our neighborhood and hopped on the ever busy boulevard Périphérique. The exit toward Goin wasn't far, but thick traffic made progress slow. Graffiti lined many of the walls facing the highway. Along the road, I spied the mounds of garbage reported on the news, which had piled up along the highway for months. Despite increasing public outcries and objections, the solid waste authority had not bothered to clean it up. After we turned on the radio, I became lost in my thoughts.

Near the town there was greenery and a less frenzied pace than on the highway. By the time we arrived at the school, my annoyance at the headmistress had waned. The security guard whisked us through, and within minutes we were seated in the Académie leader's wood paneled office, waiting for her. It was better than being in the waiting area, where I imagined naughty students cooled their heels before seeing her.

I set my still dripping umbrella at my feet. There had been nowhere else to leave it, and since it was still raining I expected I would need it again. The leather chairs were more comfortable than they looked. There was a subtle yet pleasant earthy scent. I was beginning to feel drowsy so when she entered, I was glad to see her. It gave me something to focus my attention on besides sleep. Shaking the mental cobwebs away, I straightened up, eager to know why she had dragged us all the way from Paris to her domain. Tiny strands of hair stood out at an angle from the bun atop her head, making me think she had been so busy she had nary a moment to glance in the mirror. I suspected she always looked her best in order to set an example for the rest of the staff and students. Her assistant, who had welcomed us when we arrived, and another staff person followed in her footsteps.

She stood behind her desk while her staff remained near the door, filling her in on the status of other staff members. When her assistant finished speaking, the headmistress sat down, and without so much as hello she addressed us.

"I apologize for the inconvenience, young Marshal

Poyager and your name?"

"Headmistress, may I introduce my boss Marshal Danielle Metreaux, Marshal Metreaux may I introduce Headmistress Daphne Selin-Gaspar," Sébastien said in a formal manner.

"Yes, yes, we can dispense with the lengthy introductions," she said in an impatient tone as I lifted my arm to shake hands. I moved it back and bit my tongue to avoid telling her off. There was no appreciation for our effort to rush to her aid. Other than the perfunctory apology for the inconvenience, there wasn't a single sign in her manner that she cared about our time in the slightest. "I didn't ask you for afternoon tea or cocktails. We have a situation that has become, frankly, improper. You must address it immediately to avoid a scandal."

The woman's time-lined face showed signs of tension and anxiety. Her movements mirrored the expression on her face.

"Wha—"

She cut Sébastien short. I almost said something, but I had promised myself on the drive over that I would keep my composure and not allow her entitled attitude to get a rise out of me.

"My staff will answer your questions," she said, pointing to the two staff members who remained standing in the background wearing distressed faces. "Come see me when you have resolved the mess." She turned her attention to a sheet of paper on her desk, dismissing us without a word. We were getting to our feet when she added. "I don't need to remind you the students of this academy are the crème de la crème of Weeia society. Make sure you're discrete."

I couldn't help myself from blurting, "We're not your private security guards to boss around, and it's not our job to avoid a scandal," before we exited her office.

I felt better for giving her a piece of my mind, like a weight was off my shoulders. Sébastien looked mortified as if I had ordered ketchup with the foie gras at a fine dining restaurant. Judging by his deferent attitude of late, he was under some illusion that she deserved special treatment. As far as I was concerned, when safety became an issue, Weeia politics had to be set aside. Of course, it was easy for me because I didn't have all the lifelong relationships, school and family ties he did. For a change, being an outsider was an advantage. It kept my perspective clear. Had it been anyone else, I would have rubbed it in further how the headmistress was full of herself and moaned about the way she was treating us. But it wasn't anyone else, so I let it go, gritting my teeth for a second to vent the frustration.

"So, do you know what's going on here?" I asked her staff members.

Their expressions of bewilderment told me everything I needed to know. They glanced at each other.

"I have a feeling this is going to take longer than we anticipated," I said to my colleague.

"It's starting to appear that way," he said.

"Argh, I left my umbrella in the headmistress's office," I said. "I'll be back in a minute, and I expect a satisfactory explanation of why we're here or we're leaving."

I paused to look at each of the two staff members in turn, giving them the most intense glare I could manage while holding my annoyance in check. When I knocked, the headmistress's door swung open.

"I'm sorry to interrupt you," I said, walking into the cavernous office, hoping to recover my umbrella as quickly as possible.

In place of the reply I anticipated, I heard the woman speaking across the room. She was on a wireless phone facing out past her glass wall toward the gardens and hadn't seen me.

"I've no idea what's going on," she said in an emotional voice. I was about to speak up and thought it would be better to find out what I could before letting her know I was there.

She had dragged us there and refused to tell us why, farming us off to her staff. Hearing about the problem from the horse's mouth would be the fastest and most effective way to decide what to do next. "Of course, I'm not thrilled to have the marshals snooping around the grounds, but I had no choice. Since their first visit, the number of incidents doubled and, well, severe injury of a student from one of the most prominent families in Europe isn't something I can sweep under the rug. There isn't a snowball's chance in hell that I can bottle the situation up permanently. At most, I can buy a few hours or if luck favors me, a day or two."

She paused, listening to the person on the phone. "No, no, I didn't tell them that, but young Poyager is well-connected. He'll recognize the name. It's only a matter of time. I'm confident he's on our side. He's an alumnus and his family members are major donors, but the new marshal is a wildcard. For the moment, I'm following procedure and trying to avert a scandal. If word gets out before we find an explanation, parents will fear for their children's safety. At first, I could say they were just kids getting out of hand or isolated incidents, but the injury changed that. If that kid doesn't recover quickly, the word will spread like wildfire. They'll become convinced it's an Académie wide problem and pull their precious brats out. I've dedicated my life to this place. My career is on the line."

Deciding I had heard enough, I moved toward my umbrella. As I did the old wood floor creaked. She turned around and saw me bending down to pick it up.

"How long have you been here?" she asked in a calmer tone than she had used a moment earlier.

"Long enough," I said. "You need to quit wasting our time. Where's the injured kid? We have to see him or her first."

"I have to go. I'll call you later," she said into the mouthpiece. "Yes, yes, it's fine. I'm dealing with it. Perhaps it's better this way." She breathed in, letting the air out slowly before turning her attention to me.

She walked toward a sitting area and commanded, "Sit down."

"I don't," I began to object.

Thinking better of it, I claimed a cushioned leather armchair. It was comfortable and threatened to swallow me, so I moved forward and sat on the edge. The headmistress sat across from me on a matching sofa. The indifference she had displayed minutes before had been replaced with anxiety. Tiny worry lines appeared across her forehead and on the sides of her mouth. Her shoulders were tight and her chin stiff.

"Look, it's my job to help you," I said in a harsher tone than I was looking for. Taking a deep breath, I counted to ten and released it bit by bit until I felt centered. "We came as quickly as we could and we're here to assist you and your students." Pleased that my voice was calm and, I hoped, convincing I looked into her eyes. She held my gaze. "You're right. I don't owe any allegiance to your school. On the other hand, I don't have any grudges against it and I don't want to see anyone harmed. If you want us to fix the situation you need to trust me. From what I overheard you say, this could be an escalation of what we witnessed on our previous visit. Although I was alarmed then, your assistant assured us the administration had everything under control. If you don't, we have to move quickly before anyone else gets hurt."

She straightened in her seat, running her hand over her hair in a nervous movement before stilling for a long while. I assumed she was going to turn me down and readied myself to walk out if she didn't reply soon.

"Very well, Marshal Metreaux," she said. "I'm in your hands. Let's hope I don't regret it."

Instead of saying what I wanted to say, which was snippy and less than professional, I pressed my lips into what I hoped was a confidence inspiring expression and nodded my head once. She rose and I followed her lead.

"After you left there were more incidents," she said. There was still tension in her shoulders, but the antagonism in her manner had waned. "They were different students and different situations, but my gut tells me they're related. I honestly don't know the cause. I've personally questioned each of the children. Some of them are headstrong, you know, but none dare challenge me one-on-one."

"Tell me about the injury," I said in a neutral tone to soften my command. "How serious is it?"

She was staring toward the glass wall and I wasn't certain she had heard me. A loud silence filled the room.

"How serious is the injury?" I asked.

She kept her gaze on the wall so long I thought she might not answer. Then, as if tearing her thoughts from some faraway place, she said, "He's unconscious." Regret clung to her words. "The healer thinks he'll recover."

"Yolanda?" I asked.

"No, we have a dedicated healer on staff," she said.

"Oh, I see," I said, wondering if she was as good as Yolanda. "What's her diagnosis?"

"She said he has two broken ribs and a concussion," she replied.

Out of nowhere a familiar man's voice asked, "What was the injury? What happened?"

Sébastien entered the room. He had been so quiet, I hadn't noticed him until he spoke. His lips spread a bit without showing any teeth to let me know he appreciated getting the headmistress to open up was a delicate task.

"He jumped headfirst into a partly empty pool. We don't know why," she said. Her mask of composure cracked for a nanosecond. She wrung her hands together in her lap in a nervous gesture. "It's the strangest thing. The whole school knew that pool was closed for its twice annual complete cleaning. There was a problem with one of the drains, or it would've been empty and he would be dead."

"Have you told the parents?" I asked.

"Of course," she said, looking away toward the glass wall as if she could somehow find answers in a place I couldn't see. "They're out of the country. They'll be here as soon as they can. I was hoping the boy would have recovered by the time they arrive, and to have everything under control by then."

"How?" Sébastien asked in a sharper tone than his usual.

"I don't know," the headmistress said, enunciating the words as if we were hard of understanding, and for the first time sounding unsure.

In place of her confident angelic shield, I detected frustration and fear. I had the impression those words had not crossed the headmistress's lips in many years. It must have been a jarring experience for the middle-aged administrator. If I had been able to take the temperature of the mood in the room it would have registered cool. Sébastien's mouth was open and his pupils were dilated in a surprised expression. He shifted feet as if shaking the shock away like unwanted sand from the soles of his shoes, and holding on to a stronger emotion, anger perhaps to judge by his stance.

"That's why you called our office," Sébastien said in the same tone. "You're looking—"

I caught his eyes to interrupt him. There was no point in antagonizing the woman. Whatever her intentions and political play we needed information and access, if there was any chance of figuring out what was happening and putting a stop to it before any more students were injured.

"Was there anyone with him when he jumped?" I asked.

"Yes, his best mate," she said. "They're inseparable. I spoke with him at length. He couldn't understand it either, mumbled a bunch of nonsense."

"We need to speak with him," I said, infusing my voice

with a combination of authority and empathy. "Right away."

"He's very distraught," she objected. "Is it really necessary?"

Duh, yes. We needed to trace the incident back to find out as much as possible. That was detective work 101. I held back my desire to say something snarky in response.

"I'm afraid it can't be helped," I said in my best imitation of an interrogator from a favorite crime investigation TV show who was way more patient than I would ever be.

"Very well," she said. Picking up the phone, she punched one number. Speaking in her usual commanding style she said to the person who answered, "Bring Mr. Monde to my office immediately. Yes, no matter what he's doing. This takes precedence."

"For obvious reasons, I'm pretty sure he'll relate better to you," I said to my colleague. "Take the lead. From here on we'll need to document everything. The severe injury justifies our intervention. Should his condition worsen, we have to follow the rules as much as we can." I left out how it would also protect us in case there was any wrongdoing, one of the lessons I had taken away from my most recent training at the Marshals Academy. "The headmistress's permission serves as parental consent, which allows us to question and record sessions with the students." I paused, glancing at her to confirm. She nodded her assent. "We'll interview the staff, but my gut tells me the answer will be with the students. We'll start with them after we visit the site of the injury."

"Will do," Sébastien said, looking uncomfortable.

His longtime hero had been knocked down a peg, an unfortunate side effect of the case. He had attended the Académie, as had his parents and grandparents before them. The headmistress was a larger than life figure for him. To me, she was just another Weeia in need, but to him, she was his former disciplinarian, secret keeper, and Rock of

Gibraltar, someone who was always in control. He had discovered she wasn't as solid as he expected. I could envision the cogs in his brain short circuiting and erupting with minuscule scrolling "does not compute" messages like a robot tasked with an unsolvable paradox. It had to be disconcerting.

"It's important to maintain calm," the headmistress said. "I trust you understand."

"Our priority has to be safety," I said. I was wary of her desire to maintain control of the situation. "Although we'll do our best to keep a low profile, we have to talk with students and employees to conduct an investigation. I'll leave the damage control to you and your staff."

"I remind you, young lady, that our students are the sons and daughters of some of the most remarkable and elite families," she said.

I didn't care for the young lady reference. I was tempted to reply in kind and call her old lady. I was pretty sure she wouldn't like it. For Sébastien's sake and that of harmonious work relations, I held back.

"By now, word about the injury has spread with lightning speed," I said. "They'll be afraid. I'm sure I don't have to tell you how important it is for you to reassure your students the boy is okay, and you're dealing with the issue personally."

For a flash, I saw panic in her eyes. It told me she was accustomed to ruling with an iron fist and having everyone fall in line on her say so. Asking us to investigate was conceding she had problem she couldn't resolve. That was out of her comfort zone. Too bad, she had no choice. She had to toughen up or we would be adding more incidents to the tally.

"Of course," she said. "I'll make an announcement during the dinner service."

"Good," I said. "In the meantime, we'll walk around campus. We'll need privacy to conduct interviews." Students wouldn't want to tell us about their drug use, rivalries and bad behavior in front of each other or their teachers. "What room can we use?"

"I'll organize it," she said.

The teenager who arrived a few minutes later wasn't muscular as much as athletic. His eyes were bloodshot and he wore a haggard expression. His tie was missing, his uniform had spots in places, and his shoes had scuff marks.

"Mr. Monde, come in," she said when he peered in from the door after knocking. "Good day." As soon as he replied to her greeting, she continued. "Marshals, Alain Monde was with Martin Davidi when he took a dive. Mr. Monde, meet Marshals Metreaux and Poyager." That she had introduced me first wasn't lost on me. It was a subtle acknowledgment of my higher rank. He glanced at us askance. "These marshals are here at my request to investigate what happened to Mr. Davidi. You're to answer their questions without reservation, and assist them in any way possible. Is that understood?"

"Yes, headmistress," he mumbled. "I'm sorry about my uniform. The one I had on got wet and I don't have a clean spare one. I know the rules require we have a clean uniform in addition to the one we're wearing. I—"

The words that followed were unintelligible. He hung his head low as he apologized.

"I can't hear you. Speak up, Mr. Monde," she said, her voice projecting across the room.

"I'm sorry," he said, raising his voice and pronouncing the words a smidgen better than the first time. "It won't happen again."

"Never mind that now, young man," she said in a kind voice. "We need to find out what happened for his parents' sake."

I wanted to yell it was more than for his parents, we had to ensure everyone's safety. More than four unexplained incidents that we knew of, resulting in injuries, one serious, was too many to be a coincidence. Instead, I waited for Sébastien to begin.

"I have to step away," the headmistress said, standing up and walking toward the door. "Please make yourselves at home."

It was as if an elephant had left a crystal shop. The tension in the room dropped. I watched while Sébastien connected with Alain Monde, starting by telling him he had attended the Académie. The student's nervousness remained, but was less pronounced than before.

"Please sit down," Sébastien said, pointing to one of the cushy chairs.

Sébastien allowed the student a moment before sitting down across from him. When I was tense I could be intimidating, or so people told me. When interviewing a hostile witness or someone lying, it was useful. When dealing with frail and fearful witnesses, my style tended to agitate or frighten them further. To avoid intimidating Mr. Monde, I stood a few feet back.

Chapter 13

"It would be very helpful if you walk us through the fifteen minutes before Martin jumped in the pool," Sébastien said once the headmistress had exited her office.

Observing my colleague in action made me wish I had ten percent of his way of winning over people. It wasn't a Weeia ability. It was who he was, a charismatic guy. He empathized with others rather than judging them. People could tell. It was as if he got them. I knew firsthand because that was how I felt. Being around him, and Iaen, in general had played an important role in helping me learn to keep my cool even under stressful situations. Knowing someone cared about and understood me made me feel surer of myself, less angry. And that made it possible for me to control my emotions better than I had in years. It was a wonderful improvement, I had to admit.

The student blinked several times before speaking as if clearing his thoughts. His brows edged close to each other as he spoke.

"Yeah, um, we were horsing around is all," he said. "We weren't doing anything special."

He paused, looking down at his shoes. We waited while he fidgeted with his hands.

"I know reliving it is difficult," Sébastien said. "Take your time. I want you to tell me, step by step, everything, where you were, what you were doing, what you were talking about. What you say might be key to what happened. Were you high?"

"Martin had a stash and we talked about it, but they're very strict here," he said, looking around in a nervous gesture. "It's zero tolerance. If they catch you with drugs, pills, pot, alcohol, anything really, you're out on your bum.

You won't tell the headmistress, will you?"

"We're not interested in that," Sébastien said in a neutral tone and reassuring manner. "I want to know about it only to understand if it played a role in how Mr. Davidi suffered his injuries."

The student's nervousness seemed to grow as he asked, "But you'll keep what I tell you in confidence, right?"

Sébastien nodded, replying, "I'll do my best."

Young Mr. Monde's shoulders slumped. He glanced around several times as if to make sure we were alone.

"We need to know," Sébastien prodded him. "Mr. Davidi, Martin, is in serious condition. This isn't going away. What you tell us could help your friend and prevent other students from getting hurt the same way."

Mr. Monde watched Sébastien. My colleague watched him back and waited. After what felt like a long while, he drew a deep breath and raising his shoulders a bit spoke, "We were thinking about it. We had some pills Zoe pinched from her mom. It was a new prescription and we needed a quiet place and enough time before class to find out what effect they would have on us."

I wanted to yell at him that taking pills prescribed for someone else was stupid. I wanted to shake some sense into his not anxious enough face. Instead, I remained still, allowing him to continue without interruptions.

"Is that why you were in the pool area?" Sébastien asked.

"Yeah," Mr. Monde said and nodded in confirmation. "Guillaume had told us the repairmen who clean the pool weren't due back for another week. We wanted to be alone."

"What Zoe's last name?" my colleague asked.

"Cartes," the student replied.

"Who's Guillaume?" Sébastien asked.

"Uh, you know, Guillaume, the headmistress's son," he said.

"Is he a student?" Sébastien asked.

"Yeah right," he said like that was a preposterous idea. "He does odd jobs, whatever his mom assigns him when she catches up with him. He knows what's going on."

"And in return you gave him some pills?" Sébastien asked.

"Yeah, a couple. How'd you know?" he asked. In response Sébastien half shrugged. "Anyway, we figured we would have the place to ourselves and we did. The thing is, Martin was acting weird even before we got there."

"Go on," Sébastien said.

"It couldn't have been Zoe stash that made him sick," Mr. Monde said with conviction.

"How can you be so sure?" Sébastien asked.

"Because I had the pills and we never touched them," he said. "See?"

He pulled a plastic bag, the kind you use for sandwiches, out of his pocket. In it were four pale pink pills, tiny in contrast to the oversize bag.

"This is all Zoe gave us minus the two I handed Guillaume," the student said. "The weirdness hit a peak when we sat down at the pool's edge. I tried to talk to Martin, but it seemed he couldn't hear me. He thrashed around like a fish out of water. Then he turned so perfectly still I got close to check his pulse." His eyes grew wide and his mouth opened as he grimaced. "That's when he went berserk and jumped in the pool." His eyes widened further, giving him a haunted appearance. "Maybe it's my fault. Did I get too close to him? Could that be why he jumped?"

He blinked and, like a man waking from a trance, stared at Sébastien. The haughty attitude he had brought with him had vanished. In its place, there was anxiety and something I couldn't pinpoint. I didn't have the heart to tell him he might've spooked his friend, that if he hadn't gotten close to him he might not have jumped. It wouldn't accomplish anything anyway.

Compassion filled Sébastien's face. He placed his hand on

the young man's shoulder.

"Could it?" Mr. Monde asked.

"Who knows?" Sébastien asked. "We have no clue what drove him to do what he did."

"You think if I hadn't gotten so close he wouldn't have gone into the pool," Mr. Monde said. "I can see it in your eyes."

"You can't beat yourself up for that," Sébastien said. "He might've jumped anyway. What we have to do now is try to understand what was wrong with him. Is there anything else you can remember?"

"Not really," Mr. Monde said.

"Let's go to the pool. I want you to show us what happened and where you were," Sébastien said, stealing the words right out of my head.

"Sure," Mr. Monde said.

Our path to the pool twisted and turned until I lost my bearings. A few minutes later, the three of us arrived at the pool door to discover it locked. We lost time finding a staff person who called his supervisor. The staff person asked us to wait.

It seemed an eternity, although it was probably more like fifteen minutes, before a burly man in an ill-fitting suit arrived. Even I could tell from a distance the suit was cheap and several years behind the current style. He was bald except for a crop of wiry ugly hair circling the lower part of his head. Unlike the staff, teachers, and students we had seen at the Académie before him who were all clean shaven he wore a thick, bushy, and unruly beard and moustache. Once he reached us, I noticed stains on his tie and gray suit. Scuffed up shoes and workman's hands with broken nails told me he was a handyman.

"Finally," Mr. Monde sighed when the man approached us. "What took you so long?"

He glanced first at us then at the student, moving past the

young man without a word and opened the door. He looked like he was in a hurry to return to whatever he had been doing before we called. Another man arrived soon after.

"The headmistress said it was urgent," he announced to no one in particular. "What's so urgent about a near empty pool?" Before anyone could respond, he pulled out his mobile phone and answered it. "What? No, I had to drop everything to open the West Pool for some visitors. On the headmistress's orders, that's who. I'll be there when I get there."

He hung up, harrumphing. Without another glance, he walked away.

"Who was that?" Sébastien asked the question I had on the tip of my tongue.

"Franck Pouroscure, the well, I'm not sure what his official title is, but he's the headmistress's right hand man," Mr. Monde said. "He handles everything she doesn't want to sully her manicured hands with, like maintenance, non-teaching staff, repairs, construction. Nothing happens around here without his knowledge."

"Maybe we should talk with him, if he knows about the students," I said.

"Feel free, but as you saw, he's not the friendliest of people," Mr. Monde said. "The admin staff oversee everything to do with parents and students. He steers clear of students and parents and only handles issues that require a minimum of interaction."

I was about to speak when the pool door opened and a young man strolled in with confidence, like a boxer at a geek convention. He had thick dark brown hair and a five o'clock shadow, the kind that looks casual, but requires lots of effort to maintain. He was a little taller than me, which was still short for a man. Small eyes somewhere between cinnamon and amber, I remembered the shades from Tada's children's seventy-six pencils coloring set, zeroed in on us as he approached.

"In other words, he doesn't like people much and he's not a good communicator," I filled in Mr. Monde's meaning.

"You must be talking about Franck Pouroscure," the man who had arrived said, grinning. "Not many people like him, but it doesn't matter. As long as he's in my mother's good graces, he's untouchable. He does whatever he pleases, comes and goes wherever he likes, and answers to no one but her. Best of all for him, she never intervenes in his affairs. Weird, right?" Without waiting for an answer, he went in to the pool area. "Here it is, the scene of the crime or is it the accident? Ha, ha."

His laugh was odd, out of synch with the serious injury the student had suffered. I chucked it to nervousness around marshals. It wasn't unusual for people to behave in an awkward manner around us, doing or saying unexpected things even when they weren't suspects.

"Oops, forgot my keys," the short man said. "I'll be right back. Don't go anywhere without me."

He laughed again as he dashed out of the room. Mr. Monde walked around the pool area and we followed. I wondered why the other man was there, but not wanting to interrupt Mr. Monde, I let the subject drop.

"I didn't learn anything new. You?" I asked Sébastien once Mr. Monde had left after recounting his story and walking us step by step through the episode.

"Nope," he said from across the part empty pool. "I keep thinking he had to be high. Why else would he dive in?"

"Same thought crossed my mind," I said, searching around the huge pool deck for clues, ideas, or anything that might help. "Just because they hadn't taken any of Zoe Cartes's pills doesn't mean he didn't take something on his own before he met up with his buddy. The lab results will tell us eventually, but we need to know what's going on now before any other kids get hurt."

"We should take a look at his room," I said.

I was about to suggest we walk back to the headmistress's office to find someone to take us to the boy's room when the pool door opened and the same young man strolled in a second time. He wore the same cocky expression.

"I'm Guillaume Gaspar," he said, stretching his hand toward me. A slight musky smoky body odor reached me. "You must be Marshal Metreaux, and you must be Marshal Poyager. Wait, Poyager, of the Poyagers?"

The short man emphasized the next to the last word. Sébastien nodded as they shook hands. Since we had begun working together, I had seen that reaction in people we spoke with or met more times than I could count. It was accompanied by a kind of awe. Sometimes people's eyes would stare unblinking and their mouths would remain open for seconds after speaking with or meeting Sébastien. My colleague took it, for the most part, in stride. Guillaume Gaspar's reaction was difficult to read.

"You went to school here," he said to Sébastien. I thought he was going to add that they were classmates. "I remember how excited my mom was to have you among her flock."

"How—" I began.

"Can you help me?" he finished Sébastien's question for him. "Not at all. I'm supposed to help you, take you wherever you want to go and make sure you have what you need. My mom, the exalted headmistress who runs this prison, I mean grandiose institution of learning, sent me to open doors, assist with introductions, break legs, whatever you need." He winked. "Consider yourselves VIPs. She doesn't extend such courtesies for just anybody."

"Did she explain why we're here?" Sébastien asked.

"She didn't have to," the young man said. "Things have been wacky around here lately and today a prominent kid, I know, I know they're all prominent, but this guy is extra prominent, dived into a pool without water for no reason.

Chances are he was higher than a kite, which will be bad for my mom if it comes out." He spoke so fast I wanted to tell him to take a breath. "My mom, who prides herself in never, ever, losing her cool, has been fretting. So clearly, you're here to get her out of the mess she's in, and oh yeah, without any inconvenience to her or her inmates, I mean precious students. Right?"

While they spoke I had a chance to observe him. Although at first glance I had thought him pudgy, on closer inspection I saw he wasn't thin or fat, kind of average without any obvious muscles. His movements were swift, almost jerky, making me wonder whether he had had one cup of coffee too many. His clothes were somewhat baggy as if they were hand-me-downs or borrowed from someone who wore a size larger than he did, and he hadn't bothered to take them in to fit him.

"What makes you think he was high?" Sébastien asked.

"Are you kidding? Martin lives to get high," he replied. "Everybody knows it, including my mom. Didn't the all-knowing Headmistress Daphne Selin-Gaspar tell you? No, no, I bet she didn't. She'll protect the reputations of her brats with her dying breath."

"What does he usually take, Mr. Gaspar?" I asked.

He turned to me and back to Sébastien as he replied, "Call me Guillaume. Mr. Gaspar is my father. He'll get high on anything and everything, glue, cocaine, pills, alcohol, heroin, you name it."

"Does he like speed or downers? You know, stuff that makes him mellow or hyper?" Sébastien asked.

"He's not picky as long as he gets a trip out of it, the higher and longer the better," Guillaume said. "He's a serious junkie. Everybody knows it, including his parents."

He was fidgety with excess energy seeming to seep out of his pores. His eyes danced, restless around the room. In a single long movement, they swept the entire pool area, resting on Sébastien and me at an angle on their return. Pot meet kettle, I thought.

"Are you a student?" I asked.

"Of life? Ha, ha," he said, guffawing. He stared across the pool at something I couldn't see. "If you mean here, then sadly no. My Académie days are behind me." I let the silence hang, seeking an explanation of what he did at the school. "You want to know what I do for a living. Oh, this and that, as little as possible though my mom wishes I would go to university or get a job already. I'm waiting until the hag or my old man kick the bucket so I can live the life I deserve."

He spoke with such a brash tone, I wondered if he was joking. He appeared to be enjoying himself, but there was something about him that unnerved me.

"Just kidding," he said as if reading my thoughts. "You marshals need to lighten up. It's not like anybody died, yet." He grinned.

"So you live on campus, but don't attend classes anymore," Sébastien said. "Were you around to see the previous incidents?"

"Nope," Guillaume replied. "I missed all the excitement. I was at my dad's. When I was little, they shared custody. They're divorced, you know. Now, I live here part-time and there too. Here's good because there's housekeeping and food. Rosa, the old cook from Portugal, isn't half bad, and there's lots to keep me entertained. The down side is that my mom nags me and cramps my style. Don't do this, do that, take a shower, stand straight, remember to set an example, stop smoking. She goes on and on like she did when I was a child. At my dad's, I have more space, but I have to look after myself and I get bored. I got here last night, but I didn't see Martin, in case that's your next question."

More than I wanted to know, I thought, but I kept it to myself, feigning interest or at least not disinterest.

Guillaume made twice as much eye contact with Sébastien, giving me the impression he related to my colleague better than to me. Sébastien was handling the questions well, so I let him take the lead as we had agreed en route to the school.

"We want to see his room," Sébastien said. "Do you know where it is?"

"Of course," he said. "I know every nook and cranny of this place and all the juicy gossip."

He took several long and speedy strides toward the door through which he had entered. We followed and waited while he locked the door behind us with a key from a huge keyring.

"Mom insisted we keep this place off-limits to avoid another accident," he said, making air quotes when he spoke the last word. "She thinks Martin was so well-liked that another student might try to copy what he did and dive into the pool."

"Do you think that's likely?" I asked.

He shrugged. We walked behind him until we reached the injured student's room door. I had forgotten my question until I heard his reply.

"Just because the students here are Weeia doesn't mean they're not stupid," he said. "We have our own share of morons who follow the lead of other morons. I wouldn't put it past one of them to try the same stunt."

He used a key from the large keyring to unlock the door. Moving aside he let us enter. The pleasant scent of cleaning liquids was the first thing I noticed. We stepped onto a cream colored marble floor with a matching marble table set against the wall. A chandelier above our heads lit the entrance. A hallway led into a multi-room space. As I moved closer I saw an elegant room, decorated in neutral colors, with living and dining furniture and a large kitchen in the background. To call Mr. Davidi's accommodations a room was like calling the Titanic a boat. Wherever I set my eyes there were expensive looking fabrics and furnishings. The space was posh, making me think an interior decorator had been responsible for the décor. It was excessive even for the usual wealthy Weeia homes we visited. I was lost in the thought when I heard Guillaume moving.

"Please stay there," Sébastien instructed the short man.

"It was supposed to be VIP housing for visitors," Guillaume said from behind us. "It was designed as a family three-bedroom apartment for visitors, especially for those traveling from other departments or outside of France. But, whatever Martin wants, Martin gets. He insisted that living in the apartment would allow his family to visit whenever they wanted without having to make special arrangements in advance. As I'm sure you know, his father is a big wig billionaire with a private jet and a very hectic schedule." He spoke the final three words in the sentence in a falsetto voice and winked several times in a row to let us know he wasn't impressed. "They hardly ever visit, but that makes no difference."

"If he's as devoted to drugs as you say how come it's so clean and tidy?" I asked.

"That's easy," Guillaume replied in a loud voice so we could hear him. "The Académie staff clean it daily as if he was in a hotel."

"All student rooms are cleaned by the Académie staff," Sébastien said. At my raised eyebrow he explained. "But most students don't live in apartments like this. Generally, they have rooms with en suite bathrooms. Some share with a roommate."

"The majority of the older students have private rooms," Guillaume said. "And, cleaning is twice a week instead of daily. Standard furniture like a bed, night table, and desk come with the rooms." If it was anything like what we had seen in the common areas, the quality was pretty high. "Those who want anything beyond that have to bring their own or buy it. There's a catalog to make it easier. All they have to do is pick what they want and pay for it. The school handles the logistics and in return gets a respectable cut. Interior design, additional cleaning, in-room dining, and other services are also available so the little dears don't have to suffer too much away from their loved ones."

Based on the way he spoke, it was clear Guillaume enjoyed making fun of the Académie, and was envious of the students. I made a mental note to ask my colleague about him later.

"Unless I'm mistaken, the Académie provides housing to the staff too," Sébastien said as he examined a handful of books and an electronic tablet on the dining table. "The headmistress lives in a beautiful house on the estate, and senior staff have private homes or apartments."

"You're right," Guillaume said. Sébastien and I each took a room and Guillaume remained in the dining area. I could hear him as I looked for clues about Mr. Davidi's life in what must have been the guest bedroom. The rooms, still in neutral colors, had polished wood flooring and carpets instead of marble. "I get to stay with my mom in the house rent free. The Académie pays for everything, including the gardening, meals, and cleaning. Because my mother spends nearly all her waking hours at the school, she has no time to look after her own home or her family. She can't even spare time for breakfast with me on the weekends. I guess that's why they split up."

When he exited the room he had entered, Sébastien announced, "There's not much to see there. It's mostly empty except for some clothes in the closet."

"Same with that one," I said. "The next one must be his."

We both went in, opening drawers and doors in the room, walk-in closet, and bathroom. A few dirty clothes were next to the night table. In the bathroom, a dirty razor sat in the sink, and a towel lay crumpled on the floor by the bathtub.

Sébastien drew my attention to an elegant teak chest he was holding open. It contained plastic bags with pills, dried leaves, spoons, and hypodermic needles, drug paraphernalia as my old Marshals Academy instructor used to call such items.

"Some of these look familiar," Sébastien said. "Others I can't even guess what they are."

"According to the recent updates from Portland, there are a lot of homemade drugs going around in the US and Europe," I said. "They're worse because there's no quality control. People who use that stuff are taking a huge risk because they've no idea what's in them. Street drugs might even be cut with toxic ingredients by accident or for profit. Others come from countries with little or no regulations, mainly China."

"I'll bag them in case we need to compare them with any blood test results," he said. I nodded. "Anything else catch your eye?"

"Not really," I said, circling around the room a second time. "They must've cleaned recently. There's not a speck of dust."

"My mother is fastidious," Guillaume interrupted from the door to the apartment. "She insists the Académie be as clean, and I quote, as humanly possible."

"Isn't that unusual?" I asked.

"Oh yeah," Guillaume said. "When she was younger, she studied in Finland for a few years, apparently, that's the cleanest country in Europe, and she picked up new habits there."

We browsed around the rest of the apartment for a few minutes. Finding nothing else of note, we called it quits.

"That's all we can do here for now," I said, looking forward to a warm dinner. "It's kind of late. By now everyone is likely gone to bed. We'll come back tomorrow."

"About that," Guillaume said. "My mother strongly

suggests that you spend the night here. We have plenty of room, and she wants to make sure you're nearby in case there's another incident. She's used to being in control. Having you here is as close to in control as she's going to get for now."

While her thinking was solid, I longed to return home to Iaen. In addition, I didn't have anything to sleep in or clean clothes for the following day, not even a toothbrush.

"It's a good precaution, but I didn't bring spare clothes," I objected, turning to Sébastien.

"You?" He shook his head sideways to confirm what I suspected. "We can return at the crack of dawn."

"She thought of that," Guillaume said. "She's had the staff stay late. They've been running around preparing one of the two-bedroom VIP apartments for you. There are toiletries and sleeping clothes for each of you. There are also spare clothes in the closet. If you don't like them or they don't fit, the staff will stay late to tailor them as necessary. Or they can launder and press the ones you're wearing so you can wear them again tomorrow. Alternatively, she can send someone to collect any items you wish from your homes tonight. She won't take no for an answer."

Sébastien and I looked at each other. We had a good rapport and relied on nonverbal communication. Neither one of us was thrilled with her request, but we could live with it.

"The least she could've done was to ask us herself," I mumbled to no one in particular.

"You do whatever you want, but if you leave and something happens she'll make sure you never work as marshals again," Guillaume said.

"How nice. Something to look forward to," I said.

Sébastien looked at me, concerned. It wasn't so much that I minded what Guillaume said as much as her pushy attitude.

"She didn't ask me to pressure you. I just know her," he said.

"I don't work well when threatened," I said, anger warming me.

"She's too crafty to say it, but that's how she is," Guillaume said. "She holds a grudge. I don't care either way." He shrugged. "The cook is waiting to make you dinner. Let me know what you decide."

"We don't both have to stay. If you have somewhere to be, I can stay by myself," I said to Sébastien to give him a final chance to back out, yet hoping he wouldn't.

Iaen would understand that investigating was my job. He was a good egg that way. Although the idea of spending the night at the school didn't bother me, I didn't look forward to interacting with the starched headmistress and her staff. At least with Sébastien around I had pleasant company I trusted. An added bonus was that he would deal with her.

"Nothing that won't keep," he said with a mysterious smile. "I postponed it earlier. I'll postpone it again. Absence makes the heart grow fonder."

"Okay," I said. "Lead the way."

I texted Iaen as we followed Guillaume, planning to call him when I had some privacy. Sébastien too texted someone although he didn't say who. Lucky girl, I thought. If it hadn't been because I had a wonderful man in my life already, and Sébastien was my direct report, he would have caught my attention, and not just because he was drop-dead gorgeous.

"Not bad," I said after our escort left us in our accommodations for the night.

"It's not quite as nice as Martin Davidi's place," Sébastien said in a playful tone.

"And it can't hold a candle to your house," I replied in kind.

"My parent's house," he corrected me.

"Meh, tomatoh tomahtoh, you live there and one day it will belong to you," I said.

His shrug told me he would speak about the topic no

further. I knew it made him a tad uncomfortable so I dropped it.

"If you and Iaen have plans—" he was saying when we heard a noise. I pressed my index finger to my lips and he stopped speaking.

"It's nearby. Keep talking. I'll check it out," I whispered.

"I can stay," he said. "As you pointed out, we don't both have to stay."

I tiptoed out the way we had come into the Cottage, which was more like a full-size house. Using my Weeia ability, I made myself seem invisible, circling clockwise around the structure until I found the source of the noise, two students crouched beneath the living room window.

"What have we here?" I asked as I reached down and grabbed each boy by the collar.

Their heads jerked back and their eyes widened in surprise. They strained against my hold, but I had a good grip. They were young, tweens perhaps.

"No, you don't," I said.

"How did you know we were here?" one of the near identical boys said before I could admonish them.

"I'm a marshal. It's my job to know when someone is around that isn't supposed to be," I said in a stern voice.

"If you're so good, why haven't you figured out what happened to Martin?" the other boy asked.

"What are you, twins?" I asked.

"Nope," the same boy said. "I'm a year older, but people often think that."

"Spying on marshals is punishable with public service time," I said, doubting I could get anything worse than detention for the boys.

"We weren't," the first boy began. I glared at him, making his protest wilt.

"It's late and I'm tired or I would, well never mind," I said, not knowing what I would do with them since they were so young. Taking down criminals I could handle. It was my job. Disciplining youth was more in the headmistress's wheelhouse than mine. I couldn't have them hanging around at night when we weren't sure what was going on. Plus, we needed to discuss the issues in private. "Go to your rooms. If I catch you spying on us again, you won't like what I do."

I watched them scamper away toward the main building, hoping they wouldn't return, because I didn't want to have to deal with them again. I walked around the house twice to make sure there was no one else before going back.

"It was two young boys," I said. Sébastien grinned. "What?"

"Did you startle the pants off them?" he asked.

"Not entirely, although I used my most serious tone to make them leave," I said. "Anyway, where were we?"

"Comparing notes," he said, amusement still visible on his face.

"Oh, yes," I said. "I was ready for Guillaume to leave and he lingered like he wanted to stay the night with us."

"Yes, I noticed that too," he said. "Maybe he's lonely."

"Did you know him while you were at school here?" I asked.

"Um, no," he said. "He was a year ahead of me and part of the time he went away to live with his dad."

"A year isn't that much a difference," I said.

"It is in school," he said, emphasizing the second word. "Besides, he was more of a loner. You heard that anger, right?" I nodded. "I remember him sounding worse." Silence filled the room. "Anyway, yeah he did seem like he wanted to stay longer with us."

"You could be right. Maybe he's lonely," I said. "Staying overnight should give us an early start. You're welcome to sleep in a bit since we're saving ourselves the drive."

"Thanks," he said.

Chapter 14

After dinner I called Iaen. I hoped he hadn't made an elaborate dinner.

"Hey," he said.

"Hey back," I replied. "Sorry about tonight. I was looking forward to seeing you."

"No problem," he said, understanding lining his voice, followed by a little mischief. "I get that you have to work and keep us all safe from the dangerous Académie kids."

"Funny," I said, a smile breaking through like sunshine on a clouded day.

"It's late for you and I can hear the tiredness in your voice so we'll keep it short," he said.

He always knew the right thing to say to make me feel better. I had lucked out on the boyfriend front. I couldn't wait to introduce Iaen to my aunt and uncle when they came to visit me. They hadn't decided the exact dates, but they had promised to come. I was looking forward to seeing them again.

"Thanks," I said, sighing. "How was your day?"

"Not too bad," he said. "I'll tell you about it over a nice glass of red wine."

"Oh, hoping to get me tipsy and have your way with me?" I asked, striving for a sexy voice, not sure I had accomplished it.

"Always," he said in a warm and sexy tone that sent flashes of heat down my spine. "Will you be back for dinner tomorrow?"

"I sure hope so," I said. "I'll call or text you tomorrow as soon as I know more."

"Call if you can, even if it's only for a quick hello," he said.

"Missing me?" I asked.

"Of course, and I like to hear your voice," he said. "It brightens my day."

Every so often I felt like pinching myself that Iaen had chosen me. He could have had more or less his pick of women. He was good-looking and had a way with words that could charm an Eskimo into buying ice. Besides, I hadn't been overnice when we first met.

"Really? Even when I'm in a hurry and crabby?" I asked, incredulous.

"Especially then," he said in a soft tone. "That's when I know you need me and I miss you the most."

I heard someone knocking. Assuming it was dinner, I walked toward the door and almost bumped into Sébastien.

"I got it," he mouthed.

"Thanks," I mouthed back. "Dinner is here. Sébastien and I are sharing a cottage and the cook stayed late to bring us dinner."

"I'm glad you're getting something good to eat," he said. "I'll have to work extra hard to impress you for our next meal."

"You're an amazing cook, but I can think of better ways for you to impress me tomorrow," I said, surprised at my bravado.

It wasn't like me to get suggestive on the phone. I wasn't a prude, but I didn't get all expressive and needy either. The brief silence told me Iaen was surprised too.

"I can manage that," he said, laughing. "And, dinner with my eyes closed."

"Mwah," I heard myself saying before I realized it.

Being around Iaen brought spontaneity and joy to my life. It made me do silly things like throw him kisses over the phone.

"Mwah back and more when I see you," he promised. "We'll start with dinner and work our way from there, whatever you want."

While I was on the phone Sébastien had let the two staff in with our dinner. They each had a heavy tray with two plate covers they set on the dining room table. Earlier, they had stocked the refrigerator with wine and water, covered the glass table with a tablecloth, set silverware, glassware, and cloth napkins for two, and placed condiments between the two place settings.

I felt a touch self-conscious when I noticed Sébastien watching me from across the room. I blushed.

"What?" I asked, feeling like a schoolgirl caught necking with her boyfriend by the teacher, even though I was the boss. His broad laugh reached his eyes, spreading small lines outward. I walked toward the table where he stood, waiting for him to explain as my regular skin tone returned.

"You two are such a hoot. You, at first glance, you're so no nonsense and tough. But as I've gotten to know you you're not like that at all. You're one of the kindest people I know. And, when you're with Iaen it shows. It's like you glow. Same thing with Iaen. I'm not sure he and I would've been friends if we hadn't met through you. He acts like such a player, but he only has eyes for you."

"I, uh, thank you," I mumbled, blushing again. Hoping to distract Sébastien away from my embarrassment I added, "It smells good. What's for dinner?"

"Let's see," Sébastien said. With a flourish, he pulled the top off one of the plates nearest him. "Chicken, no, Cornish hen in a mushroom sauce with a side of asparagus and sautéed potatoes." He replaced the top on the first plate and took the top off the second plate. "And, for starters there's a garden salad and a vegetable soup." He glanced around the tray and added, "There's also country bread and butter, breadsticks, and crème brûlée. I took the liberty of pouring us some wine."

"Let's eat," I said, discovering I was as hungry as a she

wolf.

Judging by how fast his food disappeared, Sébastien was also hungry. We ate in near silence. We tried to discuss the case further, but were making no headway.

"I say we call it a night," Sébastien said an hour after dinner.

"I agree," I said. My eyes were drooping and I longed for a hot shower. "We'll think more clearly in the morning and can bat around any theories we come up with then. Night."

Sleep eluded me for the first few minutes. After that, I slept like the dead. The smell of coffee pulled me like an invisible lasso into the kitchen, where I found a pot of the beverage.

"Good morning," a familiar voice said, startling the daylights out of me.

I half jumped before realizing Sébastien was sitting in the living room with a cup in his hand. Filling an empty cup I found next to the coffee pot, I turned to face him.

"I hadn't seen you," I said in a somewhat hoarse voice. "Have you been up very long?"

"Just long enough to make the coffee and sit down," Sébastien said. "Breakfast should be here in fifteen minutes. I meant to mention that last night and forgot. One of the ladies who brought us dinner asked about breakfast while you were on the phone. I wasn't sure what you wanted, so I ordered a full breakfast."

I had eaten well the previous night and I wasn't much of a breakfast person. Sébastien was like an eating machine. He could eat at any hour of the day and never gained weight, another reason to hate the man.

"Okay, thanks. I'm going to get ready," I said, walking back to my room.

I returned to a feast of hardboiled eggs, four types of fruit preserves, honey with individual wooden drizzlers, and a scoop of butter. There was warm toast wrapped in a cloth napkin in a wicker basket, baguette slices and viennoiserie, baked goods made with yeast-leavened dough, in another identical basket, deli meats and a cheeseboard spread across the table. I poured liquid from a pitcher into a small glass and took a sip, confirming it was orange juice. Two chocolate croissants, and a second cup of coffee later I was ready to turn my attention back to the case.

"She pointed out that the honey is local and extra special," Sébastien said just before taking a bite out of a croissant with a generous dollop of the thick and golden honey.

"We need to confirm what Guillaume said, but from what we found in his apartment, it seems Mr. Davidi is a frequent drug user," I announced as I spread honey on a slice of toast. "If so, he was probably in a drug-induced state and that's why he fell or jumped into the mostly empty pool. Maybe this is a whole to do about nothing."

"Yeah, but how do we explain the other incidents?" Sébastien asked. It was the same question that kept troubling me. "Don't you think they're related?"

"Dunno," I said, thinking out loud. "We need to dig around more, talk to other students. For example, let's have a chat with Ms. Cartes."

"The girl who gave the pills to Messrs. Davidi and Monde?"

"That's the one," I said.

"I'll sort it out," he said.

An hour later, we sat across from Zoe Cartes, a wraith of a girl with pale skin and stringy, shoulder length, brown gray hair, in an empty classroom. Rather than have the students parade out to our cottage, we asked for a private room within the main building. Her arms were crossed over her chest in a protective manner and she wore a sullen expression. She looked younger than the sixteen years we knew her to be. Her eyes were sunken and swollen at the same time as if she was exhausted and had been crying. Her thick synthetic fiber jacket, the kind that makes the wearer look like a blimp, hung over the back of her chair.

"Ms. Cartes, I'm Marshal Sébastien Poyager and—" Sébastien began.

"Yeah, I heard two Weeia cops were snooping around the Académie," she said in an unexpected shrill voice. "You here because of Martin?"

I wasn't surprised. Despite the headmistress's efforts at discretion, I doubted our arrival had remained a secret for more than fifteen minutes. Sébastien and I had discussed our approach in questioning the students and decided honesty was best. While we would keep certain aspects of the case to ourselves, as with any other investigation, there was no reason to hide the truth. The theory was that if they believed us they might trust us with whatever information they had that could lead to answers.

"We are," I said.

We had agreed Sébastien would take the lead, but once I saw the young student I could tell she would be distrustful and difficult out of a sense of rebellion. I had a feeling she might respond better to me than to my colleague.

"What do you want with me?" she asked.

Her voice grated on me like fingernails scraping against a metal wall. With an effort, I set aside the discomfort and looked at her. Sébastien noticed my body language and waited for me to respond.

"We're talking with Martin's friends," I said. I got the impression she wanted to respond, but she said nothing. "If we find out what happened, we might be able to help him or prevent it from happening to someone else."

"He wasn't my friend," she spat as soon as I finished speaking. "That jerk got what he deserved. If you're looking for sympathy from me, you're wasting your breath. I hope he remains a vegetable for the rest of his life."

"Okay," I said in a soothing neutral voice. "We heard you

gave him some pills."

"I didn't give him anything," she said. "He and his buddy took them. That's what they do."

"So they're bullies," I said. "I didn't know that."

"Everybody else does," she said, sinking a fraction into her seat even though she was resting against the seatback already. "Everybody knows he's the golden boy. Nobody dares to stand in his way. The teachers can't move fast enough to do what he wants." My surprise must have shown on my face, because she went on. "You really didn't know, did you?" She glanced at Sébastien. His mouth was open partway as if he wasn't sure what to say. "You're both telling the truth. I can tell. Although my ability comes and goes, when it works, I'm quite good."

I waited, giving myself a moment to process what she had said, and allowing her to decide what she wanted to do. Sébastien followed my lead.

"Why am I here?" she asked after a long while.

"We're trying to find out what happened," I said. "You probably heard already about the incidents a few days ago and now Martin's severe injury. We wonder if they're linked. Did you notice anything out of the ordinary the day he fell in the pool? Has something changed lately?"

"Not really," she said. "Same old. Can I go now?"

"Sure, thanks," I said.

We watched her walk out. She moved faster than I expected from her frail form. If the rest of the students had the same attitude, we wouldn't get far. I was about to mention that to my colleague when Ms. Cartes returned.

"The only change is that Christine Riens has become the most popular girl," she said.

"Why is that a change?" I asked, baffled.

"She did it by wearing her sister's eau de parfum," she said with a serious expression.

"Come again?" I asked. "You think that wearing a

perfume made her popular? Is it only with boys?"

"That's what she told me," she said. "She's popular with everyone, all the other students, teachers, staff, everybody. I asked her how she did it and she told me it was her sister's specially made perfume."

"And you believe her?" I asked.

"Yeah, I can tell when someone tries to trick me, remember?" she said. "She wasn't lying. The thing is, I borrowed my sister's perfume and it didn't do anything for me. I used to be really popular and nobody paid her any attention. Now, she's the one everyone turns to for everything and I'm yesterday's news."

She walked out without another word. Sébastien's lips were parted a bit and his eyes were wide in disbelief. I figured he was as baffled as I was.

"I take it you want a word with Christine Riens?" he asked.

"Yep," I replied.

Chapter 15

While Sébastien organized a meeting with Christine, I checked to see if the results of the autopsy had been released. I was distracted and almost didn't hear the knock. A staff person carrying a tray of hot beverages and baked goods arrived. I asked her to set them on the desk.

"The headmistress thought you might enjoy a snack," she said as she put her heavy burden down. "I'll pick the dirty dishes up later. If you need anything else, call the kitchen."

Before I had a chance to thank her or ask her any questions about the Académie, she had closed the door behind her. Seconds later I opened it, thinking I would catch up with her. She was nowhere to be seen. It occurred to me that I didn't know the phone number for the kitchen. Oh, well, it wasn't that pressing. If I decided it was, Sébastien would know how to reach them when he returned.

I was torn about eating any of the appetizing treats since I had already had a big breakfast. The smell of baked goods and fresh coffee convinced me. I tucked in to a cup of coffee and a *pain au raisin*, a sort of cinnamon roll with raisins, and took advantage of the break to call Iaen. He was out so I left a voicemail message on his recorder, letting him know I was thinking about him. I had thought of ending the message with a loud kiss like the one from our last conversation and in the end chickened out, not wanting to sound childish or clingy.

Ten or fifteen minutes later, Sébastien returned with a teenage girl. Her appearance was such that I had a hard time deciding what to focus on for starters. It was obvious she had spent a great deal of effort and energy on her look. The first thing I noticed about her was the amount of makeup, including seemingly mile long false eyelashes, she wore.

Her eyebrows had been plucked so thin they looked unnatural. A thick layer of foundation covered her face, making the skin appear even and blemish free. Black eyeliner circled her dull green eyes. Burgundy red lip liner outlined the contour of her lips, which were colored in a lighter shade of gloss. Her hair, dyed an unnatural red, hung loose to the middle of her back. A few months' growth of dark brown roots, identical with her eyebrows, covered her head.

Thanks to high heels, her plump frame towered over me. Although not all Weeia had abilities, when they did, the abilities manifested initially at puberty. Without drawing attention to what I was doing, I checked my marshals badge. Sure enough, it detected a third Weeia signature in addition to Sébastien and me in the room. There were four types of henki or Weeia ability categories, Emotional, Material, Mental, and Temporal. Hers was registering a mental henki. I was surprised to see a second signature for a spiritual or Emotional henki because second henkis were less common and appeared later in life.

"Hi," she said, turning back to Sébastien as if for reassurance.

"Hi," I replied. "I'm Marshal Dannielle Metreaux. Are you Christine Riens?"

"Yeah," she said, standing near the door, holding her hands in front of her in a defensive posture.

Her eyes scoured the room, landing on me as I spoke. Sébastien took the seat next to mine, inviting her with a movement of his hand to sit down across from us. She focused on him for a few seconds before sitting down on the edge of the seat and glancing at the door as if she was thinking of leaving.

"As I mentioned, we're investigating Martin Davidi's injuries," he said. He spoke in a slow soothing voice, the kind used to calm an injured animal with a thorn in its paw, which could bolt at any moment if spooked. "We heard he's popular. Since you are too, we're hoping you can help us."

"Okay, but I don't, uh, I wasn't there when it happened," she said. She spoke in a high voice that almost trembled. "I, what can I, um, tell you?"

"Perhaps nothing," Sébastien said. "We appreciate you trying anyway."

"Of course, Marshal Sébastien," she said.

She let out a breath she had been holding as if he had paid her an enormous compliment she could tell her friends about for days. There would be bragging rights for any of the lucky girls who had a chance to spend time with the handsome marshal. I could imagine it. She lifted her chin a smidgen, focusing her attention on the space between us. I wondered about her obvious nervousness.

"It seems your popularity increased recently," I said. "Is there any particular reason?"

"Uh, no," she answered as I was finishing speaking. She looked down at her shoes, which had taken a heightened importance all of a sudden. Glancing at Sébastien, who sat relaxed, looking gorgeous like a Greek god, she reversed her answer. "Maybe. I've been using my sister's new popularity enhancing potion."

She spoke the next to last words as if trying them on for size in her mouth. It occurred to me she wasn't familiar with the term.

"Did it work?" he asked.

"Oh, yeah," she said, turning her torso toward him, her eyes lighting up and her bright red lips spreading in glee. "Adrienne, Zoe's bestie, was the most popular until she transferred unexpectedly. Since then, Zoe's cred dropped and mine skyrocketed."

"What makes you think it was the potion?" Sébastien asked.

"Well, I went from like normal to special overnight,

Marshal Sébastien," she said.

"Could anything else have caused that?" I asked.

"What do you mean?" she asked.

Either she wasn't the brightest bulb in the drawer or she was playing dumb. Her open mouth and the vacant expression on her face gave me the feeling it was the former.

"Did you do or say anything different that week or did something unexpected happen?" I asked.

I wanted to ask her if she had won the lotto and split it with her classmates or gotten ahold of an important test in advance. I guessed those were the most probable reasons she might become popular since she wasn't pretty, smart, witty, or funny. Instead, I waited for her answer. I was proud of my patience.

"Uh, can't think of anything," she said, adding after a few seconds, "I changed lipgloss."

"Could the lipgloss be enhanced?" Sébastien asked.

"Naw, it's a knock off brand from a department store. There's no way," she said after pausing as if to think about it. "Half the girls here are wearing that shade and half of Paris is too. It's the in color."

She glanced at me as if I should know. She had the wrong person. I was still pondering what she meant by knockoff brand. I had heard of counterfeit watches and handbags, but never lipgloss.

When I didn't react she added, "If it was the lipgloss everyone in Paris would be popular."

"So, what's special about your sister's potion?" Sébastien asked.

"It's supposed to make her charismatic," she said, using air quotes for the final word. In response to our blank stares she explained. "You know, make people like you, a lot." Looking at Sébastien she asked, "You like me don't you?"

He got up from his chair as if to shake the awkward question off. I pressed on.

"Why do you think that it's supposed to make people like you? Did you sister tell you it would?" I asked.

"Not really, she doesn't let me in on her secrets," she said. "She thinks I'm stupid." She lowered her eyes. I felt a pang of pity. "I overheard her telling a friend about it on the phone when she didn't know I was around. She said it was custom made for her. When I went to try it on she smacked my hand, shoving me out of her room, saying it's really expensive."

"I thought you said you used her potion to become popular," I said.

"I did," she said, a grin blossoming on her face and the nervousness receding. "When my sister wasn't in her room I tried some on. Later, I took a bit for myself. I could only take a little or she would've noticed, you know? When her bottle was almost empty, I nagged until she gave it to me just to shut me up."

I nodded. Sébastien reclaimed his seat.

"How often have you worn it?" he asked.

"Uh, not sure," she said, closing her eyes and wrinkling her nose in concentration. "Not that many days. A little goes a long way. All I have to do is rub a drop on my skin and it lasts several days. If I don't shower or do PE it lasts even longer."

"What about Zoe?" I asked.

"What?" she asked, her nervous movements increasing.

"She said she tried her sister's potion too and it didn't work," I said.

"Dunno," she said, looking like she wanted to leave.

"Want a croissant?" I asked, hoping the treat would distract her.

I walked to the tray on the desk and picked up the basket. The baked goods, wrapped in a napkin, were still warm or at least not cold. Standing next to her, I pulled the napkin back so she could see inside, allowing her to pick the bread of her choice. The lingering smell tempted me, but I held strong, covering the breads and returning the basket to the tray. A couple of bites seemed to calm her down a smidgen. I handed her a paper napkin to clean the bread flakes and butter off her fingers and lips.

"Why do you think Zoe is less popular than she was when Adrienne was here?" Sébastien asked with a touch of indifference as if the answer didn't matter at all.

"Uh, I, well, she, she does drugs," she said, stumbling through the words.

It was painful to watch. I wanted to slap them out of her. Sébastien, on the other hand, sat waiting like he had all the time in the world and was keen to hear her answer.

"Didn't she do drugs when Adrienne was here?" I asked.

"Well, uh, she didn't, not as much as she does now," she said.

"What changed?" Sébastien asked.

"Hmm, I'm not sure," she said. A long moment later, she continued after looking at my colleague with an adoring gaze. I let an impatient breath out before I burst a blood vessel. "I know what it is." She lifted her hand in the air, in a triumphant gesture. "Adrienne always had money. Her parents are loaded you know. Zoe's family is well-off, but not like Adrienne's. I guess when Adrienne was around they had money for drugs. Now, she has to deal to feed her champagne habit on a beer budget."

She placed her thumb and finger almost touching to illustrate how small Ms. Cartes's budget was. Crumpling the napkin in her hand, she threw it across the room. It landed atop the tray. I noticed there was still lipgloss on her lips although it was smudged.

"What about her sister's potion?" Sébastien asked.

She shrugged. After a moment, she looked around and got up.

"Can I leave now?" she asked.

Sébastien turned to me and I moved my head up and

down in approval. He walked to the door and opened it for her in response.

"Kids," I blurted after she left. "Give me a hardened criminal any day."

He laughed. I did too. It was nice to have a partner who got me. Although we had a bumpy start, I took the blame for that, and I was his boss, I had come to think of Sébastien as my partner more than my direct report. We looked out for each other. That was what mattered.

"What do you think?" he asked.

"She's a nervous nelly, that's for sure," I said. "But, I can chuck half of that to hormones alongside developing new abilities, not an easy combo."

"And the other half?"

"To being in the presence of the devilishly handsome Marshal Sébastien," I said, chuckling.

I thought he blushed. He turned away from me, walking toward the tray and picking up a *pain au chocolat* pastry, so I couldn't be certain.

"New abilities?" he asked.

"Well, as a matter of fact, I'm baffled by that," I said. "My badge indicated her ability has already manifested. She has a mental henki."

"Why is that baffling?" he asked.

"By itself it's not, except it detected a secondary spiritual henki signature at the same time," I said.

"Could your badge be malfunctioning?" he asked.

"Anything is possible," I said, letting my answer hang between us.

"But you don't think there's a snowball's chance in the desert," he said.

"Nope," I said. "I run diagnostics on it often and if that wasn't enough Ernie, tech obsessed man that he is, checks my badge regularly."

He smiled. He had met Ernie, the second in command in

the marshals armory, when he attended the Marshals Academy in Portland, Maine; and he knew Ernie had a soft spot in his heart for me.

"Say no more," he said. "Ernie worries about you like a mother hen for her chicks."

"Don't I know it," I said, feeling guilty.

Ernie and I had met during my most recent year of training at the Academy. We had become close at the tail end. Right before I received the surprise assignment to Paris we had dared express our feelings, too late. It had been the beginning of something special, but the huge distance and meeting Iaen had thwarted whatever it might have become. Still, we stayed in touch. We spoke for work often enough, and when I could eke out time to catch up, I called him. We had never spoken about Iaen, but I knew he knew. It was the enormous elephant in the room between us.

"Could she have two abilities?" he asked.

"It happens," I said, unconvinced.

"But, you don't think so," he said.

"I don't," I said. "I can't explain it. Weeia with dual abilities are uncommon and that's usually inherited. Plus, the second ability tends to show up at an older age. Find out if her parents or anyone in her family has dual abilities or is a maximus."

"Okay. If she has a spiritshifting ability it could explain why she's popular," he said. "What if her main ability is spiritshifting and her second ability is mindshifting?"

"That might do it," I said. "If that's the case, what changed? She wasn't popular and then she became everyone's center of attention. When I asked about it, she didn't have a clue, except for that lame potion explanation. If her ability had just manifested, I think she would've boasted about it. She seems the type to do that. Don't you think?"

"Yeah, I guess," he said. "Hang on."

He stepped out of the room. Ten minutes later, he returned

with a triumphant expression on his face.

"Her parents are both mindshifters," he announced.

"Christine Riens?" I asked.

"Yes," he said. "None of her immediate family have spiritshifting abilities. That's why she desperately wants to be popular."

"I'm not seeing anything sinister here," I said. "Just a bunch of rich kids doing drugs, experimenting, and competing for most popular."

"That would explain why they're squirmy," he said. "The zero tolerance rule must have them on edge."

"I think so too," I said. "Although enforcement appears to be rather uneven. Martin Davidi does whatever he wants with no consequences." I remembered what life at the Marshals Academy had been like, how students from influential and wealthy families had an attitude of superiority supported by the administration's own policies. Expecting the Académie to be different had been naïve. "That's the way the cookie crumbles, as they say."

"What now?" Sébastien asked.

"We inform the headmistress of our findings," I said. "You're welcome to use your most diplomatic skills to let her know her school is rife with drugs and druggies."

I smiled. I couldn't help it. It felt good to know our findings would wipe the smugness off the school leader's face, at least for a while. Plus, it meant we could return to the city right away.

It was a matter of minutes before we sat in her office. I realized I was slouching when I saw Sébastien's ramrod straight posture in the seat beside mine. I didn't have to impress her, yet my colleague's eagerness to do so made me consider it. She watched us with the fixed eyes of a raptor. Before Sébastien could get a word in edgewise she asked about our progress.

"I understand you have news," she said in an inpatient

tone.

"We're pleased to report, headmistress, that there's no evidence of interference or external influence at the Académie," Sébastien said. "Based on the information we have at the moment from interviews with the students, staff, and administrators, we feel our presence here is no longer necessary."

Way to avoid mentioning the drug issue, Sébastien. He was less certain than usual, nervous of being in the principal's office, I thought.

"What, then, is the main cause behind Mr. Davidi's, uh, accident?" she asked.

"We'll know for sure when the results of the toxicology report arrive," he said. "I would rather not speculate."

"I insist," she barked.

Sébastien shifted in his seat uncomfortable. He was between a rock and a hard place. I didn't give a rat's patootie whether she liked me or not, but Sébastien did. To save him further awkwardness I answered.

"Drugs," I said. "Our investigation points strongly to a single conclusion. He was under the influence of drugs when he jumped in the pool. Apparently, he spends most of his time at the Académie in such a state."

She turned her attention toward me without so much as blinking. I got up and extended my hand as I concluded our conversation.

She glowered without accepting my hand. I could feel the warmth rising to my face and was tempted to explain, no, remind her we didn't work for her. It didn't matter. I was sure she knew it. I lowered my hand, barely managing to keep my temper in check.

"We will submit a follow up report on our findings at our earliest convenience," I said, looking at her face. Annoyance flashed through it, but she kept silent. "As my colleague explained, the situation doesn't merit our presence. We are following marshals guidelines. If we have any updates we will be in touch. Feel free to contact us, if there are any further developments here."

I stepped away from the chair and walked to the door. Sébastien followed me.

"She's not pleased," he said under his breath.

"No kidding, neither am I," I replied in a harsh tone meant for her.

It didn't seem like he was backing me up. I had the impression he was taking her side, even though I had stepped in to avoid friction for him. I didn't appreciate his attitude.

Sébastien sulked on the ride back to Paris. By the time we reached the office, I decided he was entitled to his opinion and sour mood. As long as he didn't defer to her and kept what he thought to himself, that was fine by me.

No sooner had we set foot inside than we heard Madame Marmotte's whiny voice, "Is that you, Sébastien?"

"Yes, Odile," he said. "It's the two of us."

"Where have you been?" she asked. Glancing at me, she added, "François has been looking for you all day."

"All day, really?" I blurted, feeling annoyed. "It's only lunchtime. How is that possible?"

Ignoring my reply, she fussed at Sébastien, "Are you all right? You look tired."

"It's been a long two days," he said.

"Did he say where I could reach him?" I asked, wondering what my boss wanted, he who never ever called the office.

"He said to tell you he heard about the dangerous migrants living here illegally," she said. It required a second or two for me to realize he was referring to Susanna and her children. I was about to point out it was more like without authorization, but she barreled on without pause. "You're to dispatch them immediately. He said not to bother calling back because there's nothing to discuss."

She pursed her lips together in a satisfied expression. It might have disturbed me, if she hadn't looked so tragic with caked foundation crumbling atop her food stained leopard print scarf, mascara clumps on her eyelashes, and purple lipstick coloring outside her lips.

I reached the office door in several quick steps. I was on the other side of the door when I heard her voice, "Where are you going?"

To talk to Francois, I thought, refusing to honor her bad attitude with an answer. I headed to one of his favorite haunts, a corner café on the Ile de la Cité where he and Ceri, his red poodle, often went for lunch. If he wasn't there, chances were he would be at the Weeia club on the Ile Saint Louis nearby.

On my way there, I took a detour to run a quick errand in the eleventh arrondissement. While there I saw people getting ready for the anniversary of the November 13, 2015 massacre by Islamic State extremists. It had been almost a year since they had killed 130 people in the country's deadliest attack.

It was ironic that the greatest number of victims perished in one of the most diverse neighborhoods of the city. Hundreds of balloons had been released at midday to honor the dead near the Bataclan Theater, the most notable venue the day of the attacks. At sunset, the families and loved ones of the fallen would light paper lanterns with red, white, and blue lights on the Canal Saint Martin in the eastern side of town.

Following the attacks, a state of emergency had been in place nonstop, prompting human rights advocates to complain about the ineffectiveness of the measure and the authorities' frequent violation of citizens' rights. City police and national military troops, wearing bullet proof vests and armed to the teeth, patrolled around government buildings, museums, and tourist icons like the Eiffel Tower and

Champs Elysees Avenue.

The city was on edge. Bob, a homeless man, one of my first friends when I was new in town, spoke of anxiety and fear like a living, breathing presence. It was reminiscent of dictatorships and wars past. He was part of a network of people connected by their common interests as city residents without a permanent address. It was ironic that because of their circumstances they had a better idea of what was happening around them than most urbanites rushing to and from work and their daily lives. Bob and his friends had a finger on the pulse of Paris. Although they were suspicious of strangers, he and some of his colorful friends knew me. As a result, we had candid conversations and had supported each other more than once in the past.

Chapter 16

As I neared the center of the city, the congestion worsened. Temporary tents in a multitude of colors, housing newly arrived migrants from Africa and the Middle East, lined the banks of the Seine River. Around them young men stood and sat, smoking and talking. Although I wasn't close enough to hear their conversation, I knew from the news reports they spoke in foreign tongues I wouldn't understand anyway.

The most recent grouping was the largest I had seen. According to News of France, a daily online newscast I watched, the flow of refugees into Paris had quadrupled since they had closed The Jungle. The Jungle was a tent city near Calais, where undocumented migrants camped in the hope of finding a way to cross the English Channel on their way to the United Kingdom and the promise of permanent asylum. The large flow of immigrants was one of the reasons British people had voted to exit the European Union, News of France and other websites reported.

If past patterns continued, they would remain there for days until the residents of the area became fed up with the smells of tobacco, cooking fires, and other unsavory odors from lack of sanitary facilities. When that happened, they would insist the police intervene. Hours or days after that, police vans would appear in a coordinated roundup, observed by refugee aid organizations who wanted to ensure fair treatment. From there, the men would be bussed to other temporary refuges scattered across the country and away from the heart of France.

Lady luck was on my side. Francois and Ceri were at their usual table as was Patrick Harinoir, Francois's charismatic friend. Before I reached them, Ceri barked several times until her owner shushed her.

"Speak of the devil," Patrick said as soon as he saw me. "Hello, Danni." Getting up, he pulled a chair out for me to join them. "What a lovely surprise. We were just talking about you."

Unlike Francois, Patrick always made me feel welcome. When he smiled it was like the sunlight was a bit brighter for it. He often took my side in discussions with Francois so I was glad he was there.

"Oh?" I asked.

"We were discussing the Syrian strays you took in," Francois said as if he was referring to animals instead of people.

Even if that were the case, you would think he, who was so attached to his poodle, would be sympathetic. I had seen that type of blind prejudice too many times to count growing up. People deciding I was a bad person without knowing anything about me other than my family name, had become the rule rather than the exception. Did I have a chip on my shoulder? You bet. I wanted to prove to the world and to myself that I was a good person, and a brave and fair marshal. That wasn't why I was helping Susanna and her family. Going against the tidal wave of negative opinions about refugees and the dangers they posed wasn't my idea of fun. It was the right response. I was doing my best to get other people to see it.

"Her name is Susanna," I said in the calmest voice I was able to muster. "She's the mother of one girl, Akka, and one boy, Chandi."

"We're Weeia marshals," Francois said with finality as if that explained all the conundrums in the universe.

His chin was lifted higher than normal, which was saying something since Francois walked around like a monarch surveying his subjects from high above. Francois's torso was stiff. He had crossed his arms over his chest, closing himself to what I might say next. Patrick's posture and his face were relaxed as if inviting me to speak. As usual, I was grateful to Patrick.

"Yes, and part of our job is assisting Weeia in need," I said, quoting from the marshals handbook. "Why are you so inflexible?"

"Come again?" he asked.

I thought he had taken offense to the last word. I swallowed and I was about to apologize when he went on talking.

"What are you referring to in the handbook?"

"It may not be a priority, but it's one of our mandates. This family is Weeia and they need our help," I said in a loud whisper. Where Patrick appeared jovial and interested in general, Francois was detached. Sometimes Francois gave me the impression he was made of stone. "What would you have me do, throw a family out on the streets of Paris in this climate of unrest because of the anniversary of the terrorist attacks? The children are five and two years old."

I almost asked him if he cared about anyone but himself. I made a tight fist with my left hand to keep from saying something I would regret. The gesture contained my frustration, allowing me to continue speaking with my boss without losing my temper.

"Did you say they're Weeia?" Francois asked.

"Yes," I said in a loud tone, too mad at first to realize he had expressed interest in them. As soon as I did, I explained their situation. "She's the daughter of Weeia parents who went to Syria to work for an NGO." In response to his puzzled reaction I spelled out the English word, "A nongovernment organization, a charity or nonprofit." His face turned back to normal as understanding flooded in with my words. "She married a fellow Weeia who was working there temporarily. So, yes, they're both Weeia. When the problems became too much for them, he traveled by boat, leaving his family behind to follow later because it was too dangerous for them to go with him."

I was speaking so fast the words were running into each other, but I didn't care. I felt I had to get their story out quickly before Francois and Patrick turned their attention onto something else.

"She traveled by land with the children and after many hardships made it to Paris a few days ago," I said. "He's in Germany, trying to apply for asylum there, but, as you may have heard on the news, there are more than a million refugees in Germany in the same circumstances."

"You're such a softie," Patrick said in a kind manner to me. Turning to his friend he asked, "How can you not relent?"

"And they're not even Muslim," I said.

"I thought all Syrians were Muslim," Francois said, looking like he didn't believe me.

"I think many of them are, but there are Christians and Jews, and a bucket load of flavors, for lack of a better term, of Muslim sects just like there are Baptists, Catholics, Lutherans, Jehovah's Witnesses, Mormons, and many other Christian churches," I said. "Susanna and her family are from the minority. They're Christians."

He paused as Pierre, the server, arrived. We had met on past occasions, and although he wasn't my biggest fan he had grown to tolerate me since he had seen me dine with my boss and his friend.

"Would the young lady like something?" he asked.

"Um, no, thank you," I said. "I won't be staying long."

"Nonsense," Patrick said. "Bring her some escargot and a glass of wine, Pierre." The server paid little attention to me, watching Patrick instead. Patrick turned to me. "You can join us at least for the appetizers. It would be impolite for us to eat if you have nothing yourself, and our food will get cold while we make conversation with you. The escargot is excellent this week. Besides, they're not raw. You'll see."

Patrick's amusement did little to convince me. I

remembered with little fondness the day we, well they, had raw oysters. At their insistence I tried some, but I didn't like them. In the end, they ate their portions and mine without skipping a beat. I hoped the snails were better. A minute later, Pierre set a place for me, and served me a glass of wine from their open bottle.

"So what is it that you want to do with them?" Francois resumed the conversation.

"I don't want to do anything with them," I said in a defensive manner. Taking a deep breath and releasing it in slow small even breaths I went on. "I was hoping the marshals would intervene so they can get asylum in Europe. I contacted Portland to ask how they've handled past cases similar to this one."

"And?" he asked.

"Nothing, I haven't heard back," I replied. "But, it's only been a couple of days."

"So what do you propose to do?" he asked.

"Find a way," I said.

"Let the girl try," Patrick said. "It's not hurting anyone."

"Fine, you have thirty days to figure something out," Francois said, breaking a piece of bread from his slice of baguette and buttering it as he spoke. "After that, they're out." He popped the bread in his mouth, chewing slowly. "You can't say I'm inflexible anymore."

I smiled before replying, "Thanks."

It was a big concession from him. I was confident I would find a solution before his deadline. Watching him eat was making me hungry. I took a sip of my wine. It was nice. Several bites of buttered bread and sips of wine later the escargot arrived. The smell of garlic, white wine, and butter was making my mouth water. After paying attention to how Francois and Patrick ate the snails, I picked up the special small fork Pierre had brought and stabbed one out of its shell, dipped it in sauce and took a tentative bite. Before I realized it a sound of pleasure escaped my lips. It was far less chewy, and the flavor lighter and more satisfying, than I had anticipated.

Moments after Pierre brought our appetizers, he returned with ground meat in a doggie bowl for Ceri, setting it next to the prissy dog. From her dignified sitting position by her owner's feet, she sniffed it. I assumed she hadn't liked it and returned my attention to my dish. When I looked at her a few minutes later, her plate was empty and she was running her little doggie tongue over her lips.

"How did it go at the Académie?" Francois asked.

"As well as could be expected, I guess," I said. "The only evidence we found points to an accident due to drug abuse or an overdose."

"The headmistress must've been relieved," Francois said.

"Not exactly," I said. "We were between the fire and the frying pan. I'm pretty sure she didn't want us to find evidence of any attackers from outside the school. At the same time, she wasn't happy with our conclusion of widespread drug abuse, bad for the reputation and all that."

"She told me," he said.

"You knew already?" I asked. What was he playing at? "Why ask me?"

"Just wanted to make sure I had understood her well," he said, shrugging off my question with a dull tone of voice and a wave of his hand. "Did you tell her Martin Davidi is a drug addict?"

"Sure did," I said. "I have copious notes and the testimony of several witnesses, not to mention the toxicology reports. They drew blood the day he jumped in the pool and he was higher than a kite."

"Did you file the report already?" he asked.

If he had spoken with the headmistress already he knew when we had left the Académie and probably knew our timeline. I gave him the benefit of the doubt.

"I was going to file it this morning before meeting with her, but as a courtesy I gave her an opportunity to respond to my findings in case there was anything she had to add," I said. "She didn't."

"Don't," he commanded before I finished speaking.

"You know I can't do that," I said, anger rising like a living thing. "My job is on the line. Sébastien's would be too."

Not that he cared about me or my job given his unreasonable request. He might care if Sébastien's image was sullied by a scandal.

"I gave in to your plea for the Syrians, didn't I? You can return the favor by burying the Académie report," he said.

"Is that why you caved in so easily, because you were planning to ask me to throw away my career to protect the headmistress's reputation?" I asked.

The smug expression on his face and lack of a reaction told me I had hit the bullseye. He hadn't given in to my request in a gesture of good will or because Patrick had prompted him, he had been setting me up. I took a deep breath and counted to twenty, exhaling with deliberate slowness. It allowed me a precious few seconds to calm down and come up with a sensible reply.

"You won't lose your job," Patrick said in an unconvincing tone.

I appreciated that he was a wealthy and influential man. While his pull might reach the marshals service, I doubted he would stretch far on my behalf. Ours was not that kind of relationship. I would not say we were friends. Our connection was one-sided, much more like a mentorship than anything else. He shared advice. Once or twice he had also sent me to contacts who had given me preferential treatment. I had been hesitant at first when he recommended a well-known boot maker with a three year waiting list and a huge price tag. Thanks to Patrick's say so I got to the head of the line and paid a much reduced fee. In no time, the boots had become my most comfortable and favorite item of clothing.

It cost him nothing and his contacts were more than happy to accommodate one of the wealthiest men in France with little effort. It was an all-around win for everyone. I had wondered from the beginning why he was kind to me. I had asked him and he had said that even if my boss wasn't aware of it, I was good for Francois, that I brought him out of his funk. Because of that, he was grateful to have me around.

"I'll forward the report to you to be filed, it's up to you if it sees the light of day, that's the best I can do," I said, giving him the fiercest stare I could muster.

"Fine," he said.

The interaction spoiled my appetite. I figured I had better leave while I was ahead. As soon as Pierre cleared the dishes and before he returned to ask for my order for a main dish I made my excuses and left. Ceri barked a few times. I could never tell if her barking was a form of objection or welcome. As long as she didn't bite, I didn't care.

Chapter 17

By the time I returned to the office, I had cooled down from my encounter with Francois. Plus, I had won a thirty-day extension for Susanna and the kids so I was feeling good.

The office was quiet. I assumed Sébastien and Madame Marmotte were having a late lunch. Sending the report to Francois might amount to throwing it in the trash, but I had to finish writing it. As the number two, Sébastien often filed the paperwork. Given his relationship to the Académie I had opted to handle it myself. No sooner had I sat down than Madame Marmotte's voice interrupted my thoughts.

"Marshal Metreaux, is that you?" she asked. Without waiting for a reply, she continued. "Remember Francois's orders. That family must be out of here by day's end. If you won't take care of it, I'll have the handymen do it."

Her pushy tone and threat to have Tadas and Giedrius evict the already flustered family could wreak havoc with my upbeat mood. I wasn't going to let that happen. I got up and walked to her office, placing my hands on my waist as I faced her sporting my sternest expression.

"You'll do no such thing," I bellowed, certain she was responsible for stirring Francois against the migrants in the first place. She was so concerned with appearances and what her friends would say that it never occurred to her how kicking them out would be devastating to Susanna and the children. "I've discussed the situation with him already. I have thirty days to deal with the issue. You're not to bother them in any way. Do you hear me?"

She watched me with wary eyes. I stared back, for what felt like a long while, but was only seconds.

"Yes," she said in a hoarse voice.

I finished my report and sent it to Francois. Then I went to check on the family. I found them at Giedrius' laughter-filled apartment. I didn't linger because I was eager to see Iaen and take a long hot shower.

"I'm looking for a handsome sexy guy with an attitude. Are you here?" I asked as I entered Iaen's boat.

There was no reply from the dark interior. I could smell wood polish and in the background a fragrant spice, turmeric perhaps. I waited for a few minutes until impatience got the better of me and I headed home. My mobile phone battery was dead and my charger was at home so I couldn't call him. If only I had called him before leaving the office, I might have been in his arms at that moment. But I hadn't thought about it until I had left the building. At the time, I figured I would surprise him. It didn't occur to me that he might have made plans.

I covered the short distance to my apartment in a few minutes, looking forward to a steaming hot shower. Disappointment at not finding Iaen at home distracted me, and I forgot to check the mail. I had reached my door and was fishing the keys out of my pocket when a delicious odor met my nose. It was mild but enticing. I guessed the smell of butter and white wine was wafting from my apartment. Could it be Iaen? I opened the door hoping it was. He was so engrossed in the kitchen, he didn't hear me arrive. He had his back to me as I entered and hugged him. He jumped a bit and dropped the spoon he held. Realizing it was me, he guffawed.

"You got me," he said.

"Sure did," I replied, laughing with him. "How did you know I would be home on time for dinner?"

"I didn't," he said wearing a crooked smile that made my heart miss a beat and tempted the rest of me to skip dinner in favor of flesh-oriented pursuits. "I was hoping. I left you a couple of messages to find out what time you—"

I kissed him midsentence. He kissed me back with

enthusiasm. The kiss grew into more until he turned the stove off and we made our way to the bedroom, forgetting about food in favor of other more pressing matters.

A call on my badge woke me from a deep sleep hours later as we lay entwined in bed. I looked at the clock on my night table. It was three a.m. A call at that hour of the night meant there was an emergency. As I reached for my badge, I remembered that in the heat of the moment our clothes had landed every which way on the floor. My badge was still in my jacket pocket somewhere in the room. The trick was finding it in the dark. I got up, tiptoeing to avoid waking Iaen.

"Don't worry," I heard him say in a groggy voice. "I'm awake already. Do what you gotta do."

"Thanks," I said, speeding up my pace to find my jacket and badge before the caller gave up. He turned on the light and got to his feet to help me search. "Here it is."

I went to the living room to take the audio call in private. We could receive video and audio calls on our badges.

"Yes," I said, sounding less annoyed than I was.

"It's me," Sébastien said. "Sorry to call so late. There was a report of public Weeia activity at a nightclub. I'm already dressed. If you rather I can go alone. It could be a crank call." He let the words hang as if to give me a chance to cling to the idea. "If there's anything you need to deal with tonight, I understand. I'll call you from there with a report."

Although I was not happy to be dragged away from Iaen's embrace and my warm bed, I was already awake. We learned in the Marshals Academy that late night reports were always to be taken as more serious than those at regular hours. Chances were there was drinking and substance abuse, and people's judgment was impaired. I wasn't going to send Sébastien out on his own.

"I'm not going to let you have all the fun," I said, walking back to my bedroom in search of my clothes.

I heard Iaen puttering around in the kitchen. It reminded me of dinner. A pang of guilt and regret for the lost meal he had been preparing struck for a millisecond, until I remembered how we had spent the hours instead of dining. Then a grin spread across my lips.

"You sure?" Sébastien asked.

"Yep," I mumbled, balancing my badge against my ear while I used my hands to pull my blue jeans on, zip and button them.

"I'll pick you up in ten minutes," he said. "At this hour there's a lot less traffic, but parking will still be at a premium around the nightclub. It'll be easier in one car."

"Okay, see you in ten," I said, hanging up.

The smell of fresh coffee greeted me on my way to the kitchen. My stomach grumbled in protest and anticipation. I was hungrier than I was sleepy, but there was no time for a meal. There was a sandwich on the small kitchenette table and Iaen was pouring me a cup of coffee.

"I have to go," I said. "Sébastien will be here in ten minutes to pick me up."

"I know," he said, understanding written all over his face as he turned toward me and handed me the cup. Pointing to the sandwich he added, "At least have something to eat before you go or take it with you."

"You're the best boyfriend ever," I announced, emphasizing the last word, and kissing him on the cheek as I took the cup from his hand.

"I know," he said, flashing a naughty grin and winking at me. In reply, I gave him a playful slap on his butt. "Watch it, lady, or you're not getting out in ten minutes." That won him a big smile. "Do you have time to sit or should I wrap it up?"

"If I eat quickly I should be able to finish it," I said, taking a bite. "It's so good."

While I scarfed down the sandwich, he added potato chips to the plate. Then he washed a bunch of grapes and set them in a bowl in front of me. It was the perfect combination, enough to take the edge off my hunger without making me sleepy.

"Did I mention you're the best?" I asked as I got up to hunt down my boots.

"It might have come up," he said, feigning as if he couldn't remember. "But, I never get tired of hearing you say it."

"Arrgh, my mobile phone battery is still flat," I said. "With everything going on last night, I forgot to plug it to the charger."

"You sure?" he asked like the cat who swallowed the canary.

"Uh, yeah," I said, hesitating at his expression. "Unless you know something I don't"

"Well, as a matter of fact, I might," he said.

When I found my phone, it was tethered to the cable and fully charged. It was a small detail, but it made me feel better.

"When I got up last night to go to the bathroom I noticed it on the table and plugged it in," he said.

"Thank you," I squealed. "And for making dinner."

Squealing wasn't something I did before meeting him. Iaen brought out the playful and lighthearted in me and I was glad for it. Two minutes later, I was barreling out of my apartment after delivering an enormous hug and kiss to my fabulous boyfriend. He stood at the door, watching me as I walked away down the hall and stairs. His usual appearance in motorcycle attire was of a nonchalant naughty boy. At that hour, he looked sleep crumpled and adorable thanks to the impression of the pillow still on his cheek.

Sébastien arrived one minute after I exited the building. His hair was a touch less well combed than usual. Otherwise he was as perfect as ever. I hadn't even had time to comb my hair and hadn't bothered to color coordinate my outfit. Life was too short to be preoccupied with being fashionable for strangers. After all, I didn't care what they thought. I was a marshal, not a model or a TV anchor.

"Where are we going?" I asked.

"It's called LRRR, an upscale nightclub on rue Legendre," he said, making a right to cross the Seine River on Pont de la Concorde.

"In the seventeenth arrondissement?" I asked.

"That's the one," he said. "You're getting good."

I beamed, pleased I had remembered where it was and he had noticed my geographic prowess. The city was big and its six thousand streets all had proper names, making it necessary to learn the names and locations to get around without an electronic map or guidance system. Even Parisians and cabbies struggled to find addresses without a map. I had a long way to go before I learned them all, but I had a good grasp of some of the major streets in each arrondissement.

"What kind of name is LRRR?" I asked.

"It's short for Little Red Riding Rodeo," he said.

"So what's the story?" I asked.

"Don't know much," he said. "Someone, she didn't give her name, called in an incident." She had called on the emergency number available to Weeia residents and visitors. One of us was always on call around the clock. There were few Weeia living in the city and a skeleton marshals crew of four. Since I had been in Paris, it was the first time had anyone used it. "I couldn't understand everything, and she hung up before I could get much beyond the name of the club."

"What did she say exactly?" I asked.

"That a teenager was misbehaving and she was sure what he was doing wasn't allowed," he replied. "Something to do with a fire was the only other bit I caught."

"Gotcha," I said. "Do you know the club?"

"I've heard of it," he said. Because of the hour, we had arrived at rue Legendre in a fraction of the time it would have taken during the day. "I'm going to look for a place to park. If I can't find one, I'll have to use the valet service. I know we're not supposed to when we're on our way to a situation, but it may be the only option, okay?"

"Yeah, sure," I said.

"You're in a good mood," he said. "I guess all the home cooking and loving is a mood enhancer." I punched his arm, but there was no anger in my punch. He tried to pull his arm away. Since he was driving there wasn't much room for him to move. "Don't mind me. I'm just envious."

"You've got someone in your life," I said. "I've heard you on the phone."

"Meh, it's nothing serious," he said. "Not like you two lovebirds."

"Oh?" I said. "It sounded like someone you were into at the time."

"Not the way you're thinking," he said, avoiding my gaze. "It's not someone I would ever take home to meet my family."

"I didn't think you cared so much about convention," I said.

"It's not so much that I do, although my family is somewhat uptight that way," he said. He stopped speaking to park. "When you're with Iaen, even when you talk about him, you light up. I can tell being with him makes you happy without you saying a word. It's as if it spills out of your pores."

"I do? It does?"

He nodded and grinned. I had no idea I was so easy to read.

"I've never been with someone who does that for me," he said. "I guess for the right person, I would cross all kinds of social barriers and more." The grin faded. "I haven't found anyone who makes me feel like that. What you have is special." Glancing at the street, he opened his door and got out of the car. I did the same on my side. "It should be about a block and a half from here to the club."

"What have you heard about the club?" I asked in preparation for our arrival.

"It's popular with a young crowd and Weeia students like it, not sure why," he said.

"Small, large, dark, anything else?"

"That's all I got," he said. He stopped, flicking through his smartphone screen. "I found some photos online from a year ago, not sure if it will look like that anymore, but it's better than nothing."

"You get an A for effort, but they're mostly selfies and don't show much of the background," I said. "I didn't see any police or ambulances by the door when we drove by, so whatever it is hasn't escalated to emergency services level yet."

"Good point," he said.

"Maybe we'll get lucky," I said. "It could be a prank."

"I suppose," he said, sounding unconvinced. "There's no line. That's one good bit of news."

The bouncer at the door sat on a stool, appearing indifferent and not a little bored. He was dressed all in black and held a cigarette in his hand. He perked up when he saw Sébastien and frowned when he saw me. The change in his face was so obvious it was like watching a cartoon character. Sébastien reached him before I did. After they exchanged a couple of words the man waved us through.

"What did you tell him?" I asked.

"The truth," he said, chuckling.

"Really?" I asked, incredulous.

"The version of the truth he was likely to believe," he said. "That you're from out of town and we're catching up with some acquaintances inside."

"Well done," I said, walking past the door he held open for me.

Unlike some of my marshal colleagues who refused to accept it when a colleague tried to be nice, I appreciated a polite gesture whenever someone made it. Sébastien wasn't brownnosing me. He was just the kind of person who opened doors for people.

Chapter 18

With a name like Little Red Riding Rodeo, I had anticipated a Texas or Western saloon theme. Instead of the stark and unpolished ambiance I expected, the nightclub was decorated in shades of burgundy, candy apple red and black. A statue of a woman clad Western style atop a stallion in a corner was the only indication the name had even a remote relation to a rodeo.

There was a crowded small dance floor next to the bar. Individual private rooms sprang out around the dance floor like a halo. The first one was empty except for bottles and party favors littering the floor. The second one was filled with a group wearing horse costumes. In the third room, I saw a young woman in the center of a crowd of twenty or so well-dressed people. Something about the way they stood told me that was the group we sought.

"Stop it, Cécile," an indistinct voice yelled. "You're going to burn her. Stop it!"

I couldn't see above the heads. Although the words were suspicious, it could all be innocent. Before intruding in a private event, I wanted to be sure there was a good reason. Using my badge detector, I confirmed everyone was Weeia. I showed it to Sébastien. I pressed against people until I reached the inner edge of the circle to see what was happening. A woman in her early twenties, wearing neon orange overalls with rhinestones stood across from another woman of about the same age. The second woman's left hand was outstretched, and in her palm she held a single antelope shaped origami. The tail of the antelope was on fire and then it wasn't. As I watched a thin plume of smoke rose from the charred paper, and a new fire began out of nowhere on the face of the antelope.

Across from me Sébastien observed the interaction. A sea of phones rose along the observers, capturing the moment in clumsy photos and amateur videos. That was why Weeia weren't supposed to own electronic devices. We couldn't risk those images reaching human eyes and exposing Weeia abilities. Protecting the secret of the Weeia was our number one imperative. I doubted the carefree group surrounding us gave much thought to it and the danger our people would be in if our existence were revealed.

"Had enough?" the first woman asked the woman who held the origami.

"I don't know what's gotten into them," someone behind me said. "Cécile is usually so meek and Ariadne is normally very polite."

"You think because your ability is starting to show a little I'm afraid? Bring it on, bit—" the second woman began to say.

Before she could finish, the entire origami burst into flames. She held it for a few long seconds until shaking her hand in the air, the former paper antelope fell in flames to the ground, where it was extinguished. The scent of charred paper reached me.

"Say that again and I'll teach you some respect, Ariadne," the first woman said.

She lifted her chin, looking at the second woman as if daring her to speak. Ariadne didn't say anything, but she spread her legs, and placed her hands on her waist in a defiant gesture.

Ariadne's face began to sweat and turn red. It was more than discomfort. She was in pain. Cécile's smug expression told me she was behind Ariadne's discomfort. If it was anything like the origami she had destroyed it wouldn't be good. It appeared she was a mattershifter and her element was fire.

"Enough," I said, stepping into the circle. Both women

turned toward me. I addressed Cécile. "I'm Marshal Danielle Metreaux and I'm ordering you to stop immediately."

Cécile turned back to Ariadne, who grimaced as if she was in great pain. A howl escaped Ariadne's lips. I signaled Sébastien, who was a few feet away and behind Cécile. He pressed the electric baton against her back until she fell on her knees and then sideways to the floor, gasping. Ariadne staggered as drops of blood dripped from her nose. The circle began to fall apart.

"Nobody leaves until I say you can go," I said to no one in particular. Then to a burly guy two feet away, "Collect all the smart phones and bring them to me." A chorus of objections thrummed around me. When he hesitated, I bellowed, "Now." To a woman dressed in fuchsia I said, "Get the garbage bag from that bin. Empty it in the bin, flip it inside out, and bring the empty bag for him to put the phones inside."

She hesitated for a millisecond and then began to move as if some invisible hand had poked her. When the guy returned with his arms full of phones she stretched the open bag before him.

"Yours too," Sébastien said to them when they were finished. "We'll return them once the video is wiped clean."

"We need to leave," I said to Sébastien. He nodded. "We'll take them to the car and from there go to Yolanda's." I pointed to Cécile. "Are you able to handle her on your own?"

"I think so," he said, reaching down under her arms and lifting her with ease.

"You and you," I pointed to two muscular men. "You're with me. I need a hand to get her out of here discretely." Their eyes grew wide and they stood motionless. "A hand, now."

I kept my tone level, emphasizing the last word in a higher voice. That did the trick. The two men snapped out of it. Between them, they straightened up Ariadne, who by then was leaning on someone from the circle.

"Look as natural as possible. I don't want to draw attention," I commanded. Turning to one of them I said, "Take the bag with the phones from him and bring it with you. The rest of you need to leave."

It took twenty minutes for us to reach the car and another few minutes for Sébastien to return to the club and make sure the group had left. Ariadne began to groan and Cécile started screaming so loudly, I was forced to slap her to calm her down. When we arrived at Yolanda's house it was quiet.

Seconds after I rang the doorbell I heard Sale barking. Not much later Yolanda's sleepy voice asked who it was. Before I had a chance to reply, she opened the door, beckoning us inside. Sale jumped knee-high once in greeting, circling around me and then Sébastien and the two women we had brought with us. The familiar floral and herbal scent of Yolanda's home-cum-office flooded my senses, reminding me of previous visits like a micro scent clip flashing through my nose.

"What took you so long?" she asked. I opened my mouth to explain only to realize she was pulling my leg. I appreciated her good humor despite the late hour. I might not have responded in such a positive mood had I been in her place. "There's blood on your shoulder. You hurt?"

"Not me," I said. "It must be Ariadne's."

Glancing at the women, she demanded, "Tell me exactly what happened."

The healer had a thin and ethereal appearance as if she was lighter than air. I knew from previous experience that wasn't the case. She was strong of body and spirit. Her brown hair was like a living being, held together by Rasta braids that fell to her waist. Curly strands of sun-bleached hair escaped the braids and stood at attention in no particular order away from her head. Her skin, the color of cinnamon, and her features made me think of exotic locales and sun-kissed shores. Her sole item of jewelry, a ring on her index finger, had a large sparkling see-through medium blue stone that always caught my attention.

"Uh, we're not sure," I replied. "These young women were having a disagreement when we arrived." I pointed at each of them in turn. "I believe Cécile was using her ability on Ariadne, who was injured somehow." Ariadne was dazed and seemed to be in pain. I couldn't tell what was going on with Cécile, who had remained silent after I slapped her. "Cécile what happened?"

I glared at the Weeia to prompt an explanation. The mattershifter looked at Ariadne and at us as if waking up from a dream. Ariadne's nose was still dripping blood. We had followed Yolanda into a treatment room. I called it that, although it was in no way like a doctor's office. There were glass jars, plants alive and dried, containers of varied sizes, handwritten journals and tomes, spices, essential oils, and powders lining the shelves in no particular order I could divine. Ariadne, slouching in a wingchair, was glassy-eyed and pale.

"I-uh-well," Cécile stuttered.

"Full sentences please," I said.

Straightening and taking in a breath she tried again, "I'm not sure what happened. One minute, I was fine and the next I was red-hot angry. Looking back, I realize that when Ariadne bumped into me I channeled my feelings through her. She didn't back down, challenging me instead, which added to my fury."

"Where did the origami come from?" Sébastien asked the question I had wanted to ask.

"No idea," she replied, looking baffled.

"Why did you light it up?" I asked.

"It seemed like a good idea at the time," she said. "All I wanted was to impress my friends, and it felt like Ariadne was getting in my way. I expected that burning a tiny part of the figure would win me everyone's admiration for the fine control it took, and frighten Ariadne so she would stay out of my way."

"When she didn't give in to your mini fires you blasted the whole origami," I said. "And, when even that didn't work you zapped her with your heat where it hurt, in her mind."

"I never meant to harm her," she blurted. "I swear. It was a silly prank."

I pointed at Ariadne, leaning back in the chair as I said, "That was not harmless. I think you may have burned some of her brain cells." Turning to the healer I asked, "Yolanda, is that possible?"

She hesitated, placing her index and middle finger against Ariadne's beating neck vein and lifting one of the woman's eyelids. Her usual relaxed posture and upbeat demeanor had been replaced by tight shoulders and a worried expression.

"It's possible," she said, measuring her words. "How long did the connection last?"

"Dunno," Cécile replied. She shook her head as if ridding herself of the memory or the guilt. "I stopped when—It's not my fault."

"Tell me more," Yolanda ordered.

I motioned for Sébastien to step out of the room with me while the healer questioned Cécile. He did as I asked, glancing back at the women for a second before following me. The anger appeared to be gone. They both looked the worse for wear.

"What do you think?" I asked as soon as we were out of hearing range.

I had formed an opinion but I didn't want to influence his. As his supervisor part of my job was to mentor him. Whenever possible, I took a situation as a learning opportunity. He pressed his lips together and fixed his eyes to one side in a pensive expression.

"Cécile showed no remorse and sounds like a spoiled kid, but I didn't get the impression she set out to hurt Ariadne," he said. "It's as if she wasn't entirely in control of what she was doing."

I agreed, "Yes, I got the same impression. Kinda as if she was aware of her body, but reacting on instinct or driven by strong emotions."

"That would explain why she claims it wasn't her fault," he said. "Does that remind you of anything?"

"Until recently, I would have said no, but it reminds me of those kids fighting at the school," I said. "The bigger question for now is what caused it, and is she capable of doing it again. Because if she is, we have to hold her to keep her from hurting others."

"Maybe if we question her further, we can find out what led to the incident," he said.

"Go for it," I said. "I'll stay with Yolanda and Ariadne in case I can lend a hand. Let me know if you find out anything useful."

While Sébastien took Cécile to the adjacent room to question her, I waited, helpless, as Yolanda tended to Ariadne. Sale sat in the corner, watching with interest. For a nanosecond, I wished for her blessed ignorance and carefree life.

"I've done all I can," the healer announced after administering a beverage to her patient, and placing cotton plugs in Ariadne's nostrils to keep more blood from dripping onto the floor and chair. As I drew my eyes away from the red-stained floor, I noticed I had somehow gotten blood on my hand. I inhaled the familiar scent of the red substance glad it wasn't mine. "Now, we wait."

"How severe are her injuries?" I asked, wondering when she might be well enough to go home.

Soon I would have to submit a report to our home office and deal with the devices we had confiscated. A lot of people were going to get bent out of shape about Ariadne and Cécile's behavior, not to mention all the video and photos that had resulted. And, the owners would begin clamoring for their return if they hadn't already.

"I think they're reversible, but we won't know for sure until she wakes up several hours from now," she said. "I'll examine the other woman if you like."

"Do you think she's hurt too?" I asked.

"No, it's a precaution," she said. "Besides, it'll give you an excuse to observe her before you decide if it's safe to release her."

I hadn't thought that far ahead yet. We had been lucky that someone called our office to let us know what was happening before it got out of hand. And we had arrived in time to prevent the women from killing each other. Once we returned to the office, we would have to see if anyone had posted anything about it online and deal with it.

"Do you think there could be a medical explanation for their behavior?" I asked Yolanda.

Sale raised her head, staring at me with an almost intelligent focus. I liked Sale. She wasn't spoiled like Ceri. Instead, she appeared to have empathy for her owner's moods and maybe even for her patients. I remembered her keeping me company one day when I had been feeling especially sick and groggy. That day, I had been glad she sat beside me.

"There's nothing to indicate it so far," she said. "If I find anything of that kind I'll let you know."

Chapter 19

It had been an hour since I had watched the sunrise, announced by a pallid November sun that had broken through thick, dark clouds promising rain. Sébastien lay crunched up in a loveseat too small to accommodate his tall frame. His regular breathing and the soft sounds he made every so often told me he had fallen asleep. A touch of envy assaulted me as I watched. Damn if he wasn't a hunk, even when he was slack-jawed and unaware of my unguarded inspection.

In case the two women woke up before we did, we had decided to separate them. We left Cécile in the treatment room to rest and brought Ariadne with us to Yolanda's small waiting room. She looked restful in her sleep, not unlike Sébastien.

I had not been as lucky as they had. Falling asleep had been difficult for me. I had commandeered the well-worn settee upholstered with a jungle theme that took up the left side of the room. Yolanda had said we could wait, explaining it could be several hours before the women woke. She had given them a potent herbal beverage to induce sleep. Declaring her job done and announcing that she would bill the marshals for her services, she and her furry assistant had left us to wait.

Something was bothering me. It gnawed at the back of my brain, keeping me from resting yet too distant to identify. What I wouldn't give for a cup of fresh brewed strong coffee to stimulate my little gray cells, as a famous fictional detective my uncle liked was fond of saying. I was distracted, gazing out the window into the house's inner courtyard garden. Filled with lush plants growing wild in all directions, it made me think of a tropical forest, not that I had ever seen one in person.

My thoughts strayed and I wondered what a vacation on a French Polynesian island would be like. Perhaps I needed a break. I hadn't had a vacation in five years. I could have gotten the idea from the garden or the posters featuring tanned, bikini-clad women, cloudless electric blue skies and a vacation in paradise, peppering the city buses and bus benches.

"What do you think?" Sébastien's question interrupted my wandering thoughts.

"About?" I asked, surprised but not startled.

My tired brain needed a moment to focus. I kept my attention on the garden while he replied.

"Ariadne and Cécile," he said, straightening into a sitting position and yawning broadly, covering his mouth with his hand. Leave it to Sébastien to be polite even when he was dog tired. "Since Yolanda declared them ready to go home when they wake up I assume it's up to us to decide what to do. Do you want to charge them?"

"Ordinarily something minor like that wouldn't be worth the paperwork to report it," I said, sharing what I had been thinking during his slumber. "But despite Yolanda not finding a medical reason, neither of them acted normally last night, and we can't explain what caused them to behave so, so, I don't know what to call it."

"Irresponsibly?" he offered.

"Yeah, it was irresponsible, but it was more than that," I said. "It's bugging me that we can't explain it." Like a fog clearing, the thought popped into my head. "It's like the incidents at the Académie. We assumed drugs made them do it, but what if? No, but even if they had been drinking, there's nothing that points to drugs. I didn't see anyone who looked high enough to explain last night's drama."

"I know what you mean," he said. "It was just a bunch of people out for a good time until Cécile and Ariadne had their blowout." He got up, stretching further. "The question is why." I nodded my agreement. "And, are they likely to do it again?"

"Don't have a clue about the first one, except I don't think drugs are behind it," I said. "I'm waiting to see what shape they're in when they wake up. If they're aggressive, we'll take them in to cool off in one of the cells for a day or two. We have enough to charge both of them."

"It'll appear in their record," Sébastien pointed out.

"I know, but I rather ding their record and not risk Weeia exposure and someone getting hurt," I said. "What if we're not there the next time to keep Cécile from frying Ariadne's brains?"

"Good point," he said. "Their families will raise hell."

"Let them," I said. "Maybe that'll motivate them to do something productive that leads to some answers."

"You're the boss," he said.

"Do you have a better idea?" I asked.

"Wish I did," he said with a resigned expression. "I hate to add to your concerns, but Francois isn't going to like it either."

"If he's not happy, he can get off his smug bottom and give us a hand," I said, realizing after I spoke that I had snapped and regretting it.

I couldn't blame Sébastien for Francois's behavior, but because they were friends of sorts and Sébastien was there and Francois wasn't it was easy to lash out at him. That was, as Marla might have said, not sporting of me. After that, the silence hung in the air for a while like a weight on my shoulders. I was thinking of a way to break the awkwardness when I heard footsteps.

"Hello," a woman's voice called out. "Anyone here?"

"Over here," Sébastien answered as he made his way toward the door and opened it.

Although I didn't recognize the voice, a flash of neon

orange told me it was Cécile approaching us. Her eyes were bloodshot, her hair was disheveled, and there was an indistinct print on her left cheek. Otherwise, she appeared normal or as normal as I might expect in light of recent events. She hesitated when she saw me. I watched without saying a word.

"How are you feeling?" Sébastien asked her.

"Like I had too much to drink and not enough sleep," she said.

If she was expecting sympathy, she had another thing coming. Even Sébastien, who was more forgiving than me, had a stern expression. A hint of tension in his shoulders and tiny lines around his lips told me he wasn't falling for her pathetic act.

"Do you remember what happened? How you got here?" he asked.

"Uh, Ariadne and I were, err, having a slight disagreement. Then you lot showed up out of nowhere," she said, turning her head in my direction to include me. So much for Cécile taking responsibility for her own behavior. There was annoyance when she looked at me. When her eyes lingered on my colleague I saw admiration or was that lust? Of course there was lust, maybe both. "Then you brought me, us here."

"If by slight you mean nearly burning Ariadne's brains inside her head, then that's a good description," I said in a snarky tone.

"Do you know who my father is?" she asked, speaking as if there was an audience we couldn't see.

"Not interested," I said. "What you did last night, your daddy can't get you out of. Aren't you a bit old to be calling him to rescue you?"

She opened her mouth as if to speak and closed it. Studying her nails with rapt attention, she turned away from me.

"Thanks to Yolanda's efforts Ariadne will probably be fine, in case you're wondering," Sébastien said in a neutral voice that told me he was as unimpressed by her behavior as I was. "A few more minutes of whatever you were doing to her would likely have caused permanent brain damage."

She kept her head down and her attention on her nails. When she lifted it her chin was at an angle, defiant and unrepentant.

"Whatever," she said like a petulant child. "Can I go now?"

Sébastien and I exchanged glances. While we didn't know what had led her to attack Ariadne the previous night, it was clear she had no regrets and might accost her again if the opportunity arose.

"Not yet," I said. "We need to take your statement at the office."

"What about her?" she asked, making me turn in the direction she was looking toward Ariadne's prone form.

"We've already taken her statement," I said. "We'll get her home address, and if we have further questions we'll find her. I'm sure she'll make herself available."

As Ariadne's sleepy face registered that we were referring to her, an "are you talking about me?" expression appeared. With a nod, I signaled Sébastien to talk to her. In two long strides, he reached her. Together they walked out of the room.

While we were alone, I observed Cécile. She showed no signs of illness or abnormalities. If we held her at fault for her self-absorbed personality, we would have to pursue many others for the same charge in her wake. Twenty minutes later, Sébastien returned by himself. I was convinced she was back to normal, whatever that was.

"She's on her way home," he said.

"Let's go," I said.

Cécile spent the better part of our drive to the office

complaining and reminding us of how important her father, the attorney general, didn't we know? was. At first, Sébastien attempted to calm her down with no results. By the time we arrived at the office, she had reached a fever pitch, convincing me she needed some alone time.

"Take her to number one," I instructed Sébastien once we were inside the complex.

"What about taking my statement?" she asked.

"We can do that later after you have a rest," I said.

"I'm hungry," she said. "I want some breakfast. I'm entitled to some breakfast and a phone call."

"Sure, we'll get you some breakfast and then you can have your call," I said.

"All we have is yesterday's pastry and coffee," Sébastien said. "I'll get something for her."

"There's some instant oatmeal if you rather not go out," I said.

"We could use some sugar and coffee, don't you think?" he said.

The idea hit a soft spot because my stomach gurgled in response, making me realize I was famished. What I wanted was a steak and fries. At that hour, the best I could hope for was a sandwich.

"Pick me up a sandwich if they have any," I said, handing him a twenty euro note.

Chapter 20

A belly full of pastries and decaf mellowed Cécile enough for Sébastien to take her contact information and statement. After that, she used the office phone to call her family who was surprised, judging by her reaction, to hear she was at the marshals office.

"See if she has any priors and write up the report, careful to dot the i's and cross the t's," I instructed Sébastien when he returned from taking her back to her cell. "I'll deal with CUT."

"What's CUT?" Madame Marmotte's voice asked from the entrance as she strode in late to the office.

"The Clean-Up Team," Sébastien replied. "Have you ever had them here before?"

"Never," she said. "I've heard of them. What's going on?"

"A group of people recorded an incident last night and we think some of the photos and video may be online," Sébastien said. "CUT will examine the smart phones, erase incriminating images, and if necessary, hack their social media accounts to delete anything that might expose the Weeia."

"Sounds like a lot of work," she said.

"It is, and it has to be done the right way to avoid suspicions," he said. "By the way, there's someone in the cell."

"Oh?" she said, raising her painted eyebrow.

"We don't have time to fill you in on all the details," I interrupted. I almost told her if she had arrived on time we wouldn't have to update her. It was close, but I didn't. Bully for me. "We need to file the report and call CUT."

"Fine," she said, sauntering toward her office to gossip, I was sure.

"Hello, stranger," Ernie's familiar voice said from Portland, Maine. We often spoke on a video link, but that day I used audio only. "It must be work if you're calling at this early hour."

"Sorry, I waited as late as I could," I said. "Did I wake you?"

"No," he said. His sleepy voice belied his words. "Maybe. What's up?"

"We had a severity three incident last night with a mattershifter and an injury in a public place," I said.

Anytime there was an incident in a public place in a major city it merited a severity rating. The instant we knew about postings online it became a severity one, S1, for short, which meant an emergency that required immediate attention. Since we weren't aware of any posts, I had discretion to rate it S2 or S3.

"Really?" he asked. I could hear him running water and what sounded like making coffee in the background. "How bad was it?"

"We were able to contain it, I think," I said. "Let me put it this way, nobody was badly injured."

"Paris is usually so quiet. What happened?" he asked.

"For no good reason we could find, two women had an argument at a nightclub," I said. "One of them is a fireshifter and was using her ability on the other, who refused to back down. Luckily, a responsible witness called it in, and we arrived before the confrontation peaked. Of course, everyone in the group had their electronics out to capture the moment. You know how it is these days with people sharing every moment of their lives on social media. I confiscated every device we could find, and am hopeful no one posted anything you won't be able to remove with minimum damage."

"How many devices are we talking about?" Ernie asked.

"It was a relatively small group, but some people had

more than one. Let me take a look," I said, pulling the bag that was on Sébastien's desk open. "About twenty-five."

"We'll scrub them clean and check their posts," he said. "Do you have a list of names?"

"Uh, of the owners of the devices?"

"Yes, we have the passwords on file," he said. "They're required to submit passwords for social media accounts and devices, but I need names to match them to their records. Otherwise, this will be a bear."

"I'll figure something out," I said. "You sure you have the passwords already?"

"It's a serious offense to withhold a password. The social media accounts and devices are only allowed provided the owners submit passwords to us for situations such as this one," he said. "It was the only way The Elders would bend the rule. They will come down like a ton of bricks on anyone we report. There will be fines and, depending on what we find, possible suspension of media access. They're looking for any excuse to shut the whole exception down."

"I'll get you names and as many passwords as I can," I said. "Is that coffee pouring I hear?"

"Mhmm," he moaned in agreement.

"You still drinking that smoky organic coffee from Rwanda?" I asked.

"It's from a small farm in Uganda," he said. "You should try it sometime. It'll put hair on your chest."

That won him a laugh. He chuckled.

"That wouldn't look good on me," I said. "I'll taste it one of these days when I'm in Portland."

I almost said he needed the hair more than I did and thought better than to do it. He had a full head of hair, but you never could tell what sensitivities people had. The last thing I wanted to do was hurt his feelings. I had already done enough of that when I got together with Iaen.

"Deal," he said. "I'll save a cup for you."

I was due for a break, which meant returning to Portland, but I planned to spend it helping my aunt and uncle at the farm. It was what I did on my vacation from my job at the marshals every year. I doubted I would see Ernie. I decided to avoid the topic and turn his attention back to work.

"It's my first CUT request. What do I do next? How do I get them to you?" I asked.

"I'll send someone to pick them up ASAP," he said. "Can't do much without the passwords though."

"I'll call you back within an hour with whatever I've got so you can get started," I said. "If I'm not here when they come to pick up the bag, Sébastien or Madame Marmotte will have it. Thanks!"

As soon as we hung up, I went to see Cécile. She stood in the center of the cell looking like hell warmed over.

"What's the password for your smartphone?" I asked.

"What?" she asked, looking annoyed.

"Your password, I need it now," I said. "On second thought, you better write it down." I handed her the notepad I had brought with me. "And, write down the names of everyone you remember from last night."

"What for?" she asked.

"Because I say so," I said. Taking a deep breath, I counted to twenty. Playing the tough marshal wasn't enough. I would need to convince her by means of the carrot and the stick. "Once you prove to me you're not going to attack anyone else, including Ariadne if you run into her, I'll let you go home."

Although I planned to release her as soon as possible, she didn't need to know that. We couldn't leave someone in the cells unguarded. As long as she was there one of us had to be nearby in case of a fire or medical emergency. I didn't relish spending the night at the office, and I didn't think Sébastien or Madame Marmotte would either.

"Good," she said with a smirk as if I was sharing the

outdoor temperature instead of letting her know she might return to her normal life.

"If anyone posted what you did, especially if they included photos or video, you're going to be in worse trouble than you are now," I said, hoping to prod her into giving me the information sooner rather than later.

"So what are the password and names for?" she asked.

"We need to wipe any posts about last night off the internet," I said with as much patience as I could muster. "I'm in no mood to play games with you. I need the information right away. You're the reason we have this problem, you have what we need, and you're here."

"It's not my fault," she objected without conviction.

"Whatever," I said, repeating her word from earlier in the day. "We can do this the easy way or the hard way. If you help me, I'll do everything I can to send you home today. If you make me do it the hard way, you'll spend at least one night here, and I will add this to your file." I emphasized will as I spoke. "Write, now."

"Fine, there's no need to be rude, you know," Cécile said as if I was the unreasonable person. "Handwriting is so twentieth century. It'll take forever. I can type much faster than I can write. I never handwrite anything. Can't I email them to you?"

"This is the most efficient way. I need the information now. Besides, I don't have your phone here," I said.

"Have it your way," she said. "But, don't blame me if it takes a while."

She wrote slowly with difficulty, in irregular block letters so imperfect they seemed like the work of a child with little practice rather than an adult woman. Twenty minutes later she handed me the notepad across the bars of the cell.

"My password is at the top. It's not on file so keep it to yourself."

Yeah, right. How did she expect me to do that? I stared at

her.

"Fine, give it to as few of your fellow snoops as possible. Anyway, I gave you all the names I know. There are a couple of people I only know by their nicknames. Do you want those too?"

I handed her the notebook. When she was done she passed it back to me.

"Did you know that not providing the marshals your password is a serious violation?" I asked. She shrugged to say she did. Seeking to understand why she did something knowing it could get her into trouble, I asked, "Tell me, why risk that when it's so easy to turn in your password?"

"Do they have your passwords?" she asked, lifting her left shoulder as if challenging me to deny the truth.

"No," I said.

"See? You're violating the rules too," she said, triumphant.

"No, you don't understand," I said. "I don't have any passwords to turn in. I'm not on social media."

Her mouth opened in surprise. She shook her head from side to side in disbelief.

"What about your smartphone?" she asked.

"I have an old model phone with a pathetically slow connection to the internet and very little storage space. I never take photos or video," I replied.

"You're weird," she said. "How can you live like that? How do you communicate with your friends and family?"

"Uh, you know, by phone, email, and text," I said.

"That's primitive," she said, looking as if she had tasted something bitter and couldn't get the flavor out of her mouth.

"It works for me," I said.

"What about friending and status updates, how do you do that?" she asked.

"I don't. Without an account there's nothing to post," I said.

"I met someone like that, once," she said. "I feel naked without my phone to post updates, see what's going on and connect with everyone. It's like I'm missing a limb or something. I'm kind of incomplete. What do you do when you have news to share? Do you call each of your friends one by one?"

"Sometimes," I said, smiling at her.

"You took my tablet and phone. When can I get my stuff back?" she asked.

"I don't know. As soon as they're done with it," I said.

She shook her head. I knew being isolated in a cell made people uneasy. Watching her, I realized it was being disconnected that made her uncomfortable.

"It's creepy," she said.

"What is?" I asked.

"That's why I didn't turn in my password. Don't you get it?" she asked.

"What are we talking about now?" I asked.

"It's weird that unseen forces, as my friend says, have my password and can muck around my life without my permission, seeing intimate photos, reading private messages," she said. "It's like a Peeping Tom you never see because he's hidden behind the marshals."

"What can you possibly post that would interest the marshals?" I asked.

"That's not the point," she said. Her ditzy demeanor was replaced by a more serious one. "Even if I'm not doing anything illegal, it's my life. I don't like strangers poking their nose in it."

"Isn't it all public anyway?" I asked.

"Not everything is, no," she said. "You really are clueless. How can you do your job if you don't know how to use social media?"

"I manage," I said, refusing to take the bait. "Nobody is making you share anything. All you have to do to keep your life private is keep it to yourself." She turned to me with incredulous eyes as if I had announced a unicorn stood behind her. "If you don't want strangers to see your intimate photos and private thoughts don't post them."

"I can't do that," she said, stretching out the words and whining.

"Well then don't complain that it's creepy," I said. "Has it occurred to you that once you post anything it's out there forever, as my friend Ernie says? Do you realize each website uses your information and sells it to others to create a Big Data profile on you? You agree to that when you agree to their terms." She nodded. "If someone hacks your phone or your favorite website your stuff won't be so private anymore."

"Yes, I know that, but it's never going to happen," she mumbled. "They won't let it."

I was tempted to remind her of the many times major companies and governments had been hacked in the past few years, and the millions of millions of personal records they had stolen. I didn't. She was alone in our cell and in trouble. Despite the tough act, I could tell she was concerned. It would be cruel to make it worse. Besides, I couldn't change people. I had heard my aunt say it for years, and was beginning to understand how true it was. It was hard enough to attempt to change myself even when I made up my mind to do it.

"I have to send this," I said, lifting the notepad. "Need anything before I go?"

"Bathroom," she said.

After Cécile went to the bathroom, she walked back into her cell without a word. There was something forlorn about the way she held her head as I walked out. I felt sorry for her.

Chapter 21

After I sent everything Cécile gave me to Ernie, I went over Sébastien's report, and sent it in to headquarters and Francois, who would ignore it as he did with all communications I sent. I was about to serve myself a cup of coffee when Ernie called.

"They'll be there in a minute," he said.

"Great, thanks for letting me know," I said.

"We checked the names you sent and the list is incomplete," he said. "I need the rest."

"On it," I said. Before I could finish, the CUT team appeared as if out of thin air in the office. "Gotta go. They're here."

"See ya," Ernie said as we both hung up.

The CUT team was made up of two muscular marshals, one man and one woman, dressed in black. They were nothing like what I had imagined. Scruffy was the first word that popped into my head when I saw them. Sexy was the second. Her pale skin contrasted with her jet black short hair and black eyes, making her appear exotic. She had a tattoo of a symbol I didn't recognize on her neck. Their hiking boots were well-worn and looked comfortable. If I hadn't had the most comfortable pair of boots I had ever owned already I might have been envious. He wore his dark brown hair in a tidy ponytail held together by a band of the same color as his hair. Piercing brown eyes, in almost the same shade of brown as his hair, explored the room like a laser beam. He fixed them on the garbage bag with the electronic devices we had brought back from the nightclub.

"That for us?" he asked in a hoarse voice that made me wonder if he was a smoker. Sébastien picked up the bag and handed it to him. "Anything else?"

"That's it, thanks," Sébastien said.

The guy nodded once and they disappeared in the same surreal way they had arrived in the first place. The air shimmered so briefly, I wasn't sure of what I had seen.

"Wow," Sébastien said, watching the empty place where they had stood moments earlier with a dumbstruck expression. "It was the first time I saw CUT leave. It's like science fiction."

"I know, right?" I said. "I've seen the special transports before, but they always amaze me."

"It's like when you make yourself seem invisible, except in their case it's not an illusion," he said.

"I guess," I said, not sure whether he was complimenting me. "I talked with Ernie. He said CUT needs to match the devices with names and passwords. With some prodding, Cécile gave me most of the names of the people at the nightclub last night, but there are some people she only knows by their nicknames. Call Ariadne and get her to give you the rest."

"What if she doesn't know them either?" he asked.

"We'll have to track them down one by one until we have them all," I replied. "Ernie said even a single person's posts can be very damaging if they're really into it, so this is our top priority at the moment."

"I'm on it," Sébastien said.

Sébastien was a diligent worker and between us by the end of the afternoon we had identified every Weeia at the nightclub. We had done everything we could. I was relieved that the problem was on someone else's lap, Ernie and CUT's.

Before going home, we released Cécile. She had seemed calm when I went to check on her, and I was hopeful that after enjoying the hospitality of our cells she would behave herself. Madame Marmotte had shown interest when we released Cécile since she was impressed by Cécile or rather

her family's social rank.

"It was a long day. It could've gone wonky, but it ended well, thanks," I said to Sébastien, appreciating his willingness to get the job done. He nodded in response to my praise. A few minutes earlier, I had overheard him flirting and making plans on the phone. I decided to tease him. "Hot date tonight?"

"Maybe," he said, winking. "A gentleman never tells."

"Is that so?" I asked, curious about the gleam in his eyes.

"Absolutely," he said. "What about you and Iaen? Got any exciting plans?"

"I haven't had a minute to call him all day," I said. "He texted me earlier asking if I was going to be home in time for dinner, and I said I thought so. With any luck we'll have a quiet night."

"That sounds meaningful," he joked.

"Naw, I'm looking forward to one of his gourmet fixings and a movie on the couch," I said.

"I'll drop you off," he offered.

"It's okay. I'm not in a hurry. Public transportation will be fine," I said. "Besides you don't want to keep your date waiting."

"That's not a problem," he said.

"Aren't you confident?" I teased him.

"Confident, that's me," he said. "See you tomorrow. Call if you need anything."

It took me the better part of an hour and two transfers to make my way home. I almost regretted turning down Sébastien's offer. When I called Iaen, thinking of going to his boat, I got his voicemail. Earlier he had said he would call or meet me at my apartment so I went there instead.

It felt wonderful to take my boots off at the door and pad on the old wood floors. The apartment's uneven flooring was one of the features Iaen was always going on about. He said old buildings like mine were what gave the Latin Quarter

character. Steeped in history, they infused the city with
meaning and culture. Where Iaen was romantic, I was
practical. I liked the smooth feel of the polished material
against my bare feet. The view of the Seine always took my
breath away, and after the busy day I had, the quiet was
soothing. I had just sat down on the sofa when Iaen arrived.

"Hey gorgeous," he said, rushing to my side. I got up and
he wrapped his arms around me in a bear hug. I could have
lingered in his arms, but he pulled us apart and gave me a
peck on the lips. "How was your day?" Before I could
answer he went on. "I was hoping you would be home early.
I have a wonderful surprise, tickets to a lecture on Paris
followed by the official opening of the newly renovated
Carnavalet Museum."

Iaen's enthusiasm for history was vast. When it came to
the City of Lights, it was even greater. He had been waiting
for the Carnavalet Museum to reopen, after a three-year
closure for much needed work, with giddy excitement like a
kid waiting for a new toy to be released. The idea of sitting
in a room of history buffs listening to details about the city's
distant past made me numb with boredom. Thinking of the
cocktail reception after it made me cringe, but I didn't have
the heart to tell him. I forced myself to smile and bid my
quiet evening plans adieu in silence.

"Those must've been hard to come by," I said, realizing
many people would give their eye teeth to attend the VIP
event.

"You have no idea," he said. "But I have friends in low,
and high places."

He swung his arm below his knees and then above his
head in a theatrical manner to illustrate. It was obvious he
was in an ebullient mood. I was happy for him. I wished I
had a hobby I liked as much as he did his. Most of my
waking hours were taken up by marshals duties. Whatever
spare time was left, I dedicated to working out, and the rest I

shared with him. He spoiled me with attention, cooked for me, and planned fun activities, and he never made me feel guilty when I had to leave in the middle of the night. The least I could do was accompany him to the parties and social events even if they were a bit outside my comfort zone.

"At what time is the lecture?" I asked.

"In an hour," he said.

"How soon do we have to leave?" I asked, realizing there would be no down time for me that night.

"Half an hour should be enough time to get there, if you don't mind riding in my motorcycle," he said.

"Don't overwhelm me with time to get ready or anything," I said, rolling my eyes. "How dressy is this shindig going to be?"

"Very by your standards," he said with a playful expression. I narrowed my eyes to let him know of my objection and he smiled. "That's to say you can wear anything you like, even your favorite boots."

"Really?" I asked. "Won't I be too... casual?"

"You'll fit right in," he said. "I expect it to be a mixed crowd of history professors and intellectuals, and a handful of dignitaries there to press the flesh briefly before they head on to more high profile events."

Hearing that I relaxed. Not having to fuss with what to wear took a huge weight off my shoulders.

"I'm going to take a quick shower before we go," I said, unzipping my pants as I headed toward the bedroom.

It took me ten minutes to shower and get dressed. I wore my dressiest outfit, which wasn't saying much, and the new frilly pair of shoes with heels. When I entered the living room, he got up from where he had been waiting for me and whistled, making me blush.

"I have a surprise," he announced, pulling a medium bag from behind him, where I hadn't noticed it and handing it to me.

"What's the occasion?" I asked before opening it.

"You accompanying me tonight. You must be tired," he said. "And attending a history lecture and the reopening of the museum cocktail party isn't your idea of fun."

"What is it?" I asked.

"Open it and you'll see," he said. "If you don't like it, I'll understand."

The bag was filled with tons of red tissue paper. At the bottom there was a square box. It showed signs that it wasn't new. I removed it from the bag, starting to feel curious. Iaen was generous in many small ways, but this was his first gift since we had been together. I assumed he had brought a collectible from his bouquiniste shop to decorate the apartment. I hadn't liked some of the pieces it had when I moved in and had taken them down, leaving bare walls in several places. He had insisted we had to find art to replace the items I had removed.

"It's beautiful," I said once I saw the artsy item inside. "What is it?"

"It's a necklace made of gold and silver wire, tiny gemstones and pearls," he said. "It dates back about one hundred years. I know you're not a fan of jewelry." He hesitated as if searching for the right words. "When I saw it I fell in love with it and wanted you to have it. You can keep it in the box or hang it on the wall, if you don't want to wear it. It doesn't matter as long as you like it."

It was the nicest gift anyone had ever given me. It looked expensive, unique, and delicate. Tears welled in my eyes. I rubbed them away, hoping Iaen hadn't seen them. I was a tough marshal after all, and marshals didn't cry.

"It's beautiful," I said again, finding no better word to describe it.

I was afraid to take it out of the bag in case it broke. He pulled it out with great care and handed it to me to inspect. Up close, it was even more impressive. Its intricate design must have taken hours or days to make, and who knew how many years of experience an artisan needed to make something so dainty.

"Would you like to wear it tonight?" he asked, watching for my reaction.

"What if it breaks?" I asked.

"It won't," he said. "It's stronger than it looks. As long as you don't get into a fistfight it should be perfectly safe for you to wear it."

He circled around me and clasped the necklace in place. Moving back to where he had stood he grinned with delight.

"It looks gorgeous on you," he said. "Do you like it?"

"Yes," I said a bit stunned by the surprise.

"Wonderful," he said. "I had thought of giving it to you for Christmas, but when I got the tickets for tonight I thought there would be no better night to show it off. That crowd is the most likely to appreciate it." Pulling one side, he straightened the necklace. "And now, we have enough time to get there without rushing. Shall we?"

Moments later, we were climbing on his sleek and powerful motorcycle. It was the fastest way to get to the museum in the third arrondissement. More importantly, it was easy to park. We crossed the river at the Ile de la Cité onto the Right Bank, and within minutes arrived at the rue des Francs Bourgois in the Marais. The area in front of the museum had been cordoned off for government dignitaries so we parked a block away.

"It's hard to imagine today, but Paris wasn't always the favorite destination of tourists it is now," he said as we walked to the entrance. "During the reign of Philip II in the twelfth century, there was an eight-foot-thick wall with twenty-five gates surrounding the city. At one point, Paris was in such a horrible state wolves roamed around the city."

"No kidding," I said, interested despite myself.

"Yes, by the end of the sixteenth century the country was

on its knees after decades of religious war between the Catholics and the Protestants," he said.

"That was a long time ago. I know it's your hobby, or should I say obsession, but how do you know so much about it?" I asked.

"There's lots of information from historians and writers who described it in detail," he said. "Although there were no photos back then there are reliable sources, like maps, illustrations, private letters, and even guidebooks. One historian of that era said there was nothing splendid about Paris at the end of that century. Back then, travelers flocked to places like Rome packed with history and religious monuments. In later years, the monarchs and city leaders transformed Paris until it became known as a modern and technologically advanced city."

"How was that?" I asked.

"It began with the bridge we passed on the way here, the Pont Neuf, and the Place des Vosges, two blocks from where we stand," he said. At my puzzled expression he explained. "Before the Pont Neuf was built, bridges were narrow wooden structures lined on both sides with houses that blocked the view of the river entirely. The Pont Neuf was revolutionary because it was over three hundred meters long and twenty-five meters wide, huge by the standards of the day. Also, it was paved, and because there were no houses on it there were wonderful river views, which everyone loved."

"What about the Place des Vosges?" I asked.

"It was the first plaza in the city that wasn't a religious structure or monument," he said.

"What was it for?" I asked.

"Just a gathering place, which was unheard of back then," he said. His eyes gleamed with excitement. "It signaled the birth of a new and thrilling city, and the word spread. Did you know Covent Garden in London and the Plaza Mayor in

Madrid are modeled after it?"

"I had no idea," I said. "How interesting."

Hanging out with a bunch of academics and history lovers for the evening wouldn't have been my first choice. The conversation with Iaen had piqued my interest, and the lecture about a famous resident of the Marais district where the Place des Vosges was located was more appealing than I anticipated. At the reception that followed, I learned that the reason the lecture had been on that particular person had been because she had grown up in the Marais, and lived much of her life in the house that had become the museum.

"You had a good time," Iaen said as we walked out of the museum toward his motorcycle.

"Are you asking me?" I asked.

"Nope, I could tell," he said. "I thought you might get bored, but you didn't. And so many people admired your necklace. That was the perfect group to appreciate it because they could tell it was historically significant. Thanks for coming."

With that he stopped and kissed me. It was a brief kiss, but it took my breath away, and lingered on my lips. We made our way home past the Pont Neuf, the new bridge in its day that had become the oldest bridge in the city.

Chapter 22

The following morning, I heard from Ernie saying he and CUT had done their magic and returned the devices to our office. Iaen had to go out of town for several days. I got up with him and shared a cup of coffee. He didn't know how many days he would be gone, so I wanted to see him off. After he left, I went for a run. I liked the predawn hours when the city was waking up. I felt like I was seeing a part of it that many tourists missed.

When I arrived at the office extra early I found a box with the devices on one of the desks. I was the first one in so I made a pot of coffee. Later when Madame Marmotte arrived, I assigned her to let the owners know they could pick them up during office hours that day or as soon as they were able.

Sébastien arrived midmorning after running an errand. To my delight, he showed up with a bag full of pastries. After I plucked one out of the bag, he walked over to Madame Marmotte's desk and offered her one.

"These croissants are amazing," I said between mouthfuls. "They're so buttery and crispy at the same time. Are they from the bakery near your house?"

"That's the one," he said. "They're real artists. They only sell fresh baked products, not like the chain bakeries where everything is made from frozen." He glanced back at Madame Marmotte, who was still on the phone. "What's up with her?"

"Oh, that. I asked her to call everyone to pick up their phones and gadgets," I said. "It's taking a long time to reach them because we have their phones here."

I was about to make a fresh pot of coffee and pick up another croissant when Madame Marmotte yelled from her office. We both turned to see what the problem was.

"There's something happening at the Luxembourg Garden," she said in an urgent tone. "You better head over there fast."

"Slow down, Odile," Sébastien said. "What's so urgent?"

"I'm not sure," she said. "Whoever called didn't make much sense. It sounded loud in the background like there was a crowd."

"A crowd at the Luxembourg Garden wouldn't be particularly worrying," he said. "What's the big deal?"

"I'm not entirely sure. I think some guy is using his ability in public," she said.

Concern grew on his face as he listened. Sébastien and I looked at each other.

"Let's go," I said, grabbing a croissant and a napkin.

"It will be faster in the car, except for finding a parking place," he said.

As we expected traffic was thick. It felt like it took forever to reach the park, although it was probably twenty minutes.

As we neared the famous gated park in the Latin Quarter, I said, "Drop me off by the entrance and meet me inside."

"Have you been there before? How will I know where you are?" he asked.

"No, it's on my very long wish list," I said. "I didn't realize the park was so big. Once I find them, I'll look for something distinctive and text you."

"Head for the Luxembourg Palace Senate Building," he said.

"The what?" I asked.

"It's a congressional building," he said. "You can't miss it because there are armed guards all around it and a see-through barrier."

"Do you think the gathering is in that building?" I asked.

"No, not at all," he said, frustration ringing his voice. "I didn't explain it well. Across from that building, there is a manmade pond with lots of metal chairs where people like to sit. On weekends parents and kids play with toy boats in the pond. It's my best guess of where they might be."

"Got it," I said. "I'll look for armed guards and the pond first."

I half jogged from the rue de Vaugirard entrance inward, sighting the tall sidewalls of a nonresidential building right away. I didn't want to draw attention to myself, yet at the same time I felt the need to rush. There were mothers with strollers, families, students, people with bagged lunches, and tourists along my path. As other joggers dressed in bright color-coordinated sports clothes passed me with ease, I realized I wouldn't stand out in the park because it would appear I was exercising like so many others. I was wondering if the building near me was the senate, when I spotted three vigilant guards in blue uniforms armed to the teeth and wearing bulletproof vests next to it. They stood behind a wrought iron fence adjacent to the building. A second chain link fence separated the edge of the park from the building's wrought iron fence ten feet away.

I continued jogging at a moderate pace following the wall. In addition to the guards I had seen next to the government building, more guards wearing different uniforms, patrolled the garden itself. Five minutes later, I found what I was looking for, a shallow manmade octagonal pond encircled by a one-foot-tall concrete rim within a large open space. It was the central feature of an elegant design made up of grassy patches, off limits to pedestrians, in square, rectangular, and semicircular shapes. Only a square patch of scrawny grass about the same size as the pond separated the water feature from the senate building and its armed guards. They weren't paying much attention to the garden, yet.

As Sébastien had said, there were metal chairs scattered on either side of the pond. The patches of grass were separated from the pebble pathway by narrow metal barriers

about one foot off the ground. A disorganized crowd of
rowdy onlookers surrounded the pond. I studied them before
getting closer. Rather than a pattern per se, I identified
clusters of people. I confirmed with my badge that some
were Weeia. That was not a good sign.

After I texted my location to Sébastien, I approached the
cluster nearest me. It consisted of seven young men
crouched at water level, where a lanky Weeia man with
disheveled clothes and dazed eyes sat perched on the
concrete edge of the pond. He moved his arms in the air like
a conductor following a rhythm only he could hear. Below
him, the water mimicked his movements, making peaks and
valleys, waves and flats like a liquid symphony without
sound.

"What are you doing?" I blurted in a harsh voice before I
realized it.

There was no response from the Weeia man, not even a
glance. It was as if he couldn't hear me. Some in his
audience turned to me and back to him. There were other
clusters similar to his in that section of the park, more than I
could disperse before someone saw me. All it would take
would be for one of the garden guards to notice and call the
cops, or worse yet the armed staff by the senate building,
which looked like military police.

This was bigger and more serious than we had anticipated.
Even between the two of us we wouldn't be able to shut it
down fast enough to avoid a risky situation. To prevent a
worse one, we had to request reinforcements right away. I
called Sébastien.

"It's me," I said when he answered. Keeping my voice
down, I continued. "It's way worse than we expected. Call
CUT and report a severity one situation. Have them come
immediately. You and I will deal with as much as we can
until they arrive."

"Will do," he said, and we hung up.

Rushing back to the waterside, I pushed past the observers to the center, repeating my question. Once again nothing happened. The man continued conducting. Close up, there was a certain manic quality to his movements, almost as if they were involuntary. I glanced around and behind me. Like moths to a flame, more people had come to where we were, making the half circle bigger. I was glad because they blocked other onlookers from seeing the mattershifter's odd activity. It didn't solve the problem, since people on the opposite end of the pond and the senate building had an unobstructed view. I had to stop him. It occurred to me that he might want to halt and couldn't.

"If you can hear me, blink twice," I said into his left ear. After what seemed an eternity he blinked once and again. "I'm Marshal Dannielle Metreaux. What you're doing is not allowed. You must stop immediately. If you understand what I'm saying blink twice."

My patience was wearing thin. When I was about to give up and repeat my words he blinked twice. I covered us with my illusion, projecting an innocuous false image. If anyone saw what I was about to do, they would surely call the authorities. He trembled as I pressed my electric baton against his side, and slid unconscious to the ground without uttering a sound. The water calmed and the pond returned to normal.

I straightened his head, which had landed at a ninety-degree angle from his torso, to keep him from waking up with a stiff neck. As soon as he was awake, I dropped my illusion, revealing him sitting on the ground as if he was taking a short break. Like a dog called by a soundless whistle the observers who moments earlier had been riveted to his side, walked away. One down and so many more to go.

Sébastien's voice behind me startled me when he asked, "I take it that was the only way?"

"Yes, he was out of control of his own actions," I said. "It was really weird, like that woman Ursell Morland from New York who used to make people do whatever she wanted."

A previous case we had investigated involved a powerful mindshifter, Ursell Morland, who had been forcing humans into criminal acts against their will to amass a fortune for herself. After they did the deeds they had no memory of what they had done, and often wound up in jail or worse. She lived high on the hog for a decade, traveling to Europe every so often when, after spending money like a drunken sailor on leave, she needed to refill her bank account.

She had been staying in Paris out in the open without anyone being the wiser. Sébastien and I had put two and two together, and it had almost cost me my life. Sébastien and I had been near the explosion that ended hers.

Around us the crowd had shifted. The group that had surrounded the lanky mattershifter at my feet had moved to other clusters.

"This is the most popular park in the city, and that building is an important government building with guards up the wazoo," he said. I had never heard him say wazoo before. It was amusing coming from his cultured mouth. I was tempted to tease him, but decided it could wait for another occasion. "We better do something quickly."

"I agree. I want to understand what's happening before the situation worsens and attracts the police," I said. "If we have to, we can knock the others out too." He raised his eyebrow in distaste as if there was poo on his shoe. "Unless you have a better idea?" He shook his head sideways. "It's not my favorite choice to zap Weeia out in public. Even with my illusion, after a while someone is bound to notice a litter of half-conscious people. But I don't see that we have a choice."

"You're right," he conceded.

As much to convince myself as my colleague, I went on, "The shock is painful, but doesn't cause permanent damage."

He nodded again although uncertainty clung to him. "See what those two groups furthest from here are doing while I watch the ones behind us." His mental ability could be a big help. "Once we know better what's going on, we can figure out what to do. As soon as you form an opinion find me. Hopefully, CUT will be here soon."

"Do you think a mindshifter is behind everything?" Sébastien asked.

"Uh, I hadn't gotten to that yet," I said. "It was when I described it to you that it gelled. It's possible and might explain the sudden weirdness, if not necessarily its purpose. At the same time, it would be a bigger problem than I had anticipated." He watched the crowd while he waited for me to finish. "It would be good to know what the heck we're dealing with this time, even if it's another mindshifter."

In the middle of the circle to my right, a woman about my age, though taller and slimmer and with no muscles to speak of, lifted a man twice her size several feet in the air with her index finger. Where a weightlifter might have grunted with the effort, she giggled every so often like a child with a new toy. The man cooperated or rather didn't object.

"Do two," someone instructed.

Another man, shorter than the first one yet still much bigger than she was, raised his hand to volunteer. The gesture caught her attention and she beckoned him with her eyes. As I got close to her I saw that she wasn't touching the first man. Her finger stopped the movement for a second and the man she was lifting stood unmoving as she positioned the second man next to him. Lifting her finger again, she seemed to raise both men without effort.

"Higher," someone demanded.

She obliged by raising the men waist high. Except when she giggled, her face was expressionless.

"Higher," a voice called.

When she raised them shoulder high their eyes widened

with fear. One of them moved his arms as if reaching out to balance himself on an invisible bar. Not finding anything to hold on to in thin air he tumbled to the ground instead, landing at my feet, and screaming in pain. Before the other man dropped, she lowered him until he stood up on his own and rushed away.

"Are you badly hurt?" I asked, concerned for the man's well-being and the attention he might draw. "Can you get up?"

He grimaced. I wasn't sure what caused the facial expression, the loss of face at falling in front of everyone or an injury.

"Did you break anything?" someone asked him. In response, he straightened up from the horizontal position he had been in, and touched his ankle. "How bad does it hurt? If you can walk we should go."

With slow deliberate movements, he stood up, favoring his right leg. The man who had been peppering him with questions approached, and raising the injured man's arm over his shoulder made him lean on him. They walked at a faster pace than I expected toward the nearest street.

The woman was impassive as if she was ready to lift someone else at the first opportunity. I took advantage of the lull to reach her and look into her eyes. They were vacant, like the man by the pond a few minutes before.

In the background where Sébastien had gone, I heard the sound of scuffling. Turning, I made sure he was unhurt. He caught my gaze and gave me a thumbs-up to say everything was okay.

"Can you hear me?" I asked the woman. She nodded without looking at me. "I need an answer." She said nothing. I spoke in measured tones to make sure she understood, and kept my volume low so only she could hear. "I'm a marshal. I think there's something the matter with you, that you're not yourself. But what you're doing is against the rules. If you don't answer me by the time I count to ten, I'll have to do something to keep you from using your abilities in public. You probably won't like what I do. Understand?" She nodded again. "One, two, three, four, five, six, seven." People around us began to disperse when they heard me counting. I reached ten and she didn't say anything. "I'm going to shock you. That should fix whatever is going on with you. It's going to hurt a bit. I'm sorry."

As soon as she nodded and before the fear I could see blossoming on her face grew further, I wrapped us in an illusion that made it appear we were having a simple conversation. In reality, I pressed the baton to her skin. She shook for a moment and stiffened, dropping into my expectant arms. I set her on the ground against the stone base of one of the statues strewn around the park. I waited a few minutes for her to come to, making sure she was breathing and unharmed. She was flushed. I hated to leave her there by herself.

"I'm going to call someone to come here," I said as I searched for identification in her pocket and found her smartphone instead. "Does it have a password?"

She didn't answer. It was fortunate that it didn't need one. I pulled up her recent text messages and found an exchange with what seemed to be her husband. I texted him to come pick her up at the park as soon as he could. Tucking the phone back into her bag, I walked away.

Chapter 23

Before I reached the next group, Sébastien was by my side. His furrowed eyebrows and the fine tension lines around his lips told me he was worried.

"The people acting weird are out of control, like zombies," he said, pointing to the Weeia that remained.

"Oh please," I said. "There's no such thing as zombies."

"I didn't mean actual zombies," he said in a soothing tone. "What I mean is the Weeia I see have dazed eyes, and when I talk to them it's like they can't hear me."

"The ones I spoke to heard me, but couldn't answer me," I said. "The only way to stop them so far has been to knock them out."

"Do you think Ursell is alive and doing this?" he asked.

"I don't think she could've survived the explosion," I said.

"What if she had?" he insisted.

"No, even if she had, which I doubt, I don't think she would've been behind this," I said. "She was so good at what she did she escaped detection for ten years, maybe longer. What happened here, this…," I paused to gather my thoughts, "wasn't organized. At best it was an accident and at worse it was amateurish. She was a lot of things, amateur wasn't one of them."

"What do we do next?" he asked. "We need to find the source, the reason they're all behaving oddly. Then, instead of putting out a bunch of small fires, we would take out the source of the fire."

"Yeah, that would be the ideal solution," I said. "We need to squelch this quickly before it gets out of hand. But how?" I thought some more. "What if only certain henkis or abilities are affected? Maybe if we identify Weeia by their henkis we could narrow down possible suspects from everyone here."

"Then?" he asked.

"With any luck we can diffuse the whole situation by catching the person who's controlling them," I said, starting to like the idea. "It'll save us time and effort. At worst we'll take the three we found here in for questioning, if we have to."

Pulling my badge out, I stood so Sébastien's tall frame sheltered my actions from curious eyes. I could have used my illusion again, but it required energy I might need later. Once I had adjusted the setting to reveal the information I wanted I took off my jacket, using it to cover my badge beneath it.

"Feel that?" he asked.

"What?"

"The subtle pressure against your mind," he said, looking from side to side. "CUT must be here."

"Now I feel it," I said, emphasizing the first word. "It's like a soft wave surrounding us."

"That's it," he said, excited. "I've never felt anything like it before."

Around us we heard people talking. The thrill we had seen in their eyes when they thought they were witnessing extraordinary feats was gone.

"It's just a trick," one chubby woman told her friend.

"She's studying to be a magician," someone I couldn't see said behind me.

"The park must've wired the water fountain in the pond with special effects," a middle-aged man with a Roman nose said to the woman holding his hand. "That's how that man made it seem he was controlling the water. It was all a water feature."

One by one the voices around us explained away what they had seen moments before. The excitement faded and the regular movement of people back and forth resumed.

Seconds later we heard complaints.

"Oh no!" one well-dressed woman yelped, shaking her smartphone hard against the palm of her hand. "There's something wrong. It's broken."

The person next to her asked, "Is your phone out?" Before she could answer he went on. "My phone made a humming sound I had never heard before it went black. Now it won't start back up."

Around the pond we heard the same sentiment repeated. People were staring aghast at their smartphones and electronic devices almost in shock.

"CUT?" Sébastien asked.

I nodded. "That would be my guess. I bet our phones are down too while our badges are unaffected."

"I can't pick them out in the crowd. Can you?" he asked. I shook my head. "Wha—"

"Bingo," I said, excited, before he could finish his question. "There are three, no two, maybe three mindshifters. I'm getting a flickering signal on one. We need to gather them. Even if CUT is helping we still need to squelch any remaining Weeia public displays."

"Got it," he said. "What can I do?"

"They may resist our kind request. It's better if we approach them together in case they try to flee," I said.

"You're in charge," Sébastien said, following my lead.

Within ten minutes we rounded up three others with minimum resistance. They appeared as confused as the other Weeia we had intercepted by the pond. After getting their names from their French National ID cards, we sat them down together at a table, and went back to deal with the remaining clusters. That ate up another hour, between snapping them out of their odd state and reuniting them with friends and loved ones to make sure they returned home unharmed. We questioned many of them, but not a single one of them had anything useful to say to explain what had happened.

"The good news is that we were able to handle whatever that was before it got out of hand," I said, once we were finished and the Weeia involved had scampered away.

"The bad news is that after all that work for us and pain for them we haven't a clue how it started or why," Sébastien added. Turning his attention to the table where we had left the three mindshifters he added, "And, they left."

"We've got their info," I said. "It won't be hard to track them down. Although I suspect they won't know any more than the others, we should question them on the off chance they do."

"CUT?" Sébastien asked.

"Yep, let's hang back a bit before we go back to the office in case they have questions," I said. "This is going to be a long report."

"And it's going to draw attention to our little office. It's like there's something in the water," he said, half joking.

We each circled one half of the pond, watching the garden for any stray Weeia or abnormal behavior. When we were done we leaned against one of the stone statues. For thirty minutes nothing out of the ordinary happened and no Weeia appeared. We were getting ready to leave when a tall muscular man who walked with a purpose approached us. I didn't need the triple buzz of my badge announcing a fellow marshal was nearby to know he was one of us.

He moved his jacket aside for a millisecond, allowing us a glimpse of a CUT seal embroidered on his polo shirt. I could have sworn I saw his lips part in a tiny smile. I shifted my badge from my left hand to the other, drawing his attention to my right hand.

"Roger Sanders," he said, extending his hand to me as if he knew I was in charge.

Close up he was even more physically fit than I had realized at first glance. His clean-shaven face, blue jeans and leather jacket may have fooled other people into believing he was just another guy, but I knew a well-trained man when I saw one. While he wasn't handsome in the classical sense, he was attractive thanks to his rugged masculinity. I had a feeling he was a man of action and few words. There was tension to his body, as if he was ready to spring into battle at a moment's notice. His pale eyes evaluated me from head to toe. I wondered why he didn't repeat the gesture with Sébastien.

"Dannielle Metreaux," I said, shaking his proffered hand. "My colleague, Sébastien Poyager."

After they shook hands he glanced behind him toward someone dressed in a similar style across the pond from where we stood. The man nodded. As required by the marshals guidelines, we kept the conversation casual and refrained from using titles in public, in case someone was watching or overheard our conversation.

"That was an impressive illusion you used earlier," he said. "I was paying attention and was still surprised with the level of detail it had."

"Uh, thank you," I said, blushing.

I so seldom received compliments from peers, let alone superiors, I didn't know how to react. It made me self-conscious.

"Unless there's something else you need, we're leaving," he said.

He exuded authority and energy. Standing next to him I felt puny, an odd sensation for me. Despite my lower-than-average height and some might say chunky body type, most of the time when I faced a potential opponent I was confident in my fighting skills and Weeia marshals training. Something about him made me nervous.

"No, I don't think so," I said, a bit flustered.

Without a word he turned and walked away. It wasn't until he and the other man reached the nearby rue de Médicis and disappeared from our sight that I realized I hadn't thanked him. Like me Sébastien watched them leave, lost in his own thoughts.

"We better make a stop at Francois's to bring him up to speed," I said when we reached the car. "This time, the camel manure is going to hit the fan and I doubt he'll be able to ignore it."

I hoped he wouldn't dump said manure on our shoulders, mine in particular. To avoid placing Sébastien in an awkward spot, I kept that to myself. Besides, he knew what a lazybones Francois was. I didn't need to remind him.

It took forever to find a parking spot near Francois's apartment on the Ile Saint Louis. As luck would have it, he was at home alone. Ceri barked her head off at me. She jumped with joy on seeing Sébastien, going as far as falling on her back and exposing her belly for him to rub.

"What's up with you two?" he asked.

The scent of expensive cologne and saliva-inducing food odors were mingled in his apartment. From that and his better than usual disposition, I guessed he had had company for lunch.

I had contemplated letting Sébastien explain. It would have been easier for me to take the coward's road, and Sébastien wouldn't mind. He was such a ham that way. But I was the boss, and it was my job, so I took a deep breath, and explained the events at the Luxembourg Garden.

"And you're sure that was everything?" he asked when I finished recounting the events of the day.

"Pretty sure," I said, striving to keep my composure.

It wasn't anything he said at that moment that threatened to upset me. It was everything he had said and done since I had arrived. It was such a disappointment to have a boss who not only didn't back me up, but I was sure was willing to place the blame on me if it gained him advantage.

"You're missing something," he said. "What caused the

problem in the first place?"

The words stumbled out of my mouth before I could catch them, "No kidding. If I knew that I would've mentioned it." I was talking so fast the sentences ran into each other. "We're down there doing the grunt work and the thinking. I don't hear any bright ideas from your cozy corner."

When I raised my voice, Ceri raised her head. It was uncanny how she knew when I was upset at her owner. Or maybe it was my briny tone that did it. Francois absentmindedly reached down to sooth her. A moment later she lowered her head.

Sébastien filled the awkward silence asking, "Have you come across anything like this before?"

"Can't say I have," Francois replied. "I would remember. You better call it in. There's bound to be video or photos or something they'll need to deal with pronto."

"We did already," I said, getting up from the stylish armchair that probably cost more than a year of my salary. "As soon as I saw what was happening, I requested CUT assistance."

I made it my decision in case Francois thought I had jumped the gun. I didn't want Francois to give Sébastien a hard time for something I had decided.

An hour later we were back at the office. Madame Marmotte had gone home early. What a surprise. We split the report writing task, and by the end of the afternoon sent everything to Portland. I had a feeling we would receive a follow up message with questions. Before calling it a day we spent an hour training in the workout room. Our gym had been a work in progress for weeks, but there was a well cushioned tatami mat so we could spar with ease.

"Tomorrow we can follow up with those mindshifters," I said.

"They all live in the city, which makes it much easier than if they were from out of town," Sébastien said after looking at their addresses.

"I feel better," I announced when we called it quits.

Wiping the sweat off my forehead before it fell into my eyes I watched Sébastien drinking half a bottle of water in one long swallow.

"Yeah, me too," he said. "Even when I'm dog tired a bit of sparring releases the tension." As he was putting his shoes back on, he looked like he had a question. I waited. "Heading home?"

"Not yet," I said. "I'm going to check in on Susanna and the kids. Wanna come?"

"I would," he apologized. "I have fun horsing around with them, but I have plans I've canceled three nights in a row."

"No problem," I said striving for an island accent and sounding like I had a speech impediment. "I'll tell them you had better things to do."

"You wouldn't," he said.

"See ya," I said, heading toward my old apartment.

He knew I was kidding. Besides, they wouldn't believe me. They adored Sébastien.

"Danni!" Chandi said with glee when he saw me.

His older sister Akka gifted me a smile as her mother opened the door, beckoning me inside. Susanna also appeared pleased to see me.

"You look tired," she said.

"It's been a long day," I replied.

"Is everything okay?" she asked.

"Yes, fine," I said. "I'm just checking in to make sure you're all right."

"With everything you have to do I feel bad that you have to deal with us too," she said.

"Don't," I said. "I could've called, but I wanted to see you. I like to see the children. They're always happy. How are you?"

I had been with the migrant family for a few minutes

when Tadas came looking for them. Little Akka opened the door.

"Dinner?" he asked as he entered.

"Yes, yes, please," the little girl begged her mom in broken English.

"Are you sure it's not a problem?" Susanna asked the handyman.

"Yes, wife cook ten people," he said, beaming with pride. "Danni, you come. She happy you come."

"That's so nice, Tadas," I said. "I'm exhausted. It was a long and tiring day. Next time, thanks."

That morning I had taken public transportation to get to work so to return home I had to go back the same way. An accident on boulevard Henri IV held up traffic, and it took me longer to get home than I expected. I was inserting the key in the door of my apartment when I got a call.

Chapter 24

"Yes?" I answered.

"It's me," Sébastien said, sounding less cheery than usual. "Sorry to bug you, but we have another situation."

"You're kidding," I said, opening the door and entering the empty apartment. "What is it this time?"

"I'm not sure. Some disturbance at the Chatelet-Les Halles subway station," he said.

"Hard to be much more public than that," I said.

"I bet they have cameras covering every corner of that place," he said. "Should we call CUT now?" I mulled his question over while I grabbed a clean top. "You there?"

"Yes, thinking," I said, setting my badge down while I changed tops. "Let's have a looksee first. I hate to drag them all the way over here for the second time today for nothing. Once we're sure we can call them."

"Okay," he said.

"Do you know the area well? What's the best place to meet?" I asked.

"It's not a place I hang out often, but I know it," he said. "Half the station is under construction, especially because the shopping center above the subway station is still unfinished." He was silent for a few seconds. "I know, meet me at the corner of rue de Turbigo and rue Rambuteau, at the church. It's on the tip of my tongue. Give me a minute."

While I waited I pulled out my Paris by arrondissement map. It was more of a map in book form Iaen had given me. It was most useful in finding places when I was offline. What I liked about it was that it showed each arrondissement spread over two pages so that the details were easy to see. As I found the intersection of the two streets he had mentioned and the church Sébastien interrupted my thoughts.

"Saint-Eustache," Sébastien said.

"I see it," I announced. "It's in a triangle next to rue du Jour and rue Montmartre, by the Nelson Mandela Garden. In the first arrondissement, right?" I asked to be double sure.

Paris was one of those cities with similar named streets, odd angles, extra short streets that dead ended unexpectedly, and many one-way streets, where even taxi drivers had to rely on maps to get around. I had been studying the city by neighborhoods since I had arrived so I could find my way, but every so often I got lost or disoriented.

"Yes," he said. "You're closer. You should be there before I am. I'll be there as soon as I can. It can be a bit dodgy, especially at night when the dope dealers, pickpockets, and potheads come out. You might want to leave your car at home."

"Thanks for the heads-up," I said. "I'll be extra alert."

I planned to nose around a bit, depending on how near the entrance to the station the church was, but I wouldn't tell him that so he wouldn't feel he had to rush more than he already did.

While I could take the subway, I didn't know what the situation was within the train station so that was less than ideal. There were also buses, but they ran with little frequency after nine p.m., not to mention that they often ran late. I could be standing at a bus stop for half an hour or longer waiting for a ten-minute bus ride.

So I walked to the nearest taxi stand. Taxis weren't supposed to stop when you hailed them in Paris. You could call them or find a taxi stand. If you were lucky, there would be taxis at the stand. It was expensive to take taxis and we weren't allowed to use ride share services. In an effort to save money, I tried to take public transport whenever possible. It helped that the marshals provided me with a transportation allowance, although it had taken months of being stationed in Paris to see the first euro cent of it.

I caught the next to last taxi waiting for passengers. From the Latin Quarter where we were, he took boulevard Palais on the Ile de la Cité across the Pont au Change north onto the Right Bank past the Théatre de la Ville on the Place du Chatelet and rue de Rivoli. After that I became distracted and stopped paying attention until he stopped in front of the church to drop me off.

It was quiet outside the church and across the street by the Nelson Mandela Garden. Other than a handful of teenage boys playing with their skateboards in front of the garden, there wasn't much activity on that part of the street. Instead of standing there, I decided to jog around the block to get a sense of where I was.

I crossed rue Rambuteau and followed a short street without a street sign until I reached rue Berger, where I turned left until rue Pierre Lescot, circling back to the church. The construction site was like a cavernous open maw in the center of the city, interrupting the flow of people with its ugly, menacing cranes, tall fences, and beware-of-the-danger signs. Along my way I saw an entrance to the Les Halles subway station, which connected to Chatelet, forming the extra-large Chatelet-Les Halles station. There was also a movie theater, tons of shops, cafés, and fast food restaurants, even a hip hop cultural center. I walked in and took a quick look. Not seeing any sign of a disturbance I went back out to wait for my colleague.

Fifteen minutes later when Sébastien arrived looking flustered, I was ready to find out what the fuss was all about. If we were lucky it might be a false alarm, and we could head home for a well-earned rest. I wasn't counting on it, but a girl could hope.

"Whatever is going on doesn't seem to be outside," I announced as soon as he was close enough to hear me.

"There are several entrances, so it's possible it's at one of them, but I agree with you," he said. "I think it's in the subway or train area."

"I understand it's huge," I said, moving out of the way of a rowdy group of teenagers. "Is it a subway or a train station?"

"I think it's the largest subway station in the city, where the greatest number of lines cross each other," he said. "I said train station too because there are three RER lines."

"I've never taken one of those," I said. "What exactly are they?"

"They're commuter trains that connect the city proper with the suburbs," he said.

"What does RER stand for?" I asked.

"Réseau Express Régional, but I bet most Parisians don't know that," he said.

"Aren't you a font of knowledge?" I asked to lighten the mood.

"I aim to please," he replied.

"So we have an oversize subway-cum-train station and no idea where the problem might be," I said.

"That sums it up," he said. "What do you want to do?"

"We can scan the station for Weeia signatures with our badges," I said, feeling uncertain about how to approach such a thorny situation. "Is there a particular entrance we should use?"

"Not that I can think," he said, looking as baffled as I felt. "There are nine or ten entrances for Chatelet-Les Halles."

"How confident are you that the report was legitimate?" I asked.

"I can't make any guarantees," he said. "It could've been a prank, but the woman who called sounded frightened. I heard sounds in the background that could've been from a train station." He hadn't mentioned that when he called me. "She hung up before I could get any specifics. More importantly, the previous two calls turned out to be the real deal."

"Good point," I said. I had thought the same about the

calls before that one while I was waiting for Sébastien to arrive. "We're going to play it safe."

"How so?" he asked.

"I'm going to call CUT," I said. "Let's find a private corner where nobody can eavesdrop."

"I know just the place," he said, taking the lead.

I followed him down a street so narrow that it was more like an alley. It was dim and empty of people. Large garbage bins, half-filled and half emptied on the street, made long shadows. There were no sounds around us, assuring me we had found the privacy I wanted. The smell of rotting garbage mixed with the stench of old urine was strong. I placed my hand over my nose and mouth.

"I'll keep watch," he said, planting himself a few feet away like a sentinel.

"Paris calling," I said when a man answered the CUT line after several long rings.

"What's the emergency?" he asked.

There were restaurant noises in the background. I got the impression I had caught him at dinner somewhere. I guessed he was the lowest on the totem pole so he was assigned the dreaded on-call duty.

"We have a potential situation in the busiest and largest subway station in the city," I said, keeping my voice low. "We're about to investigate. Before we risk losing connectivity below ground I'm calling to let you know there could be a severity two or one situation coming your way."

"How many in your team? How much backup?" he asked.

Was he kidding? Backup, really? You would think CUT had information on office resources. I was tempted to snap at him, but I couldn't risk making him mad. We needed their help or we might soon.

"There's two of us," I said in a meek voice I regretted the instant I heard it.

"And your backup?" the man asked again.

"None," I said, that time in a flat tone. "That's why I'm calling you now, to warn you. If it's bad down there, we won't be able to control an entire station between two people, we'll need help in a hurry."

"And you are?" he asked as if paying attention for the first time.

"Metreaux," I said.

"How likely do you estimate the situation is to become a severity situation?" he asked.

If I knew that and the right numbers for the next lotto I would be a winner. I took a deep breath to keep from getting so annoyed I let it show.

"It's likely enough I'm calling to let you know it could happen," I said. "It's up to you what you do about it."

"What will you do now?" he asked.

"We're going into the station to search for and if necessary identify the problem," I said. "If we find one, we'll deal with it."

"Hold a moment," he said, without waiting for my reply.

A drunk entered the alley. He walked with confidence like a man returning home after a long day out. I could tell from his relaxed movements he hadn't seen us, and because we were quiet he didn't know we were there. I had a feeling I knew who was responsible for the smell of urine. Sébastien took several long strides until he reached the man. He handed him something, and seconds later the man was gone.

It was a while before the CUT man returned. I was starting to think about hanging up and heading down when I heard his voice.

"Ma'am?" he asked.

"I'm here," I said.

"My boss wants to speak with you," he said. "I'm patching the call to him."

"Marshal Metreaux?" a man's voice, deeper than the first man's voice, asked.

"That's me," I said in a faux jovial tone.

"We met this afternoon at the Luxembourg Gardens," he said. "Marshal Hall tells me you might have another situation."

"That's what I explained to him," I said.

"Are you in a public place?" he asked.

"Yes," I said.

"I understand that you're limited in what you can say," he said.

"Exactly," I replied.

"On a scale of one to ten, where one is least likely and ten is absolutely certain, how sure are you that there is a second situation?" he asked.

"Seven," I said. "But, once we are below ground if the worst happens and we are unable to contain the problem, we may not be able to call you."

"I take it it's still just two of you?" he asked.

"Yes," I said.

"Do you have any idea what the nature of the problem is?" he asked.

"No," I said, feeling stupid at not being able to answer what seemed like a simple question. "If it's anything like this afternoon it could get messy."

"I take it you have no new information on that either," he said.

"Nothing," I said.

"I tell you what we're going to do," he said. "Given the sensitive nature of the station, we're going to take preemptive action. We'll disrupt their camera systems to start with, and if it doesn't endanger lives we'll also shut down electronics system-wide." I wasn't sure how difficult it would be to do what he proposed. I had a hunch it was something they seldom did. "I can't stress enough how important it is for you to call in as soon as you have something to report."

"Yes, of course," I said.

"You have thirty minutes before we send a team," he said.

If someone had told me a week earlier that we would need CUT twice in the same day, I would have laughed in his or her face. At that moment I was relieved to know he was taking my concern seriously.

"Understood," I said. "We will report as soon as possible."

"CUT is going to scramble their cameras," I said just above a whisper after we hung up.

If anyone suspected we were talking about messing with the city's transit system, they would label us terrorists or strikers. Given the continuous state of emergency and public paranoia the country was in, there was no knowing what they might do to us. Not only would we not be able to do our jobs, but we risked major problems.

"Oh?" he asked incredulous. "I didn't know they did that."

"I don't think they usually do," I said. "The first man who answered sounded like he wanted to blow me off. He passed me onto another more senior man, who turned out to be the same guy we met this afternoon. He took our concerns seriously. Anyway, we have half an hour to find out what's going on down there and fix it. If he doesn't hear back from us by then it's going to escalate to a CUT visit."

"Then we should get going," he said. As soon as I nodded he turned toward the side of the alley we had come from. "Down?"

"Yep," I said. "Keep your eyes peeled."

Chapter 25

Metal and glass doors led to a modern entrance hallway, where new looking public transport blue and green signs confirmed we were in the right place. The largest had white letters set against a royal blue background spelling "Chatelet" on top and "Les Halles" below. To the left, two signs listed the RER and subway lines available at the station. At the top, blue letters spelling RER were in a circle next to the letters A in orange, B in blue and D in green, each in a circle of the same color. One line beneath there was a blue M within a circle next to the numbers 1, 4, 7, 11, and 14, each in a circle of its own with a different color. The numbers matched to colors made it easy to find a line at a glance. So 1 was in a yellow circle, 4 in a fuchsia circle, 7 in a pastel pink circle and so on.

It had been six minutes. I was monitoring the time since I had spoken to Roger Sanders. To enter the bowels of the underground we needed tickets. Neither of us had brought any, so I bought a pack of ten from the vending machine. It was cheaper than buying single tickets. The tickets were valid on all the subway lines, RER trains, trams, and buses. Even the Montmartre cable car accepted them. To enter the station, we would have to feed a ticket for each of us into one of the automated turnstiles.

After we passed the turnstiles we faced several choices. I recognized the familiar signs with the subway line numbers and matching colors. Signs listing the stations each subway line had remaining before the terminus station pointed to the platform for that train. Tunnels had signs pointing at connections with corresponding lines, and signs for the connecting buses outside. For arriving passengers, there were blue *sortie* exit signs. At that hour of the evening, station traffic eased in comparison to the daytime crowds. Chatelet-Les Halles was thrumming with commuters going in all directions as if someone had yelled fire. Most were distracted on the phone, wore headphones, wireless or wired, or texted as they walked.

The cavernous central area was bright with artificial lights. It had multiple levels and so many crisscrossing escalators it was hard to keep track. Within the first two minutes I heard five or six foreign languages, some I couldn't identify.

"Do you want to split up to cover more ground?" Sébastien asked.

"This place is too confusing and large for that to work with two of us," I said. "Besides, when we find whoever is causing the problem, who knows what we'll have to deal with, and we'll need to back each other up."

Neither one of us said it, but I was sure Sébastien, like me, was wishing Francois was with us. I wasn't afraid for my safety, although as his supervisor I felt some concern for his. I could take care of myself. In hand-to-hand combat I beat Sébastien every time. Eyes would be on us if things went south in the best known Metro station in the city. I didn't want to make a mistake. Nor did I want anyone to get hurt.

We had walked around for twenty minutes without seeing anything out of the ordinary, for Chatelet-Les Halles. From the little I knew about it, the busy station attracted many shady characters selling drugs and questionable merchandise as well as vagrants, pickpockets and drug addicts.

I was preparing to make the call to CUT as we turned a corner when a tween boy on a motorized board ran into us. He was moving fast and looking away from the direction he was traveling, so he never saw us. We landed on the floor, a bit worse for wear. Although Sébastien shoved me aside and took the brunt of the hit, the side of the board smashed my shin. It left a deep welt sure to hurt and result in a purple bump for days. Without so much as an apologetic glance at us, the kid hopped up with his board in hand, and took off like a bat out of hell.

Sébastien and I got up at the same time. My annoyance dissipated when I looked at my watch.

"I need to call CUT or they're going to show up," I said, searching for a place where I could have a private conversation.

"How about the bathroom?" he asked.

"That could work if I had any clue where it was," I said, sure there was one somewhere. "By the time I find one, it'll be too late."

"I have an idea," he said, heading to one of the many shops, where he spoke with the attendant.

The man's tired expression shifted a fraction as Sébastien handed him something. He looked like he might argue, but didn't. A second later my colleague beckoned me to enter. He headed to the rear of the shop, past flower arrangements and water filled pots with roses and other flowers. Closing a small privacy curtain, he faced me.

"This should be okay," he said.

"Yes," I said, flipping out my badge as I spoke. Once Roger Sanders picked up I identified myself. "Paris calling."

"Their cameras should be down," he replied. "Can you tell?"

"Not really," I said.

"Did you find anything?" he asked.

"Nothing," I said. "It's a big place. They could be anywhere or they could've left. We'll continue for another thirty minutes."

"Don't hesitate to call," he said. "I rather have to show up for a false alarm than have to clean up a big mess."

"Understood," I said. "Thanks."

"You bet," he said.

After I hung up, Sébastien asked, "Anything new?"

"Cameras should be down," I whispered into his ear.

"Great," he said. "Shall we?"

"There sure are many colorful characters here," I said fifteen minutes later.

"Is this your first time here?" he asked.

"I think I changed trains here in the past, but I was so focused on finding my way I didn't notice the station," I said. "Over there."

I was going to point at the young woman walking across the hall from us and thought it better not to draw attention to what was going on. She wore clothes that would fit in well at the Weeia Club on the Ile Saint Louis, the kind that cost more than most Parisians earned in a month. Compared to the crowd around us, she looked too clean, for lack of a better word.

"What?" he asked.

"Look closely at the people who pass by her," I said.

"They're breaking out into some sort of a rash," he said, crossing his arms against his chest in a protective gesture. We kept watching for what seemed a long time, but was only a few minutes. "Every single person that crosses her path has the same redness on his or her skin."

"Some of them turn into black boils," I said.

"What on earth?" he asked. There was confusion and fear in his eyes. Lines appeared on his forehead and his mouth was open in a stunned expression. "I've never seen anything like that. Have you?"

"No, but I read about it at the Academy," I said. "I'm willing to bet she's an unhealer."

"A what?" he asked, staring at the woman.

"An unhealer, it's the opposite of a healer," I replied. "Where a healer can make you better an unhealer can make you ill. I didn't understand everything the instructor said, and because they are rare she didn't spend much time on it in the course."

"It can't be a coincidence that she's the only person

without a rash. And, she's definitely Weeia," he said. "She doesn't even seem to be trying to harm them. She seems, uh, I don't know, detached from what she's doing, almost unaware of it."

"It takes a lot of energy to heal someone. To make them sick is easy," I said. "Maybe she's not doing it on purpose, like the people at Luxembourg Garden."

"How can we tell? What do we do?" he asked.

"I'm sure she's causing the rash," I said. "I checked my badge and she's using her ability. There are no other Weeia signatures near her. As to what we do, we could approach her and ask her to stop, nice and careful so we don't end up with a rash ourselves."

"What if she doesn't want to stop?" he asked. "What if she attacks us with something worse?"

"That's the rub," I said. "We can't risk it. We have no clue what she's infecting people with as she walks along so merrily. For all we know, we might not be able to recover from it, and this could be the start of an epidemic. If she knocks us out with something nasty, when CUT arrives it could be too late to treat us, and to keep it from spreading citywide."

"Is this a case of zap now and ask questions later?" he asked.

"Maybe," I said. "I'm going to give her the benefit of the doubt. Here's what we're going to do. I'm going to walk up to her, slowly, and ask her to stop. If she doesn't, or if she attacks me and I can't recover, it will be up to you to take her out."

As I spoke I found that what I was planning would be risky. That was my choice to make, but if the unhealer reacted in a bad way, it would leave my colleague to confront a dangerous Weeia alone. It was something he wasn't ready for yet. I hated to accost the woman, who could be a victim herself, without asking her what she was doing, but the alternative wouldn't be fair to Sébastien. He was only an L1 with little field experience.

It took years of training to become a seasoned Weeia marshal. Relative to the human population, only a few were Weeia, and fewer still marshals. As hard to replace, valuable assets, the service frowned on us risking our safety when it wasn't essential. Going against policy could earn me a ding in my record. That was nothing, if my actions saved lives. I didn't care much what my slacker boss would say. I knew without asking him that he would protect Weeia, and not care much about the loss of human lives. Regardless of his antiquated attitude, it was our job to protect all lives.

Sébastien waited in silence as if he could sense my internal turmoil. Some of my concerns were reflected on his face. His wider than usual eyes and dilated pupils gave away his fear. To his credit he didn't object. The more I thought about it the more I decided I simply didn't want him hurt. If there was a way to avoid it, that would be my first choice.

"Change of plans," I said, in a voice that sounded way more confident than I felt. "While I use my illusion to distract her, you, quiet as a mouse, approach her from the back, and zap her unconscious."

"What if it doesn't work?" he asked.

"We'll go to Plan b," I said in the same confident voice, as if I had one. "With any luck the cameras are out. Before we do anything, I'll contact CUT and make them aware of the situation."

That was the closest to a backup plan I had. It would have to do. I had just updated CUT when a deafening crack that sounded like the air around us was alive filled the station. I jumped, at least in my head I did. Years of marshals training had kept my feet on the ground. My initial thought was that there was an earthquake, but I dismissed it as I had never heard of earthquakes in Paris. It occurred to me that a train crash might sound like that. A glance at Sébastien confirmed he was unhurt. Some of the passengers near us were rising from the ground, others remained where they had fallen. In the distance a child cried.

More stentorian sounds followed the first one. One train crash was possible. Two was much less likely.

"What was that?" Sébastien asked as if I knew everything.

"Dunno," I said. "I have a feeling it could be Weeia related."

"How do you know?" he asked.

"I don't," I snapped. "I just said I didn't know. I'm speculating since we have no idea what else it—"

I couldn't finish my sentence because another louder sound swallowed my voice. Was it closer to us than the first sound or further away?

"The wacky thing is that woman is the only person I see who hasn't reacted to the noise," he said. "She appears to be in her own private Idaho. I don't think she even slowed down."

"Do you think they're connected?" I asked.

"Not necessarily," he said. "I've been watching her closely. She acts like she's in a trance, unaware of where she is or what she's doing." I had the same impression. "While everyone else was startled and afraid, she kept walking the same way as when we arrived."

"I guess it's a good news bad news situation," I said, watching the woman pass by more people, leaving a trail of rashes along her path. "She's not the cause of the horrible banging, but she's still making people sick, and nobody seems to realize what's happening except for us."

"At least there are fewer people walking in this direction right now than a few minutes ago," he said.

"I noticed that too," I said. "Let's take advantage of that while we can. You ready?"

"As ready as I'm going to be," he said.

"Make sure not to touch her," I said. "From what I

remember skin to skin contact is the worst. Cover your hands with your jacket or better yet if you have gloves put them on."

"It hasn't been cold enough for gloves," he said as if apologizing for not having them. Taking off his sweater he motioned to it. "I'll wrap it around my hands."

Arming myself with courage I made my way toward the unhealer, wondering all the while what kind of illusion to use. As I approached her I saw her eyes were puffy and red, and her mascara was running as if she had been crying. On a whim I made myself look like Sébastien. I had a feeling she would respond better to a handsome well-dressed young man than to me.

"I'm sorry to bother you," I said to her in a manly voice, keeping what I thought of as a safe distance. She didn't respond. She didn't even look toward me. "I'm looking for RER B. Can you point me in the right direction?" As soon as I saw Sébastien behind her, I covered him with my illusion in case anyone was watching us they wouldn't see him knocking her unconscious with his marshals badge. To make sure she was distracted I raised my voice, "Hey, I'm talking to you."

There was no reaction from her. Sébastien was almost within reach when he fell. I felt the adrenaline spike course through my body, signaling for a fight or flight response. I hesitated for a nanosecond, tempted to run to his aid, but I held fast to the illusion, giving him a chance to get up before losing our opportunity. He regained his footing with a motion so swift it made me think if I hadn't been focused on him I might have imagined the fall.

There was no sign that she had noticed him behind her. He glanced at me for confirmation. I nodded once. Using a maneuver we practiced often when sparring he pressed his badge against the back of her neck. She stiffened, but in lieu of the scream I expected or even turning around to face her attacker she dropped like a heavy lump. The whole exercise was over within seconds. No sooner had she fallen than the loud noise started up again. I kept my illusion over the three of us, making it appear we were walking together while in reality Sébastien and I were dragging her to a corner as far from people as possible.

"Our first present is by the shoe repair shop," I said as soon as someone answered the call at CUT. I had to be careful about what I said because we were in a public place. The cameras might be off and the electronics with them, but we couldn't take any chances. "We have to run to get a second present we didn't know we needed. Please come pick it up as soon as you can. We wouldn't want someone to see it. Make sure not to touch it to avoid, well you know."

"Damn," the voice on the other end said. "You have another one?"

"We're not sure yet," I said. A loud hard to describe sound made it impossible for me to hear. It was similar to the previous ones and yet it was different. I waited for it to end. "Did you hear that?"

"Yes," the man's voice said. "What is that?"

"Tell your boss," I said. "We don't know what's causing it."

"A Weeia?" he asked.

"It's possible. We have to go," I said. "Repeat my request." He did. "Great, thanks. I'll call as soon as I know more. Get the present."

"Are they coming?" Sébastien asked.

"I sure hope so," I said. "Do I have a rash?"

"No, I don't see anything," he said. "What about me?"

"Nope," I said. Lowering my voice, I added, "I guess if we don't have symptoms soon, we're not infected."

That was a relief. There was no time to appreciate it. Once again the noise started up. It had a metal quality to it.

"I think it's coming from that direction," Sébastien said,

pointing behind us to where the unhealer had come from.

"Let's find out what it is," I said.

As we walked toward the noise we crossed people running away from it. They were so intent on fleeing they weren't paying attention to where they were headed. More than one of them bumped into us.

"Excuse me," I said, trying to get a burly man's attention.

He turned to me, shook his head and kept going. Others behind him behaved in a similar way.

"He looks like a cop," Sébastien said, focusing his attention on a uniformed man wearing a bullet proof vest, knee pads, and more weapons than I could count at a glance. Drawing his attention, he called, "Officer."

The man was stocky and about my height, which was short for a woman in North America. He had a clean shaven face and his black hair was cut military style. It struck me as unusual to see him alone. Most police officers I had seen in France were in pairs or groups, never alone.

There was a wild expression on his face when the man looked at Sébastien.

"Run," he said, following his own advice before we could ask him anything.

Our progress was impeded by the people bolting toward us. It was like an obstacle course where the obstacles moved quickly and of their own accord. The noise started and stopped. Each time it sounded a bit different. The pace of the crowd accelerated whenever the noise restarted.

A scrawny man, about Sébastien's age, stood in an open space where several hallways crossed. He didn't look dangerous, but I had the distinct impression he was the one who had caused the noises we had heard. Around him the station was broken. It was the best description I could come up with for what I saw. There was a huge pile of debris at his feet. Pieces of concrete, metal, glass and other items I couldn't identify were strewn about in every direction, in no particular order or size. The floor was slippery with spilled liquids. Smoke spewed out of a cable and long lightbulbs dangled useless from ceiling fixtures. The smells of coffee, burnt electrical wiring and unidentified chemicals mingled in the air, making me rub my nose. The signal on my badge indicated he was Weeia.

Unlike the woman we had tackled minutes earlier he appeared furious. He screamed something over and over again, but the words were garbled, making it impossible to understand what he was saying. If he was aware that we were the only ones walking toward him I couldn't tell. An older woman with gray hair tied up in a bun was on the floor to our right, dragging herself away from the screaming man with her arms. Her left leg was twisted at an impossible angle, and every time she moved, a hand's breadth at a time, she grunted in pain. Several other people lay where they had fallen, unmoving. I assumed they were dead or unconscious.

"I'll help her," Sébastien announced.

"Be careful," I said, focusing my attention on the man in the center.

When I stepped closer to him I noticed a line of blood dripping from his head onto his right shoulder. I assumed he had been hollering out of anger. Had he been screaming in pain? A long gash crossed his right leg, leaving a gap of flesh exposed and blood seeping out in spurts. I was about to try to talk to him when he mouthed "help." By then Sébastien was back by my side.

"I got her as far back as I dared," he said. "She passed out."

"I don't think she had any life threatening injuries," I said. "There isn't anything else we can do. CUT will get to her soon. We have to stop this, whatever it is, before anyone else is hurt."

He turned to the Weeia in front of us, asking me, "Was my mind playing tricks on me or did that guy just beg us for help?"

"You saw it too," I said, relieved. "Him mouthing 'help.'"

"Definitely," he said. "I thought he caused all the destruction, yet he's asking us to do something, not sure what exactly. It's confusing."

"I've been thinking about that," I said. "What if it's not so different from the unhealer who didn't appear to purposely be infecting anyone? I'm starting to think this man is a mattershifter who was going about life like any other day, minding his own business. What if someone or something triggered his ability without his knowledge or worse yet without his control?"

"That would be a problem," he said, rubbing his chin like a much older man contemplating a difficult decision. I suspected it was a mannerism he had learned from his father. "I expected the person behind all the destruction to be evil or angry. Instead he seems afraid and weary."

"Which makes our jobs that much harder," I said, thinking out loud. "If he's a bad guy we're well within the guidelines to execute him."

"We are?" he asked. His eyes widened and he focused his attention on me. "I thought only L5 marshals were authorized to execute Weeia."

"Under the right circumstances, marshals may execute humans without prior approval and Weeia with prior approval," I said, quoting from the Marshals Guidelines, and remembering a previous case of ours in Paris. The scumbag I killed preyed on a whole neighborhood, and while justified, his execution still weighed on my conscience.

"He could be asking for help to trap us somehow," he said. "Or if someone else is controlling him he might not be able to stop himself from attacking us."

"I thought the same," I said. "I want to believe the best, but we have to think about what he's done and the risk involved first." I left out the part about not wanting to die that day. "If he incapacitates us, he'll be free to continue the destruction until a backup arrives to stop him."

"What do we do?" he asked.

"Our best approach is to neutralize him so he can't cause any more damage or hurt anyone else, preferably without killing him," I replied. I thought for a moment. "While I distract him with an illusion go around behind him. As soon as you see an opportunity, take advantage of the moment to zap him unconscious. He's lifting his hands as if he's going to restart. You up to it?"

"Yeah, I think so," he said, hesitant.

"We can wait for CUT if you rather," I said, not wanting to push him too far beyond his already maxed out comfort level.

"Others might die," he said. "I'll do it."

Distracting him was a bit trickier than I had thought. It was as if he was aware of everything around him, including Sébastien's and my every movement. Visual illusions did not seem to fool him, he kept tracking the real us. We could not approach him from behind and he kept blowing up objects with these huge explosions as he moved. Just trying to avoid shrapnel and keep up with him was taxing us both.

Finally I remembered a trick I had not tried in a long time. Crouching down, I placed my hands on the floor and pushed an illusion of pain through the solid matter directed at his feet. I was sweating from the effort and for several minutes it did not seem to have any effect. He blew up a candy vending machine into the tracks. It landed with a huge crash, spraying us with glass and metal shards. After I pushed my illusion again he stopped walking and stared down at his feet, hopping from one to the other like a man standing barefoot on hot sand. The distraction slowed him down long enough for Sébastien to zap him with his badge, and he dropped boneless to the floor.

Both of us were exhausted and bleeding from minor cuts

and scrapes on our exposed skin. We walked up together out of the tunnels, leaving the CUT staff to sort out the remaining mess.

"Wow," Sébastien said as we headed away from the well-known station. "That was wild. I wasn't sure I would get him. Interesting trick you used to draw his attention."

"I know what you mean," I said. "I don't know whether my illusion distracted him or he ran out of juice and let us capture him. See you tomorrow."

"Remember I'm taking the morning off to help my sister," he said as we parted. "Of course, if there is an emergency I can come in."

"Now that this is sorted I hope there are no emergencies tomorrow," I said, sounding more energetic than I felt. "By the time you get up it will be late. Don't worry about coming in at all. I'll be at the office in case there are any follow-up issues."

"Thanks," he said. "You're the best, boss."

Chapter 26

When I arrived back at my apartment on the Left Bank, the sun was rising. Muted light filled the cloudless sky. When I moved to Paris, I thought skies like that one lasted the whole day, only to discover an hour or two later the heavens had clouded over.

Paris was blessed with a quality that made it beautiful and timeless regardless of the weather. Still, I loved the way the city sparkled when the sun was out, making everything bright and extra pretty. In my short time living there, I had discovered the weather was fickle. Whenever I wanted to bask in the sunlight I rushed outside before conditions changed, sometimes in the blink of an eye.

It might be days before I caught another glimpse of blue skies. For an instant I thought of jogging along the riverbank and surprising Iaen. The thought of his clean, manly smell and the scents of his boat popped into my head, goading me. My eyes closed and I imagined him hugging me. I could use a hug. But, the adrenaline that had kept me running had worn off and I was dead tired.

I took off my boots, throwing them by the door and made my way to the bedroom, promising myself I would stop by Iaen's bouquiniste stand later on my way into work. It was early afternoon when I woke up. A quick shower and a strong cup of coffee got the cobwebs out of my head.

Then I remembered Iaen was still out of town. The soft bell on my phone indicated there was a voicemail. He had called while I was sleeping. I sighed, wishing I had been able to hear his voice live and not on a recorded message. Keeping busy would make the time pass faster so I didn't miss him so much. I headed to work.

"It's nice of you to grace us with your presence," Madame

Marmotte said in a snippy tone as soon as she spotted me in my office. "It's past lunchtime."

She was one to talk. She made a point of leaving the office for lunch every day, and most days she took an extended lunch hour or three.

There had been a time when comments like those would get under my skin. It happened less often ever since Sébastien arrived, both because she poked me only when he wasn't around, and because I didn't care much anymore. I was about to ignore her and settle down at my desk when I heard voices. I couldn't make out what they were saying or who they belonged to. It sounded like two or more men. I followed the sound to the storage room past her office.

She crossed her arms over her chest as she watched me, a satisfied expression blossoming on her face as if she thought I would get my comeuppance. When I looked at her, I noticed her manicure set, which was almost always on her desk, was nowhere to be seen. She had tidied her desktop and pulled her scarf straight. Her scarves often had the appearance of a last minute addition that didn't match the rest of her outfit.

"As I mentioned before, although we have taken care of the worst of the situation, we're still following up on several leads," a man's voice said. "We take these incidents very seriously."

It wasn't Sébastien, but the voice was somewhat familiar. I had heard that person speak before. From where I stood I couldn't see the man, and he was too far away to be speaking to Madame Marmotte.

Although I knew the voice that replied, it took a moment for me to place it because I was so unaccustomed to hearing it. It was my boss, Francois.

"We appreciate your efforts, Marshal Sanders," he said. "I've heard you have an exceptional team, the elite marshals, they say."

It was odd to hear Francois at the office, and sounding professional rather than bothered or downright irritated at the trouble marshals matters represented for him. I took two steps in the direction of the conversation, curious about what had drawn him to work. Since we had met, he hadn't worked a single day at the office, let alone had meetings there; not to mention I had no idea why they were in the storage room.

I had heard the same thing about CUT, only the best and brightest selected; most applicants washed out; and the training grueling, but if you made it, you had reason to be proud. Everyone admired CUT members.

"Go on then," Madame Marmotte said in a soft tone. "They were waiting for you to attend the meeting, but you strolled in so late they had to start without you."

I was tempted to reply that I hadn't received any messages about the meeting. There was a chance she knew and had "forgotten" to tell me, so I decided to keep my thoughts to myself. There was no point in arguing with her. It was like wrestling in the mud with a pig, as my uncle liked to say. You both got dirty and the pig enjoyed it. With rare exceptions, it didn't seem to matter what I did, Madame Marmotte was always trying to trip me up.

"I want to take this opportunity to compliment you on your team's outstanding handling of a rather delicate situation," the man with the familiar voice said.

The voice belonged to Marshal Sanders, the CUT leader I had met at the Luxembourg Garden the day before. I was surprised he was at our office.

"We do our best," Francois said, taking credit for our hard won praise without missing a beat.

He might not show up at work, but he sure was ready to accept kudos that didn't belong to him. It made my blood boil. Before I realized what I was doing I had walked into their conversation. Francois directed his attention toward me as I entered a handsome office I had not seen before.

Marshal Sanders, seated facing Francois, followed my boss's gaze, turning to me.

"Ah, Marshal Metreaux," he said, a smile spreading across his face and up to his eyes. He rose, extending his hand. I stepped forward to shake hands with him. "You've met my number two, Marshal Johan Dinkey." He glanced at a young and muscular man standing beside him. I recalled seeing him at the Luxembourg Garden. The man nodded at me. I nodded back. "I was just telling your superior officer how well you de-escalated the recent incidents."

I blushed. Feeling the heat reach my cheeks and knowing I was turning red, I mumbled something unintelligible. Marshal Dinkey grimaced as if his teeth hurt. It didn't take Weeia abilities to guess he wasn't in my fan club.

"Our junior marshals, they're quite a team," Francois said with the same enthusiasm he might use if he was describing a vacuum cleaner and its hose extension to a housekeeper.

Francois's office looked like the centerfold out of a decorator's magazine. The antique style wood furniture alone must have cost a small fortune. The workmanship and detail required hours of work from one or more people. I was no expert, but a friend of my uncle's dabbled with wood when he could. I had learned a little about the craft when I went with my uncle to visit him as a little girl.

I had no idea what the value of the Persian rugs, porcelain, crystal, and other furnishings was, but I was willing to bet it was a worthy match for the furniture. Francois's desk stood out as the most important piece in the room. It was shiny and had an intricate design. It was so gorgeous; I wanted to run my hand over the surface to find out if it was a trick or the real deal.

"Definitely," Marshal Sanders replied. "Marshal Metreaux's performance was exceptional. If you don't mind my saying so, I think she should seriously consider applying for CUT. We can always use marshals like her in our team."

Marshal Dinkey made a grunting sound. It was high praise for a CUT commander to reach out to my superior the way Marshal Sanders had done. Inviting me to apply was, as far as I knew, unusual. From what I had heard through the grapevine there were so many applicants CUT didn't need to make any outreach effort. Marshals tripped over themselves just for an opportunity. Francois's smile didn't reach his eyes. If Marshal Sanders noticed the two men's reactions he didn't let it show.

I was tickled pink. I could have jumped out of my skin I was so elated.

"Thank you for your time," Francois's words filled the room. It could have been my imagination, but he looked eager for the CUT marshals to leave. "And, for all your team's efforts on the recent emergencies." As he and the men shook hands he addressed me, "Marshal, would you be so kind as to escort them to the circle?"

The circle was a designated place cleared for teleportation arrival and departure. While it was possible to teleport elsewhere, from what little I knew, the circle was the safest and best option. Marshal Sanders was relaxed as we made our way to our office circle in the complex courtyard. He peppered me with questions about my experience and skills as well as my professional goals. I was glad Marshal Dinkey trailed us so at least I didn't see his envious stares. He was already in CUT. Why did he care?

"I meant what I said," Marshal Sanders reminded me as he left. "Think about it."

I walked on a cloud for the rest of the day. I was giddy and wanted to share the news with someone who would be happy for me. I couldn't tell my human friends about the opportunity without lying about the specifics way past my comfort level. Ernie was eyeball deep in a big project and asked not to be disturbed, and I didn't want to interrupt Sébastien on his day off. I decided to call Marla, who lived in San Francisco, when I returned home. The nine hour time difference meant it was morning and she might be available to talk.

Chapter 27

When I arrived at my apartment I discovered I had missed a call from Iaen. I must have hit a cell tower vacuum on my way home because his call went to the answering system. He went on and on about an antique he had found that would resell for a fortune. It was a deal he had been after for months. The part about what he planned to do when he sold it caught my attention.

"Let's take a real vacation. We can travel around France or Europe or to a tropical island, wherever we want. How does that sound? Say yes! I'm so sorry I missed you. I wanted to hear your voice and tell you all about my finding. I'll be here for another five minutes and then I have to go out again. I'll call you again as soon as I have a minute, if it's not too late. Can't wait to get back. Mwah."

My call to him went straight to voicemail. After leaving a short, but mushy message I played back his message three times, trying not to get too excited and failing. Next I called Marla and got her voicemail too. After letting her know the latest and greatest news in my life in a long message I took a hot shower and climbed in bed.

All my life I had been independent. I decided at a young age that becoming a marshal was a priority. While I longed to be with someone, it had always been difficult meeting Weeia men to date. Graduating from basic training at the Marshals Academy did nothing for my love life. As soon as a potential date found out who I was, his interest waned. If we made it past that obstacle, they felt threatened because I outperformed my colleagues in almost every testing category.

Dating led to disappointment. Besides, relationships were a distraction I could do without. When Ernie and I became close while I was at the Academy I considered being more than friends. Unfortunately, my assignment to Paris got in the way. Things had been rocky when Iaen's and my paths crossed during a case. Except for Ernie, Iaen had been the first guy I wanted to go out with in a long while.

When we met I didn't dare dream that Iaen liked me. It was hard to believe that in only a few months he had become an essential part of my life. I hated admitting that I missed him something fierce.

***

Sébastien greeted me with a giant grin when I arrived at the office the following morning. I assumed it was because his family gathering had gone well or he had met someone special.

"Congratulations," he blurted as I was pouring myself a cup of coffee. "I heard the head of the CUT team came especially to the office to sing your praises."

"He what?" I asked. "Not that I know of. He was meeting with Francois and mentioned us at the tail end."

I had planned to tell Sébastien what Marshal Sanders had suggested over lunch. By the time I arrived at the office he had already heard a blow-by-blow description of the entire conversation from Madame Marmotte. I should have known she would suck the joy out of my news. It was unavoidable, gossip was her superpower.

"Apparently, he asked for a meeting with Francois to brief him on the Luxembourg Garden and Chatelet-Les Halles incidents," he said. "My source says his real motive was to steal you from under Francois, who is none too happy about it."

"Really?" I asked. "Inviting me to apply via my boss hardly seems like stealing. Besides, Francois would be pleased if I left town. Why would he care if I joined CUT?"

"Perhaps because you've become a valuable resource

someone wants to take away from him," he said. "It's like a little kid who ignores one of his toys until someone else wants to take it away and suddenly it's his favorite."

I hadn't thought of it that way, not that the possibility of being Francois's favorite toy had ever entered my mind. I had been too preoccupied with Iaen's news to mull over the offer. I couldn't keep the idea of a vacation with Iaen out of my head. I was daydreaming of white sand beaches on Pacific islands, hiking adventures, a safari in Africa, and plain old touring around Europe. I couldn't help it.

"I had no idea Francois had an office, a really nice one," I said, giving myself a moment to think about what Sébastien had said and wonder how it might affect me. "Did you know?"

His trapped expression told me he did. He was too nice to say Francois had confided in him. It still bothered me that while Francois wouldn't slow down to give me the time of day if he could avoid it, he treated Sébastien, who was junior to me, like a VIP. Sébastien being the son and only male heir to one of the largest business empires in Europe impressed Francois, no matter how much Sébastien tried to shrug off the importance of his family's company. I, on the other hand, had no money or family connections and a tarnished family name. That didn't impress my boss at all.

"It was custom made for him by the best interior decorator," Madame Marmotte said from her office as if she had been part of the conversation all along. "The desk belonged to Louis XIV, you know." That was why it was so elegant. It had been created for a king. "The chair came from the Chateau de Versailles. Everything in there is a work of art or an antique. He used to be into all that back in the day." She sighed like a schoolgirl. Her deep admiration was incongruous with her harpy attitude. But then I remembered she was nice to Francois and Sébastien, just not to me, or anyone or anything related to me. "I wish he would spend more time in the office like he used to."

Yeah, it would be nice if the boss honored us with his presence once in a while or took an interest in work. We dedicated the next few days to answering questions and following up on issues referred to us by CUT from the incidents at the Luxembourg Garden and Chatelet-Les Halles. We worked long hours, but I didn't mind. Judging by Sébastien's mood he didn't either.

"I had no idea how much effort CUT gives to each tiny part of the puzzle," Sébastien said, after he tracked down one of the subway passengers who had been at the station that day. "Even with the electronic signals and camera system down, there were thousands of people in the station around the time of the incidents. Some of those people captured audio and video on their personal devices and posted clips, which have been viewed all over the world through social media. The vast majority of those have nothing to do with what happened that night, but even one could be a problem, so we have to find them all to make sure."

"Come up with anything yet?" I asked.

"There were a few legitimate posts," he said. "I don't know how, but CUT destroyed the original files. Marshal Sanders explained that in the rare cases where they're unable to beg, borrow or steal the files they go after all copies until there is no trace of the clips anywhere. If it means taking down entire websites and servers, and intercepting internet service providers, they'll do it. They're ruthless that way."

"That's a good thing," I said. "If CUT wasn't here to help it would be an impossible task for us. We would be near retirement age before we finished tracking everyone who was at the station that night, and that's not even counting all the tech know-how and support they have at their fingertips to deal with electronic surveillance and erase unwanted files."

"Speaking of impossible, how are Susanna and the kids?" he asked. "Are you any closer to finding a solution for them?"

"Not yet," I said, wishing I felt more hopeful. "The powers that be in Portland are dragging their feet, what a surprise."

I didn't know how Sébastien felt about my request for asylum for the Syrian family. While he hadn't been discouraging he also hadn't been encouraging. Given the fear of anything related to refugees, who many assumed were terrorists in disguise, few in France liked the idea of welcoming them as neighbors. The apprehensive attitude was worse among Weeia, many of whom didn't like change or strangers in general. I imagined it was a sensitive topic for him. I didn't want to make him uncomfortable by asking him to get involved so I hadn't brought it up. I was surprised he had.

"How did it go at your sister's event the other day?" I asked to change the topic.

"Pretty good," he said. "She launched a line of bespoke home furnishings. The first store opens in January. She's giddy with excitement and I'm happy for her."

"It's so nice that you have each other," I said, wishing I had a brother or sister who was as supportive of me as Sébastien was of his sister.

"That's what brothers are for," he said, smiling. "I expect you and that no-good boyfriend of yours to come to the opening reception, right?"

"Oh, you know how I love social occasions of any kind," I said in a syrupy tone. "I'll be fretting for days, trying to decide whether to wear the sequined evening gown or the feathered one."

He guffawed. I mock curtsied for comedic effect and was rewarded with more laughter.

"Please?" he pleaded. "You don't really care where you

are as long as Iaen is whispering sweet nothings in your ear."

"With so many important people, why do you want us there?" I asked.

"My whole family and their friends will be gushing over my sister's success," he said.

"That's not a bad thing," I said. "You're not answering my question."

"Of course not," he said.

"You're still not answering my question," I said.

"Yes, they'll be there for her," he said. "While at the same time they'll be wondering when they'll get to celebrate mine. As the heir apparent there's tremendous pressure for me to follow in my father's footsteps. There are those who would rather I leave the position vacant so they can fill it. Everyone there will have a side, even my sister. They all have vested interests. I'll be caught in the middle. I desperately need someone in my corner. Who better than you and Iaen?"

"Why us?" I asked. "You have tons of friends."

"Correction, I have tons of acquaintances," he said. "When things are going well everyone stands by you. When you put your foot in your mouth, you stand alone, assuming you don't tip over." He winked as if that had been funny, but it didn't appear to amuse him. Although every once in a while I got the impression he was lonely, I had always assumed it was a fleeting emotion. I took it for granted that Sébastien's life was easy and he was happy. Growing up he had had every privilege I had not. "It's hard to tell who's really your friend, when there's so much at stake." He paused as if searching for the perfect argument to convince me. "You and Iaen are impartial. And more importantly, you're my friends and wish me well."

He fixed his eyes on me, waiting for an answer. What started out as light banter had taken on a serious tone.

"Fine, if it means that much to you," I caved.

"Thank you," he said.

"Don't thank me yet," I said. "They're all going to be horrified when I wear my feather and sequin cowgirl gown."

"It would almost be worth it to see the shock on their faces," he said, ending with a grin.

"You think I'm kidding," I said. "It's L'Unifolié."

"The Canadian Maple Leaf?" he asked.

"One and the same."

I laughed at his shocked expression. His puzzled expression added to my amusement.

"I can't tell if you're serious," he said. "But, I'm completely serious. I don't care what you wear as long as you come."

Although Sébastien fit in high society, he wasn't stuck up like many of his peers. In his company, I never felt inadequate the way I did when I was with Francois and Madame Marmotte. My aunt had once told me that true class was making those around you as comfortable as possible. For the first time I understood what she meant. I appreciated that about him. It was one of many qualities he had that was much more important to me than his fashion-model looks. Of course I wouldn't embarrass him on purpose. On the other hand, there was no way I was going to spend a month's salary on a pricey dress to wear for a single event. I would figure something out now that I understood it meant so much to him.

"Great, it's settled then," I said. "I'll muddle along and I'm sure Iaen will be happy to attend. You might not have noticed that he's more sociable than I am." His lips spread revealing perfect white teeth. "And he'll have something more suitable for the occasion than the Maple Leaf."

He sighed with relief. I wasn't looking forward to it, but it seemed unavoidable.

Chapter 28

Life at work had calmed down from the rushed pace after the subway station incidents. Since the day he met with Marshal Sanders, Francois had not been back to the office, not even once. Sébastien and I sent him regular reports as usual, but there was no indication he read them. That week Sébastien had been leaving work as early as possible to assist his sister with her big opening. I had become excited about the vacation Iaen had proposed although I couldn't settle on where we might go.

I had returned from jogging on one of my favorite routes on the south bank of the Seine. I was always surprised by how many other joggers, dog walkers, and pedestrians were on the streets before the sun rose. If I hurried I had enough time to shower, get dressed and reach the office. I was about to jump in the shower when my mobile phone rang. Usually when I was strapped for time I let the call go to voicemail, but Iaen and I had been missing each other, and I hoped it was him so I picked up.

There was silence on the line so I hung up, assuming the signal was poor or it was a prank call. When it rang a second time I watched the small screen for the caller's number. It was Iaen's.

"Iaen?" I asked. Nothing. "Hello? Iaen?"

"Madame, I'm sorry to disturb you," an unfamiliar woman's voice said. "I hope I didn't wake you."

"Uh, no," I said.

"I noticed you called an hour ago so I assumed you were awake," the woman said. "This is Agnes Solene at the police department for the fifteenth arrondissement."

My heart sank. Why was a woman at the police department calling from Iaen's phone? Was he in trouble?

Even if he was, why would a policewoman use his phone to call me?

"Yes, I'm awake," I mumbled.

"Madame Metreaux, is that right?" she asked.

"Yes, how did you know?" I managed to ask while my mind raced, seeking explanations.

"The caller ID shows the name of the last caller," she said. "Are you a friend of Mr. Fleming?"

"Yes, yes, I'm his girlfriend. Why do you ask?"

"I'm sorry to inform you he was in an accident," she said in slow measured words. "The paramedics did their best to revive him, but I'm afraid it was not possible." I took a deep breath. I felt like someone had punched me hard in the chest. The shock was so severe my senses were on hold for a millisecond. The woman's voice sounded far away, disembodied. "He sustained fatal injuries... a truck... last night... on boulevard..."

I interrupted her explanation, asking "Did you say Iaen is dead?"

"Yes, I'm sorry for your loss," she replied. Without pausing, she went on, "If you provide me with contact information for his next of kin, I will contact them to make arrangements for his remains."

His remains? I couldn't get my head around Iaen being dead. My heart beat loud in my eyes. I had seen him a few days earlier, we had been together, we had held each other, and we had spoken on the phone after that. We were going on a dream vacation when he returned. He couldn't be gone. How long had I been trembling?

"Ma'am? Are you there?" she asked. "Madame Metreaux, I need to contact his family to plan the disposal of his remains." I hated that she used the word remains. I couldn't think. I wanted to cry and scream at the same time. All I managed was silence. "Ma'am?"

"He had no close relatives," I mumbled after a long pause.

"I'm it."

"If you lived together you may qualify as his common law consort," she said. "Did you live together?"

"Practically," I said, realizing as soon as I did that I should have lied.

"Did you both live exclusively in one household together?" she asked, sounding as if she had memorized the words or was reading. At my silence she continued. "If you can prove you lived together, as husband and wife or its equivalent in the eyes of your friends and family for six months or longer, you may have rights."

"Uh, I'm not," I said, struggling to understand. "What kind of proof would I need?"

"A rental agreement, utility bills, a joint homeownership deed, notarized statements from your relatives and friends, that sort of thing," she said as if I kept those in my bedside drawer.

"Without such proof I'm afraid we may only release his remains to a family member," she said.

"Like I said, he didn't have any living relatives," I replied, miffed.

"I see," she said as if she didn't see at all.

I asked in a little girl voice. "What will happen to his, um, body?"

"The authorities will follow procedure," she said in a neutral voice as if we were talking about a car parked in a no parking zone or a zoning violation.

"What does that mean?" I asked. "I've never, nobody close to me has died before."

My parents didn't count. I had been too little to be aware of what was happening around me then.

"Well, since he died in a public place, the public prosecutor will be responsible for issuing a death certificate and a burial permit," she said.

"A public place?"

"Yes, ma'am, it was an accident on a public street," she replied in the same neutral voice. "That is a public place and falls under the jurisdiction of the public prosecutor. Once he issues the death certificate and burial permission the notification process will commence."

"What notification process? You already told me," I said. "I'm the only person he was close to."

"There are legal requirements we must meet," she said.

"Like?"

"The appropriate authorities will notify interested parties within seven days of his death," she said.

"What interested parties would that be?" I asked.

"His employer, his health and life insurance companies, and his bank," she replied. That made me laugh. Iaen lived off the grid. I was surprised he had government issued ID with his own name. I wondered if he had any kind of insurance or a bank account. "In time, his assets will be disposed of per his wishes. The unemployment office and tax authorities will also have to be informed."

"I would like to bury him," I said with difficulty.

I couldn't believe those words had left my lips about Iaen. I walked to the window, looking out, but not seeing anything in particular.

"It's not possible," she said. "You'll have to prove a family relationship in order to do that."

The conversation went around in circles until I couldn't take it anymore and hung up. I realized it was childish and regretted it the moment I did, but I wasn't sure I would be civil with her if I called back right away. Thirty minutes later when I was calmer I attempted to reach her by calling Iaen's number. If they wouldn't let me bury him, perhaps the government would do me the kindness of informing me when and where they were going to bury him so I could attend. My call went straight to voicemail.

I paced around the apartment not sure what to do, how to

feel or who to tell. After a while, I wasn't sure how long, although the sun had risen and was hidden behind thick gray clouds, I called the office. Madame Marmotte answered. After I hung up I couldn't remember what I had told her.

A knock woke me. I had fallen asleep on the floor in the living room. Once the disorientation passed the horrible memory flooded my mind. The persistent knocking was annoying. I got up to make it stop. All I wanted was to forget, to feel nothing, to go back to the way things had been before the call that morning. Had it been that morning?

My grief was reflected on Sébastien's face when I opened the door. Well, not my grief, but sadness, his own. He knew. I stood there still in my jogging clothes with my arms hanging down my sides not sure what to do. Without saying anything he walked in, closed the door behind him, and wrapped his arms around me in a big hug. His personal scent, I knew it from the many workouts we had shared, citrus scented deodorant, and a hint of lingering expensive cologne enveloped me. The familiar smells were comforting. I hung on to the feeling.

I had put off calling Sébastien or anyone else, as if somehow that put off accepting Iaen was gone. As long as I was the only one who knew it could have been a bad dream, except it wasn't. Perhaps it was the nearness of someone else who knew Iaen or having a friend beside me after the impersonal exchange with the police officer. I began to weep. Sébastien held me steady like a bay sheltering a ship from a storm. The weeping became sobbing. Not wanting to step away from the safety of his embrace I rubbed the liquid that poured from my eyes and my nose against my sleeve.

A long while passed during which I cried until my tears ran dry. I remembered vaguely parting from Sébastien's side. When I looked around I was on the sofa and Sébastien was sitting in the armchair watching me. Night had fallen and I hadn't noticed. My nose was so stuffy I had to open my mouth to breathe. When our eyes met pity filled his face. Tears gathered in my eyes ready to spill. I refused to let them. My eyes were sore, but that wasn't why I held them back. I had to be strong. Crying was for sissies. I was a tough marshal, not a sissy.

Sébastien got up, returning a moment later and handing me a glass of water. He had been to my apartment for get-togethers in the past, and was familiar with the kitchen, where he and Iaen often had hung out chatting like old school pals. I accepted the glass, grateful. I was aware that my mouth was dry, but it wasn't until he gave me the glass that it dawned on me it was the source of my discomfort.

"Can I get you anything else?" he asked. I looked at him lost in his words. "Danni, did you have anything to eat today?"

It took me a moment to focus. He sat down in the armchair and asked me again.

"Not hungry," I said.

My stomach gurgled as the water made its way through my system. Food held no appeal.

"Is there anything you need?" he asked.

"I don't think so," I said. "Thanks."

"Do you want to talk?" he asked.

"Not really," I said, fearing another tear fest. It occurred to me he might leave. The only thing worse than the way I felt would be to be alone with my memories. "Do you mind keeping me company for a while longer?"

"Of course not," he said, reaching over and placing his hand over mine. "I'm here for as long as you need me."

He sat with me late into the night, offering me food several times, and holding me when I cried. I had tried to be brave, discovering instead that I was weak. I missed Iaen and it hurt so much I didn't know what to call the pain. I hated crying, but I felt I would burst with unspent anger if I didn't let my sorrow spill.

When I woke Marla sat in Sébastien's place. Her legs were scrunched up under her chin and her arms were crossed over her legs. Concern and sadness marred her face. As soon as I moved she stirred.

"Hey, sweetie," she said in a soft voice.

"Hey. Where's Sébastien?"

"He went home to shower," she said. "You were so tired we decided not to wake you. I had to force him to go, promising not to leave you alone for a single minute. He's a good egg, that guy. You have the most amazing luck with men."

I was tempted to yell at her that I didn't feel lucky. Instead, I got up.

"I'll be back," I said, heading to the bathroom. "What are you talking about?" I asked when I returned.

"Sébastien is devoted to you and Ernie worships the ground you walk on," she said, ignoring the elephant in the room.

If she mentioned Iaen, I was sure we both would have begun reminiscing. I preferred to avoid what was at the end of that path. I didn't think the time would come when I could do that without so much pain.

"Sébastien is just a friend," I objected.

"I wasn't saying otherwise, but he's a really good friend," she said. "Those are few and hard to come by, trust me. Finding one is hard, finding three, wow!"

"You have nothing to complain about," I said, referring to her boyfriend.

"I'm not," she said. "He sends his love, by the way."

I nodded my appreciation asking, "Everything good with you two?"

"Yeah, you know, we have our ups and downs like everybody I guess," she said. "But mostly. Sometimes he's a selfish thoughtless blockhead." She shrugged in a what-you-gonna-do manner. "When it matters, he's as solid as the

Rock of Gibraltar."

"How did you find out?" I asked, returning without thinking to the lump in my heart.

"Sébastien contacted me as soon as he heard from Madame Marmotte," she said, sympathy appearing on her face. "He said Iaen was in a car accident." I nodded to confirm in response to her questioning gaze. "I called your aunt and uncle and Ernie. Is there anyone else who needs to know?" I shook my head no. "What about Iaen's family? Does, did he have any relatives?"

"Nobody," I said.

"When is the funeral?" she asked.

"Dunno," I said. "Since I'm not related the police won't let me bury him."

The feelings of anger started to rise. I got up to push the strong emotions away from me before I said something I regretted. Marla got up too.

"Oh, sweetie, I'm so sorry," she said. After a pause she added. "In the end, what matters is saying good-bye one last time. Let's go wherever they hold the service, wherever they bury him."

"I hung up on the policewoman before I could find out what they will do with—" I said. My composure broke before I could finish the sentence. "Him. I called back, but she had called me from his phone and it went straight to voicemail. I left a message, but she probably can't pick those up without his password."

"Maybe she doesn't have the phone anymore or it ran out of battery," she said.

"I hadn't thought about that," I said. "I assumed she was annoyed at me because I hung up on her."

"I wouldn't worry about it," she said. "If she does this for a living, she's used to people's reactions when they receive bad news. All we have to do is find her so we can find out where Iaen is. Did she tell you her name or what police station she was at?"

"She said a bunch of stuff I didn't catch," I said.

"If we have to, we'll call every police department in the city," she said. "Do you remember anything at all? Her first or last name maybe?"

"She had two first names," I said. "You know, one of those people whose last name could be a first name. Her first name began with an A, but that's all I remember."

"It might come to you when you're not trying," she said. "If worse comes to worst we can use marshals resources, after all Iaen is, was a Weeia. Let's give it a while longer to see if you remember."

I was about to say I agreed when there was a knock on the door. My stomach tightened. I must have grimaced because Marla placed her hand on my arm in a reassuring gesture.

"It's probably Sébastien," she said. "I'll get it."

"Hi," she said, exchanging cheek kisses with Sébastien once he was inside.

"I come bearing lunch," he said, raising his arm laden with two bulging bags. "Anybody hungry?"

"I'm starving," Marla said. "Danni's stomach has been growling like a wild beast too."

"I picked up some of Danni's favs. I didn't know what you might like so I got several different things," he said.

"You feel like going to the dining room or would you rather eat here?" she asked me.

The dining room made me think of Iaen. I preferred to stay where we were.

"Here," I said with more force than I meant.

I started to get up to get dishes and cutlery. Sébastien set the bags down on the table and started toward the kitchen.

"Don't move a muscle," he said. "I'll yell if I have any questions. Besides, I probably know your kitchen layout better than you do."

A pang of sadness hit me. What he said was true because

he had helped Iaen out with meals and set the table more than once. I dropped down on the sofa. Sébastien and Marla served lunch for the three of us. I played with my food to humor them, but although my stomach growled, I wasn't hungry. Worse yet, when I tried to eat the food had no flavor. Neither said anything. I didn't resent them for eating their food. When they finished they cleared the coffee table, and we sat down in companionable silence for a few minutes.

"Solene," I said as if someone had poked me with an invisible cattle prod. They stared at me, a touch startled. "Agnes Solene. That's her name."

"The policewoman?" Marla asked.

"Yes, I don't know why, but it just popped into my head," I said, feeling a smidge better.

"We'll track her down," Marla said. "That's the name of the policewoman who called Danni about Iaen. We need to find her so she can tell us where they're going to bury him."

"I'll start calling," Marla said, grabbing her phone.

"Use mine," I said, handing her my phone. "If you use your US phone it will cost a fortune."

"Thanks," she said. "It's out of juice. Where's your charger?"

"Sorry. On the table," I said.

"I know a guy who might help," Sébastien said.

The thought of hearing those conversations didn't appeal to me. I needed some air. I threw my jogging clothes on and headed toward the door.

"Guys, I'm going for a run," I said.

It was only halfway through my run that I realized I had yet to thank them for dropping everything to be with me. That made me cry. On my way back home I walked by Iaen's boat. It looked just like the last time we had been there. If I closed my eyes I could remember it in detail. I could replay our time together like a video in my mind. I let my memories run wild. It was nice to forget the bad news even if it was only for a minute. Maybe if I kept them closed a little longer, when I opened them everything would go back to the way it was, and Iaen would greet me with his usual banter. I stood in front of the boat for a long time, afraid if I went inside the loss would overwhelm me, and unwilling to tear myself away to return to reality.

"We have it," Marla shouted as soon as I walked through the door. "We know when and where they'll set him to rest."

I had meant to thank them both. Instead I burst into tears. I had promised myself I wouldn't do that, but there were moments when I couldn't help myself. I would feel calm until something would remind me of Iaen, and a torrent of grief would pour out of me despite my best efforts.

"It's sorted. We'll go with you," Sébastien, who had been standing quiet like a statue in the corner, announced.

The burial service was simple and brief. Getting there, being there was a blur. Hours and days passed almost without my noticing. It was as if time moved at faster than normal and slower than normal. I would be distracted, lost in thought and the morning disappeared without my having done anything. On the other hand, sometimes I felt stuck like an insect trapped in honey.

At my insistence and after I assured them I would be fine if they gave me half a chance, Marla returned home and Sébastien went back to help with his sister's big event. I missed them. They had fussed over me, and even when it annoyed me I was glad for their company. When they left I felt desperately alone.

Chapter 29

Iaen's death left me behind a wall of grief and emptiness I struggled to understand. Before we had met, I had been a strong determined woman. I tried to return to that person to take refuge from my loneliness and couldn't find her. I paced around my apartment and when I couldn't take it anymore walked around the Latin Quarter. I lost myself running without direction, time keeping or fixed thought. Night was the worst. Sleep was always at arm's length, and when I woke the sadness returned, aching all over again like the first day.

I pushed my badge aside and let the battery die on my phone. One morning melded into another until I had no idea what day it was. When I returned from a long run midmorning on a rainy day Marla was sitting at my door.

"Hey," she said. "You look pretty good for a ghost." I must have seemed puzzled because she continued. "Rumor has it the Danni I knew and loved has become a phantom. Nobody has seen or heard from her in days. There's no reply to badge calls, and regular calls go to voicemail right away like when a phone is switched off."

"Oh that," I said, opening the door and waiting for her to enter. "Sorry."

"Everyone is worried about you, sweetie," Marla said, wearing a concerned expression. I had no reply. "You've lost weight."

I looked down at my body, asking aloud, "Have I?"

"Definitely," she said. "When was the last time you ate?"

I shrugged. Nothing tasted good. Plus, food made me think of Iaen and that made me sad. I was tired of being sad, but I didn't know how not to be sad. I didn't feel like being around people. I didn't want anyone to see me so down.

She walked to the kitchen. I remembered it was a mess. There were dirty cups and dishes in the sink. I heard the refrigerator open and close.

"I'm famished," she announced. "Let's get some lunch."

I opened my mouth to object and closed it without saying a word. I raised my hand for her to wait, changed out of my sweaty running clothes, grabbed my wallet, and we went out.

"There's a place I liked the last time on the quai des Grands Augustins," she said. "The food and service are good and it's quiet enough to talk. That okay?"

I nodded. We both ordered the lunch menu. I didn't plan to eat it, but I figured she would fuss if I didn't order something. I took the path of least resistance. After making small talk for five minutes she surprised me.

"I'm not going to lecture you about what you should or shouldn't do," she said. "You're a big girl and it's your life. I'm here to remind you that there are people who love you and care about you. Your aunt and uncle are worried and on the verge of coming over."

I hadn't thought about that. Traveling to France would be expensive for them. And, it would cause them all sorts of problems to part in a rush, leaving everything unattended. Guilt pulled at my heart strings.

"I'll call them," I said. She stared at me with an unbelieving expression. "Really. I will."

"Do what you have to do," she said. "I promised to call them, and if I can't reassure them they're flying over on the next available flights."

"Oh, no," I blurted.

I went to look for my phone, remembering it was in my apartment with a dead battery. I had to call them right away to stop them.

"The incidents multiplied," she said before I could ask to borrow her phone to call them.

"What?" I asked, not knowing what she was referring to at

first.

"The odd incidents you and Sébastien had been dealing with," she said. "They got worse. There are more of them, all over Paris. They don't know what's causing them or how to stop it. If you're up to it, they could use a hand. I know you're grieving, but this seems important."

She let the words hang in the air. The food arrived, giving me a moment to think while the server set down the plates, described the dishes, and refilled our glasses.

"Did Sébastien ask you to come?" I asked.

"We've been in contact," she said. "He's come by to see you a bunch of times, but there is never an answer when he knocks on your door."

"I haven't been—" I left the sentence unfinished.

Brushing my explanation aside with a flick of her hand she continued, "Anyway, I volunteered to check in on you. It was a great excuse to come to Paris. You know how much I love it here. Plus, I get free room and board with you. What's not to like?"

I waited while she took a bite of her duck salad. Leaving mine untouched, I ripped off a chunk of baguette and popped it into my mouth, more to do something than because I was hungry.

"If what you're asking is whether Sébastien told me to hound you to return to work, the answer is no," she said. "Although he has his hands full, he's been coming over to check on you. That guy is a sweetheart and he thinks the world of you. You going to eat that?" She pointed at my salad. I nodded to say no. "I'm famished. We wrapped up a big case before I came to see you. Using my abilities always makes me hungry. May I?"

"Feel free," I said.

"Aren't you going to eat anything?" she asked, swapping her empty plate with mine.

"I don't feel like duck," I said.

"So don't have duck," she said as if I was dense. "Order something else. Who cares if it's not the special? If you feel like having French fries, have that. Eat whatever you want, just eat something."

"I'll have a potato and leek soup," I ordered from the server.

That was all I might be able to stomach. Marla ate with such gusto it made me wish I could too.

"Work would take your mind off things," she said, hesitating between the last two words. "I'm not putting any pressure on you. It's no skin off my nose either way. I'm just a tourist in town to see my bestie. I'm fine hanging out at home with you. But, if you're up to it, I think you should at least talk with Sébastien, be there for him. He's in way over his head."

I felt better after I finished the bowl with a slice of bread. By the end of the meal I had decided I wanted to talk about the case with Sébastien.

"Excellent," Marla said when I told her.

"You staying the night?" I asked.

"Maybe," she replied. "Why do you ask?"

"I'm going to the office," I said, making up my mind as I spoke. "You can join me or I can give you my keys and meet you at my apartment later."

"I'll go with you," she said. "Here." She handed me her phone. "Press redial to call your aunt and uncle's number."

"Thank you," I said.

"Let's take a taxi," she said. "You make the call and I'll take care of paying for lunch."

Turning to the server who had come to collect payment she asked, "Do you know where there's a *tete* around here?"

The fastest way to get a taxi in Paris was to find a *tete de taxi* or taxi stand. While she listened to the directions I called my aunt and uncle.

"It's me," I said when my aunt answered.

"Danni?" she asked. "It's hard to hear. There's so much noise."

"I'm in Paris, having lunch with Marla," I replied. "Sorry about the noise."

I was going to explain that Marla had made me call and decided not to. I didn't want them to think I didn't care about them or worse yet that I was too depressed to call.

"It's good to hear your voice," she said. "How are you?"

"Uh, okay," I said.

"You don't sound okay," she said, cutting to the chase.

"I've been better," I said. "I, uh, well, you know."

"We could visit you for a few days," she offered. "Would you like that?"

"No," I blurted. "I mean I would rather we plan a visit at a better time. Besides, we're in the middle of a complicated case. There are few of us at the office. If you come now I might not be able to be with you."

I knew from the heavy silence she wasn't convinced. It would take a long conversation and a more upbeat tone on my part to get through to her.

"Danni," she began.

"I have to go now," I interrupted her before she could get going. "I promise to call as soon as I have a moment, this weekend at the latest. We can discuss it then, okay?"

"I'll tell your uncle you'll call this weekend," she said.

Woven between her words was the expectation of my call, and what they would do if they failed to hear from me. They wouldn't hesitate to drop everything, even if it was expensive and inconvenient, and catch a flight to Paris if they thought I needed them.

"Kisses," I said with as much enthusiasm as I could muster.

"Kisses back," she said. "Talk with you soon."

After I hung up with my aunt we walked to the nearest taxi stand. There was a cab available so we didn't have to wait for one to arrive. Waiting at a stand was such a waste of time. I was grateful that Marla spent the entire ride on the phone dealing with work stuff because it gave me a chance to gather my thoughts before we arrived at the office.

Madame Marmotte and Sébastien were nowhere to be seen. Several people I had never met were spread across the desks and tables, working on laptops and electronic devices. They paid no attention to us.

"Excuse me," I said to the nearest one. She turned toward me with impatience.

"Yes?" she asked.

"Uh, who are you?" I asked.

"Who are you?" she replied.

What the heck? She was in my office. I pushed down the anger that had begun to bubble in my belly.

"Marshal Dannielle Metreaux," I said in a calm voice. "This is my office. Would you please—"

"Danni?" a familiar man's voice interrupted me. I turned around to face the owner. He hugged me. I stood there limp and unsure what to do. His scent, a blend of metal, gunpowder, solvents and soap, surrounded me. It was reassuring, pleasant. "How are you? I'm so happy to see you."

"I had no idea you were in Paris," I said, pleased and surprised to see him.

"CUT called me in," he said. "It's been pretty wacky around here. They said you were on bereavement leave. I'm so sorry."

Tears welled up in my eyes. I rubbed them before they grew. It was nice to see Ernie. He was second in order of importance after the weapons master at the armory at the Marshals Academy, our headquarters in Portland, Maine. He didn't work in the field. He was always in his office. Him being in Paris meant things had gotten far worse than I had thought. Still, if someone had to be there I was glad it was

Ernie. Although he was more geek than warrior by far, what he lacked in athletic build and skill he made up for in tech smarts and pigheaded determination.

He had disarming guy-next-door good looks and a smile that warmed me. I had underestimated him when we first met in Portland. Before Iaen had come into my life, Ernie and I had sort of dated. He didn't have Iaen's ease in social situations or his knack for squeezing every ounce of joy out of life, but I liked being with Ernie. When I was with him I felt grounded and self-assured with nothing to prove.

Chapter 30

"No, not there," Francois's bellow interrupted my conversation with Ernie. "Tell them to move the boxes out of the way. Set up on the other side."

A second later, Madame Marmotte and two CUT women hurried by us. Madame Marmotte, walked at twice her usual speed, and was so engrossed following his orders, she didn't even notice me. I was going to ask her where Sébastien was and thought better than to stop her midstride.

"Francois has been running the office since the crisis started," Marla said, as if in response to my surprise at seeing him at our headquarters.

"You and Ernie in Paris, Francois running things, and Madame Marmotte working diligently, how long was I gone?" I asked Marla. She and Ernie smiled. "Next there will be unicorns feeding on raspberry bushes in the courtyard."

"There's more," Ernie said. "CUT brought in a full team. Sébastien has been working night and day to get them settled in. He and your Lithuanian staff converted the training room into barracks barely in time to accommodate them."

"Ernie showed me around," Marla said. "This place is a worse mess than you had described. I don't know how on earth you managed to get so much done on your own when you arrived."

That seemed like another life, years rather than months in the past. One of the people in my office had stopped what she was doing and was listening to our conversation, making me feel self-conscious. Ernie and Marla hadn't noticed.

"Where's Sébastien?" I asked.

"Around somewhere in the apartment building, finding a

way to fit everyone in the complex, answering questions, dealing with whatever fires pop up," Ernie said in a voice filled with admiration.

"What are you doing?" I asked Ernie.

"I'm helping out with all things technology, portable devices, and online and social media containment," he said. "The events increased in frequency and number. Because of the six-hour time difference between the east coast and Paris it was difficult for me to keep on top of the situation from Portland. Yesterday, when Francois asked me to come over I agreed. Contamination events expand exponentially and require multiple coordinated vectors to create firebreaks, and channel the linguistic threads to intercept and break up the viral memes without revealing our intervention, which would of course be self-defeating."

I tuned out the last part as he began slipping into technobabble. Although I was sorry the situation had worsened I was glad to have Ernie in Paris. Francois popped out of his office at that moment. Seeing me he stopped in his tracks.

"I thought you were on leave," he said, without so much as a good afternoon greeting.

"I heard you needed me," I said, expecting him to try and push me out of the case.

His expression was unreadable. He was dressed in his usual casual style, but his body language and the energy he suppressed with difficulty belied the superficial nature of his wrinkled social club attire.

"You heard right," he said. "I'm less thrilled than you are about what's going on, but we can use all the help we can get."

Color me surprised thrice over. I was sure he would tell me to go home. Had Francois just said he wanted me to stay?

"What should I focus on?" I asked, deciding to set aside my grief for the moment.

"Between us, the CUT team and now with Ernie here we're managing the situation, but only just," he said. "If the incidents increase, we won't be able to keep up." He thought for a moment. "We still have no idea what's causing this or how to keep any other cases from starting. That has to be the top priority."

"Sure, hand me the impossible task," I said in a soft voice I didn't expect him to hear.

"I realize it's asking a lot, but you have a good investigative nose," he said. That was the best and only direct compliment he had given me since I had been working under him. "I can't spare the time for anything more right now. Any headway you make could be instrumental in finding a solution, which we desperately need. Do what you can."

With that he turned around and walked out. Wherever he was headed he was in a rush.

"Yeah, go ahead, overwhelm me with details, why don't you," I said to his disappearing figure, confident he couldn't hear me, and feeling better for having aired some of my frustration.

"I can fill you in on what we have," Ernie volunteered. He was such a sweetheart. "Everything crosses my desk on its way in or out. What would you like to know?"

"Everything," I said. He and Marla laughed. "What?"

"You, you're always ready to slay the dragons, no matter how big and ferocious they are," Marla said.

"It's just good to have you here," Ernie said.

"Okay, I get it," I said, amused despite myself and elated at being welcomed by my boss. "Let's start with the basics."

"You know most of that already," Ernie said. "Francois, Sébastien, and CUT have been working together, clamping down on incidents, bringing affected Weeia in for questioning, suppressing information, shutting down rumors, and starting new ones to distract people from the truth."

"I have it from a reliable source that Ernie has made a huge difference," Marla said.

"That's not surprising," I said, meaning it. "He's the best at what he does."

Ernie almost glowed with pleasure at having his contributions recognized. He was one of the unsung heroes who often faded into the background during an operation. Later, people forgot how valuable his support was.

"I've mapped out the location of all the known incidents," he said, filling the silence.

"And?" I asked.

"I can't see any patterns," he said. "While they're not exactly everywhere, they're not predictable or at least I haven't found any way to predict them."

"What's new?" I asked.

"Hmm, I can give you a list of incidents, if you think that would help," Ernie said. "In addition to examining locations, I've looked at type of ability, duration, level of Weeia affected, and effects to find any patterns."

"And?" Marla and I asked at the same time.

"Nothing definitive," he said.

"I'm going to get a cup of coffee," I announced.

"I could use a cup," Ernie said, glancing at his watch.

Marla followed us into the breakroom, which looked like a storm had passed by, filling it with discarded paper cups and empty food wrappers. There were fresh coffee supplies, unused paper cups, and two dozen or more unopened snack bags on the shelf. Madame Marmotte had been busy.

"Have the lab results come in?" I asked as I served myself some of the hot liquid.

"For?" he asked.

"The man who died, Robert Previn," I said.

"Not sure," Ernie said, picking up a cup of his own. "I'll be back in a minute."

A minute turned into ten and twenty and there was no sign

of Ernie. I knew from experience when I was a student in my last year at the Marshals Academy that Ernie was capable of becoming lost for extended periods when he was focused on a problem. He was like a dog gnawing on a bone. It was difficult to pry his attention away from whatever he was working on until he found a solution.

"We could go find him," Marla offered when Ernie failed to return after thirty minutes.

"Naw, he'll be distracted and possibly annoyed," I said.

"Does he get annoyed?" Marla asked, amusement ringing her voice.

"He's mostly good natured, but mess with his toys or interrupt him when he's knee deep in a project or on deadline at the armory and he'll bite your head off," I said.

"Goes to show you can't judge a book by its cover," she said. "So whatcha gonna do? I can help while I'm here."

"Those results are important," I said. "Let's give him an hour. While he finds them I want to check on Susanna, Akka and Chandi. Since they arrived, I had been checking in on them at the end of the day. With everything that's happened I haven't even called to make sure they're okay, and with Francois here things could get wonky."

"He promised you a month, didn't he?" she asked. I nodded. "Do you think he would go back on his word?"

"I don't know," I said. "He's hard to read and I'm far from his favorite person. Without me around to play interference it probably wouldn't take much for him to change his mind. I could be wrong."

No one answered when we knocked on my old apartment door. We were walking away when a squeaky child's voice called out, "Danni."

I turned back and waved to Akka at the door. The five-year-old smiled and waved back.

"Hello," I said to her.

She glanced at Marla. When Marla looked at her she ran

away, leaving the door ajar.

"She doesn't speak English and she's never said my name before," I said, delighted. "I didn't think she even knew it."

Susanna appeared at the door, opening it when she saw me. Akka, cute as a button, stood behind her mother.

"Danni, how nice to see you," she said.

I thought she might be upset that I hadn't looked in on her since I had said I would. If she was, it didn't show. Instead she beckoned us inside.

"Susanna, this is my friend Marla," I said. "Marla meet Susanna, Akka, and Chandi."

The children giggled and shrieked when they heard their names. They had gained weight since the last time I had seen them. They were calmer, showing far less fear than the day they had arrived. It seemed a distant memory.

"I'm sorry I haven't been by in a few days," I said. Was that all it was, a few days? My life seemed to have been turned upside down since the last time I had been there. "I, uh—"

I couldn't finish the sentence. My voice began to crack. I didn't want to talk about it. I was afraid if I did the tears would start to flow. I didn't want to cry in front of Susanna and her kids. Besides, they had suffered enough for a lifetime already.

I was thankful when Marla finished for me, "She hasn't been in the office in several days. I heard all about you from Danni. How are you and the children liking it here?"

The felt a bit awkward asking the question, and I could see in Susanna's eyes that she had picked up on my distress. It didn't matter. I would tell her another day. At that moment I couldn't face the sadness.

"Good," Susanna said, pushing the hair away from Chandi's eyes with her hand before the boy squirreled away from her. "Your friends have been so nice to us. Every day they bring us food, or have us over for dinner so the children can play together. The kids love going there."

"Look," Akka commanded in French, showing us a doll.

"French too?" I asked.

"They're picking up a bit of everything," Susanna said. "English, French, and Lithuanian."

"Lithuanian?" Marla asked.

"Yes, the Lithuanian children don't speak English and are only beginning to learn French," she said. "They gave her the doll and bought a truck for Chandi. They also gave us all clothes. My children are the happiest they have been in months." She turned away as her voice broke. "I can't thank you enough." She took my hand in hers and looked into my eyes. "I know this hasn't been easy for you."

I guessed the Lithuanians had told her it was difficult to get permission for her to stay. I thought of asking if she had heard from her husband and figured if she had she would have said something. Why spoil the moment?

"Would you like some tea?" she asked.

The children's joy was contagious. I was tempted to say yes even if we only stayed for a cup. Ernie's call interrupted my thoughts.

"Excuse me. I have to take this," I said, stepping a few feet away.

"I have some information you're going to want to see right away," he said. "Where are you?"

"With Susanna and her kids," I said. "We'll be right down."

"Ernie?" Marla asked after I hung up.

"Yep, he's back," I said, intrigued by his words. "Susanna, I'm sorry. We have to go. It's urgent. We're in the middle of a difficult situation, but I'll be back as soon as I have a chance. Do you have everything you need?"

"More than enough," she said.

"If you need food, money, toys, anything at all ask Tadas or Giedrius," I said. "They'll take care of it and I'll sort it out with them later."

"We're fine. Don't worry," she said, taking my hand in hers again.

The children were playing with a jigsaw puzzle, happy and carefree, when we left. Susanna watched us go from the door.

"Now that I've met them I can see why you had to help them," Marla said once we were out of hearing distance. "I hope everything works out."

"Thanks," I said. "I hope so too."

"So what did Ernie say?" she asked.

"Not much," I said. "He was excited though. He's pretty thorough in his work, so if he gets excited there's usually a good reason."

Chapter 31

"What you got?" I asked as soon as Ernie was within sight. "Were the autopsy results interesting?"

"Better," he said, looking pleased.

"Spill," I said, eager for a clue.

"The lab found common organic compounds on the deceased," he said, reading in part from his tablet.

"That doesn't sound extraordinary," Marla said.

"Not by itself," he said, smiling like the cat who had the canary in its mouth. "They have distinctive markers, which have also appeared at the incident sites. On their own they're meaningless. Anyone else would probably have missed it." He raised an eyebrow to indicate he was special. I rolled my eyes, making him smile. I nodded my head, prodding him to continue. "Combined they're worth a second look. Multiply the results across town and bingo, we have a pattern."

"I'm not following," Marla said. "What does it mean? Do we know what's going on?"

"Not exactly," he said, sounding a touch disappointed, like a kid whose balloon had popped for no apparent reason.

"It's the first promising lead we've had in days," I blurted, excited.

"It is?" Marla asked.

"Yes," I said.

"What does it mean?" she asked.

"I believe some substance has been making Weeia ill," Ernie said.

"Why?" she asked.

"I don't know why it's making them sick, but from the descriptions and the video we have the Weeia appear unwell," he said. "Once they bring them in their symptoms go away. When questioned they have no idea what happened or how."

"That makes sense," I said. "We don't have the answer, but I think we know where to look next."

"Where?" they asked in unison.

"At a perfume maker we questioned in relation to Robert Previn's case," I said. "At the time, we could only question him on a volunteer basis, and he blew us off. If the organic compounds you identified from the incident sites match any of his fragrances, we have probable cause to bring him in formally. How long will it take you to—"

Before I could finish Ernie interrupted me, "If you bring me a sample, I'll fast track it. You'll have the results as quickly as I can process them. Keep in mind chemistry is not my area of expertise, not even close."

"Will do," I said. "I'll get the cologne Robert Previn borrowed. That's a direct link."

"That should work," Ernie said.

"Want to come with me or would you rather stay here?" I asked Marla.

"I'll go with you," she said.

We had to wait for someone to arrive at the Previn home. It took some nudging to obtain the cologne, but two hours later we handed it to Ernie.

"Did they give you any trouble?" Ernie asked.

"She was so diplomatic, I thought I had banged my head and was hallucinating," Marla said, earning her a soft smile from Ernie and a punch in the arm from me. "Ouch."

"I'll take that," Ernie said, reaching for the bottle of Parfumerie Tartan cologne in my hand. "You'll have to be patient until I can get ahold of someone in Portland who knows about this stuff."

"I thought you were going to fast track it," I said.

"I'll process the samples immediately, but for anything meaningful that will stand up to scrutiny, we need a chemist who can interpret the results," he said. "There's nobody here who can do that so I'll have to rely on someone back home."

He was about to walk away when I had a thought. The more I rolled it around in my head the better it seemed.

"Wait up," I said to Ernie. He paused. "I have an idea. We have a chemist right here." In response to his surprised expression I said, "Susanna, the refugee from Syria. She's upstairs. Assuming she agrees to work on the case for free, all we need to do is find someone to babysit so she can review your test results."

"She's Syrian," Madame Marmotte, who had been listening without my noticing, protested. "Does she even speak French?"

"Even better, she speaks English," I said.

I was glad when Marla added her two cents worth, "Chemistry is chemistry no matter where she's from. We'll ask her. She can always turn us down, but she seems like a good person, and I bet she'll say yes. If she has experience with analysis, how complicated can it be?"

My gut told me Susanna would pounce on the opportunity to do something productive and to be useful. And I was certain the Lithuanian ladies would be delighted to look after Akka and Chandi while she was working.

"She's not a marshal. She has no business looking at confidential marshals documents," Madame Marmotte said.

"It's no big deal," Ernie said. "We sometimes send out samples to human labs when we have staff shortages, and when we want to double check our results. She's Weeia, so that's better than a human lab already." He shrugged. "If she's willing and able, it will speed up the process. I have no objection. Your call."

"Great," I said. "Go ahead and get started. I'll talk to her."

Within minutes Marla and I were knocking on the door of Susanna's temporary home. She was wearing an apron and had pulled up her sleeves the way someone does when they don't want them to get wet or dirty. There were bits of flour and dark spots on her apron. She looked surprised to see us, although that didn't diminish her delight.

"Come in," she said, stepping out of our way, and allowing us to enter.

The children were still playing on the floor with the jigsaw puzzle. They looked up when we arrived. When they saw it was just us they returned to what they had been doing. Judging from the bowls and plates, eggs and flour, and other ingredients on the table, we had interrupted Susanna while she was in the process of baking something.

"Did you change your minds about the tea?" she asked in a jovial tone.

"Not exactly," I said. "We need your help with something."

"Oh?"

"It's for a case I'm working on," I said, searching for the right words to explain what we wanted from her.

"They need a chemist to help with the analysis and comparison of samples," Marla said. "Instead of delaying the results until they find someone stateside, Danni thinks you might be able to pitch in since you're a chemist."

"What she said," I added. "You told me you're a chemist, right?"

Susanna nodded in agreement and her face brightened like a room in shadow when the sun lights it. I shouldn't have worried about choosing the words.

"I don't think it will take more than a day," I said. "The children can stay with the Lithuanian families. They'll be in good hands so you don't have to worry about them. The only thing is that there's no budget to pay you."

"That's not a problem," she said, brushing aside my concern with her upbeat tone. "Although for the last years I've been working in a management position rather than as a chemist, if you think I can help I'll do my best."

"Let's find out," I said. "I'll call Ernie and he can explain exactly what he needs. Then if you're comfortable that you can do it we'll go from there."

"Okay," she said.

"Let's go to the kitchen," I said, seeking privacy. "It shouldn't take long."

I had noticed from past visits that the children listened to our conversations even when they appeared to be distracted, and later they repeated what we had said, sometimes in front of other people. Given the prejudice some people had against Susanna I didn't want that to happen with the case. I didn't want to give the naysayers any way to object to her participation.

"I'll keep an eye on the kids," Marla said, standing at the kitchen door.

"Thank you," Susanna said.

"It's me," I said when Ernie answered my video call. "Ernie, meet Susanna, our recently arrived chemist. Susanna, meet Ernie, our all-around genius. We're in her kitchen. I thought you two could discuss what you need first, and if you decide to give it a go we can sort out the next step."

"Hi," Ernie said in a shy voice.

"Hello, Ernie. It's nice to meet you," Susanna said. "Danni thinks I can help with your project. What do you need?"

"Someone who can interpret lab results," he said.

"That sounds easy," she said. "Is that it?"

"There are dozens of chemicals, but in a nutshell, yeah," he said. "If you can tell me what the results mean I think I can take care of the rest."

"Do you have any kind of equipment in case we need to run additional tests?" she asked.

"I have a portable GC-MS," he said. "Will that be enough?"

"I've never worked with a portable unit, but I imagine unless you require a high degree of detail it should be fine," she said. "When do you need to start?"

"Yesterday," I said before Ernie could reply. "Can you start right away?"

She looked in the direction of the living room, although the kitchen walls blocked her from seeing her children. I understood.

"Hang on a minute," I said.

I dialed Tadas on my smartphone. He answered on the fourth ring.

"Hi, it's Danni," I said.

"Danni," he said, drawing in a breath, buying time.

Because he wasn't fluent in English when he had to think about how to say something he paused. Before he could mention Iaen and I got all sad again I spoke, "I'm at the office. Actually, I'm at Susanna's apartment. I need her to help me with something, but she can't leave the kids alone. Can your wife babysit the kids?"

"When?" he asked.

"Now," I said. "Sorry, it's urgent or I wouldn't ask."

"I call back," he said and we hung up.

"He's going to check," I announced. "What's a GC-MS?"

"A gas chromatography mass spectrometer, a long word for a machine that can identify substances with great accuracy," she said.

"Is that good?" Marla asked.

"Yes, excellent," she said. "That's the kind of equipment all chemists want, especially for organic analysis."

While we waited Susanna checked on the children. Two minutes later my phone rang.

"Yes," Tadas said. "Giedrius pick children today."

"Thanks," I said. Turning to the others I explained. "I think Giedrius is on his way to pick up the kids."

"I'll get them ready," Susanna said.

"See you as soon as Giedrius comes to get them," I said to Ernie and we hung up.

Chapter 32

As soon as Susanna and I arrived, she and Ernie got down to business. It was as if someone had switched on an invisible button and she had come to life. Her manner became businesslike and her movements more efficient and economical than usual. It wasn't that she was slow at other times, but rather that she was relaxed and nurturing around her children.

"We'll call you when we have something to share," Ernie said, dismissing me.

"In an hour, a day, a week?" I asked.

"Soon," Susanna said.

Marla was distracted, chatting on the phone with her boyfriend in the only quiet corner. I was wondering how to make myself useful while I waited. Before I had a chance to get very far, a man's voice drew my attention.

"Danni," Sébastien said, swallowing me into a huge bear hug before I could protest. "It's good to see you."

"You too," I said into his ear.

The human contact felt good. It also reminded me of Iaen's absence. Afraid the tears would rise I turned my mind to the case. As long as I was working I only thought about Iaen every other minute instead of every minute.

"Let me guess," he said. "Marla dragged you in?"

"Who else?" I said, grateful she had.

The sadness was still there even when I hid it from others, but it felt good to be useful and away from the memories of Iaen that filled my apartment.

"Did I hear my name used in vain?" Marla asked as she walked in.

"Not in vain," Sébastien chuckled. "It's good to see you both."

While they exchanged the usual cheek kisses, I had a chance to observe Sébastien. For once his shirt and pants showed signs of wear, no hard wrinkles or stains mind you, just less than perfect. That was unusual for him. Small bags under his eyes told me he had not slept well or at all on recent nights.

"Catch me up," I ordered.

"I'm sure Marla told you what happened to win your cooperation," he said with a knowing smile. "The number of incidents has multiplied. We have no idea why. Francois got involved. He's been running the office for two days. All we've been doing is running interference so far. What we need to do is catch the culprit before he or she attacks again."

"So you think it's a person," Marla said.

"We don't know," he said, running his hand through his hair in a nervous gesture. "All we know so far is that someone or something is triggering weird and out of control reactions from Weeia. We've brought them in, of course, to stop them and to question them. But, they're as clueless as we are, if not more."

"Like the kids at the Académie," I said, thinking out loud.

"I hate to admit it, but yes, I think they're connected," he said. "We found evidence of drug use in one case and presumed the incidents were all related. What if the other cases had nothing to do with substance abuse?"

"Do you think the Académie is where it started?" Marla asked.

"It's hard to say," I replied. "It could be coincidence that we happened to be there to see them. Otherwise, the incidents could've gone unnoticed and unreported."

I emphasized the final word to remind Sébastien how hard Francois and he had pressured me not to file my report with headquarters. It wasn't so much that I wanted the satisfaction of being right. I already knew I had been. It was meant as a lesson to Sébastien about the importance of filing reports because they provided data points that could prove crucial in a case like the one we were facing.

"There could've been similar situations in other places we were unaware of until the number grew, making it impossible for us to miss them," Sébastien said. "The million-euro question is who is behind it all and for what purpose."

"What if it's accidental?" I asked out loud.

"What do you mean?" Marla asked.

"What if nobody purposefully meant for them to happen and it was a side effect of an experiment of some sort?" I asked.

"What kind of experiment?" Sébastien asked.

"I don't know," I said. "I'm speculating, thinking out of the box because the usual reasons don't fit. Nobody is benefiting, that we know of. We can't even link the incidents to a person or place."

"I thought they were all in Paris," Marla said.

"All except the first incidents, which were at the Académie," I said. "Still, it's close enough to say they have been in the greater Paris area. The only death so far was in the city, right?"

"Yes," Sébastien said. "There have been a lot of injuries, some serious, among the humans at the train station, but no more deaths."

We went on speculating and throwing out ideas and possibilities for the better part of an hour. No matter how hard we tried nothing made sense.

"We have something," Ernie said. He had entered the room and we were so wrapped up in our discussion we hadn't noticed. "We're not sure what it means, but it's pretty clear there is a common element to all the incidents, a sort of signature."

"Was it in the Parfumerie Tartan cologne?" I asked.

"Definitely," he said.

"That's enough to pick up that smelly man," I said. "What was his name?"

"Mathis Tartan," Sébastien said. "Do you want to get him now?"

"Yes," I said. "If he's behind this or involved in some way we don't want him to skip town."

"Bring us some samples from his shop," Susanna said. "Since the bottle you brought belonged to a customer, the shop owner could argue it was altered after he sold it. If the tests on the samples from his shop match the ones we ran on Robert Previn's bottle, we'll be one hundred percent sure of the connection."

"I'll get the car keys," Sébastien said, walking out.

"I'm not sure what time I'll be done," I said to Marla. "Do you want to wait here or at my apartment?" Her expression told me the answer. "You're going home." She nodded. "Tonight?"

"You're pretty busy so if you don't need me, I'll head back as soon as I can," she said.

"Is your boyfriend the teleporter coming to get you?" Ernie asked.

"Yep," she said. Turning to me she added, "He can pick me up after work west coast time so I might be able to have dinner with you before leaving."

"Great," I said. "See you in a little while. If he has a break and you want to go home, it's okay. I don't mind."

Before Sébastien and I went to get the samples Marla and I hugged in case she left before we returned. The moment tugged at my heart strings. I walked away at a fast pace to avoid her seeing my tears.

On our way to the shop Sébastien's phone rang. He glanced at the caller ID, announcing, "I'm going to take it it's my sister." I nodded. "Hiya. No, I haven't forgotten. I've been too busy to answer texts. Yes, I'll drop them off after work. How late will you be there?" While I could hear her voice I couldn't make out the words. "I'm working. I'm in the middle of a case. I'm in the car with Danni on our way to the Island." He stiffened for a moment. "Okay."

He moved the phone away from his ear and turning to me said, "I have a set of keys I promised to give to Caroline today. She's in the Marais. Would you mind very much if we swing by there? It's on our way."

"Sure," I said.

Caroline was a bit high strung and spoiled, but she was his only sister, and he was devoted to her and his family. He sighed with relief before placing the phone back against his ear.

"We don't have time to park," he told her. "I'll text you when we're near so you can pop out. See you in a few."

As he had said, it didn't take long to reach the Marais. He texted her as we approached the Place des Vosges. Although the building where we stopped looked old the walls were spotless, giving me the impression it had been renovated in recent months. Caroline, dressed like a fashion model as usual, smiled on seeing her brother.

"Thanks," she said as he handed her the keys. She waved at me. I waved back.

"Caroline, Sébastien mentioned that you shop at Parfumerie Tartan," I said.

"Yeah," she said, watching me with an inscrutable expression.

"How long has it been popular?" I asked.

"I think the shop has been around forever, but it only became popular recently, about six months ago maybe," she said, looking to one side as if searching her memory.

"Good to know, thanks," I said.

As we drove away Sébastien said, "Good thinking. That confirms what I picked up from Mr. Tartan during the interrogation."

"If the shop is closed we'll have to return in the morning," I said as we walked toward Mathis Tartan's Ile Saint Louis shop after parking three blocks away.

"Maybe not," Sébastien said. "I did some digging on a hunch. He and his mom own the building. He lives in an apartment above the shop."

"Wow, they own the whole building," I said, impressed despite myself. "A building on the Island has to be worth a fortune. Is it family money?"

"I'm not sure," he said. "The perfume business runs in his family. According to the city records, his great grandfather was among the first tradesmen to buy land on the Ile Saint Louis in the mid seventeenth century when it developed as a planned neighborhood for the filthy rich."

"You mean like your family?" I asked to tease him.

"Kind of," he said, refusing to take the bait. "In the early days of the country, most of the wealth belonged to the crown and the nobility. When they needed money they borrowed it from rich barons without title or lineage called parvenus. The island was built for them. To lure them to buy land and build their mansions, the developers sold affordable land to tradesmen. They were the first inhabitants."

"Why would the parvenus want tradesmen in their exclusive neighborhood?" I asked.

"Back then there were no bridges to connect the island to the rest of the city," he said. "The only way to reach the Ile Saint Louis was by boat. Having tradesmen onsite meant there were supplies for your mansion nearby, and that was important. Having a baker, produce seller and cheese vendor on hand was convenient, for example."

"Got it," I said. "So his family has been on the island for several generations."

"It appears that way, though I'm not sure of the whole story," he said.

"Seems we're in luck," I said when we arrived to find the

shop door open. I pushed it and went in. Sébastien followed. The reception area was empty. "Hello?"

Chapter 33

A long moment passed. It might have been a minute or two, but I'm not in my element in shops. When I'm standing in a boutique waiting for a salesperson time seems to slow down to an impossibly boring pace.

"Yes?" a man's voice called from inside.

I waited for him to enter the area where we were before speaking to avoid spooking him. His eyes grew wary on seeing us.

"Mr. Mathis Tartan, we would appreciate it if you accompanied us," Sébastien said in such a polite manner it sounded like an invitation to a gala rather than to the questioning that was in store for him at our offices.

"Do I have a choice?" he asked in a defiant tone.

When he opened his mouth his ugly teeth showed. A foul smell spilled out and mingled with his pungent body odor, making me want to gag. Instead, I stepped back before I could stop myself.

"Not really," I replied. "On our first visit speaking with us was a courtesy. Today, we're here officially."

"It's in your best interest to join us," Sébastien said in the same polite manner. "Should you have pressing matters let us know. We'll do our best to expedite the interview, if possible."

"Well, since you put it nicely, I'll go with you," the man said. "Give me a moment while I close the shop."

Before we could reply he scurried behind thick brown velvet curtains I didn't recall from our previous visit. Sébastien indicated he was going to follow him. I nodded. The sounds of scuffling made me wonder if I should follow. Moments later Sébastien and the perfume maker reappeared.

"Problem?" I asked.

"Not at all," Sébastien replied with a satisfied look and a half grin. "Here are the samples."

Handing me the heavy bag, he pushed the man back into the small reception area by the scruff of his jacket. Mathis Tartan was disheveled. His tight lips and sideways glance told me he had lost face in the confrontation. My first thought was that poor Sébastien had been forced to touch the icky man. Despite the chill outside, I opened the windows as soon as we were inside the car, wondering if we would ever be rid of the stench.

When we returned I didn't see Marla so I assumed she had returned home to San Francisco early. We were taking a coffee break while letting Mr. Tartan cool his heels before questioning him, when Ernie and Susanna showed up in the breakroom. Their eyes were restless and they couldn't stand still for long. Their nervous energy told me they had news.

"There's no doubt about the connection to the perfume shop," Ernie said in a confident tone. "We're almost sure it's the source or a big part of the problem."

"We found the same markers in the cologne that are present at the incident sites," Susanna said.

"What makes you think the perfume shop is the source?" Sébastien asked.

"The concentration is much higher in the cologne than in any of the other samples from across Paris," she replied. "That means the cologne came from the source of the problem."

"Is the marker causing the problem?" I asked.

"We don't know for sure, but I doubt it," she said. "I think the marker is a harmless substance used to stabilize the blends."

"Why are Weeia the only ones affected?" Sébastien asked.

"We don't know," Susanna said. "We have some theories, but nothing solid yet."

"Let's see what the perfume shop owner has to say,"

Sébastien said.

"If he was involved in making the cologne he probably knows something," Susanna said. "Is he a chemist?"

"That's an interesting question," I said. "We'll start with that. If we discover anything useful we'll come find you. By the way, we brought back the samples you requested."

Sébastien handed them to Susanna. She and Ernie looked pleased, like kids with a new toy.

"We'll start running tests right away," she said.

Before returning to Mr. Tartan, Sébastien and I sat down for a couple of minutes to discuss our strategy. Despite the physical signs of tiredness, he appeared full of energy.

"This is the first break we've caught in days," he said. "I'm glad you're back."

Feeling awkward at the compliment I mumbled thanks and changed the topic back to the pending interrogation. He didn't seem to mind.

"Based on our last encounter I doubt he's going to tell us anything, if he can avoid it," I said. "Are you able to use your ability on him?"

"I think so," he said. "I picked up snippets of his thoughts without much effort today and the last time we went to see him."

Weeia rules prohibited the invasion of another Weeia's mind without justification. It was the first opportunity we had to question a person of interest where Sébastien could apply his mindreading ability. I was curious to know how well it would work.

"What is the best approach?" I asked. "Do you need to go in alone to question him?"

"I don't think that's necessary," he said. "It's better if you talk to him. That way I can concentrate. If he realizes what I'm doing he'll probably get spooked and that will make it more difficult. On the other hand, if you make him think about what we want to know, even if he doesn't tell us anything the thoughts will pop into his mind. As long as they're there I can pick them up."

"We're not required to disclose your ability to him," I said. "That's our advantage. In his case we can use all the advantages we can get. I want to get through it as quickly as we can. That man's smell is hard to bear."

Sébastien's smile told me he agreed. I breathed long and deep before entering the room where Mr. Tartan was waiting for us.

"Mr. Tartan, do you know why you're here?" I asked the perfume shop owner five minutes later.

He sat with a sullen expression across the table from us without saying a word. He avoided my gaze by staring at the floor.

"It's your right not to answer our questions, but we have to ask them," I said. "We'll be here as long as it takes to do that. The less you cooperate the longer it will take. I promise I'm enjoying this less than you are." I leaned in to make my point. "A man lost his life so this is a very serious matter. Since we visited you, the situation has worsened. You must know that all across Paris Weeia have been behaving in odd ways for no reason. When I say for no reason, I mean for no reason we could find until earlier today when we discovered a common link." He looked up. "Yes, Mr. Tartan. Our lab tests found a common element between a bottle of your cologne and the incidents. Not only that, but your cologne has a huge quantity of the element. That is a problem."

I let my words hang in the air, making him stew. He shuffled in his seat, turning his gaze away from me. He pulled a small bottle of cologne out of his jacket pocket, showing it to me for permission. I nodded. He had my vote for anything that improved his smell. A moment later the mild woody scent reached my nostrils making me sneeze. Sébastien rubbed his nose.

"I have an easy question for you," I said. "Are you a

chemist?"

"Uh, what do you mean?" he asked.

"Did you study chemistry in college, did you train to be a chemist?" Sébastien asked.

"Not exactly," he said. "I'm self-taught."

"How does your business work, Mr. Tartan?" I asked. "A customer walks through the door and wants one of the popular Parfumerie Tartan products, what does he get?"

"It depends on the customer," he said in a shaky voice.

"What does?" I asked.

"The product," he said. "I use the customer's personal scent profile in my work. I listen carefully to them. I ask them what they want from their cologne, and how much they're willing to spend."

It sounded like sales speak. Buying perfumes seemed like a huge waste of money to me. As a marshal, I never wore scented products because they could give me away during a case at work.

"With the exception of our line of soaps all our products are custom blended for customers," he said.

"Do you really blend a unique cologne for each person who walks through the door?" I asked.

"Yes, of course," he said.

"Completely unique?" I asked.

"Perhaps not unique, but bespoke, designed to match a customer's ability, personal scent and goals," he said in a confident sales-like manner, which was the opposite of the near hostile attitude he had before. "Human customers are the simplest. I can see their scent spectrum easily. Weeia customers present greater challenges. That's why the prices are higher for their line of products."

"I see," I said, not seeing at all how that had anything to do with the crisis we were facing. "How do you decide what ingredients go in a customer's perfume?"

"It may be an eau de toilette, an eau de parfum, or a

parfum, depending on the needs and budget of the customer," he said, smiling like a benevolent monk.

"What's the difference?" I asked to allow more time for him to think about the issue so my colleague might find answers.

"Eau de toilette has the mildest scent, eau de parfum can have up to 30 percent fragrance, and parfum has the highest concentration of fragrance," he said. "The more concentrated the product the pricier it is."

"That's all well and good, but how does that explain what's been happening?" I asked in an exasperated tone.

Sébastien scribbled on a piece of paper: You're doing great. Keep him talking. I nodded.

"I have no idea," Mr. Tartan said.

"You're a scent expert. There must be something you know that can help us," I said, appealing to his sense of importance. "What should we look for?"

"I don't know," he said, spreading his arms to emphasize his words. "Smells are produced by tiny chemicals that float in the air currents. Did you know scents also travel underwater? What science knows about the other senses is vast by comparison to our sense of smell, which is a virtual mystery. While we're aware that nasal neurons make it possible for us to smell, we don't know what part of our brain recognizes a particular odor."

"What makes you special?" I asked.

"I have an overdeveloped sense of smell and I know how to use it," he said, looking down his nose at me as if I had asked a stupid question.

"What does that mean?" I asked.

"Like any business, I match people and their needs," he said.

"Let's try this another way. Is what you do possible because of your Weeia ability?" I asked.

"You could say that," he said.

I was beginning to see red from all the obfuscation. Sébastien pushed the piece of paper he had scribbled in front of me. At least he was getting something productive out of Mr. Tartan's ramblings. To avoid an outburst, I got up and stood against the wall for a moment. Stretching my legs, I took a series of deep long breaths and let them out. Once I felt calmer I returned to my seat, where the man's offensive odor struck me.

"What would you offer me if I went to your shop?" I asked on a whim.

A puzzled expression spread over his face. He inhaled, letting the air out slowly, and narrowed his eyes.

"I find it unlikely that you would," he said. "You don't wear any perfume. Except for your natural body smells, the only odors attached to you are tobacco from your mouth, food smells from lunch, laundry detergent, cheap personal care products, and contact residual smells."

"Full marks," I said, impressed despite myself. "What if I wanted people to like me, to be popular or lucky? That's what people ask for, right?"

"Some of them," he said with a cryptic smile.

"Well, what ingredients would you put in my blend?" I asked.

"There are many possible combinations," he said. "I would have to think about what you want and how it would interact with your existing ability. Illusions, right?" He didn't wait for an answer. "Then I would have to see if I have the ingredients in stock."

"Oh?"

"There are recipes that require perishable, expensive or hard to find ingredients," he said. "In those cases I have to make sure I can procure the necessary items before quoting a price and date to a customer."

"Let's take a break," I said, getting up.

"Would you like a cup of coffee?" Sébastien asked Mr.

Tartan.

"A glass of wine would be better," Mr. Tartan said.

"We're fresh out of wine," I said in a snarky tone.

"In that case I would like to go home," Mr. Tartan said.

"Please be patient for a while longer," Sébastien said.

Although we weren't required to be polite to suspects, polite marshals received higher scores overall when it was time for promotions and raises. It was no surprise Sébastien had it nailed, not only because he was way politer than I was in general, but because he sympathized with people too.

"Did you get anything useful?" I asked as soon as we were alone. "Between his stuck-up bad attitude and his smell, I'm ready to throw a bucket of cold water on this guy."

"Yes," Sébastien said. "We were right to bring him here. He's been telling us the truth, just not all of it. He uses his Weeia ability to identify a customer's type and blend a custom scent. Like he told you, for Weeia customers it's more complicated than humans. He doesn't know what's causing the problems, but he suspects it's got to do with his products. He sees no benefit if he tells us, and he fears being blamed so he prefers to keep his suspicions to himself."

"How does that help us?" I asked, feeling like we had been going around in circles for nothing.

"While you were talking he thought about his process," he said. "If I'm interpreting what I picked up from his thoughts correctly, his ability is amazing. He can tell all sorts of things from people's odors, like he demonstrated with you. He can prepare blends that alter a Weeia's natural energy, converting it for a brief time into spiritshifting energy. If I'm right, his perfumes give new abilities to the wearer for as long as the scent lasts on his or her skin."

"He's giving abilities to Weeia only, right?" I asked.

"Yes," he said.

"How?" I asked.

"That's where it gets complicated," he said. "The recipes

are in a journal from one of his ancestors."

"I knew that twit didn't have it in him," I said. "Any idea why this is happening now?"

"Yes, I think I do," Sébastien said as his eyes widened and his lips broke into a grin. "After his father passed away without sharing the family heritage he and his mother struggled to keep afloat. He tried his luck at running the shop, but it was a failure. Customers didn't like him, his smell, his appearance or his bad attitude. For a while, he took odd jobs, though that didn't go well, judging by his thoughts of disappointment."

"What changed?" I asked.

"He found the journal when they were working on renovations to his basement," he said. "It took him a while to figure out what it meant, but once he did Weeia customers started seeking him out, and the business took off. His shop has been booming ever since. He can hardly keep up with demand."

"That explains a lot," I said. "He won't hand the journal over to us."

"He doesn't have to," Sébastien said. "I know where he keeps it. All we have to do is go to his house and get it."

"You're kidding," I said. "No way it's that easy."

"Way," he said, triumphant. "He thought about it while you were questioning him. I know where it is."

"What are we waiting for? Let's go get it," I said, giddy with excitement. "This could be the clue we've been looking for all this time. Put him in a cell. I'll get someone from CUT to monitor him."

Returning to the shop meant crossing town to the Ile Saint Louis a second time, finding parking, and walking back to his shop. It was a matter of two minutes to trump the lock on his shop door. The state-of-the-art security he had boasted about posed no difficulty for us.

"Now what?" I asked.

"We find the basement," Sébastien said.

"Really?" I asked.

"Yep, that's where he found it when they were expanding the shop two years ago," he said. "Nobody is allowed there. This way." I followed him down steep stone steps. The temperature dropped a few degrees and the air was thick with humidity. "The staff don't even know there's a room there. He waits until he's alone to look at his ancestor's journal. It should be behind this wall."

I began to ask how we would find our way in when he pushed aside a curtain, revealing a musty and dust-filled, closet-size room. He crouched down in one corner, inspecting the floor, poking and prodding until he found a loose stone. He pushed it to one side to reveal a thick leather bound notebook.

"Looks like he hasn't done much to the place," Sébastien said, lifting the tome out of an opening only wide enough for the notebook.

Sitting on the floor he opened it. I stood beside him, looking over his shoulder.

"This is all handwritten," Sébastien said. "Look at these frail pages. It's old. There are new slips of paper here and there with notations, probably from Mr. Tartan."

"Do you understand it?" I asked.

"I understand the words, but the meaning is not entirely clear," he said.

"We'll take it with us," I announced. "Hopefully we can figure out enough of what it says to find a solution. If we have to, we can show it to him and ask him about it."

I looked at it in the car on our way back to the marshals complex, but it was too hard to read in the moving car and I had difficulty making out the words. We showed the journal to Ernie and Susanna when we returned.

"We found this at the perfume shop owner's house," I said.

"It looks old. What is it?" Ernie asked.

"We think it's a journal written by his family members and passed down through the generations," Sébastien said. "The oldest entries date to the first half of the seventeenth century."

"Maybe this will make sense to you in light of what you know from the test results," I said. "Please be very careful. It's an antique and it might provide useful information for this case."

"We should scan the whole document," Ernie suggested. "It will protect it from being handled and preserve the data."

"Good idea," I said. "Do you have a scanner?"

"Sure," he said. Of course he did. "I'll send you copies once I do."

Two hours later Ernie and Susanna found me. They looked tired.

"I sent you the file," Ernie said. "Did you get it?"

"I'll check," I said. "What did you think?"

"Neither one of us speaks fluent French," Ernie said. "We tried to use translation tools, but it's been slow going because it's not just French it's archaic French. The handwriting is hard to read and often the terms are unfamiliar. Plus, there are handwritten chicken-scratch like comments on the margins and edits from different people that make it even more difficult to understand."

"We needed help," Susanna said, cutting to the chase.

"Susanna found a crusty old scholar of French history to help us interpret and understand it," Ernie said. It was like him to give her credit, although I was surprised at how well they seemed to be getting along. "He wouldn't give us the time of day. I mentioned the problem to Sébastien when he popped by for an update. He offered to try to convince him. We have no idea what he said, but in less than an hour the guy was here. You should see the guy. He's like a caricature of an eccentric professor. He's glued to the journal now."

"Is there anything you can tell me?" I asked, impatient for

an update.

"Give us a couple of days," Ernie said.

"Days?" I asked.

"Yes, we need time to decipher and interpret the document, and figure out if it means anything important for our case," Ernie said.

"Akka and Chandi," Susanna began.

"Don't worry," I said. "Take a break anytime you want to see them. And, I'll find out from Tadas if they're okay babysitting them until you finish." Judging by how well they seemed to get along with the children, I didn't think it would be a problem. "If for any reason they can't, I'll sort out another solution."

Susanna let out the breath she had been holding as relief flooded her features. She gave me a grateful look.

Chapter 34

The marshals complex had become a beehive of activity. While Roger Sanders and his CUT team squelched news of the incidents, making do with only a fraction of Ernie's attention, Francois, Sébastien and I filled in as necessary.

Sébastien and I had gone home only to shower and return. I managed three hours of rest. What few meals we had, we ate at the office. Although we were all doing our best, running on adrenaline, with our combined efforts we were barely keeping ahead of the crisis.

While Sébastien looked in on Mr. Tartan and Susanna checked in on her kids, Ernie and I went to pick up pizza for everyone, which turned out to be a rather large order. I was glad Ernie was in Paris.

Ernie, Sébastien, Susanna and I had gathered around the pizza when Francois showed up. We made room for him, although I was not expecting him to eat with us. To my surprise he picked up a slice from the still warm box and gulped it down in several quick bites.

"Any news?" he asked.

We all started talking at once. Then we all stopped.

"Ernie and Susanna, with the help of an expert, have been studying a journal we found in Mr. Tartan's home," I said. Francois raised an eyebrow at the mention of an expert, but didn't interrupt me. "They have also reviewed the test results from samples of the cologne used by the deceased man, Robert Previn, the incident sites, and the new samples Sébastien and I brought back from the perfume shop. We've been waiting for an update. Ernie?"

"We're not finished with the journal yet," he said, hesitant. He had come in for a snack and was being roped into a status update. "We're still double-checking the results."

"You've been neck deep in this for three days. Is there anything you can tell us?" Francois asked.

Ernie and I exchanged glances. He nodded once to let me know he would try. As I signaled for them to share their findings I saw Marshal Sanders enter the room.

"Go ahead," I said.

"You analyzed the test results," Ernie said, inviting Susanna to tell us what they thought.

"There's no doubt they're all connected," she said. "The original source is the perfume shop. We know because all the samples contain a common organic compound, and the samples from the shop have the highest concentration. Something in the samples is reacting with Weeia energy."

"How?" I asked.

"We're not—," Susanna said without finishing the sentence. She paused as if to gather her thoughts. "We don't know."

"When we questioned him, the perfume maker explained that he custom makes his orders for each individual," Sébastien said. "He uses his Weeia ability, an enhanced sense of smell, to identify the buyer's henki, and blend a fragrance to produce the effect each customer requests. He strongly recommends they not gift or lend their cologne to others."

"Could he be doing that because he knows they have side effects?" Ernie asked.

"It's possible, but during questioning we found no evidence that he knows what's causing the incidents," Sébastien said. "Although he suspects they're connected to his products, he doesn't know in what way exactly."

"Look," I said. Pointing to a page in the journal on my tablet I continued. "There's a warning in the journal about side effects. I think that's also why he labels the bottles, in tiny print, for use by the customer only."

"Does it say anything else?" Francois asked.

"Not that I can see," I said. "It's at the bottom of a page, and the next page is about a different topic." Turning to Ernie and Susanna I asked, "Did you find any other reference to that?"

"None," Ernie replied.

"There were fewer Weeia in Paris back then," Francois said. "Maybe whoever wrote the journal suspected there could be problems, but didn't witness any himself."

"Fewer products and fewer customers would mean a lower likelihood of something going wrong," Ernie said.

"What can you tell us about the compound that reacts with Weeia energy?" Francois asked Susanna.

It was the first time I had seen him speak with or recognize her. She straightened and took a deep breath.

"Before I reply I want to stress that this is only a working theory," she said. She glanced at Ernie and me for support. He held her look. I nodded encouragement. "We're not ready to present our results yet."

"We get it," Sébastien, ever the understanding one who knew what to say, said. "Tell us whatever you can. We won't hold you to it. We're overwhelmed out on the streets and need to try something before this gets worse, and the higher-ups force us to take drastic measures."

Reassured, she continued. "We believe something is interacting with and modifying Weeia energy. His colognes seem designed to interact with a Weeia's Emotional henki rather than Material, Mental, or Temporal henkis. For those who don't have an Emotional henki the cologne alters the Weeia's essential energy temporarily to mimic an Emotional henki. We believe this in turn produces the Weeia trait desired by the wearer."

As she explained their theory, her confidence grew. "For example, someone might go to the perfume shop and ask the owner for a scent that gives her charisma. Using his very particular super smell and the recipes in the journal, Mr.

Tartan will mix a blend of natural substances as common as chamomile and as exotic as Madagascar lemur dung into a cologne that will produce the desired effect on that customer when she applies it to her skin."

"In other words, the cologne will make her charismatic while she's wearing it," Ernie said.

"That sounds benign," Francois said.

"It should be," she said, "but, if someone else wears that person's cologne the effects will almost certainly differ."

"Fair enough," Marshal Sanders said. "How do you jump from a benign product that adds a hint of charisma to a Weeia personality while she wears the cologne to the situation we have right now?"

"That's where it gets complicated," she said, looking at the CUT leader. "The people who wrote the journal referred to the interaction between Weeia smells and abilities in a way we don't understand, at least not entirely. It has something to do with the way they perceive Weeia energy and smells. We think they see smells."

She glanced at Ernie, who nodded in agreement. "We believe the ability of the journal authors and Mr. Tartan allowed them to identify henkis and combine different scents into a cologne that modified a wearer's henki temporarily. If what the journal says is true, using their sense of smell they found a correlation between a person's henki and a base ingredient. By adding a second ingredient they were able to produce a particular effect, such as charisma, for example, for a given person's henki. Each perfume they formulated contained the base ingredient along with added ingredients to modify each individual's own henki to obtain the desired effect. Because nearly all the ingredients varied with every wearer, there are thousands of possible formulations."

"Nearly all?" I asked.

"There is a stabilizing agent common to all the samples," she said. "It's an inactive ingredient."

"Is what the journal proposes merely theory?" Sébastien asked.

"It's impossible to answer that question with one hundred percent accuracy at the moment," Ernie said. "The closest to their ability that we know of in nature is bioluminescence, which converts chemical energy to light energy in the ocean. From what we know, it seems likely Mr. Tartan has been relying on the journal in combination with his ability to prepare the formulations he has sold to Weeia customers."

"Assuming that's the case, what does that mean for us right now?" I asked, hoping somewhere in all the scientific analysis there was information useful to resolving our crisis.

"In simple terms, when the person the perfume was made for wears it he or she should obtain the desired result without any issues," Susanna said. I was growing impatient. When I opened my mouth to ask another question she held her open palm up facing me. "If the wearer has a henki that doesn't match the base ingredient it was made for, the fragrance produces the wrong energy." She emphasized the next to last word. "In extreme cases, like poor Mr. Previn, it can drain the person of all energy before he or she knows what's happening. In other cases, that wrong effect generates random Weeia energy."

That reminded me of Yolanda's description of Mr. Previn when she used her second sight. She had said it was unlike anything she had seen before.

As if reflecting my thoughts Ernie added, "We believe such random energy probably has unpredictable and uncontrollable results."

"The theory is exciting," Susanna said. "If this wasn't happening randomly in front of the general public…the research possibilities are seemingly endless."

"Let me see if I understand your explanation," Marshal Sanders said. "You're convinced the perfume maker blended fragrances that specifically bonded with a wearer's own

Weeia energy resulting in a particular effect, such as making people like them." Ernie and Susanna nodded. "The problems started when Weeia began wearing someone else's fragrance because it wasn't a match to their Weeia energy."

"Exactly," Ernie said. "We believe if an unintended person wears the fragrance he or she risks an unknown effect, which could be lethal. In addition, anyone else who is exposed to that person while they're wearing it may also suffer an unknown and unpredictable effect."

"That's why even though you have a complete analysis of the chemical composition of the samples you can't predict the results," Francois said.

"Yes," Ernie replied.

"But there have been lots of incidents," I objected.

"All it takes is for one person to have an unexpected reaction that turns on an ability he or she doesn't normally have for things to go awry in a major way," Ernie said. "Also, the compound might push a Weeia ability into high gear, stimulating a Lowes Weeia to Medius, for example."

Most Weeia had a minimum level of ability, known as Lowes. Others had a middle range, called Medius, and a few had the highest level, Maximus.

"We aren't aware of that having happened, but if it did, it would cause a serious problem," Ernie said. "It's especially bad because the victims, the ones who have the reaction, are often unaware of what's happening, and probably weren't ever in contact with the person who wore the fragrance originally. Even if they realize there's an issue, so far they haven't been able to control their ability."

"I think I understand," Sébastien said. "That's the effect Mr. Tartan's ancestors thought possible, but may have never witnessed."

"That's what we theorize," Ernie said. "If this was happening in a small or isolated community, say Paris of the seventeenth century, it wouldn't be the crisis that it is here.

Everything gets magnified in big cities like modern day Paris."

"Why did it happen now?" Sébastien asked.

"His shop is new," Ernie answered. "As far as we know he only started selling his products recently."

"Assuming you're right, how do we stop it?" I asked.

"Susanna has an idea," Ernie said, turning to her. She hesitated so he continued. "She may be able to synthesize an antidote of sorts to neutralize the effects of the stabilizing compound common to all the blends. Once they become unstable our hope is that the blends' effectiveness will fizzle out."

"How long would that take?" Francois asked.

"We're not sure," Ernie said. "Although the journal has been a big help in speeding up the process, we're learning and testing as we go along."

"Assuming we're successful in distilling a substance to interfere with the stability of the products, we thought you could use a dart to administer the antidote," Susanna said.

I guessed that idea had been Ernie's. He spent most of his waking hours in an armory, after all.

"Ordinarily that would work well, especially for a single individual," Marshal Sanders said. "Under the current circumstances darting groups of Weeia in public would present a significant challenge. Is another method possible?"

"How about liquid or spray?" Susanna asked.

"That would be perfect," Marshal Sanders said.

"What are you thinking?" Francois asked Marshal Sanders.

"It would be a lot of work, but I'm confident we could administer the antidote to those affected so far," he said. "Such an approach would halt the situation as it stands. But, if someone wears the cologne again, we'll be right back where we started."

"We would have to confiscate and destroy all the products Mr. Tartan sold to Weeia," Francois said.

"And shut him down," I added. "He can't sell any more either."

"Where is he now?" Francois asked.

"In a cell," Sébastien replied, looking at Francois and Marshal Sanders. "He's been complaining that he's uncomfortable, that we've held him unlawfully for three days, and that he's losing business. While it's true that the cell is barely adequate, it's the best we have. With cause the period is well within our discretion." Was he hoping to impress them? "Under the circumstances and given the direct link between his perfumes and the incidents we thought it prudent to hold him."

"Good thinking," Francois said.

Chapter 35

It took a week and all the resources of the CUT team temporarily assigned to Paris, plus the hard work of our entire staff, including Francois and Madame Marmotte, as well as Ernie and Susanna, to track down and destroy all the bottles of Mr. Tartan's expensive cologne in the city. Everyone exposed to cologne worn by the wrong henki was treated with Susanna's antidote just to be sure. It worked.

"They're gone," Sébastien announced as he entered the breakroom, making a beeline for the box of doughnuts and snatching one with the elegance and speed of a cheetah hunting prey in the African savanna.

"CUT?" Ernie asked.

"Mhmm," Sébastien managed despite the half a doughnut wedged in his mouth.

"I'll be heading home soon too," Ernie said, his voice ringed with regret. "As soon as Susanna and I finish analyzing the last samples and writing our joint report."

I had known that would happen and was dreading his departure, not only because I would miss his cheerful company, but because it signaled the end of the case. The crisis had distracted me, and with them all gone I would return to my grief. I felt a pang of guilt for wanting to push the pain away, because I stored my memories of Iaen with the pain.

"That's a shame," Sébastien said, echoing some of my thoughts. "We'll miss you."

I was about to agree when Sébastien's badge chime went off, indicating a call. He flipped it open, answering without hesitation. His enthusiasm reminded me of myself in my first year as a marshal.

The expression on his face darkened in an instant. He

signaled the call was important and stepped out of the room.

"It was the headmistress," he said. Before I had a chance to moan about her disrespect for the chain of command, he went on. "There's been a death at the Académie."

"Mr. Davidi?" I asked.

"No, someone else. He recovered enough to return home to his parents," he said. "By the way, one of the substances we confiscated from his room was a powerful hallucinogenic, a variant of bath salts. So drugs are confirmed in his case, not the perfume."

"Is it related to the incidents we investigated?" I asked.

"She doesn't know," he said, hesitating for a nanosecond more than necessary. I prompted him to finish his thought by remaining silent. "It's likely that there's a connection because the deceased is one of the students from the incidents we witnessed."

"I suspected the other three incidents stemmed from the same problem," I said.

"Didn't you and CUT track down all the perfumes?" Ernie asked.

"We thought we did," I said. "And, at our request, Madame Marmotte spread the word far and wide for Weeia to steer clear of Parfumerie Tartan products, explaining they're toxic and possibly lethal. She's fast and more effective than social media." Sébastien chuckled. "But the headmistress runs the Académie like her private fiefdom, protecting her secrets fiercely." I left out that my boss and colleague enabled her behavior through their own efforts. "It's possible something escaped us."

"Should we contact CUT?" Sébastien asked.

"Not yet," I replied. "Let's find out exactly what happened." Turning to Ernie and Susanna I added, "Stand by in case we need you."

"Will do," Ernie said.

The last time we had been there we had to stay the night

so I took my overnight bag just in case. I had refreshed it after spending a night at the office.

Two hours after her call to Sébastien we arrived at the headmistress's office. On our drive over to the Académie I had instructed Sébastien to take the lead. Her haughty attitude annoyed me and didn't bother him at all. She communicated better with him and preferred his company to mine. The goal, I decided, was to solve the case rather than to win a popularity contest with the headmistress. If having Sébastien interact with her served that purpose it made the most sense. Besides, I didn't care overmuch whether she liked me or not.

"Coffee?" the headmistress's assistant asked before we had a chance to sit down.

"Yes," I said, grateful. "Black."

"Another one for me, thank you," Sébastien said.

"One of our young students, Bruno Malesherbes, passed away," the headmistress said without preamble.

Passed away sounded natural, expected even. I doubted that was the case. I pressed down my desire to point that out.

Instead I asked, "What was his ability?"

"Gravity," she said. "You met him the last time we had those unfortunate incidents."

Unfortunate sounded like an act of nature. I doubted nature had much to do with the student's death. Remembering Sébastien was to take the lead, I waited. He looked unsure, which she took as a cue to assume control of the conversation.

"In case you're wondering why I asked you to investigate, Mr. Malesherbes was missing for several days before one of the instructors found his body this morning," she said as devoid of emotion as if she was discussing the type of wood floor in her office.

"Why didn't you call us when he went missing?" Sébastien asked.

"As you may recall, young man, from your days at the Académie, we give wide latitude to our students," she said. I didn't appreciate her attempt to return him to his former status of student. For the briefest of moments, I was tempted to let her know what I thought of her tactic. Instead I waited, allowing Sébastien to respond for himself. "At the time, there was no reason for alarm."

"Had he gone missing before?" he asked.

"Not that I'm aware," she said.

"Have other students gone missing recently?" he asked.

"No," she replied.

I didn't believe her. She was too much of a control freak not to know what was happening at the Académie. She turned her head toward the window as if the answers were outside somewhere. After a long silence she returned her attention to us.

"I'm very busy with the Académie's burdensome administrative duties," she said. "I don't have time to keep track of each student's movements. You'll have to ask the staff."

"Where was he found?" Sébastien asked.

"In the pool deck area," she said.

"The one that was closed before?" he asked.

"Yes, it's still closed," she said. "Now, if there's nothing further, I trust you'll handle the situation with the utmost discretion, and protect the reputation of our institution to the best of your ability."

Not trusting myself to keep quiet I bolted from my seat and walked out of her wood paneled office. Seconds later Sébastien followed me out.

"That woman is unbelievable," I blurted once we were out of hearing range from her office. "Not once did she express concern for the dead student or the rest of her students."

"It's not that she doesn't care," he said. "That's her style. Women of her generation keep their feelings private.

Expressing emotions in public is considered a weakness and impolite."

"Even if that's true, she didn't ask us to find out how her student died," I said. "She asked us to protect the school's reputation."

"She's responsible for the entire school," he said.

"Doing one doesn't automatically make the other impossible," I replied.

The more he defended her the more it annoyed me. I pushed the feeling aside.

Her assistant's voice startled me. I hadn't seen her standing in the corner watching us.

"The headmistress asked me to escort you to the pool," she said. "This way, please."

She unlocked the door to the pool and left us to make our way in, turning back in the direction we had come from without a word. Franck Pouroscure, the handyman, was in the pool area. He shifted position when we entered as if he had been waiting for us. He wore the same sour expression I remembered from the day we had met him.

"Hello, Mr. Pouroscure," Sébastien said.

The man watched my colleague without replying. We walked to the body, which was uncovered on the floor.

"I'll call Body Retrieval," Sébastien announced after we examined the body.

While we waited for their arrival, we circled the pool area, looking for anything that might point to the reason for the young man's death. Sébastien was quieter than usual. I had a feeling the headmistress's words and my criticism were swirling around in his head.

"Anything?" I asked.

"Nothing," he said. "It's really clean."

"Same on this side," I said. "As if someone cleaned recently."

If Mr. Pouroscure knew anything he didn't say. He stood

like a guard, out of our way, yet within hearing distance of our conversation. I didn't appreciate having a spy for the headmistress underfoot. I was tempted to kick him out. The problem was that we needed someone from the Académie to take us around and open doors for us during our investigation.

"Is there anything you can tell us?" I asked the groundskeeper.

"Nothing," he said.

"Listen, Mr. Pouroscure," I said, becoming annoyed at his lack of cooperation. "This is a murder investigation." His eyes grew a bit wider than before, which did nothing to improve his odd appearance. "We're not kidding around."

"Murder," he repeated.

"Yes, there is every indication his was not a natural death," I said. "When was the last time you were here?"

"I was looking after my mother," he said. "She's not been feeling so good lately. The headmistress gave me permission. You can ask her."

"How long were you gone?" I asked.

"Three days," he said. "I came back after they found the body."

An hour later the Body Retrieval staff had completed their preliminary examination of the body. Sébastien and I watched as they readied Bruno Malesherbes's remains for removal.

"Marshals, if there is nothing else, we're leaving," the man from the Body Retrieval staff said.

"Is there anything you can share with us?" I asked in a soft voice.

"He was restrained in some manner before his death, for twenty-four hours or so," the man said. "He was unable to move. Also, the forensic evidence indicates he died somewhere else and the body was moved here postmortem."

"Did he suffer?" Sébastien asked.

"At this time, I'm unable to answer that question," the man said, wrinkling his nose in displeasure. "You should have my preliminary report by the end of the day, my time, tomorrow."

"You know what bugs me?" Sébastien asked me after the Body Retrieval staff had gone.

"Uh, no, what?" I asked.

"If he was killed somewhere else, how did the killer get the body here and why?"

"Why seems straightforward," I said. "To hide his or her identity. We find the place where he was held and we'll have the killer's identity or be pretty close to finding it."

"You think?"

"Yes," I said. "Your other question intrigues me too. How did the killer move the body?"

"I suppose it could've been more than one person," he said.

"Yes, that's entirely possible," I said. "We'll keep an open mind about that. Either way, it would be difficult to carry a body across the Académie grounds without being seen. How much do you think Bruno Malesherbes weighed, one hundred and fifty pounds?" He nodded his agreement. "That's a lot for the average person to carry more than a few feet alone."

"You're right," he said.

"Call the headmistress and verify Mr. Pouroscure was away," I said. "It will help us eliminate suspects."

Thirty minutes later she called him back. Given how long it took her to respond, I was glad it wasn't an emergency we had called her about that day.

"He was away three days and returned after they found Mr. Malesherbes," he said. "It couldn't have been him."

"It makes you wonder why he's not eager to help us," I said.

"Ever since I was a student here he was never eager to help anyone, except the headmistress," he said. "He's loyal to her for some reason. It's not about us. It's who he is."

Chapter 36

As I had feared, we ended up spending the night at the Académie in the interest of furthering our investigation. We worked into the early evening interviewing staff, faculty, and students. The staff assigned us the same cottage as on our previous visit. When it was too late for interviews we sat down to dinner, reviewing the information we had and discussing the case.

"I've been thinking about this all night," Sébastien said, as I took my first sip of coffee the following morning. "There's no convenient place in the main building where the killer could've kept Bruno Malesherbes for long without risking someone noticing. Even the closed swimming pool was risky because the students like to hang out there and get high, especially after Mr. Davidi's accident. Now the pool itself is a draw because of his accident."

"Okay," I said, waking up faster than I had anticipated as a result of the conversation with Sébastien. "There's no housing in the main building so that doesn't shorten our list of suspects."

"That's just it," he said. "It means the killer, or killers, had to have carried him to the main building. I think they used equipment to do that." I must have looked unconvinced or confused because he raised his voice a notch the way people do when they're excited. "That amount of dead weight would be difficult to move around unaided. The killer could've stolen or borrowed yard equipment to move the body. Only Mr. Pouroscure would notice a wheelbarrow in the yard and he was away."

"I bet he would notice if someone used yard equipment without asking him," I said. "He might not volunteer to tell us, but if that's what happened the equipment will still be around somewhere." I emphasized the last word. "Maybe we can find evidence of that."

"Anything that heavy would leave noticeable traces on the soil," Sébastien said. "I'll take a look."

"No lone rangers on this one," I said. "Give me a minute and we'll go together. Whoever is behind this isn't just a killer. He, she or they are calculating and patient. Mr. Malesherbes was held for hours. We need to be extra careful."

No matter how well we got along it was my responsibility to supervise Sébastien and ensure his safety. I had every intention of doing that. As much as I was willing to offer him learning opportunities, I wouldn't knowingly allow him to get in harm's way by himself. Within minutes we were both scouring the Académie grounds for suspicious tracks.

We circled around the buildings, looking for any indication a body had been moved around. It was early and few lights were on inside. Fifteen minutes into our search we found what looked like wheelbarrow tracks. They stood out because they had left much deeper marks in the soil than other wheelbarrow tracks would have.

"They look relatively fresh," Sébastien said in a soft voice.

"Let's see where they lead us," I said. "Be alert."

"How far can they go?" I asked after five minutes.

"There," Sébastien said, pointing to an entrance on the side of a small building.

"It doesn't look like much of a place," I said, walking to the building, Sébastien close behind me.

I knocked on the door. There was no reply.

"If it hadn't been for the tracks we never would've looked there," I said, waiting in case there was someone there. I knocked a second time with the same result. "I'm going to try the door. Are you ready?"

"Yes," he said.

The door was locked. I pulled out my lock picking toolkit.

Under the circumstances I didn't want to wait for one of the staff to bring a key. Five minutes later the door was open and we walked into a dark foyer.

"You're good," Sébastien said about my lock picking.

"It's an old lock," I said, shrugging off the compliment.

"This hasn't been used for years," he said, examining the interior. "This campus is big and there is more space than the school needs. It could be a former workshop."

The dim light from a single bare lightbulb illuminated the middle of the room. Dilapidated work benches, broken bottles in a corner, yellowed newspapers, and spider webs confirmed our initial impression.

"Somebody was here recently," I said, pointing to dirt footprints on the floor leading to one side. "Over there."

Sébastien followed my gaze, walking to and past the footprints to a door I hadn't noticed. It opened when he turned the knob.

"There is a basement," he said. "The light is on, but I can't see much from here. I'm going down."

"Be careful," I yelled. I didn't like him descending to an unknown basement alone. He hadn't waited for approval. "We can't both go down. I'll stand guard. Keep me updated."

"Will do," he said from the dimly lit staircase. He disappeared from view as soon as he reached the bottom.

Sébastien sent me a telepathic message saying, "Nobody in the room at the bottom of the stairs, but someone disturbed the dust and dirt. There is a short passage with a light on, going to investigate."

After a few long moments of not hearing anything further I was jittery. I resisted the temptation to descend until my badge vibrated with a short staccato pattern signaling a marshal was in trouble. It had to be Sébastien. That he had used his badge in such a fashion meant he was injured or incapacitated. Concerned about my partner, I projected my cloaking illusion and stepped down the stone staircase, to search for the source of the alert.

When I reached the bottom of the stairs, I found myself in an ancient basement with stone walls and floor. Squinting in the dim light, I spotted old broken down furniture, and a row of bottles in various shapes and sizes on an old worktable. The floor was cluttered with debris, some of it decades old, but mixed in were more recent garbage and food wrappers. As I moved close to the table I found a clean area at one end with a small cluster of familiar bottles, three of Mathis Tartan's infamous perfumes near a dark leather bag or backpack.

From a passage to the left out of sight beyond the table I could hear voices but I couldn't distinguish the words. Then I saw several bright flashes of brilliant blue light reflected on the walls, and someone cried out in pain.

Since the incident in the subway, I carried a lipstick size energy tube prototype Ernie had made for me with my regular gear. The device allowed me to store energy and blast it in a single burst at a target. I readied the weapon and projected an illusion of myself remaining still while I walked down the hallway to where the flashes of light originated. Almost instantly, I heard a shout and blue light arced out through my projection and onto the walls. My hair was stood on end as the smell of ozone filled the tight musty space.

Feeling less confident than before with my tiny tube of energy, I kept myself cloaked behind my own projection, and peeked around the corner. Sweat poured down my back from the effort of maintaining my illusions. I was wary. The enemy in the next room had not spoken a word before the last pulse.

Keeping to the shadows in the corner, at last I could see into the room and the scene was not reassuring. A teenager lay flat and unmoving on an old table with a faint blue light outlining his body while a figure dressed in baggy clothing held his hands over the boy. Something about the figure's movements gave me the impression it was a man. He seemed to be gathering energy like someone inhaling smoke. The light in the room was from a bulb hanging behind the figure collecting the unusual emissions. Something was wrong with the shape of his face, it was impossibly long, like a big cat or a wolf.

"You can come out now marshal, or I am going to finish off your partner," the strange figure called out in a man's voice. He sounded strained, no, over excited like someone who had too much coffee. It didn't escape my notice that he recognized me, although I couldn't identify his voice. "That clever illusion of you peeking around the corner won't fool me again."

I realized the man wore a rubber mask when I heard his garbled voice. I could just make out one of Sébastien's shoes, he was lying on the ground behind the masked figure, unconscious or worse, I couldn't tell. Reaching forward with my energy weapon through my own illusion in the doorway I must have looked like a ghost trying to match up to its own body. I fired.

The blast had a satisfying effect as the jerk flew back into the corner, falling over the prone figure of my partner behind him. Instead of catching himself, he pointed his hands towards the doorway and let loose more lightning like energy. As I jolted back around the corner to avoid electrocution, I realized my mistake. The blue bolts of energy kept coming, and I could hear manic laughter from the little room. My energy burst had charged him up, not take him down. He sounded giddy with power.

"Thanks for the extra juice, that was high quality stuff," he chortled as he continued to blast the walls and his voice grew closer.

Fearing he would reach the doorway at any instant, I sprinted down the short passage I had come from, and crawled under the table with the bottles on it. In my haste for cover I bumped against a table leg causing a couple of the bottles to fall. One smashed to bits when it hit the floor, spraying shards of glass in all directions. I felt minor cuts in my neck and cheek from the tiny shrapnel.

The wolf figure was an impressive sight coming toward me. He was floating above the floor and drifting forward as if he had wheels on his feet. Azure bolts flew out in front of him, lighting his path. He paused at the opening, looking into the cluttered room. Spotting the broken bottle, he headed in that direction.

I threw out several small, shadowy illusions across the room to distract him. It's not easy to ignore shadows moving in your peripheral vision. Although he twisted back and forth, he kept calm. I could see the tension in his body. He held his hands ready to blast a real target.

"Danni, can I call you Danni? When we met I thought we had a lot in common. I imagined us becoming good friends. I know what it must've been like for you, being an outcast in your peer group because of your parents. The unfairness chafes. It stays with you for a long time." His voice sounded labored. He was breathing heavily in the mask, making me think the energy bursts were heating him up. "So what do you think of my little experiments? I used to sneak small quantities out of the perfume bottles from the kids here. They never noticed. It was easy. But once the official word came out, Mother confiscated every bottle the staff found. That gave me an idea, and I started my experiments. It was rather fun." Mother? His voice ran along my spine, giving me goosebumps. "If my subjects remembered anything, they thought they had been hallucinating. Who would believe those who shared their story about being captured by the infamous wolf-man? Nobody would take them seriously."

As he chattered on, he floated around the table to the far side. I could hear him approaching, but there was nowhere for me to hide. He crouched to where I was under the table.

"And today I get to see what makes marshals so special," he said with glee.

Once his vulnerable bent knee came within range, I mule kicked him with all my strength, sending his feet out from under him. I heard a satisfying grunt as the fall knocked the wind out of him. I crawled out from under the table, feeling more cuts from the broken glass on my hands. I grabbed three bottles of Tartan perfume and headed for the passage. I stopped next to the entrance and cloaked myself with darkness, blocking the light from the little back room. Pulling the tops off the bottles, I hurled the glass stoppers at the junk along the wall, and was rewarded with a crash of broken glass.

He stepped into view, a bit worse for wear, to check the location of the crash. The light was in my eyes, making it difficult to identify the man. As if reading my mind he pulled the mask back into position. He stumbled over something on the floor and cursed as he blew the offending objects across the room with a flash of blue. I wondered how much energy he had stored. Flying bits of wood and rock went in all directions.

Cloaking myself required concentration. Any movement would reveal my position so I had to ignore several new cuts and scratches, including a wood splinter as long as my finger that had become embedded in my arm.

He fumbled with the mask. Unable to get it to align properly, the man removed it. My mouth opened in surprise when I realized it was Guillaume, the headmistress's son. Grunting in pain, his hands roamed over his face, wiping blood from under his eyes and nose. His eyes were glowing blue and his nose was broken, but it was him. I was sure.

Seeing the dark fluid on his hands, he screamed "I'm going to kill you both and drain all your energy, you cow! You don't know who you're messing with here, this is my domain."

As he started moving toward the passage I stepped out of hiding and kicked him between the legs before he could lift his arms to release any lightning. Once he fell to the floor, I poured the contents of the bottles over him, dousing him from head to toe in a mixture of the three perfumes.

He began convulsing and a rainbow of energy bursts sparked around him and crackled to ground. He kept trying to cradle his injured tender bits, but convulsions kept clenching and relaxing his muscles making that impossible, so he curled up into a fetal position and shuddered.

To be safe, I slipped my collar around his neck and fastened it as quickly as I could. The device prevented him from using any abilities and allowed me to track him with my badge. I left him writhing on the floor to enjoy his personal light show, and went to check on my partner and the teenager in the back room, hoping for the best.

I checked the boy's pulse. It was steady. Sébastien was still as I stepped around the table with the teenager on it. I got a jolt of electricity when I reached down to check for a pulse on his neck. When he rolled over and opened his eyes they were glowing and blue like Guillaume's had been a few minutes before.

"You're absorbing loose energy," I told him.

"I dropped my spray bottle when he zapped me, it must be here someplace," Sébastien rasped in a hoarse voice.

Looking around on the floor, I found one of the familiar sprayers distributed to the Paris intervention teams with Susanna's mixture to counter the effects of Tartan's Weeia perfumes.

A few pumps of the spray on the teen and the wisps of blue energy stopped clinging to him. Checking his pulse again, I was relieved that he appeared unharmed. After I sprayed Sébastien his eyes lost the blue glow. I helped him up into a chair and let him rest.

"I guess I should spray the wolf-man out there too," I said. "I doused him with three bottles of perfume. He was convulsing and pulsing with multiple colors of light."

I headed toward the outer room with the spray in hand. With the amount of perfume he was covered with, it took the rest of the bottle of the antidote to quiet him down. After a while, the light show ended and he collapsed on the floor.

Chapter 37

Sébastien, still unsteady, kept an eye on our prisoner and the boy while I went upstairs to find help. I didn't want to call the headmistress since her son was involved. The boy needed medical attention pronto, and Sébastien could do with a healer himself. Guillaume remained prone. When I stepped out into the daylight, I found Mr. Pouroscure studying the tracks we had followed.

"Thank goodness you're here," I said, relieved. "We have a situation and need the healer right away. What is her number?"

Without a word or any gesture of disagreement he started walking between the two buildings. I assumed he was going to get help. While I waited for his return I used the time to call Francois and left a message. Then I called Portland to request a dangerous prisoner retrieval.

"It was a busy night. We won't have anyone qualified to pick up your prisoner for a few hours," the dispatcher's voice came back, sounding exhausted himself. In response to my silence he added, "Sorry, that's the best I can do. We'll call when we have an ETA."

"Understood," I said, realizing it was early morning in Portland. "We'll expect your call."

As I hung up, Mr. Pouroscure and a middle-aged man hurried across the lawn toward me. The well-dressed man was of medium build, wore wireframe glasses and a lab coat.

"Hello marshal, my name is Dr. Jules Des Richel, are you the patient?" he asked as he looked me over. "You have several lacerations."

"Are you a medical doctor?" I asked.

"Yes, and before you ask, I'm a healer too," he said.

I had heard that was the perfect combination as it allowed

healers access to medical facilities, whereas healers without medical degrees couldn't get privileges at hospitals. It was expensive to hire a healer doctor. Leave it to the academy to have one on call. I shook my head from side to side to indicate I wasn't the one who needed him.

"I'm not the priority, Dr. Des Richel," I said.

"Where is the patient and what are the injuries?" he asked.

"It's easiest if I show you. Follow me, please." I motioned to the building. "Mr. Pouroscure, if you please as well."

I led them downstairs, leaving Mr. Pouroscure to watch the prisoner, while the doctor and I walked to where the student and Sébastien were waiting. I was thankful that Guillaume, still out for the count, faced away from us. As far as I could tell, neither the healer nor Mr. Pouroscure had recognized him. Sébastien had leaned back against the wall and his eyes were closed. I waved the doctor to the figures on the table and floor.

"The student is unconscious and my partner took a serious lightning blast from our friend down the hall," I said, avoiding mentioning that the attacker was headmistress's son for as long as possible.

"What happened to the student? Why is he unconscious?" he asked.

"We don't know," I said. "His pulse was steady when I went to get you. My partner had an irregular heartbeat and difficulty breathing."

Dr. Des Richel had the competent manner of a capable healer. I sighed with relief as he bent down to examine Sébastien first. Two minutes later, he pulled out a syringe and a glass vial from a black bag he had brought. I held his arm, preventing him from moving.

"What is that?" I asked before allowing him to inject my partner.

"It's an herbal stimulant," he said. "I'm hoping that is all he needs. If that doesn't work, we'll have to consider something stronger."

I released my hold on his arm, observing him as he plunged the sharp needle into Sébastien's muscular upper arm. His expression grew concerned when he focused on the boy.

"Will he be all right?" I asked.

He nodded, adding, "I think so. I'll know more after I run several tests."

Once the doctor had assessed everyone, including my superficial cuts and scrapes and our prisoner, he called the infirmary. When he saw Guillaume, he drew in a sharp breath, but didn't comment. He placed his hand under Guillaume's nose. It must have been smelling salts because the young man stirred awake with a moan.

"He'll be fine," the healer announced when he concluded his examination of our prisoner.

Within minutes Dr. Des Richel's assistants showed up with a gurney and carried the boy away. The prisoner sat on the floor under the watchful eyes of Mr. Pouroscure, who held the leash from the collar.

"Get a good night's sleep," the doctor said as he took his leave. "We doctors can stitch up wounds and patch you up, but you need to give your body a chance to finish healing the trauma at its own pace. Take it easy for a few days."

"It's going to be a few hours before Portland can pick him up," I pointed at Guillaume. "This is too cold and uncomfortable. Where should we wait?"

Sébastien looked exhausted. Anger poured out of Mr. Pouroscure's eyes, although he was silent.

"In Guillaume's apartment," he said.

"Take us there," I ordered Mr. Pouroscure.

Without a word, he handed the leash to my partner and started climbing up the stairs. The four of us walked across the nearly deserted commons to a large house inside its own iron fence. He unlocked a door on the side of the house and held it open.

"Why are we here?" Guillaume asked in an insolent tone.

It was the first time he had spoken since our fight. Of the three of us he looked the best.

"We have some questions for you," Sébastien replied.

"Does he have to be here?" he asked, glancing at Mr. Pouroscure. We didn't answer. Mr. Pouroscure didn't either. From the men's body language, it was clear there was no love lost between them. The older man stood against the wall, his eyes fixed on Guillaume. "What about?" he asked, trying to look relaxed and failing.

"The death of Bruno Malesherbes," Sébastien said.

"Oh that," he said. "Poor chum."

"Frankly, we're impressed," I said on impulse. "We're looking forward to hearing it from you." I gave him a meaningful look, hoping it conveyed suitable admiration. I thought he would want to show off. "You can fill in the blanks while we sit comfortably."

"Oh, all right," he said. "It's not like I tried very hard to hide my identity. I frankly didn't think you would be so smart or move so fast. What do you want to know?"

"Record it," I instructed Sébastien, who turned on the recording feature on his badge.

"Why did you kill him?" Sébastien asked.

"I didn't really kill him per se," Guillaume said, staring at the badge. In response to Sébastien's disbelieving stare he went on, "Well, it wasn't my intent for him to die. He wasn't strong enough, is all."

"Strong enough to what?" Sébastien asked.

"Survive the effects of the high," Guillaume replied. "You know, the perfume high. It's the most amazing sensation."

"What are you talking about?" I blurted.

"You mean you don't know?" he asked.

"Know what?" Sébastien asked.

"About the perfumes," he said. "Of course you do. You're

not thinking. Come on marshals, I know you can do it."

"The Tartan Perfumes?" Sébastien asked.

"There you go," he said. "They produce the most amazing and powerful high you can imagine."

"Are you saying what I think you're saying?" I asked.

"If you think I'm saying I fed off the effects of the perfume to get a high, then yes," Guillaume replied. "You haven't lived until you feel the thrill, go on the joyride of your life."

"But the effects of the perfume on other people can be deadly," Sébastien said.

"Sadly, that's true," Guillaume said. "Although in fairness, most of the students were only ill temporarily before, with a little help from yours truly, they forgot the whole thing. I let them enjoy a mild high initially, and then I fed off their energy. In the end, we all got what we wanted and nobody was the wiser."

"Until Mr. Malesherbes," Sébastien said.

"Yes, that was unfortunate," Guillaume agreed as if he was referring to a sudden rain shower rather than the death of a student at his hands. "But, you can't pin all the blame on me. They knew it was risky to be exposed to other people's perfumes and they bought them anyway. They sought out the experience. Whose fault was it that they ran toward the toxic products instead of away from them? I only took advantage of a situation of your own making."

"How was it of our own making?" Sébastien asked.

"Because we made a point of warning everyone to stay away from them," I said, understanding flooding my mind. "While it had the desired effect on most people, and they kept away from the fragrances, others were drawn to the idea of a scent Russian roulette with unpredictable yet powerful, even potentially deadly, side effects."

"Exactly," Guillaume said.

It made me feel sick to think of their reckless behavior.

And I felt foolish for failing to anticipate their reaction.

"How many were there before Mr. Malesherbes?" Sébastien asked.

"A few," Guillaume said.

"How many?" Sébastien asked in a menacing tone.

"Well there were a few mild ones early on," he said in a calm tone as if Sébastien's insistence was unimportant and he had answered of his own accord. "Six, no, seven once the real fun began. It was easy. Besides, Mom made everyone keep quiet about the blackouts, thinking it was her precious students getting high. In her defense, with all the heroin, cocaine, prescription pills, and designer drugs floating around campus how was she to know what was going on?"

He guffawed. It was a painful sound, not merry at all.

"What did you get out of it?" Sébastien asked.

"You mean in addition to the pleasure?" Guillaume asked. "Oh, let me think. The satisfaction of having those wretches helpless under my thumb for as long as I wanted. I may have purloined some of their assets along the way, but that was merely a bonus and not my main purpose at all. Oh, well. It was good while it lasted."

"Turn around and put your hands behind your back," I ordered Guillaume.

"Why?" he asked.

"Why do you think?" I replied, pulling a zip strip from my bag.

A sullen expression appeared on his face. It was sudden and darker than I would have expected. He complied without protest. I had just tied his hands together when Mr. Pouroscure appeared out of nowhere and punched him. He fell on his butt. A shrill laughter erupted from Guillaume a moment later. It was creepy. Before I had a chance to say anything to Mr. Pouroscure, he left.

Chapter 38

Two hours later, after a team from Portland had picked up Guillaume, we made our way to the headmistress's office. Sébastien wanted to tell her in person. She would only see him alone. That was fine by me. Afterward he kept silent until we were in the car returning to Paris.

"Thanks," he said.

"What for?" I asked.

"For letting me be a part of the investigation, giving me an opportunity to learn, treating me like an equal, for your patience with the headmistress, and most of all for trusting me despite my divided loyalties," he said.

"Sure," I said. "You know we're going to have to testify at the hearing in Portland. I'm sure the headmistress will do everything in her power to get him off. That's not going to be a problem for you, is it?"

He turned his attention to me from the road long enough to let me see his eyes. The answer was clear, but I needed him to say it for both of our sakes.

"No," he said. "As much as I respect her I know my duty. I won't let you down."

Silence filled the car after that. I was tempted to turn on the radio. I could use a mental break, but I had a feeling there was something else on his mind.

"On the subject of Portland," he said. "I got my papers while you were out."

"Huh?" I managed. "Do I have any idea what you're talking about?"

"There's a slot in the next L2 class," he said. "I thought I had mentioned it."

"Last I heard you were happy as a clam in Paris," I said, fearing the answer that was coming.

"I was. I am," he said. "But I've learned a lot during my months here. If I have a chance to go to the next level, I want to take it. I'll be back in a year."

I turned away so he wouldn't see the disappointment in my face. I was happy for him. I was.

"Is that alright with you, boss?" he asked in a soft voice.

When I was sure my voice wouldn't break I replied, "Of course." I said. "I'm excited for you. You're going to blow them away. You're a great marshal already." I owed him an honest reply. "The timing sucks."

"I'm sorry, Danni. If you need me here," his voice trailed away as he waited my reply.

"No, no. It's a good opportunity," I said. "Of course I would prefer to have you here, but you should go." I struggled to keep the pain from showing. I would miss him. I managed a weak smile. "I'm happy for you."

He averted his eyes. I turned away to keep my feelings in check.

"So whatever happened with the invitation for you to try out for CUT?" he asked after a few minutes of awkward silence.

I had not even thought about it since before Iaen had died. Maybe I should pursue it, since everything around my apartment and half of Paris reminded me of him. Just thinking about him had me on the verge of tears again. I choked out a few syllables. "Nothing definite."

More awkward silence filled the car until Sébastien broke it, returning to the case, "That's one dark and twisted guy."

"Yeah," I said.

I didn't want to dwell on the subject. It was depressing, and more than anything I wanted it out of my head, at least for a little while. He took the hint and changed the subject.

"Have you heard anything from Portland about Susanna's application?" he asked.

"Not a word," I said. "Though I'm not surprised. It's a

political hot potato. If they turn it down, I'll appeal. Her help with the case made a difference. I've made sure it was reflected in the reports I filed. It could make a difference in the appeal. I wish I could offer her a job, but we don't have the budget. The problem right now is that Francois only agreed to let them stay thirty days and it may be longer before we hear back."

"About that, I have some good news," he said. "I spoke with Francois."

"About Susanna and her kids?" I asked, surprised.

"Yes," he said, sheepish. "I know I kind of went above your head, but in this case I didn't think you would mind." I wondered where he was going. "He agreed to let them stay for as long as necessary until Portland replies."

"He did?" I asked. "I hadn't realized you cared as much about them as I did." He shrugged. "How did you get Francois to agree to that?"

"Like you said before, her help made a difference in the case," he replied. "I pointed that out to Francois."

I wasn't convinced that had been all it had taken. Francois wasn't a pushover.

"And?" I asked. I let the question hang. When he didn't answer I added, "What else?"

"I asked him to let them stay as a personal favor to me," he confessed.

"You're right," I said.

"About?"

"I don't mind that you went over my head," I said, smiling.

I was thankful. It didn't make up for his announcement, but it took some of the sting out of it. I could live with that.

"I promised Ernie and Susanna dinner if we got back early tonight," he said.

"And they agreed?" I asked.

"I told them it was your idea and you were coming," he replied.

A sly grin appeared on his face. I smiled in return.

"You can tell Susanna at dinner," I said.

"Not a chance," he said. "She'll appreciate it more coming from you."

As I looked at my own reflection on the side view mirror it occurred to me how much my life had changed since our first visit to the Académie. I was glad we were leaving that place, and hoped it was a long while before I had to set foot there again. I was looking forward to dinner.

Thank you for taking time to read
Smells Like Weeia Spirit

If you enjoyed it, please consider telling your friends or posting a short review. Word of mouth is an author's best friend and much appreciated.

Sign up to receive updates and news of upcoming releases on Elle's website:

http://elleboca.poyeen.com/smells-like-weeia-spirit

About The Author

Elle Boca is the author of the Weeia urban fantasy series about superhumans. The Unelmoija Series is set in Miami. In the Garden of Weeia, a novella, is set in Portland, Maine, and her newest Marshals Series is set in Paris, France. Elle makes her home with her king cat husband in South Florida. When not writing and creating fantastical beings she likes photographing nature and wildlife, pastries, movies, and dreaming of going on safari.